NOT A
WORD

OTHER BOOKS AND AUDIO BOOKS
BY STEPHANIE BLACK

The Believer

The Witnesses

Rearview Mirror

Cold As Ice

Methods of Madness

Shadowed

Twisted Fate

Fool Me Twice

Played for a Fool

NOT A
WORD

a novel

STEPHANIE BLACK

Covenant Communications, Inc.

Cover image: *The Bridge in the Dark* © Supercel7, courtesty istockphoto.com

Cover design copyright © 2016 by Covenant Communications, Inc.

Published by Covenant Communications, Inc.
American Fork, Utah

Printed in the United States of America
First Printing: November 2016

22 21 20 19 18 17 16   10 9 8 7 6 5 4 3 2 1

ISBN 978-1-52440-124-5

To Amelia Kathleen Black, my firstborn. I knew those two-and-a-half hours of pushing would be worth it.

ACKNOWLEDGMENTS

THANK YOU TO SUE MCCONKIE, Jean Newman, Amy Black, and Dianna Hall, who kindly gave of their time to read the manuscript and provide feedback.

Huge additional thanks to Amy Black, who answered my endless questions about the work of a psychologist and didn't even block my messages, change her phone number, or move to Antarctica to get away from me. She deserves eight million awesomeness points, plus chocolate. Thank you also to Sarah Lucas, Suzanne Lucas, Irene Klinger, Jennifer Clark, Laure Ginestet, and Marshall McConkie for the information they provided.

As always, much gratitude goes to my editor, Samantha Millburn; working with Sam is a delight. Thank you also to cover designer Christina Marcano and to all the marvelous people at Covenant Communications. I appreciate all you do for me.

CHAPTER 1

WINCING, LACEY EGAN RELEASED HER grip on the fence and thumped down onto the sidewalk a couple feet below. After ten minutes of trying, *that* was how far she'd made it up the fence? Her tennis shoes couldn't secure stable toeholds, and the wires gouged her fingers. She couldn't risk injuring her hands. Jonas would watch her work tonight, and if her fingers were bruised, fumbling with the tiny glass tiles and scattering them across her worktable instead of arranging them perfectly in place, he'd ask questions. *"What happened to your hands? You look nervous. Is something wrong?"*

She massaged her fingers and scanned the fenced-in renovation site. Framed by a storm-gray sky and dampened by drizzly rain, the Victorian office building reminded Lacey of a haunted mansion. Ghostly souls, cold with hate, drifting through cobwebbed corridors. Vampires craving blood. Murderers with axes and knives.

She batted those fantasies away. *Camille Moretti wouldn't stew about monsters.* Lacey pictured Camille's confident stride as she'd walked toward the trailer that had to be the construction office. Lacey wished she could have crept through the gate after Camille, but the security guy had closed the gate after Camille had driven inside. Lacey had to find another way into the site so she could witness Camille reporting to multimillionaire Robert Chapman.

He must have arrived before Camille; Lacey had spotted an electric-blue Volkswagen Beetle convertible, sparkly and eye-catching even in the rain. That had to be Chapman's car. She'd heard rumors that he drove a wacky assortment of cars, everything from million-dollar Lamborghinis to Honda minivans and Ford trucks. What would it be like to have as much money and power as he did? Could he do anything he wanted? Did anyone ever try to stop him?

Lacey clutched the phone in her sweatshirt pocket. If she could record even a snippet of Camille's conversation with Chapman, it would be gold. She could get over this fence; she *had* to. Anyone could climb a chain-link fence.

She backed into the middle of the street, inhaled, and sprinted toward it. As she neared the wire, she leaped and reached upward. Her fingers caught the links; her toes slammed into the fence and slipped. The fall jerked at her shoulders, and the wire scraped her chin. Hanging by her fingers, she kicked at the fence, trying to push herself up, but she couldn't do it. She crashed to the sidewalk, this time losing her balance and landing on her backside.

She remained hunched on the wet sidewalk, catching her breath, her burning fingers shielded under her arms. Her chin stung. She didn't dare touch it; she didn't want to know if she'd given herself a visible welt or a scrape deep enough to bleed.

Maybe creeping around the renovation site after Camille had been a dumb idea from the start. With the rain, the site wasn't as busy as it had been when she'd walked past here before. If she'd made it over the fence, someone might have noticed her and gotten suspicious, even if she'd tried to look official by carrying the clipboard and wearing the reflective workman's vest and hard hat she had hidden in her backpack. Maybe it was better to observe Camille from outside the fence. Even if Lacey couldn't hear the conversation, she could still gather information: Camille's posture, what she did with her hands while she talked, whether or not she smiled.

Lacey stood and wiped her glasses on the lining of her sweatshirt, relishing a tingle of rebelliousness. Jonas would be shocked at her appearance—costume-shop glasses with thick black rims, a big, grubby sweatshirt she'd pilfered from the back of his closet, her platinum hair in a tight braid hidden under a knit beanie. Nobody would recognize her. She poked her earbuds into her ears, pulled the rain-dotted hood of Jonas's sweatshirt farther over her face, and ambled along the fence. Ignoring the pain in her tailbone, she imitated the gait of those teenagers who'd swaggered out of their classroom after her visiting-artist presentation, not thanking her or even glancing at her. Lacey was now an oblivious kid surfing on her own coolness.

She rounded the corner and passed the closed gate. The office trailer was near the fence on the opposite side of the grounds from where she'd tried to climb in. Casually, she advanced to the next corner and turned left to walk past the trailer. Spying on Camille here was riskier than observing her through her office window or at her house or the gym or the grocery store. Lacey's heartbeat clobbered her eardrums, the noise trapped by earbuds that weren't playing any music.

It was kind of a thrilling sound.

The chance to see Camille report to real-estate mogul Chapman—Chapman had hordes of people working for him in Ohneka . . . in the whole Finger Lakes area, actually. Probably in all of New York, maybe even across the whole country. How often would he meet personally with one of his property managers? It was crazy lucky that the call from Chapman's secretary—Lacey assumed Chapman's secretary—had come while Camille had been sitting on a bench in the park near her office, eating lunch in the afternoon's prestorm sunshine. Lacey, on the grass behind the bench, dressed in jogging clothes and pretending to do stretches, had overheard most of the conversation.

The back of the trailer had two windows. The blinds were half closed over one window and completely open on the other. She slowed her pace and peered through the windows. The view wasn't great—the trailer was too high off the ground, and rain beaded the glass—but she could see inside. Camille stood next to a man who must be Chapman. He was the same height as short Camille in her heels; Lacey had expected him to be bigger than that. His longish white hair was so tousled that she wondered if he'd driven over here with the top of his convertible down despite the rain.

Neither Camille nor Chapman was facing the windows, so Lacey felt safe stopping and studying Camille. Camille's shoulders were straight—not stiff, not bowed forward. One arm was bent—was she pointing at something? Her head was slightly tipped toward Chapman, and the gloss and color of her hair made Lacey think of the citrine quartz she'd used in that vase she'd made for Jonas's mother.

Lacey leaned her shoulder against the fence, pulled out her phone, and pretended to text. If Camille or Chapman glanced out the window they'd see only an anonymous skinny figure—probably a teenager—in an old hoodie and ratty jeans, ignoring everything but her smartphone. No one to notice or worry about. She nudged her hood back far enough that she could keep watching Camille out of the corner of her eye.

Camille pivoted, and Lacey caught a profile view of her face. The corner of her mouth was raised but not too far. Eyebrow a little arched—was she asking a question? Doubting something, even? Challenging Chapman? Would she dare?

Lacey tried out the expression, but shaping it on her own face felt like creating a portrait with awkward chunks of glass. She could shape a smile, but it was a surreal Picasso smile. She relaxed her face and tried a second time.

Camille turned so she was fully facing the window. Hastily, Lacey bowed her head lower and tapped frenetically at her phone screen. A texting teen, part of the background, uninterested in the lit windows of the trailer.

Around the edge of her hood, she could barely see Camille still standing there. Was she looking at Lacey or gazing absently at the misty rain? She wouldn't turn her back on Chapman to stare at the sky. She must be looking at Lacey.

Lacey wanted to run, but if Camille saw her fleeing, she might be alarmed. Still pretending to text, Lacey meandered along the fence, passing the trailer and continuing until she was out of sight of the windows. Once she was confident

Camille couldn't see her, she sprinted around the block to the back of the construction site and stopped to catch her breath.

Hot under her sweatshirt, she leaned against a telephone pole and turned her face up toward the rain. Her chin still hurt. It must have a scrape—one big enough for Jonas to notice. She'd have to think of a way to explain it.

Loitering and trying for another glimpse of Camille was too dangerous; she'd better get out of here. She started to walk away, but the elbow of her sweatshirt snagged on something—a rusty staple sticking straight out of the telephone pole. She ripped her sleeve loose and hurried toward the plaza where she'd left her car. Jonas wouldn't notice the tear in the sleeve. He used to wear this old sweatshirt for yardwork, but she hadn't seen him wear it in years.

For long, dreary minutes, she sat behind her steering wheel and watched rain trickling down the windshield. She'd been wildly reckless today for only a tiny amount of information, but she didn't regret trying.

She didn't *think* she regretted it.

She twisted the rearview mirror so she could assess her chin. A red mark marred the bottom of it, but it wasn't bad. She could conceal it with makeup. It was time to slump back home, clean up, hide the wet, dirty clothes, and go back to being worthless Lacey Egan.

No . . . today's research didn't have to end yet. Jonas had a meeting in Buffalo, and he wouldn't be home until around eight. She had time to go to Camille's house. She could sneak through that garage side door with the broken lock. She could hide, wait for Camille, and study her as she got out of her car. Seeing her arrive home wouldn't be as useful as seeing her with Chapman, but it would still be valuable. Confidence, triumph, satisfaction—whatever showed on her face, it would be an expression Lacey could practice in front of the mirror tomorrow while Jonas was at work.

Reenergized, she drove to Camille's neighborhood, parked a block down the street, and strolled toward the two-story house with unblemished white siding and yellow shutters. Camille had decorated her porch for autumn with a scarecrow in a wooden rocking chair, pumpkins, and a basket of apples.

The wind blew harder, scattering maple leaves across the grass. Most of the tree was still green, but soon the whole thing would be red-gold fire. When the color peaked, she'd have to take pictures of it; it would make a breathtaking mosaic. If she was careful not to get the house in the background, Jonas would never know she'd taken the picture at Camille's. There were plenty of sugar maples around Ohneka.

Taking strong, confident steps, she followed the flagstone pathway along the side of the house. At the side door, she paused, opened it, and stepped into the dim garage. Noiselessly, she settled into the spot she'd staked out two weeks ago when she'd discovered the unlocked door: a snug hiding place between bins labeled *Christmas decorations* and wall shelves holding camping equipment. When Camille drove into the empty bay of the garage and stepped out of her car, Lacey could get a view of her face, illuminated by the bulb on the garage-door opener.

From her backpack, Lacey took her pen and fabric-covered notebook and started recording what she'd observed today, lighting the pages with her phone flashlight. Huddled on the concrete in her damp jeans and damp sweatshirt, she grew colder and colder. What if Camille had gone out to dinner after work?

The grumble of the garage door opening heated her discouragement into glowing anticipation. Instantly, she stowed her phone and notebook. Peeking between the boxes, careful to keep her breathing silent, she watched Camille's car glide into the garage and stop the perfect distance from the back wall.

With her face angled away from Lacey, Camille stepped out of the car, a leather briefcase in her hand. Lacey flexed and relaxed her arm, imagining carrying a case like that. Camille walked toward the house, her face still averted as though she was examining the hood of her car or checking out the shelves on the opposite wall. Lacey glared at the back of Camille's head, eagerness breaking into fragments of anger. After the time spent hiding and shivering, this was all she got?

She could make Camille look in her direction.

Using one knuckle, Lacey rapped twice against the nearest plastic bin. It wasn't a loud noise, but Camille started and wheeled around. Lacey flinched, startled herself at Camille's expression—mouth gaping and ready to scream, eyes bugging. Camille scanned the boxes, gripping her briefcase like she planned to swing it as a weapon.

"Is someone there?" Camille yelled. "I have a Taser."

Lacey crouched, dead artwork instead of living flesh. She hadn't expected to frighten Camille. She'd thought Camille would glance in her direction, then shrug off the tapping noise as raindrops.

Camille scanned the garage for another moment, then rushed toward the door to the house, unlocked it, and disappeared inside. She slammed the door, and the dead bolt clacked.

Lacey wormed between boxes, slipped out the side door, and closed it. It made a slight thump; had Camille heard it? It would be . . . a little fun if she had.

She'd never planned to scare Camille; she'd never planned to let Camille know anyone was watching her at all. Was she calling the police? Or was she now persuading herself the sudden noise had been the rain?

Lacey had scared her. *Scared* her. With a couple of taps of her knuckle against a storage bin, she'd shaken a woman who thought it was nothing to hobnob with a multimillionaire. An intelligent, strong, independent woman.

Two taps of her knuckle.

CHAPTER 2

"MORNING, NAT." SKYLER HUDSON SETTLED into a chair in the break room. "Curls today, huh?"

Natalie Marsh bent her head and shook her brown hair forward so she could see it around her face. It hadn't been this wavy when she'd left her house. "Apparently," she said. "It's the humidity. My car's in the shop, so I was waiting at the bus stop in the rain this morning."

"What's wrong with the car?"

"Old age. It'll be done this afternoon." She pushed the napkin dispenser toward Skyler. "You might want to wipe that chocolate off your chin."

"Eh, my clients won't care. They'll be too busy developing their Jedi mind powers."

"Is that what you do in biofeedback? You should charge more."

"Free light saber with every ten sessions." Skyler took a napkin and cleaned his chin. "Though if it's Jedi we're talking about, it's you who should be seeing them. They're prone to mental instability, right?"

Natalie swallowed the last bite of her yogurt. "I don't feel good about seeing clients who could strangle me with their minds if I annoy them."

"It'd make a good research topic though. 'Anger Management Issues in Jedi Knights: The Lure of the Dark Side.' You should write a paper."

"I'll make you second author," Natalie said.

Kirk Valdez walked through the door, sleeves rolled up, insulated travel mug in his hand. "Good morning, youngsters."

Skyler tipped back in his chair and squinted at Kirk. "The humidity didn't curl *his* hair."

Kirk patted his bald head, then stroked his graying black beard. "The beard's not curlier?"

"The beard is still a sad imitation of Freud's facial hair, revealing your insecurities as a psychotherapist."

Kirk unscrewed the lid on his travel mug. "Better Freud's beard than the hair of some tweenage boy band."

Skyler touched his auburn hair, short on the sides and long on top, drooping to his eyebrows. "Eh, you're jealous because you're an old bald guy. Nat, settle this. The hair is better than the beard, right?"

"If you think I'm getting involved in this, you're delusional." Natalie's phone buzzed. She checked the screen. "Camille will be here in a moment. She wanted to stop in and chat before the office opens."

"Drawn by my hotness," Skyler said.

"To chat with *me*," Natalie said. "How does Vicki put up with you?"

"She considers it a privilege."

Natalie believed it. Skyler's easygoing charm and sense of humor made up for his cocky vanity; everyone liked him. Even her mother had adored him—despised her own daughter but adored the biofeedback and physical therapist who'd eased her pain in the last year of her life.

A year in which Natalie had played no part.

Natalie smoothed and folded her napkin as though it needed to be tidy before she dropped it in the trash. She *was* glad Skyler had joined the practice, and she was over feeling awkward around him—mostly over it. Sometimes she still wondered if her mother had told him horrible stories about her, but after nearly a year of working in the same office with him, she hoped he knew she was a decent person notwithstanding whatever her mother had said.

"A privilege, huh?" Kirk drizzled creamer into his mug. "I didn't realize Vicki's psychosis was that severe. Tell her to make an appointment."

"I'll tell her to make an appointment with the state board to tell them you printed your license off the Internet," Skyler said.

"How long are you here at the office today?" Kirk asked. "Because we have a party scheduled for as soon as you leave to go flirt with the knee-replacement brigade."

"No physical therapy appointments until two, but if there's a party here, maybe I can bail out earlier. I know how you psychologists party. You sit around analyzing each other's childhoods, then dump your drinks on napkins and analyze the blots." Skyler looked at Natalie. "How's Camille doing?"

"She's okay. Busy with work. Too busy."

"She seeing anyone?" Skyler asked. Kirk glared at him, and he cringed. "Whoa, Valdez, I didn't mean it like that. I'm taken. I'm not chasing her. I'm just asking how she's . . . you know, healing. Poor girl. They weren't even married a year, right?"

"Just over six months," Natalie said.

Skyler grimaced. "Awful stuff."

Natalie's phone buzzed again. "I'll let her in." She exited the break room and passed through the waiting room to open the outer door.

"Good morning." Camille entered the office, her raincoat draped over her arm. She wore a teal blouse with a beaded gold-and-coral scarf, a coral pencil skirt, and six-inch snakeskin heels.

Natalie hugged her and relocked the outer door; the office didn't open for another forty-five minutes. "You look great. I love the shoes."

"Aren't they fabulous?" Camille lifted one foot and swished it back and forth. Natalie was impressed that she could balance on one stiletto. "On clearance at DSW."

"Sweet. Come on back." Natalie led her out of the waiting room.

Kirk and Skyler were standing outside the break room. Kirk had rolled his sleeves down and buttoned the cuffs, and Skyler had finger-styled his hair. Kirk was married, and Skyler was engaged, but male preening seemed to be an irresistible impulse when Camille was near. Vibrant, funny Camille was a Renoir painting come to life, with her graceful, rounded face and full lips, curvy figure, and flowing blonde hair.

"Guys! How are you?" Camille smiled at them, and they trotted toward her. "It's been awhile." She hugged both men.

"The renovation's looking good," Skyler said. "I drove past it the other day."

"Can you believe he's honestly naming it the Stoker Building?" Camille asked. "That's Bob Chapman in a nutshell."

"What's wrong with 'Stoker Building?'" Skyler asked. "Who is Stoker? Some investor?"

"No. The building was originally built in 1897, which was the year *Dracula* was published."

"And?" Skyler said.

Kirk snickered. "*Dracula*," he said. "By Bram Stoker, you ignoramus."

"He named it after the vampire-novel guy? Because of the date?"

"That's Bob," Camille said. "Most people will never know why it's named that, which he finds even funnier."

"The Stoker Building." Skyler brushed his bangs off his eyebrows and grinned at Natalie. "You're lobbying this rich dude to fund a mental health clinic in a vampire's castle?"

"Vampires need psychological services too," Natalie said.

"Vampires and Jedi." Skyler waved farewell. "Good to see you, Camille." He headed toward his office.

Kirk smiled and retreated as well.

Natalie ushered Camille into her office. "I can't believe how smoothly you walk in those heels," she remarked as Camille passed her.

"Practice. You should wear heels. They'll make your legs gorgeous."

Natalie eyed the portion of her legs that showed beneath her knee-length gray wool skirt. Navy tights, low-heeled, brick-red pumps. "Next time I have a date, I'll think about it." Given the deadness of her recent social life, she'd be safe from stilettos forever.

"Not that your legs aren't already gorgeous," Camille said. "Wear what you want; that's how I feel about it. I hate fashion police. Or at least I've hated them since I realized how obnoxious I was in high school. Your hair is darling. Did you get it cut?"

Natalie flipped her fingers through her shoulder-length bob. "Nope. The curl makes it look shorter. How is everything? Your text sounded stressed."

"Curt and rude, you mean. 'I'm coming over! Make time for me or else!'" Camille sat on the couch and dropped her raincoat and purse on the floor. "Sit on the couch with me. If you sit in your Dr. Marsh chair, I'll think you're diagnosing me."

"I'm listening as a friend no matter where I sit." Natalie settled on the couch. "What's up?"

"I'll get to the point since I know you have clients arriving soon. Something weird is going on." Camille played with the wedding ring she still wore, rotating the diamond-loaded band around her finger. "I think someone is stalking me."

"Stalking you! What's going on?"

"It's . . . well, for a while, it was small things. Silly things that might not have been real issues, if you know what I mean."

"Like you might have imagined them?"

"Yes, or misinterpreted them. Like I'd be shopping and I'd get this feeling that someone was watching me, but there wouldn't be anything definitive—just hints of motion out of the corner of my eye. Or I'd be walking in the park and would keep seeing the same person, but they were wearing a hooded jacket, and if I looked toward them, they were always looking down or in the other direction, and I never saw their face. I figured I was being paranoid and didn't worry about it too much. But over the past couple of weeks, there have been a few times when I had the windows open, when the weather's been so nice, and I'd see little movements outside my study window or hear weird noises."

"Weird noises?"

"Rustling or twigs breaking."

"Noises that a cat or raccoon couldn't have made?"

"I did figure it was an animal or my imagination. But yesterday, Bob wanted a face-to-face update—which businesses have signed leases for space in the Stoker Building, what the latest proposals are from the interior design team, and so on. We met at the renovation site. We were in the office trailer, and I glanced out the window and saw someone standing there. Right behind the trailer."

"Inside the fence?"

"No, outside, but . . . right there."

"Peeking in the window?"

"I think he had been. I think I saw him turn—or her—I couldn't tell if it was a man or woman; they were wearing a loose hooded sweatshirt. I think they were facing the trailer but turned away when I looked."

"They were standing there doing nothing?"

"Well, texting."

Natalie imagined the scenario; she'd been to the renovation site a few times and could picture the trailer and the fence. "Did you get a look at their face or part of their face?"

"Just a glimpse . . . I think they're . . . Caucasian?" She sighed. "I know that's useless."

"Did you try to confront them yesterday?"

"No. What could I say to Bob? 'Excuse me while I run outside and ask that person in the hoodie if they're watching me'? Besides, they walked away a few seconds after I looked out the window. I think they knew I'd noticed them."

Natalie was starting to understand why Camille had been apprehensive about her shifting into psychologist mode. "Okay. Let's break this down. The hooded sweatshirt—was it raining while the lurker was there?"

"Yes, but . . . okay, yes."

"So there's another reason for the hood. If he was looking in the window, is there anything besides you that could have drawn his interest?"

"Maybe he wanted a peek at my eccentric boss or was nosy in general, but I felt so uneasy. Weird vibes. Come on, it's intuition."

Natalie contemplated Camille's words. Yes, she believed in intuition. Yes, it was possible someone was obsessed with Camille.

Yes, Camille had some leanings toward melodrama and tended to jump to conclusions. Yes, she was under a lot of stress.

"Stop that," Camille snapped. "You're running everything I told you through your DMV book, or whatever, and trying to label my brain malfunction."

"You mean DSM," Natalie said. "Diagnostic and Statistical Manual. Though the Department of Motor Vehicles is a lot scarier."

Camille laughed. "Freudian slip."

"Camille, you know I have the capacity to listen as a friend. Stop being so defensive. You're worried someone is stalking you. Is there anyone you've been in conflict with lately? Anyone who's threatened you?"

"Oh . . . no . . . There were people who were bent out of shape when I got the Stoker management job, too big of a promotion, they deserved it more, or whatever, but I have a hard time imagining any of them hanging around and spying on me."

"Do you feel like the stalker wants to harm you?"

"I have no idea what he wants. I was guessing he just wanted to watch me—believe me, I've been keeping my curtains closed when it's dark outside—but last night when I got home after work, someone was in my garage."

Alarm flashed in Natalie's mind. Up till now, Camille hadn't offered any evidence heftier than imagination, but an intruder was different. "You saw someone?"

"I heard them. A noise from behind my storage bins. And *don't* say it was a rat because it wasn't a rodent noise. It was two knocks."

"Knocks?"

"Like knocking on a door, only not a door. A knock on something hard, probably one of the bins. Two even, clear pops."

"What did you do?"

"I yelled that I had a Taser, ran into the house, and locked the door."

"You have a Taser?"

"I was bluffing. I don't want a Taser; I'd electrocute myself."

"Did you call the police?"

"I called my neighbor. He's an ex-Marine, big muscly guy. He searched my garage and house and yard but didn't find anyone."

"Any footprints? Like wet footprints in the garage?"

"No, but maybe the stalker was waiting for so long that they'd dried. And don't tell me I imagined that knocking noise because I didn't. You don't believe me, do you? You don't think there's a stalker."

"Have I said that?"

Camille crinkled one side of her face, pondering the question.

"I haven't said it," Natalie said.

"I'm reading your mind. You thought it."

"Why didn't you call the police?"

"Because I was afraid they wouldn't believe me about a creeper in my garage. I was afraid they'd write up a report and file it in the 'Drama Queen' archive."

Natalie refrained from joking that if she were chief of police, she'd definitely be tempted to create an archive like that.

Camille fidgeted with one of the gold beads that dangled from the hem of her scarf. "All right, I'm sorry for being so testy. I do want to know what you think about all this, so chuck it at me. Be frank."

"All right. I think *you* doubt there's a stalker."

"So I'm paranoid, and I'm paranoid about being paranoid. Meta-paranoid."

"No. I think you're excited and stressed about your new job responsibilities. You're feeling overwhelmed but don't want to admit it to yourself because you're superwoman."

"Do you think the scenario of an evil stalker dogging me is easier for me to cope with than the scenario of being dogged by insecurity and possible failure?"

"Do *you* think that?"

Camille glowered at her. "I knew you didn't believe me."

"I can give you sympathy and hugs if you want them, but I don't think that's why you came to me. You know better than I do that every incident you've told me about could be harmless coincidence—someone doing their shopping, a random passerby curious about the Stoker renovation, a couple of supersized raindrops falling from a tree branch and smacking your garage roof. If you thought there was more weight to your fears, you would have called the police, not your neighbor."

Camille rubbed her thumb against the largest diamond on her ring, her gaze focused past Natalie. "I don't know. This is giving me the creeps. Could it . . . be grief related, do you think?"

"Sure. You want to share your stress with Dante and get his support, but you can't. You want him to see how you're succeeding and be proud of you, and instead you're coming home to an empty house."

"I've been coming home to an empty house for nineteen months," she said curtly. "What makes you think I'm having a worse time now?"

"Intuition," Natalie said. "Weird vibes."

"You're a brat."

"You're wearing the pearl earrings he gave you for your first Christmas and the blouse you wore in your engagement pictures, and you keep playing with your wedding band."

"Grr. Look who's going all Hercule Poirot." Camille held up her left hand and studied her ring. "Do you think it's unhealthy that I still wear this when it's been a year and a half since some anonymous weasel ran my husband down in a crosswalk?"

"Unhealthy in what way?"

"Like I'm supposed to move on. Like I've been mourning him three times as long as we were married."

"The fact that you were only married for six months is irrelevant. Grief isn't a mathematical equation. Wear the ring as long as you want. Only you can say if and when it's not healthy for you."

Camille lowered her hand and sighed. "It *has* been tough lately. I wonder if it's fallout from what happened to your neighbor's husband . . . your neighbor from when you were a kid, I mean. Felicia Radcliffe."

Pain gouged Natalie. "I can see how you'd relate to that."

"Right? Kissing your husband good-bye in the morning with no idea you'll never see him alive again . . . that he'll fall off a stupid ladder . . ." She gave Natalie a bleak smile. "You collect more than your share of widowed-too-young friends. Find a new hobby, Nat."

Camille's black humor usually amused Natalie, but this time it made her feel illogically culpable. "That's what Skyler said. And he asked me to please visit my bad luck on someone who wasn't his client next time because he'd done great work with Wade and now it was wasted."

"Wade Radcliffe was his client?"

"A couple of years ago, in PT. He got hit in the head with a softball while playing in that local-business-owners league."

"Ouch."

"Serious concussion, but he recovered."

Camille shuddered. "That makes me feel like the Grim Reaper was already following him around. When his first try didn't work, he clonked him a second time. And that was a punk comment from Skyler."

"Teasing is his way of coping. And he apologized for it even before Kirk threatened to knock his teeth out."

"You know what's weird? You know how I told you I met Felicia's husband for the first time at his store not long before he died?"

"Yes."

"It was bugging me, so I went back and looked at my receipt, and I looked up the newspaper reports on his accident. I met Wade the *day* he died. That day! First time I'd ever shopped at MaryLisa's. I was there late in the day too, near closing time—what if I was his last customer? What if I was the last person he talked to? I saw him after his wife saw him!"

"And you feel guilty about that."

Camille groaned. "Yes. And I was a piece of work too. I got all tense and emotional because I was there to buy myself my birthday present from Dante, and I ended up having to flee to the restroom to get control of myself. What if the last woman's voice he heard was mine haggling over the cost of that fancy purse and trying not to break down in front of him? I've always wished I could go back in time and call Dante at the end of the day so I could tell him I loved him, that those could be the last words he heard instead of whatever random last words he heard from whoever. Which is a silly wish; if I could go back in time, I'd prevent him from getting run down at all. And yes, I know feeling guilty is irrational; you don't need to tell me that."

"Here's something to help you ditch that irrational guilt: Felicia probably *was* the last person Wade spoke to. At the funeral, someone—her sister, maybe?— told me he called Felicia after work to tell her he was staying late and that she'd offered to bring him dinner, but he'd said he was fine."

Camille's face brightened. "Really? Oh, I feel so much better. How is she doing?"

"I wish I knew. She's been avoiding me."

"I thought you guys were close."

"We were when I was a kid, but I don't see her very often anymore. I keep trying to reach out to her, but when I call or text, she usually doesn't answer. If I stop by her house, I'm lucky if I get a chat on the doorstep. She did mention that her stepson has been helping her out, so I hope she has the support she needs."

"Good, I'm glad to hear that."

"I'm not surprised she's choosing to grieve mostly on her own. She's a private person."

"She knows you're there if you need her. It's only been, what, a month since Wade died?"

"Yes, six weeks or so. But back to your current stress. What can I do to help you?"

"What do you think would help?"

"How about some mental time off? You need a break. What are you up to tonight?"

"Work."

"Forget it. Lock your work in your desk, put on some old sweatpants, and pop some popcorn. I'll come over. We'll binge-watch Netflix."

Camille twitched one eyebrow up and down. "Do you seriously think I'm imagining my stalker?"

"I wasn't there for any of it. I don't know. But frankly—you said be frank—none of it seems conclusive enough to be worth worrying about. How about we bring your stress level down and then see if someone is still playing the bongos on your storage boxes?"

"You are a brat *and* a punk." Camille stood up. "Bring those chocolate gingerbread squares; I'm craving them."

"Deal." Natalie rose to walk Camille out. One young friend, one older friend, both widowed and grieving. And Natalie offered calls and texts and chocolate and Netflix parties, hoping that would help. *You're offering friendship. Love. You're doing what you can. You can't wipe the pain out of their lives.*

You ought to know that.

CHAPTER 3

"YOU MAKE THE BEST CINNAMON apples." Jonas spread another spoonful on his waffle.

"Thank you." Lacey smiled at him. Eight years of cinnamon apples twice a week. *This* was the morning she'd change things. She'd tell Jonas that on Saturday when she made waffles again, she wasn't making cinnamon apples. She was making raspberry sauce. Camille wouldn't keep making cinnamon apples if she were so sick of them she'd rather eat a bowl of cement, and Lacey could be strong like Camille. She'd even spooked strong Camille with only a small noise; Lacey wasn't powerless.

She cut off a corner of her waffle that she hadn't contaminated with the apples. Scaring Camille hadn't been nice. She wouldn't do it again.

"You should finish that milk." Jonas forked another waffle onto his plate. "Calcium for those pretty bones."

Lacey lifted her glass and took a gulp of milk. She'd take three swallows of milk, two more bites of waffle, and then she'd tell him about the raspberry sauce. If he said to do the apples instead, she'd refuse and give him that smile she'd practiced, the smile Camille had given them when Jonas and Lacey were leaving her office and Jonas had asked her to call him as soon as she had a decision. *"Jonas, I'll be blunt. Don't wait by the phone. I like the samples of Lacey's work, but the odds of Mr. Chapman commissioning one of her mosaics aren't high. He loves personally finding original art for his properties, which is good news for Lacey, but every artist in the country knows it and pushes their work at him, so that's the bad news. He has unlimited choices. I'll make sure to show him her portfolio, but that's the only promise I can make."*

Jonas's response had been calm and respectful: *"I understand. Thank you for taking the time to talk with us. It's good to see you again."*

Calm and respectful. Lacey would give him that firm smile and friendly refusal, and he'd be calm and respectful like he'd been with Camille. She would make the raspberry sauce. He would love it. Maybe he'd compliment her for branching out.

She took her third swallow of milk and set the glass down, readying herself.

Jonas reached across the table and placed his hand on hers. Her fingers felt squashed under his, and she wanted to wriggle her hand free, but she didn't move.

"There's something I want you to do this morning," he said.

"I'm sorry I'm so slow," Lacey said. "I *am* working on ideas for the Stoker project in case they're interested. I'll work hard to finish one of the designs this morning."

"Not that," Jonas said. "Baby, you're keeping secrets."

Sweat broke out under her shirt, tiny, hot drops of confession. "I . . . I did want to tell you I found this recipe for raspberry sauce . . ."

With his free hand, he touched her chin where she'd painted foundation makeup over the scrape from the fence. "How did you hurt yourself?"

Lacey pressed herself together: ankles joined, knees pushing against each other, elbows squeezing her sides. In a light voice, she recited the lie she'd prepared in case Jonas noticed the scrape. "The phone rang while I was working, and it made me jump. I hit myself in the chin with a tile scorer. Silly."

Jonas scrutinized her. His eyes were two shades of brown, lighter in the center, darker on the edges. They reminded her of stained wood. The polished walnut stock of her father's rifle.

"What really happened?" he asked.

"That's what happened." She pushed her feet harder against the tile floor, but the fabric soles of her slippers skidded. She imagined Jonas knocking his chair over, smashing his plate to the floor. Ramming his fist into her face.

She tried to breathe slowly. Jonas had never hit her. Why did she fear he'd start today?

Because she'd never lied to him before, but she was lying to him now. And he knew it.

His hand constricted around her wrist. "What's wrong? What are you hiding?"

"I'm not hiding anything! What do I have to hide? You know everything about me."

"Baby, you're jumpy. You toss and turn and wake up at night. You aren't eating enough, and you're already too thin. How much weight have you lost?"

"I don't know. None, I think. I haven't stepped on the scale in a while."

"I checked the scale log this morning. You weighed yourself three days ago, and you're down 6.2 pounds."

Lacey focused on the iridescent blue tiles of the fruit bowl she'd made to accent the kitchen decor. "I'm fine. I . . . think I'm wound up about the possibility of a commission for Robert Chapman. That would be a huge break for me."

"I ran into Camille the other day. She said your portfolio is on Chapman's desk now."

The sharp, fast pounding in her chest made her feel her heart might crack. "Thank you *so* much for introducing my work to her. You're always looking out for me."

"Is that all that's on your mind? Stress over your work?"

"Yes, that's all." *I'm not cheating on you. I swear I'm not cheating on you.* Lacey pushed her tongue against the roof of her mouth, squashing the defensive words before she could speak them. Jonas hadn't directly accused her of infidelity, and if she brought it up first, it would sound suspicious. He must be thinking it though. *Cheating, mangy cat in heat, prowling the neighborhood.*

Jonas released her wrist, reached into his shirt pocket, and took out a folded piece of paper. He opened it and set it on the table in front of Lacey.

In Jonas's handwriting was a local phone number and two names: Kirk Valdez and Natalie Marsh.

"They're psychologists," Jonas said. "I got a personal recommendation to make sure I found someone good. Both are great therapists."

Therapists? Psychologists? Lacey tried to sort her jumbled thoughts and arrange them into a picture that made sense. "I'm not crazy!"

"I never said you were crazy, baby. You don't have to be crazy to talk to a pro."

"I don't need to talk to anyone. I'm fine."

"I know you don't like making phone calls, so I tried to make an appointment for you, but the receptionist said you'd have to call the office yourself." Jonas reached into his pocket again and pulled out his phone—no, that was *her* phone. Why did he have her phone? He set it in front of her. "Call now," he said.

Lacey's tongue was a piece of broken glass. "It's . . . it's . . . too early."

"The office opens at eight thirty. It's eight thirty-four now."

Lacey pictured herself lying on a couch, observed by a man in a high-backed armchair. *"Your husband tells me you are disturbed, Mrs. Egan, and I see he's right. An ambulance is coming to take you to the hospital. Please cooperate; this is for your own good."*

"I don't need a shrink," she said.

"Baby, you have a multimillionaire art aficionado reviewing your work, but instead of stepping up your game, you're unfocused and unproductive, and you look worried all the time. I ask you what's wrong, and you tell me lies."

She let the words loose. "I'm not . . . I'm not cheating on you."

"I never said you were. But something's wrong inside of you, and it's my job to see that it gets fixed." He tapped the paper with his index finger. "Call now. I'll sit here with you so you won't be so nervous."

Lacey edged her still-full plate away, nauseated by the smell of butter and cinnamon. She didn't have to call. He couldn't make her call. He couldn't make her go. She didn't have to talk to anyone.

Firm smile. Use that firm smile. She tried, but her lips squiggled into a mushy curve. "I need to think about this."

"Call now. Lacey, the other night you were saying you thought it was time to try for a baby. I want kids as much as you do, but I can't bring them into a situation where their mother can't handle her own issues. Let's get your head straightened out before you end up like the rest of your family."

Lacey's face was so hot she felt his gaze had sunburned her. *I don't want to do this. You can't force me to do this.*

"I'll dial for you." Jonas took the piece of paper and the phone and tapped the number onto the screen. He passed the ringing phone to Lacey.

"What am I supposed to say?" she rasped.

"Just that you want to make an appointment." He rested a hand on her arm, as heavy and cold as cast iron. "I'll stay right here with you."

* * *

Gideon Radcliffe grinned at his stepmother. She smiled back, to his relief. She looked better tonight—not as pale, not as tormented, and she met his gaze as though glad to see him instead of just wishing he were his father. "Hey, Mama Felicia," he said. "How are you?"

"Come in, Gideon. Have you eaten dinner?"

"Not yet, but don't worry about it. I'll throw something in the microwave when I get home." He stepped into the entryway and removed his loafers.

"I have leftover beef and barley soup in the fridge. Would you like some?"

Nothing he could microwave would be anywhere near the quality of Felicia's soup. "Heck yeah, I would." He followed her to the kitchen. Felicia poured the soup into a saucepan and ignited the gas burner. "Can I help with anything?" he asked.

"No. Sit down and relax. Are you coming straight from work?"

"Yeah." He settled into a kitchen chair. "The city wants to redo the medians on Main Street and make some changes in traffic flow, so I was downtown today. I passed MaryLisa's a bunch of times. Kept hoping I'd see Dad through the window."

A slight silent smile was Felicia's reply, but Gideon could read it: she kept hoping she'd see his father not only at his store but everywhere.

"That sweater's a good color on you," she said, stirring the soup. "The cadet blue matches your eyes."

Gideon lifted an arm and admired one of the wool, cable-knit sleeves he'd pushed up on the drive over here—the evening was warmer than he'd anticipated. "Thanks. You gave it to me."

"Because I knew it would look good on you." The motherly approval in her voice made Gideon want to sit with good posture, run his hand over his dark hair to make sure it wasn't sticking up, and share everything he'd done at work today in a quest for her praise. If he gave her a printout of the Main Street layout, maybe she'd stick it on the fridge.

Felicia cut two slices of oatmeal bread and put them on a plate. She set the plate on the table along with the butter dish.

"Thank you." Gideon picked up the knife. "Sit with me while the soup heats."

She filled a glass with water, set it in front of him, and sat down. "The autopsy results are back," she said. "Finally."

The load of grief inside Gideon increased. "And?"

"Acute subdural hematoma, resulting from a fall."

"So no surprises."

Despondency in her eyes, Felicia didn't answer. Had he guessed wrong in thinking she was doing better tonight? No, she definitely looked more grounded than she had in the first weeks after his father's death. Less lost inside her grief, more engaged with reality.

"It must be rough, seeing it in clinical terms," Gideon said. "Even though we knew from the start what killed him."

Felicia spoke quietly. "I don't think we do know."

"Do you think the autopsy missed something?" he asked.

No answer.

"Felicia, we know exactly what happened. He was up on the ladder in his storage room, getting a box down. The old ladder broke, he fell, and he struck his head. Second traumatic brain injury in the past three years, after getting slammed with that softball. This time it was too much." His voice was getting choky; Gideon paused and inhaled, hoping his throat would relax. It had shaken him, seeing his father in the hospital after that first concussion, then on bed rest, slowly struggling back to health with the aid of physical therapy. This time Gideon had had no time to be shaken—he'd vaulted straight to devastated. No sight of his father in a hospital bed. Just in a coffin. "What could the autopsy have missed?" Gideon asked.

Her fingertips tapped the tabletop—touched more than tapped—in repeated, silent motions. "That the injury was deliberately inflicted."

"What? Like . . . he fell on purpose? He wouldn't—"

"No. No. That someone caused it to happen."

"Who else was responsible for the ladder? Dad had had it forever; it was old. He probably never thought to check the rungs or the bolts." Guilt kicked Gideon, a blow he'd felt so many times that he didn't bother trying to parry it. His father had had a multitude of skills; he'd been adept at running a business, and his clothing boutique had been the delight of Ohneka's wealthier women. But his abilities hadn't included any handyman skills more advanced than jiggling the handle to make the toilet stop running. "I should have told him he needed to check—"

"It's not your fault," Felicia interrupted. "Not your fault at all. The ladder didn't collapse due to neglect."

Gideon studied her, trying to process what she'd told him. Her expression was stoic, but her cheeks were red.

"You said someone caused the ladder to collapse," he said. "Are you saying someone sabotaged it?"

She ran her pinky across her forehead, lifting her bangs and letting them settle again as though wanting a breeze on her skin. Her prematurely silver-gray hair was so smooth and shiny it always reminded Gideon of cold-rolled steel.

"That doesn't make sense." He spoke the dismissive words as gently as he could. "Who would sabotage the ladder? Nobody had a reason to hurt Dad."

"There . . . is a reason."

"What reason?"

"That's not for your ears."

Boggled and irritated, Gideon fought to respond like this was a sensible conversation. "He's my father. Everything about his death is for my ears. If you suspected sabotage, why didn't you tell the police? They never said anything about foul play. Why didn't you tell *me*? I threw the ladder away, hauled it to the dump. I didn't want you to have to deal with it. If the police knew you had reason to suspect sabotage, they would have examined it more closely."

"It took me a little while to realize . . . It doesn't matter anyway. I'm sure the saboteur was clever enough not to leave evidence."

Evidence of murder? This was ridiculous. Who would want to kill—or injure—Wade Radcliffe?

No one.

Gideon looked down and occupied himself by buttering his bread. Felicia had always been a reasonable person. If he stayed calm and spoke rationally, whatever grief-warped theory she'd erected in her mind would collapse before he'd finished his soup.

"Why would someone hurt Dad?" Gideon started buttering the second slice of bread. "Clearly robbery wasn't a motive—nothing was missing from the store.

And he wasn't a guy to get mixed up in anything dangerous. He loved his family, he loved his store, and he loved kicking my trash in one-on-one basketball. He didn't like drama, any kind of drama. You know that. You guys were married for . . . was it eleven years?"

"I know he didn't like drama," Felicia said. "But that doesn't mean he couldn't be hurt by someone who does like drama."

"Who? You suspect someone."

"I don't know her name. A woman bought an expensive purse at MaryLisa's not long before Wade died." Felicia's tone was grim but so composed that Gideon felt he was the only one rattled by the suggestion that his father's death was a homicide. "When he called me at closing, he mentioned this woman and the transaction."

"What did he say about her?"

"She acted strange. Both pushy and nervous, and at one point, she asked if she could use his restroom. He got busy with another customer, he said, but when the woman finally returned to the front, he realized she'd been gone a long time. He was joking about it with me, saying he hoped she hadn't gotten trapped in the bathroom because sometimes the lock sticks, and she'd seemed so edgy that she'd probably be traumatized by the experience and sue him."

"You think she was back there tinkering with the ladder?" Gideon pulled down the sleeves of his sweater. He was colder in here than he'd been outside. "Okay, let's talk about this woman. I know Dad didn't have security cameras, but can't the police track her down with her credit card information? If you think she set up Dad's accident, that's a police matter."

"She paid cash," Felicia said. "For a royal-blue silk evening clutch that cost nearly seven hundred dollars."

"Seven hundred dollars! For a *purse*? That's nuts!"

"It was rare for your father to have a cash transaction that large. Why would this woman have been carrying such a large sum? Maybe she'd recently been paid in cash for an illegal transaction? Maybe she didn't want to leave traceable evidence?"

"That's a leap to assume the cash means something shady. She could have sold a couch on Craigslist."

"On its own, it doesn't mean much. It's the timing that makes it suspicious. The purse is one-of-a-kind, handmade by a local mosaic artist."

"Mosaic?"

"Decorated on both sides with winter landscapes made of tiny glass tiles. It was a foolish purchase for her to make."

"Because it identifies her as the saboteur?"

"Yes."

Gideon wanted to point out that it was absurd to view this woman's actions as though they were living in an Agatha Christie novel, but tact was a better approach. "Is there any way to track her down? Through the artist, maybe?"

"I spoke to the artist. She doesn't know who bought the purse but promised to call me if she finds out. She seems spineless and wishy-washy though, so I doubt she'll take the initiative to follow up with me. I'll contact her myself later."

"Have you told any of this to the police?"

"No." Felicia went to stir the soup. "I can't explain why, but it's not a good idea to talk to them right now. I've only told you this much because you need to be on guard. You might be in danger."

"Me? In danger? Why would a killer target me?"

With her back to him, she kept stirring the soup, her posture pillar-straight. She didn't answer.

Gideon picked up his glass, swished water around his dry mouth, and swallowed. This conversation had moved past improbable theory to bizarre paranoia. Time to get them back on a straight, level road instead of following Felicia on these hairpin curves. "We need to look at this logically. Is it possible that grief is leading you to jump to conclusions? Blaming a mysterious woman doesn't make sense. There's no evidence the accident was staged. It was just an accident. A horrible accident. We need to accept that."

She shut off the flames under the soup and pivoted to face him. "Do you think I came to this conclusion without good reasons? I know it isn't rational to blame a stranger simply because she was there. That's not why I suspect her. I know why she killed him."

Felicia spoke with such conviction that Gideon felt he'd clipped the guardrail, sending his car skidding out of control again. *Was* this more than grief? Had someone wanted his father dead?

"Why would she kill him?" he asked. "What was her motive?"

"Her motive was money, I assume." Felicia opened the cupboard and took out a bowl. "But she wasn't the one who wanted him dead; she was only doing a job." She filled the bowl with soup, brought it to the table, and returned to her chair.

"Who did want him dead?" Gideon half expected another "not for your ears" response, but her answer was solid and clear.

"Robert Chapman," she said.

"Chapman! The multimillionaire guy?"

"Yes."

"Why would he send someone after Dad? I didn't know Dad had dealings with him besides the store lease."

"You don't need to know the rest."

"He's my father. Yes, I do."

"Knowing details wouldn't change anything for you," she said. "This is the only warning you need: be wary around anyone who has a connection with Chapman."

Gideon goggled at her. "Beware of the whole city?"

"Not everyone is his puppet. But if someone works for him or has other connections with him, be cautious."

Baffled, Gideon mulled over the facts—*tried* to mull over the facts but couldn't find any, except that his father was dead and Felicia was withholding information.

"Eat your soup," she said.

"This is absolutely crazy. You have to tell me—"

"If it would do any good, I'd tell you. It won't; it would make things worse. Trust me to do what's best."

"I trust you. I love you. Top-ranked stepmother in the galaxy. You brought my father a lot of happiness, and you were a godsend to a nerdy, motherless teenager who was blundering his way into adulthood. But trusting you doesn't mean I agree with your keeping secrets about—"

"There are private matters involved, factors that are none of your business."

Gideon had never been a tantrum-throwing teenager, but he was tempted to belatedly offer his stepmother some yelling and door slamming. "We're talking about the possibility that my father was murdered. How can that not be my business?"

She leaned her elbows on the table and peered into Gideon's eyes. "You need to keep what I've told you completely confidential. Do you promise?"

Gideon picked at the crust on one of the slices of bread, tearing it away until he had a ring of crust in his hand. "I've heard Chapman is eccentric, but I've never heard he's deadly."

"He does things his own way, and not all those ways are harmless. He gets the media to present the image he wants to present, but don't underestimate him. Be careful and don't let on that you suspect anything. Agreed?"

Gideon wanted to shout that he *didn't* agree. He disagreed, to the nth degree. "Felicia—"

"I want your agreement, Gideon." Her stern voice made Gideon feel he'd time-traveled back to adolescence. "You won't speak to anyone about anything I've told you. Not a word."

He *needed* to speak to someone. He needed outside input, an opinion from someone who wasn't messed up with grief. Which both he and Felicia were.

"Gideon!" Anger boiled in her voice. "Answer me!"

"Uh . . . okay, agreed," he said, unnerved at how rapidly she'd lost her composure. He didn't want to agitate her. He needed to think about this, and he didn't know whom to talk to right now anyway.

"Thank you." Her voice calmed. "You won't have to be on guard forever. Things will resolve. But for your own safety, keep quiet."

"Mama Felicia." He reached across the table and rested his hand on hers. "I'm worried about *your* safety. If there's danger, let me help you. I'm good at helping. Good at defeating enemies and huge armies. The sword of the Lord and of Gideon and all that."

"I'm not a target. I'm not in danger." She pulled her hand away. "It's not something you can help with. The issues involved aren't yours to deal with. Trust me." She gestured at his bowl. "Eat your dinner, and tell me about the Main Street project."

CHAPTER 4

A YOUNG WOMAN—LACEY'S AGE, maybe? Late twenties? Early thirties?—smiled and held out her hand. She had friendly hazel eyes and sepia-brown hair that was cut so it didn't quite reach her shoulders—shorter than Jonas had ever allowed Lacey to cut her hair. Her nose had a slight curve in the bridge. Aquiline. It was a strong nose; Lacey admired it.

"Good morning," the woman said. "I'm Natalie Marsh."

This was Dr. Marsh? Lacey had figured she was an assistant to the Frida Kahlo look-alike sitting behind the sliding-glass reception window—Frida Kahlo if she'd lived to reach her late fifties. Lacey had imagined Dr. Marsh as older. She'd also imagined her wearing a white coat, but psychologists probably didn't do that. She was wearing a sunflower-gold cardigan over an ivory blouse and an ankle-length brown skirt with multiple angled layers. Lacey recognized that skirt: it was from MaryLisa's. Shards of anxiety poked at her stomach as she thought of Felicia Radcliffe's phone call demanding information about the purse Lacey had placed at that store.

"Jonas Egan. This is my wife, Lacey." Jonas shook Dr. Marsh's hand, despite the fact that she'd been offering it to Lacey. He'd intervened because Lacey was gawking blankly at a skirt instead of responding to the greeting.

As Jonas released Dr. Marsh's hand, Lacey reached hurriedly to shake it. She needed to act like a normal person so she could convince Dr. Marsh she was fine.

Dr. Marsh's hand was firm and warm. She must have noticed immediately that Lacey's hand was quivery and clammy. All of Lacey was quivery and clammy, her body a limp water plant that could move only with the currents.

"Jonas, you're welcome to have a seat." Dr. Marsh gestured at the uphol-stered chairs in the empty waiting room.

Lacey wished she could have a seat out here instead of going with Dr. Marsh. This was a pretty room, with pale-turquoise paint, light-gray Berber carpet, and

Monet reproductions on the walls. In one corner sat a water dispenser and a small granite-topped table that held a coffee maker and baskets of teas and coffees.

No, she didn't want a seat in a pretty waiting room. She wanted a seat in Jonas's car as they drove home. Right now.

No, not in Jonas's car. She wanted to run out of here and sprint through the chilly September morning, escaping to . . . where? Jonas was all she had.

Jonas rested his hand between Lacey's shoulder blades. If she tried to leave, he'd grab her. She pictured him dragging her into Dr. Marsh's office.

"It would be better if I came in with Lacey," he said.

"Lacey and I need time to get to know each other. Help yourself to coffee or tea or water."

"Lacey's nervous." Jonas wrapped his arm around her. "She'll feel safer if I come with her."

No, I won't. Lacey's heart was a blob of glass, heavy but ready to shatter. She didn't want Jonas in there. He'd tell Dr. Marsh she was mentally ill.

"I need to speak with her alone first," Dr. Marsh said pleasantly.

Jonas's arm tightened, squeezing her shoulders. "She's my wife. She's had a tough life. She needs me."

"She knows you're right here. Lacey, if you would come with me."

Jonas turned Lacey around and hugged her, squashing her against him. "See you in a few minutes, baby."

He released her. Dr. Marsh opened a door that led to the back and smiled at Lacey. Lacey stepped gingerly through the open door. When it closed behind them, it sounded heavy. Reinforced.

She followed Dr. Marsh along a corridor decorated in pastel hues. It was so quiet back here. Was she the only patient? Did they schedule them one at a time so no one else heard the screaming?

Dr. Marsh opened a door and gestured Lacey inside. The room had a blonde oak desk, armchairs upholstered in a lavender and blue pattern that reminded her of the impressionist prints in the waiting room, and a blue couch—a regular couch, not the reclining couch she'd always seen in cartoons poking fun at shrinks. Was she supposed to lie on the couch?

"Have a seat wherever you're most comfortable." Dr. Marsh closed the door.

Would the door lock automatically, trapping her inside?

Dr. Marsh stood waiting for Lacey to choose a seat. Lacey licked her lips and scanned the office. A water bottle, a closed laptop computer, and a notebook sat on the side table next to an armchair that was solid lavender instead of patterned. That must be Dr. Marsh's spot. Lacey hurried to sit in one of the patterned chairs.

Dr. Marsh sat in the lavender chair. Lacey edged backward so her shoulders touched the upholstery. The chair was comfortable, and for a moment, she wanted to slump in it and close her burning eyes. Jonas had forced a sleeping pill on her last night, but one night of rest wasn't enough to make up for weeks of poor sleep, and even with the medication, she'd woken up at four and couldn't get back to sleep.

Dr. Marsh gave Lacey another smile. "Feel free to call me Natalie. Or if Dr. Marsh is more comfortable for you, you're welcome to use that as well. Whatever you prefer. I answer to anything."

Lacey nodded. Calling her Natalie would make it sound like she was a friend, which she wasn't; calling her Dr. Marsh would make her sound intimidating. Lacey didn't want to call her anything. After today, she never wanted to see her again. What did Dr. Marsh know about her? Lacey had no idea what Jonas had written on that paperwork the office had e-mailed to them—e-mailed to *her*, but Jonas had filled it out. Had he written embarrassing things about her childhood? Theories of whatever he thought was wrong with her mind?

"Have you ever been in therapy before, or is this a new experience for you?" Dr. Marsh hadn't opened her notebook yet, but Lacey figured it would flap open at any second and that pen would be in her hand.

"Um . . . it's new." When Jonas had rescued her from her miserable life, he'd told her many times that she should see a counselor, but she'd talked him out of it. *"I don't need a shrink. I just need you, you're enough, you're everything. I know I'm safe with you."*

"Then let me give you an idea of what to expect," Dr. Marsh said. "Today is a chance for me to get to know you a little and for us to talk about why you're here and what you'd like to accomplish through therapy. I'll be asking you a lot of questions, getting some background and learning more about you. Please feel free to ask me any questions you have as well."

Lacey nodded again. The only question she wanted to ask was *"Can I leave now?"*

"You came with your husband," Dr. Marsh said. "I see he's interested in being involved in your therapy. How do you feel about that?"

"Oh, he's . . . always helpful. He takes good care of me. He's . . . worried about me, but he doesn't need to be because I'm fine. I don't need to be here."

Dr. Marsh watched her with a patient, thoughtful gaze.

Lacey fiddled with her wedding ring. "I . . . uh . . . I made the appointment because he wanted me to, but he worries too much."

"Why do *you* think he thought you needed help?"

"Um . . . well . . ." Lacey wanted to say she didn't know, but what if Dr. Marsh responded with, "I'll ask him, then" and went to fetch Jonas? "Um, he thinks I've been absentminded lately. Not very productive. I'm an artist. He thinks I've been slow about finishing things."

"Why else?"

Lacey traced her thumbnail over one knee of her gabardine dress pants. She'd tried to dress as professionally and sanely as possible. "Um, he thinks I've been . . . anxious or something." Her cheeks felt cold. How could she tell this stranger that Jonas had brought her here because he thought she was keeping secrets?

"Do you feel you've been anxious lately?" Dr. Marsh asked.

Lacey wanted to say no but suspected she looked petrified, and the lie would sound so silly that Dr. Marsh would run for Jonas to find out what was truly going on.

Dr. Marsh waited for her to speak, but it was a gentle silence; she didn't look irritated by Lacey's hesitation. The tired stinging in Lacey's eyes became the wet stinging of tears. *No. Oh no, you stupid girl, don't cry, don't cry, don't cry.* She blinked, but that wasn't enough; tears kept rising, and she had no idea how to hide them. They fell down her cheeks, dribbles of weakness.

"There are tissues on the table to your left, if you need them." Dr. Marsh didn't sound bothered. Apparently, weeping didn't faze her.

Lacey grabbed a tissue from the box. "I'm . . . a little wound up, but I don't think it's anything I need a psychologist for. Jonas is overreacting."

"Do you feel that anxiety is interfering with your life?"

Difficulty planning projects, difficulty concentrating on them, difficulty finishing them. Hiding everything from Jonas, wanting to flee from him and wanting to cling to him, making stupid cinnamon apples twice a week. Shadowing Camille Moretti, unable to stop even after she'd scared Camille. *Liking* that she'd scared Camille.

More tears waterfalled down her face. She snatched a second tissue. "I'm . . . just . . . I'm just tired." She was sobbing. Sobbing in front of a stranger.

Dr. Marsh rose to her feet and switched chairs so she was sitting next to Lacey. "Can you tell me what's upsetting you right now?"

She wasn't buying Lacey's excuse of exhaustion. "Please don't . . . tell . . . my husband I was crying. He'll think I'm . . . falling apart. I'm not."

"Are you worried that what you say in here will be shared with him?"

"He . . . Yes . . . He'll want to know everything."

"Lacey, you're my client. I won't tell your husband anything at all without your permission—your written permission, in fact. And he won't come in here without your permission. These sessions are confidential. *You* set the boundaries of what he finds out."

This surprised Lacey. "He thinks he'll be involved in it all."

"He'll only be as involved as you want him to be."

"He'll ask you about everything. When we go out there."

"I won't tell him anything without your permission."

Lacey swabbed her face. "You won't tell him *anything*?"

"No. I'm ethically bound to keep what we discuss private."

"He'll ask you. He'll push you."

"He can push, but I won't tell him anything without your approval."

Lacey sniffled. "He won't learn anything I say in here?"

"Not unless you want him to know."

"I don't . . . really want to say anything in here. I want to get out of here. I'm sorry. You seem really nice, and I'm sure you're a good psychologist . . ."

"I'm not offended. This is about you, not me. You feel you're fine, then? The anxiety your husband is worried about is not something you want to seek help with? This is your choice."

Her choice. How was it her choice? Jonas wouldn't let her squirm out of this. "I'm not crazy," she whispered.

"What do you mean by crazy?"

"Crazy! Insane, lunatic. Like I should . . . be locked up."

"Do you think you need to be crazy to talk to a psychologist?"

"I don't know."

"Do you think Jonas thinks you're crazy?"

Lacey pressed a tissue against her closed eyelids. "I'm not sure. He didn't say that."

Dr. Marsh's voice tapped softly on Lacey's eardrums. "I'm not implying that anything is going on, but this is a question I ask all new clients. Are you experiencing abuse in any of your relationships? Do you have any reason to fear for your safety?"

"No." Lacey lowered the tissue. "Jonas would never hit me. He . . . protects me."

"Okay. Lacey, therapy can be helpful for anyone. It's not reserved for people so disturbed that they can't function. Seeking help is a wise, courageous thing to do for yourself, and the earlier the better. It's not something to be ashamed of."

Lacey nodded, though that didn't make sense to her. If her brain wasn't sick, why would she need an expert to fix it?

"But therapy is only effective if we work together, and you'll be doing most of the work," Dr. Marsh said. "I'm not a medical doctor giving a shot of antibiotics to cure an infection while my client waits passively to feel better. If you don't want to be here—if you're only here because you feel pressured into it and you're not willing to participate in therapy—you're wasting your money. If you like, I can tell that to your husband."

Hope steadied Lacey's composure. "You'll tell him I don't need this?"

"I won't tell him you don't need this because I don't think that's true. I think therapy would benefit you. But I will tell him there's no point in forcing you to come here, that I can't help a client who doesn't want to be helped, and it needs to be your choice."

Hope shattered and made a heap at the bottom of her stomach. She knew how Jonas would interpret those words: "*Your wife isn't cooperating. Take her home and convince her to cooperate.*"

"I'm not crazy," Lacey said again.

"Who told you that you are? You said Jonas didn't."

"No one . . . told me that." Not recently. Not since her father.

"Are *you* worried that you're crazy?"

"I said I wasn't!"

"You said you weren't crazy. Are you worried you *might* be crazy?"

"No!" She stared at Dr. Marsh's tiered skirt, the bottom tier draping over her feet. Stalking people wasn't normal, but she wasn't stalking. She was watching, learning . . . but what about yesterday when she'd gone to Camille's house while Camille was at work and had rearranged the autumn decorations on her porch? That wasn't learning anything; that was playing with Camille's mind. If the police had caught her, they'd have arrested her. If she'd insisted she wasn't stalking Camille, that she was only admiring her, the cops would have locked her in a padded cell.

Stalking Camille. She *was* stalking her, stalking the widow of her husband's old running partner, stalking a woman she'd met face-to-face only twice: once at Dante Moretti's funeral, once when Jonas had taken her to Camille in hopes that Camille's boss might be interested in her mosaics. Lacey had told herself she'd stop, but when she tried to, she ached like she was starving or addicted to a drug she couldn't get.

Tears plopped onto her blouse.

"Lacey," Dr. Marsh said softly. "What makes you think you might be crazy?"

Lacey blinked and focused on the toes of the shoes showing beneath Dr. Marsh's skirt. They were nice shoes, wine-colored leather flats. "What would . . . happen if I . . . was crazy?"

"Crazy isn't a diagnosis. It's a catch-all word that's completely useless here. Something's bothering you, interfering with your life. If you're willing, I can help you work through that."

Help. What kind of help? Locking her up so she couldn't peek in Camille's window? Doping her until her brain was so foggy she couldn't do anything at all?

"I have a suggestion," Dr. Marsh said. "I'll go tell Jonas that for now, I need to meet with you one-on-one so he doesn't pace out there, expecting me to call him in. I'll tell him to return in"—she checked the clock on the wall—"in an hour. Then we can chat for a while. You don't have to tell me anything you don't want to tell me, but I think I can give you a better idea of what therapy involves, and you can decide if you want to continue with it."

Jonas wouldn't want to leave the office. He'd protest. He'd demand to join Lacey. But Dr. Marsh wouldn't get intimidated. She was a confident woman, like Camille.

Are you going to stalk Dr. Marsh too? The thought whirled through her mind. What if she *did* get obsessed with Dr. Marsh like she was obsessed with Camille?

"I'll go talk to him." Dr. Marsh stood.

Lacey swallowed. "Could you maybe . . . could you tell him . . . he doesn't need to pick me up? He should go to work. Tell him . . . tell him I'll take the bus home."

"Of course. I'll be right back." She walked out of the office and closed the door behind her.

Lacey thought about getting up to test the doorknob to see if the door was locked but realized that didn't make sense. Dr. Marsh hadn't unlocked the door before going out, and Lacey hadn't heard any lock click after she'd closed the door. She wasn't trapped. She could leave whenever she wanted. She didn't have to be here.

Yes, she did, because she didn't have the guts to tell Jonas she'd fled while Dr. Marsh was out of the room. She tried to visualize herself as Camille facing Jonas, shaking her head and smiling. "Jonas, I appreciate your concern, but I'm fine. I don't need a psychologist."

She'd already tried to say those words, and they hadn't worked; if she tried them again, they still wouldn't work. Even if she held out for a day or two, that wouldn't be enough. She'd earn herself weeks of Jonas's lectures, his interrogations, his watching her, his promise that he wouldn't even consider having children until she cooperated. Eventually, she'd shatter, and he'd sweep up the broken mess and carry it back to Dr. Marsh's office. Or to the hospital.

Maybe it was better to stay here today and learn more about what Dr. Marsh wanted to do in therapy. She'd said it would just be questions. Talking. Maybe Lacey could even share *some* of the things that bothered her. Like the way she was terrified to go into their basement, even though her brain knew there was nothing dangerous down there. It wasn't like her father had slithered in through a window and set up camp next to the storage boxes.

This might be okay. Lacey could talk to Dr. Marsh without telling her about the stalking. No matter how much Dr. Marsh swore to keep confidences, Lacey could never tell anyone what she'd done.

What she was doing.

CHAPTER 5

IN THE TWILIGHT, NATALIE PARKED in front of Felicia's house and picked up a gift bag from the passenger seat. After too many days of useless worrying, she'd decided to try to make contact with Felicia again, this time by dropping off a small gift. She'd chosen a book of famous poems about animals, an easy book to read in small doses and to pick up or set down according to Felicia's mood. Felicia enjoyed poetry, loved animals, and would appreciate the original watercolors illustrating each poem. Natalie wasn't confident her old friend would want to talk to her, but she was confident she would like the book.

As she walked toward the house, the man raking leaves off Felicia's lawn stopped working and smiled at her. He was wearing jeans and a Georgia Tech T-shirt and had damp dark-brown hair sticking up unevenly in front—Natalie guessed he'd messed it up when wiping sweat off his forehead. He must have been working hard to be sweating that much; it was a chilly evening.

Wade's son. Natalie had met him at the funeral but only for a few words of condolence and a handshake.

"Hi," he said. "Looking for Felicia?"

"I am, yes."

"Unfortunately, she's not home." He pulled off his work gloves and held out a hand. "Gideon Radcliffe. Felicia's stepson."

"Natalie Marsh." She shook his hand. "We met briefly at your father's funeral."

"Oh, right. I'm sorry I didn't recognize you."

"I don't know how you could. You shook hundreds of hands that day."

"But I've heard Felicia talk about you. You're the one whose family lived next door to her when you were a kid, right?"

"Yes." Natalie kept a neutral expression on her face, wondering what Felicia had told Gideon. About the yelling she could hear through her windows when Roxanne Marsh was in a manic phase? About the times Natalie had crept to Felicia's door to ask if she had any cereal and milk they could borrow because her father was on a business trip, her mother hadn't gotten out of bed in two weeks, and she and Andrea couldn't find anything for breakfast?

About the fact that Natalie had ended up the family outcast, cut from her mother's life, disinherited at her death?

"I'm so sorry about your father," Natalie said quickly. "How are you doing?"

"Ah, you know, day by day. Push on. Keep working. That kind of thing. I decided to move to Ohneka to help with selling or closing down the store and to be here for Felicia." He lifted the rake and shook a few yellow leaves off the tines.

"Where were you before?" Natalie asked, then remembered Felicia talking about it. "Ithaca, wasn't it?"

"Yeah. But I found a good job with the City of Ohneka; I'm a civil engineer. This is a great place to live, and I found an apartment not far from here, so I can help Felicia out if there's a plumbing emergency or something. It was a . . . good time for a new start."

That reminded Natalie of another reason he'd probably wanted to leave Ithaca: when she'd been on a lunch date with Felicia last summer, Felicia had mentioned that her stepson's fiancée had dumped him mid-wedding-planning. What a rotten year for Gideon. "I'm sure Felicia is grateful to have your support."

"Hey, she's family. My dad would haunt me if I didn't look out for her." His face changed, right brow dropping and right side of his mouth stretching in what looked like half contemplation, half wince. "His death devastated her."

"I'm so sorry."

"Thanks." Wind blew a layer of Gideon's leaf pile around the yard. He shivered. "Gets cold once I stop moving." He dropped the rake, walked to the porch, and grabbed the sweatshirt draped over the rail.

"I'll let you get back to work," Natalie said. "I'll stop by another time."

"Hey—" Gideon yanked the sweatshirt over his head and shoved his arms into the sleeves. "You . . . you're a psychologist, right?"

"Yes."

"Do you . . . ? This is awkward. I'm going to sound like the guy cornering the doctor at the ball game and asking about his heartburn. But I'm worried about Felicia."

Natalie slid the gift bag handle onto her wrist so she could button her long sweater. "Worried in what way?"

"Hey, uh . . . as long as the theme is 'awkward,' how would you feel about coming inside for a few minutes? You must be cold out here. No problem if you'd rather not. I realize I'm a stranger, and I'm imposing on you."

"You're not imposing. I'm worried about Felicia too. And I've heard enough about you to not consider you a stranger."

From his uneasy smile, she knew she'd provoked the same concern she'd had when he'd recognized her name: *How much did Felicia say about me?*

"Thank you," he said. "I'll keep it short." He picked up his rake and leaned it against the tree. Natalie headed up the stairs to the front door; he followed.

In the house, a savory aroma nudged Natalie's hunger and made her contemplate what in her fridge she could fix in a hurry. Gideon shed his shoes in the entryway. Natalie started to do the same, but he said, "Don't bother; you're fine. My shoes are a mess from the yardwork."

"I don't mind. I know Felicia prefers no shoes on her carpet." Natalie left her flats near the coat tree. The tiled entryway chilled her stocking feet.

Gideon led her to the living room, where she sat on the couch and adjusted her skirt to cover her toes, glad for the thick pile of the carpet. Gideon sat opposite her in the green leather armchair Natalie had loved when she was a child. She'd been pleased when she'd first visited Felicia in the home she'd bought with Wade and had seen Felicia had kept the chair. A decade later, it was still in superb shape.

"Thanks for taking the time to talk to me," Gideon said.

"I'm glad to do it." She set the gift bag on the cushion next to her. "Tell me about Felicia. I've tried to connect with her, but she doesn't usually respond."

"Is it cold in here?" Gideon rubbed his hands together. "If she's going to be gone for hours, she usually turns the thermostat down. Let me fix that." He stood and jogged out of the room. The furnace kicked on.

"Should warm up soon," he said as he reentered. "Felicia is off meeting with a woman in Rochester who is interested in possibly buying my father's store."

"All of Ohneka will appreciate it if the store stays open," Natalie said. "Though it won't be the same without your father at the helm."

"Yeah. Financially, it would be nice for Felicia if she could sell it. She doesn't want to run it herself. She was a big help with it, but it was his passion, not hers."

"I remember when she owned The Chicken Noodle," Natalie said. "She used to bring us leftover soup or cookies or bread, and the food was always marvelous. I still like the café, but I don't think it's ever been as good as it was before she sold it."

"That's what people tell me. I was surprised when Dad told me she'd decided to ditch it. I thought she was still going strong."

"Yes, it surprised us too. I was away at school, but I remember my mother telling me Felicia was hitting the big-time, getting hired to cater the opening of Maison du Canard. Though that might have—" She stopped. Gideon was part of Felicia's family; why was outsider Natalie telling him this? "I'm sorry. You must already know this story."

"I don't think I do. And I can't remember what Maison du Canard is, though I've heard of it."

"You've probably seen it. It's that glass-walled reception hall built on Kahrakwa Pond, next to the art museum."

"Oh yeah, yeah. Cool building. She catered the opening?"

Natalie fingered the raffia handles of the gift bag. She felt gossipy, but she'd stirred Gideon's curiosity, and it was better to finish the story than refuse to explain. It would be pointless to act like something that had been local headline news was private. "The man who'd donated the money to build the hall—Robert Chapman, I'm sure you've heard his name—loved Felicia's food, and he hired . . . " She hesitated, thrown by the change in Gideon's expression. He'd been listening with courteous attention, but now he'd averted his eyes, and an emotion darker than interest or concern shadowed his face. "Do you know Robert Chapman?" she asked, unsure what she'd said that had disturbed him.

Gideon picked a twig off one sleeve. "I know of him. I haven't met him."

Natalie hastened to finish, wanting to change the subject. "Unfortunately, there was an accident at the reception, and Mrs. Chapman—Sheryl, his first wife—died. Felicia witnessed it, and from what my sister told me, it was traumatic for her."

Gideon's brow wrinkled. Should she tell him he had a leaf fragment clinging to one eyebrow? "That's right; I remember my father mentioning it. Do you think that stress had anything to do with her deciding to sell the café?"

"I don't know." Natalie felt foolish for bringing it up. "I admit I always assumed the stress of that experience was a factor, since she sold the café a few months after that, but I don't have anything definitive to back that up. She's never been willing to talk to me about Sheryl's death, and I've seen her change the subject if anyone else asks."

"Huh." Gideon finally resumed eye contact. "Do you . . . do business with Robert Chapman?"

"We lease our office space from Chapman Development. Is that what you mean?"

"Do you know him? Personally, not by reputation?"

"Yes. His company is renovating an 1890s building, and I've been meeting with him about the possibility of opening a mental health clinic there. I've been seeking funding from him, actually. Clinic fees would be on a sliding scale—everything from free on up, according to a client's financial situation. My goal is to make mental health services more available and affordable."

"That's a great goal," Gideon said, but he sounded guarded. "What's he like?"

Natalie pictured short, wild-white-haired Bob Chapman. "He's quirky. Doesn't care about conventions or expectations. He's a fascinating, sometimes overbearing, funny guy. He married again and adores his wife; he also has an adult daughter, but unfortunately, they're estranged. Let me apologize; I've been rambling instead of listening to you. How is Felicia doing?"

Gideon pushed up the sleeves of his sweatshirt, then pulled them down again. "Have you talked to her much lately?"

"Unfortunately, I haven't. Since your father died, we've only had short conversations. Like I said, she often doesn't answer her phone or respond to texts. That's why I stopped by with this." She touched the gift bag. "I understand if she doesn't feel like talking to me, but I want her to know I'm thinking of her and I'm here if she needs a friend."

"She always told me nice things about you."

"I appreciate that." Natalie smiled at him and sat silently, waiting for him to continue. He averted his eyes again and rubbed his thumb on the face of his watch as though cleaning it. If he'd been a client, Natalie would have waited longer, letting the silence coax him into speech, but in this context, the silence made her uncomfortable. "Is she taking care of herself?" Natalie asked.

"Yeah, sure, she's fine physically. Exercises, eats well, I think. In fact, she's okay all around, as okay as she can be right now. Just needs time. Speaking of eating well, she left soup in the Crock Pot. She made a ton of it and told me to help myself. Have you had dinner? Might be nice for you to taste her soup again."

"It smells delicious," Natalie said, puzzled. Gideon had invited her in here to listen to his concerns about Felicia, and now he didn't seem to want to share those concerns. "But I don't want to intrude on your evening."

"You're not intruding. It's split pea with ham. When I was a kid and my mother would make split pea, I wouldn't touch it because it looked disgusting. I'm glad I got past that. I was missing out. Give me a minute to get things ready." He sprang up and hurried out of the living room.

Natalie debated what to do. Did he want to talk about Felicia over dinner, had he changed his mind about confiding in Natalie at all, or was something else going on? *You mean is he the first guy in history to use his stepmother's grief and split-pea soup as a ploy for hitting on a woman? Dream on.*

Did she want to stay? Yes. Felicia had always spoken highly of Gideon, and it wasn't her style to gush insincere praise, even about a family member. Natalie was willing to give him the benefit of the doubt and see if he relaxed enough over dinner to tell her what was worrying him about Felicia.

Even if he didn't open up, she'd still get a bowl of Felicia's homemade soup. That alone made the evening worth it.

* * *

His brain slamming him with insult after insult, Gideon trudged into the dining room, grabbed the empty soup bowls off the table, and shoved them into the dishwasher. No wonder Tamara had dumped him; he was an idiot.

Over the past week, he'd pondered Felicia's theory that his father had been murdered and had convinced himself it was absurd. He'd wanted to discuss it with Felicia, but she'd mostly ignored his calls, and when she had answered her phone, she'd insisted she was too tired to talk or too busy for visits. Her avoiding him had strengthened his conclusion that grief was making sensible Felicia irrational. For her sake, he couldn't keep his promise to hide what she'd told him, allowing her to suffer alone. When Natalie had shown up, she'd seemed like the perfect person to confide in—Felicia's long-time friend and a mental health professional as well.

If he'd made up his mind, why had he flip-flopped the instant Natalie had admitted her connection with Robert Chapman? Felicia's warnings had stabbed into his mind, and he'd panicked and put himself in the running for Nincompoop of the Year by railroading Natalie into staying for dinner. He'd been desperate to shift the subject away from Felicia, and dinner was the only diversion he could think up.

Natalie had been so kind as he'd spent the entire dinner prodding the conversation away from Felicia, even resorting to analyzing every type of soup he'd ever eaten. Natalie had courteously joined in the soup analysis, sharing her own thoughts on minestrone and french onion, but she must have been privately analyzing him—how could she not? *Erratic behavior. Poor social skills. Wearing argyle socks with running shoes.* He wished for a moment that he'd explained to her that the dress-socks-and-athletic-shoes combo was because when he'd changed clothes to rake the leaves, he hadn't bothered to change his socks.

Who cared? His socks were a lot less dorky than his claiming he wanted to talk to her about Felicia, then doing a bait and switch. He must have come across as a sleazeball who was using his worry about his stepmother as a ruse for hitting on Natalie. And after he'd gotten the heebie-jeebies, why had he thought he needed to pretend Felicia was fine and avoid talking about her completely? Why hadn't he shared some generic worries like "I'm afraid she's spending too much time alone," or "I'm afraid she's working too much," so Natalie wouldn't wonder why his worries had magically disappeared?

Natalie hadn't even left the gift she'd brought for Felicia, claiming she wanted to deliver it in person. Was that the reason she'd taken it, or did she think Gideon was too much of a loser to handle the task of passing it on?

At least the split-pea soup had been great.

Gideon stuffed the remaining rye crackers back in the box, put it in the pantry, and wiped the table. He'd better get that leaf pile swept to the curb, even though it was dark outside. He should have finished the raking earlier rather than leaving it unfinished so he could focus on making a fool of himself.

Would Natalie tell Felicia what he'd done? What if Felicia's fears *weren't* imaginary and he'd almost screwed up catastrophically?

He hurried outside and put on his gloves. Working fast, he raked the remaining leaves toward the curb, hating that he was vacillating again. This whole thing was ludicrous. How could Felicia tell him someone had maliciously caused his father's accident but the specifics were none of his business? What were these "private matters" she'd refused to discuss? Something must have happened in his father's interaction with Chapman that she'd twisted in her mind, and the nervous, purse-buying woman had sparked her theory about sabotage. Even Felicia must know her reasoning wasn't valid. If it were, she'd have told the police everything. She'd have insisted an expert examine the ladder for deliberate damage instead of saying nothing while Gideon had chucked the evidence. She wouldn't value hiding *any* private matter more than she'd value getting justice for her husband. Right?

Mrs. Chapman's death. The accident Felicia had witnessed . . . how long ago had that been? Seven or eight years, maybe? He couldn't remember how she'd died. Something to do with water. Drowned? Had the trauma of witnessing that accident now linked to his father's accident in Felicia's mind? Was that why she'd mentally entangled the Chapman family in her grief?

Gideon flipped a clump of leaves into the gutter. If there had genuinely been trouble—dangerous trouble—wouldn't his father have told him? Gideon had talked to him the week before his death, and he'd been fine, telling Gideon the shop was thriving and asking if Gideon wanted to come camping with him in August; Felicia wasn't a fan of dirt.

Sweating now, Gideon raked faster, gathering leaves from the last corner of the yard and directing them into the gutter. What was Felicia up to now? She was a tireless, organized person, and even if grief had fogged her logic, it hadn't changed her personality. She wouldn't be sitting home, passively lamenting his father's alleged murder. She'd mentioned following up with the artist who'd made that incriminating purse. Had she done that? Had she learned anything?

Gideon's rake scratched along the sidewalk as he clawed a few damp leaves loose and added them to the pile heaped near the street light. Why was he always so clueless? He had no idea how to help his stepmother. He'd had no idea how to handle the conversation with Natalie tonight. He'd had no idea his fiancée was cheating on him. He hadn't seen anything coming before Tamara had handed his ring back and said, *"There's someone else."* He'd gaped at her, a deer in the headlights, thinking, *Someone else you want to invite to our wedding?*

Get a grip. His father would want him to help Felicia; he had to figure out how to do that. Why did she think Gideon might be a target—but she wasn't? Wasn't that evidence that this was traumatized imagination? She'd lost her husband, and now she was afraid of losing all she had left of Wade: his son. She wasn't scared for herself because intellectually she knew there was no danger.

Or maybe she was right, and he was naïve, thinking picturesque Ohneka couldn't harbor deadly evil or that his father couldn't have crossed a ruthless, conscienceless man. But sabotaging a ladder was an odd way to murder someone. His father could have received only bruises or a broken arm. Maybe it was meant more as a warning than attempted murder?

He needed to talk to Felicia again, and this time he wouldn't back off until she gave solid, provable evidence for her theory. He wished he could call Natalie and apologize for his behavior, but how could he do that without admitting why he'd acted weird? Nothing he could say would purge her memories of his dorkiness anyway. He'd wrecked his chance to get help from her, but maybe he could get on a better track with his stepmother.

At any rate, when he confronted Felicia, he could wear better socks.

CHAPTER 6

WIND PLUCKED RED LEAVES FROM the maple tree in Camille's front yard and scattered them over the lawn and driveway. The rustling branches and leaves fluttering and swooping in the dark sky gave Lacey a thrill. It was a spooky night, and she was slinking right through it, not scared. Plus, with the wind noises, Camille couldn't possibly hear her approach.

All the curtains on Camille's front windows were closed, but light glowed in the entryway, the living room, and her office. Camille would be in her office; Lacey had learned that she always left the living room lights on when she was home at night, but only turned her office lights on if she was working in there. Good thing she'd learned that before Camille had gotten vigilant about closing her curtains. She used to leave gaps sometimes, but now she never did.

Beneath the excitement, guilt nibbled at Lacey, taking tiny but poisonous bites that she knew would burn later. What would Dr. Marsh say if she knew Lacey was creeping toward Camille's house? What would Jonas say? He'd tell Dr. Marsh, call and inform her Lacey had a problem with stalking and Dr. Marsh needed to fix her.

Fix her. Nobody could fix her. She was born warped and weak and rotten.

She'd been determined not to tell Jonas what she and Dr. Marsh had discussed, which wasn't anything earthshaking—mainly basic stuff about her background that Jonas already knew—but she'd still wanted to keep the conversation private. On the bus ride home from her appointment, she'd told herself over and over that when Jonas asked what they'd talked about, she'd say, "It's confidential." She'd thought about lying and saying, "Dr. Marsh said I can't tell you," but that wouldn't have worked. Jonas wouldn't have believed her, and if she'd insisted, he'd have called Dr. Marsh and asked. Even though Dr. Marsh was adamant that she wouldn't tell Jonas anything without Lacey's permission, would she be willing to cover for Lacey and say she'd forbidden her from sharing?

Her plans had ended up useless anyway. When Jonas had arrived home yesterday evening, he'd asked her about the appointment, saying how disappointed he was that he couldn't be with her and it must have been stressful and what did they talk about? She'd told him she was fine, that she didn't want to discuss it, but he'd insisted. She'd given him short answers; he'd pushed; she'd given him longer answers; he'd pushed harder; she'd blabbed everything, despising herself.

Why hadn't she kept her mouth shut? Why couldn't she tell him she wanted her sessions to be private, that she needed something in her life that wasn't under his control?

She walked along the driveway at a normal pace so if a neighbor saw her, they'd assume she was a friend visiting Camille. At the corner of the house, she stopped and glanced around to check for any passers-by or open curtains in surrounding houses. No one was watching her.

She slipped behind the bushes lining the front of the house and ducked so they concealed her. From inside her long, hooded coat, she pulled out the telescopic rod that had once been part of a duster she'd used to clean ceiling fixtures. To the tip of the rod she'd glued a pebble.

She extended the rod until it was about five feet long, positioned the end of it near the side of the window opposite from where she crouched, and tapped the pebble against the glass.

Taptaptap tap tap tap taptaptap.

Morse code. SOS. Camille might or might not recognize it, but she'd know it wasn't a branch hitting the window or debris blowing against it.

One more time to make sure Camille's fear was surging: taptaptap tap tap tap taptaptap. Finished, Lacey began backing away, smoothing the mulch as she went, keeping the rod below the level of the windowsill. The curtains swooshed open, and light illuminated the bushes. Lacey glimpsed Camille facing the wrong way—the direction from which she'd heard the tapping.

Lacey snaked around the side of the house, collapsed the rod, and sped through the back yard. She passed through the yard of the house that backed on Camille's, jaywalked across the street, and hurried through a park where empty swings swayed in the wind. On the next street over, she started walking along the sidewalk at a normal pace, the cleaning rod concealed inside her coat. Her insides jumped and rattled like a bag of beads, but she smiled. She pulled the rolled-up, reusable shopping bag out of her pocket and shook it out.

Strong Camille couldn't manage everything, could she? The abrupt wrenching of those curtains open . . . She was scared. She'd probably called 911 by now, but when the police came, they wouldn't find anything.

A car passed, and Lacey maintained her brisk pace, a confident woman heading to the grocery store on a windy September evening, enjoying the exercise. More headlights approached, but she didn't care. Even if it was a police car—which it wouldn't be; she was already half a mile from Camille's—there was nothing suspicious about her.

She should call it quits with Camille now, but she'd think about it later, after she'd finished savoring tonight's triumph. Maybe she was crazy, but wow, she was good at this spying and stalking. She'd never been caught. Jonas had no idea what she was doing. She *could* keep a secret. One secret. She hadn't told Dr. Marsh, she hadn't told Jonas, and she never would. This was hers. She owned it. She was strong enough to—

The car swung toward the curb and pulled over a few yards in front of Lacey. Fear rolled through her. What should she do? Ignore the car, or look toward it?

Keep walking. Head up. It has nothing to do with you. Someone's visiting one of the houses near you.

Lacey kept walking, her empty shopping bag flapping in her hand. Something brushed against her hair, and she started but recovered without slowing her gait. It was only a leaf tumbling from the tree overhead. *Confident.* She passed the car, not even glancing at it.

A car door opened behind her. "Lacey!"

Lacey whirled toward Jonas's voice.

He barreled toward her. "What are you doing here?"

Lacey's thoughts stuck to each other and froze into chunks of ice.

He reached her. "What are you doing here?" he repeated.

He thought she was sneaking out to see a boyfriend. Her father's voice thumped into her brain: *"Where've you been this time? Thrashing around with some pretty boy you think's better than me?"* Denials from her mother. A slap. A cry.

"Lacey." Jonas grabbed her shoulder. "What's going on?"

He'd followed her. He must have followed her. He knew she'd been at Camille's. Wait, did he know that house was Camille's? Had he ever met Dante Moretti there when they were training for that marathon? It didn't matter. Even if he'd never been there before, by now he'd looked up the address to find out who Lacey was spying on . . . but *had* he spotted her there? She hadn't seen any cars on the street while she was nearing Camille's house. A car had driven past while she'd been behind the bushes, but she'd glimpsed it; it had been a pickup truck. She hadn't seen Jonas's car at all. Or maybe she had and hadn't noticed it. She hadn't noticed it *now*, hadn't recognized it even when it had pulled over. So many people drove that model . . . She couldn't even remember what model of car it was; she never paid attention . . .

He was still gripping her shoulder, staring at her. She needed to answer him. "I'm . . . going shopping." She held up her empty bag. "At The Antipasti." She named the Italian specialty market a few blocks away. "You love their soppressata.

I wanted to make pasta tonight—tomorrow night. I thought . . . didn't you have a work dinner tonight?"

"I didn't feel like going. The Antipasti is on Melrose Street. Why did you park there and walk over here?"

Glass cut into her chest with each thump of her heart. How did he know she'd parked there? "I was feeling, um . . . It was stifling in my workroom, and I needed some exercise. I thought I'd walk around a little before I shopped."

"In the dark?"

"It's not very late. This neighborhood is safe." Beneath her gloves, her hands swam in perspiration. Was he testing her? Did he already know everything she'd done? "I'm sorry. I had no idea you'd be home tonight, or I would have had dinner ready. I can go grab that sausage and do a quick pasta."

"Where's your purse?" he asked.

My purse. She'd left it in the car, under the seat, not wanting ID with her while she was on the prowl. Left her purse and brought a shopping bag. That made no sense. "That's a good question," she said. "I wasn't thinking about it. I guess I left it in the car."

Jonas shifted his hand to her elbow and led her toward his car. He opened the door for her, and she slid into the passenger seat, all but splashing in the sweat running down her body.

Jonas drove toward The Antipasti, not speaking.

"How was your day?" Lacey tried to sound nonchalant.

He didn't answer. Lacey's tongue went dry and still, a stone cemented in place.

When they reached the store, Jonas drove into the parking lot and stopped behind her beige Kia. She started to open her door, but Jonas grasped her arm.

"You stay here," he said. "Give me your keys."

Did *he* want to drive her car home, leaving her to drive his? She never drove his car. "Why don't you head home?" she said. "I'm sure you're tired. I'll grab the stuff for the pasta and follow you. I can have dinner ready in half an hour."

"Give me your keys."

Afraid to ask why, Lacey dug her keys out of her coat pocket and handed them to him.

"Stay here." He opened his door. At her car, he slid into the driver's seat and leaned to the right. What was he doing?

Within thirty seconds, he stepped out of the car, holding her purse, and locked the doors.

He climbed back into his own car and slammed the door. Trying for a Camille-confident gesture, Lacey held out a steady hand for her keys. "I'll see you at home," she said.

Jonas flung her purse into the backseat, accelerated past her car, and headed toward the exit on the other side of the parking lot.

"Honey, what are you doing? I need my car!" She faked a laugh. "I don't want to walk miles back here tomorrow to get it. My legs don't need *that* much stretching."

"I'll get the car later so you don't have to worry about it."

"Oh, thank you," she said, pretending to be grateful for his thoughtfulness, pretending she wasn't terrified. She didn't dare look at him, even out of the corner of her eye. Why was he leaving her car behind? Because he knew she was lying about her impromptu walk. Because he was afraid if he let her drive herself, she'd return to the lover he thought she'd visited.

"Did you get much done today?" He spoke in an even, almost monotone voice.

"Actually, I did," she said, relieved that this was a question she'd prepared for. She'd pulled some old sketches out of her files, sketches she'd never turned into mosaics, and had left them on her desk, along with the beginnings of one new sketch. "I've been sketching some ideas. I did a bunch of them."

"I saw them," he said. "On your worktable."

"Oh, do you like them?"

"I still like them," he said. "I liked them when you sketched them years ago."

Lacey's face heated. Out of the hundreds of sketches she'd done, how could he possibly remember that he'd seen these before? "Do you think they're too much like some of my old stuff? They're rough; I know they need work."

"You did one of them three years ago, one of them four years ago, and four of them seven years ago."

Was that right? She did remember taking four from the same file, and one each from two other files. She thought about insisting he was wrong, but that would sink her deeper into quicksand. He must have marked the sketches—had he written dates on the back? He was the one who always filed her sketches. "I . . . thought they might give me ideas. That I could modify them—"

"What have you been doing today? You weren't working."

She pulled her icky, sweaty gloves off her hands. She *had* tried to work, tried a bunch of times, but she hadn't been able to concentrate. She'd done a frenzied cleaning of the house, striving to relieve her stress through mopping and vacuuming until she couldn't focus well enough even to scrub toilets. Finally, she'd paced the house, tension escalating until she either had to explode or bleed off stress under Camille's window.

"I did a lot of cleaning," she said.

"Who did you come here to visit?"

"I didn't visit anyone." Lacey pressed her shoulder against the door. "I honestly didn't visit anyone. I just walked. I'm . . . I felt restless."

He didn't respond. He'd already nailed her lie about the sketches, and he wouldn't buy her hole-filled story about going on a walk either.

She glanced at him. His face was marble. She *couldn't* tell him the truth— that his quiet, pretty wife was a crazy stalker. He'd already forced her to go to Dr. Marsh because she'd seemed anxious and secretive. If he found out the truth, what would he do? Have her committed? But if she didn't confess to her obsession, he'd think she was cheating on him.

"I'm not cheating on you," she said. "I swear I wouldn't do that."

He didn't answer. He didn't look at her. His rage must be mounting as he pictured her sneaking away to meet a lover. After the way he'd taken care of her, she'd betrayed him.

She had to tell him the truth. If she didn't want her nose smashed, her eyes blackened, her ribs cracked, she had to tell him the truth.

She couldn't. She folded her arms tightly and thought about the pain. She'd been through it before, many times. She could survive it.

Jonas pulled into their garage and closed the door behind them. Paralyzed, Lacey waited as he retrieved her purse from the backseat, stepped out of the car, and came to open her door. He held out his hand. She didn't want to touch it, but rejecting him would be foolhardy. She shouldn't have taken her gloves off; he'd feel her sweaty fingers.

She clutched his hand. He didn't comment on how wet her palm was, but there was no way he hadn't noticed.

"I'll get started on dinner right away," she said as he led her into the house.

He released her hand and removed his jacket. Lacey ripped off her own coat, not wanting Jonas to help her with it and notice the rod in her pocket. She couldn't think of any credible lie to explain why she'd glued a stone to the end of a telescoping cleaning rod and taken it with her. She reached past Jonas, grabbed a hanger, and hung up her coat while he was busy with his.

"Come with me," he said, closing the closet door. He was still holding her purse.

Her legs were so weighty and wobbly that she might as well obey him— she certainly couldn't run away. She followed him to his study.

"Take my chair," he said, pulling the high-backed executive chair away from his desk. "You're tired."

Lacey settled into the chair. He unzipped her purse and began removing her belongings and setting them on the desk.

She tried not to breathe loudly. Thank heavens, she hadn't taken her note-book this time. She'd known she wouldn't be at Camille's long enough to write anything, and she'd planned to record her notes after she got home. Jonas would never find the notebook. She'd hidden it at the back of the bathroom closet in a canister that had once held disposable cleaning wipes.

Jonas set her wallet to one side and sorted everything else: old receipts, a hairbrush, a pot of lip moisturizer, a flyer advertising the new exhibit at the art museum, spilled change, breath mints. He dropped the trash into the can next to the desk and put everything else except her wallet back in the purse.

He walked toward a wall-hung mosaic she'd done of a sunset on Lake Ohneka. He lifted the mosaic off its hooks and rotated the dial of the wall safe hidden behind it. He set her wallet in the safe, closed it, and rotated the dial.

She didn't have the combination to the safe—she'd never wanted or asked for it. Her car was miles away; he'd taken her keys; now he was taking her credit cards and ID.

He faced her. "Something's wrong with you. It's good you're seeing Dr. Marsh, but you need more than that. You shouldn't be on your own right now. I'm going to take some time off work and stay here with you. Whatever's messing up your mind, baby, we'll fix it. I'll take care of you 24/7, if that's what you need."

At least he didn't sound angry, and he wasn't making a move to attack her. But 24/7! He was locking her up, making her his prisoner. Lacey scrounged for firm words to say, but her protest was a feeble stammer. "What . . . Jonas . . . you can't do that; you have responsibilities—"

"You're more important than work." He grasped her hand, her clammy, guilty hand. "Come lie down on the couch and rest. I'll go fix you some dinner."

CHAPTER 7

"IF WE WERE WILLING TO drive a few miles down the shore, we'd see more stars," Camille said. She sat on the fleece blanket Natalie had spread over the warping boards of Beau Lac pier and hung her legs over the edge.

"Mmm, true." Natalie sat beside her. "But is stargazing the point? I thought we were here for tranquility."

"I thought we were here for yappy girl talk." From the fidgety way Camille kept bumping one tennis shoe against the other, Natalie knew the stars overhead and the moonlight glimmering on Lake Ohneka wouldn't be enough to bring her serenity.

"It's a beautiful night," Natalie said. "Not cold at all."

Camille stretched a toe downward, nearly touching the surface of the water. "Remember how we used to come here on winter afternoons?"

"Before we decided we didn't like frostbite?" Natalie opened her tote bag and removed a compact LED camping lantern that she set between them and switched on so she could see what she was doing.

"It was so beautiful though." Camille watched as Natalie opened a Thermos and filled a foam cup. "With the ice around the shore and the snow on the trees . . . How cold do you suppose the water is right now?"

"If I push you in, you can find out."

"Try it. We'll see who gets wet first." Camille shivered. "Never mind. Two lone women splashing around in deep black water sounds like a scene from a horror movie."

"You're wrecking the tranquility." Natalie offered the filled cup to Camille. "Mexican hot chocolate. Cinnamon and a dash of cayenne."

"Cayenne?" Camille tasted it. "Turbo hot chocolate. Thanks for bringing it. And thanks for agreeing to a last-minute stargazing session. I hope you didn't cancel any plans."

"My social life is jam-packed with my one date per year. It was tough to fit you in."

"Stop it. Hey, that reminds me. You know who I've decided you should chase? Skyler Hudson. He's a smart-alecky punk, but he's cute. And fun. And sweet."

"He's engaged."

"*What?* As of when?"

"A month or two ago."

"Why didn't you grab him first?"

"Not my type," Natalie said. "And I'm not his."

"He's a nice guy though. You knew him before he joined your practice, right?"

"No." Natalie watched ripples move through the silver swath of moonlight. "I knew *of* him."

"Through Felicia's husband?"

"No. He was my mother's physical therapist and worked with her up until she died—she's actually the one who recommended him to Wade and Felicia. I'd never met him, just my sister had. Andrea is the one who dealt with him. And she told him we were looking for a biofeedback therapist; that's how he ended up joining us."

Camille face-palmed. "I am *so* sorry. I remembered there was a personal connection but didn't remember what it was, and here I am pushing him at you. You *should* throw me in the lake."

"No, thanks. What if you need help and I have to jump in after you?"

"I'm sorry, Nat. I'm a total nitwit."

"No, you're not. I don't expect you to keep track of everything in my life, and it was a busy time for you when . . . this was happening."

"You mean I was so busy falling in love with your mother's hot young lawyer that I couldn't pay attention to *your* situation with your mother."

"You make it sound like you ignored me crying in my pillow while you chased Dante. That's not how it was at all. And neither of us knew your guy was my mother's lawyer until after you were engaged."

"Which is just as well because that would have been awkward."

"A little." Natalie used the light, casual tone she always used when discussing Dante's link to her family—the light tone she'd used even at that jolting moment when Camille had first introduced her to Dante and Natalie had finally made the connection that Camille's beloved Dante was the Mr. Moretti whom Andrea talked about—the lawyer who knew every financial detail of how intensely Roxanne Marsh despised her oldest daughter.

A light tone. Polite, interested, amused at the "small world" nature of the connection. The gush of humiliation inside her hadn't been Camille's or Dante's fault; the illogical urge to be angry at Camille's choice of husbands had been

Natalie's problem too. Neither Camille nor Dante had done anything selfish or devious, and Natalie refused to let her negative emotions escape to taint Camille's happiness.

Or—now—to taint Camille's memories.

"Has it been weird working in the same practice with Skyler?" Camille asked.

"I was a little uncomfortable at first, wondering if Mom had told him anything about me, but it's fine now. He's fantastic at his job and connects well with clients. It's no wonder my mother adored him. So, thank you, Andrea, for recommending him to us."

"Wow, your sister did something *nice* for you? That must have been a mistake."

Natalie laughed. Someday, she hoped she could laugh about her family without a spiky layer of pain underneath, but for now, she was grateful she could laugh about them at all.

Camille reached into the backpack she'd brought with her. She took out a blue candy box. "Chocolates. The de-stresser collection."

"Perfect." Natalie poured hot chocolate for herself and replaced the lid on the Thermos. Camille set the candy box between them and clicked the button to shut off the camping lantern. Wordlessly, they gazed at the sky.

"You'd think after all these years I'd be able to identify some constellations," Camille said.

"I don't think it was ever about the stars. I'm guessing it's not about the stars tonight either. How are you?"

Camille sighed. "You know, I tried telling myself you were right and I was overworking my imagination due to stress, but let me tell you, Dr. Marsh, something weird is definitely going on."

"You've seen new evidence that someone is stalking you?"

Camille picked up a chocolate and held it to the sky, apparently trying to discern the flavor by moonlight. "I have some harvest decorations on my porch. Two orange pumpkins, one white pumpkin, a basket of wooden apples, and a scarecrow sitting in a mini rocking chair. Somebody messed with them."

"Vandalism?"

"No, nothing was damaged. But someone moved the whole set-up to the opposite side of the door."

"Moved it . . . ?"

"All the decorations were in the same spots in relation to the others, like the white pumpkin was still to the left of the basket. But when I set them up, I arranged them on the right side of the door. Someone moved them to the left."

Frowning, Natalie pictured Camille's porch. "Was there anything about the new arrangement that seemed threatening?"

"Like a death threat magic-markered on a pumpkin or a knife stuck in the scarecrow's chest? No. Good grief, don't you think I'd tell you up front if there were something that overt? I'm not one of your clients burying my real issues and waiting for you to pick the important stuff out of my soul with tweezers."

"That's not a—"

"Sorry, I'm not dissing your clients. I'm just creeped out. Nothing damaged, no threats, no reason on earth for someone to teleport my decorations five feet to the left. And no, I didn't immediately call the police because what was I going to say? 'Officer, someone moved my harvest decorations.' 'Do you want me to cite them for a Pinterest fail, Mrs. Moretti?'"

"If that's a thing, they'll lock me up for life."

"Me too. But it doesn't make sense. If it was a practical joke, it's so tame it's pointless."

"It's a strange choice of pranks." Natalie sipped more hot chocolate, the cayenne spicy on her tongue.

"Then something else happened," Camille said. "Last night when I was working in my study, I heard tapping on the window. Yes, I *know* it was windy last night, but no, it wasn't a branch or anything natural. It was an SOS."

"An SOS?"

"Morse code. SOS."

"You recognize Morse code?"

"Doesn't everyone know SOS? Dot-dot-dot dash-dash-dash dot-dot-dot. Someone tapped that on my windowpane. The first time, I didn't recognize it, but they did it twice." She tapped her fingertips against the chocolate box in rhythm. "*SOS*. Pause. *SOS*. I looked out the window, but I didn't see anyone. This time I did call the police, and they sent an officer over, but he couldn't find anything, not even footprints below the window, and I could tell he thought I was this fragile widow living alone, imagining spooky noises, and wandering decorations."

Natalie looked at Camille's profile, clear in the moonlight. "There is no way he thought you were fragile."

"Okay, fine. But he did think I was imagining things because who would randomly tap SOS on someone's window, and what is a distress call on my window supposed to mean? If someone is stalking me, shouldn't *I* be the one sending a distress call? Is this a hint that I'm going to *need* to send a distress call soon?"

"Do you have a ship heading for an iceberg?"

"Metaphorically?"

"Or literally."

"Since I lost the *Titanic*, I've been afraid to invest in another luxury liner." Camille took another chocolate. "Listen, I've analyzed all these incidents to death—ugh, that wasn't a good choice of words. I'm still spooked. I know the SOS seems silly, but it freaked me out. After the police left, I packed an overnight bag and went to a hotel."

"A hotel! Why didn't you call me? You could have spent the night at my place."

"I know. I just wanted to figure out what was going on, and I didn't want company yet."

"Were you afraid I'd tell you you'd imagined it?"

"Would you have?"

"No."

"You finally believe someone's stalking me?"

"Finally?" The question stung. "You're the one who's experienced these things, not me. When you came to me last week, you described what was going on and wanted my opinion. I did the best I could. I didn't realize you thought I was being dismissive of your experiences."

"I'm sorry. I'm being a grouch. But don't you think these new things are clearer evidence than the person outside the construction trailer? Some psycho *is* messing with me. It's creepy."

"I'd be creeped out too," Natalie said, knowing it wasn't as strong a confirmation as Camille wanted from her. She resisted the temptation to ask if Camille had considered that these incidents might not be linked—that some of them might have been imagination or personalization on her part and some might have been the work of a bored neighbor kid.

"I know it sounds like I'm overreacting," Camille said. "There hasn't been any damage or threats—unless the SOS was meant as a threat, but it's a lame threat. I guess I'm scared, worrying the person will escalate. And I'm angry, wondering why they're messing with me."

"I assume you've thought a lot about who might want to spy on you or upset you."

Camille groped inside her backpack and took out her phone. She lit the screen and passed it to Natalie. "Read the first list of names there. Our old high school friends. I wrote down everyone I could think of who's still in Ohneka or in a town nearby. People I knew at least fairly well."

Natalie read the list. "Okay."

"Use your psychologist brain and tell me if there's anyone on that list who you think could turn stalker."

Internally, Natalie groaned. Camille ought to know better than to treat her like a mind reader. "I haven't seen some of these people in over a decade, and even the ones I do see, I don't see often."

"Make some guesses. This is friend to friend; I'm not asking you for something you could back up in court. This is anything-goes brainstorming. Here, do it this way. Look at the list again. If you *knew* the stalker was on this list but didn't know who it was, pick the three people you'd investigate first."

Reluctantly, Natalie read the list a second time. "Fine. I'd investigate Griff Norris. Maybe he never got over you, and after you lost Dante, he wanted to see if he could start something with you again, but he was still bitter about being dumped, so he decided to stalk you instead."

"Good job. Who else?"

"Uh . . . Tanner, because he was Griff's best friend, and I think he had a crush on you but never could admit it. Maybe he's obsessed with you now. And . . . Sierra, because she used to make snotty remarks about you."

"Yeah, the fat jokes."

"Because she was jealous that the most beautiful girl in school wasn't a size 0, wasn't ashamed of her body, and annihilated her in the senior class elections."

Camille laughed. "She's still a size zero. Or maybe a point five—the point five is her belly; she's pregnant. She friended me online a few years back, and I thought, 'Bring it on, sister,' and accepted."

"Yes, I'm friends with her too. She seems happy. Thrilled about her pregnancy."

"No kidding. If she posts one more pic of her husband's manly hand resting on her baby bump, I might puke, but other than that, I actually like her now. So those are your top three?"

Natalie handed the phone to Camille. "My *forced* top three. I was trying to think of anyone who might be ambivalent toward you or who might have been ambivalent toward you a decade ago."

"Anybody else you want to add to the list?"

"I didn't want to add anyone to the list in the first place. Don't you have any current-life suspects we could pick apart?"

Camille tapped the screen on her phone. "You mean, am I dating, or was I dating, or have I rejected anyone recently?"

"Sure."

Camille held up her left hand, tilting the diamonds toward the moonlight. "This scares off most guys. If they know I'm a widow, sometimes they try to hit on me, but I can handle it, and it doesn't go anywhere. Nobody's been weirdly persistent, so if it's a sick romantic obsession, they're sneaky about it." She passed her phone to Natalie. "I wrote down the names of anyone I could remember asking me out or trying to flirt with me in the past few months."

Natalie read the list and couldn't restrain a smile. The list was long. "A few of the names are familiar but only vaguely. Like I've heard of them or met them in passing but don't know enough about them to be helpful."

Camille took her phone. "I was hoping you'd recognize someone on the list as a client who struggles with an obsession over beautiful, not-size-zero widows."

"You do realize that if I recognized one of them as a client, I couldn't tell you."

"I know you couldn't tell me anything you've discussed—"

"I couldn't even confirm they were a client. Have you thought of hiring a private detective?"

"Yes, but . . . I don't know. Maybe I can't face the fact that it's time to let Dante go and move on, so I'm imagining someone stalking me because then I can be scared instead of dealing with the fact that I'm lonely. How's that for analyzing myself?"

"Deep. Well done."

"I'm developing an obsession that someone is watching me. I'm developing a phobia of self-propelled harvest decorations."

"I doubt that."

"Did you know Bob Chapman's first wife had a phobia of cats?"

"I didn't."

"Adorable, fluffy, Internet-meme-worthy cats. Cat phobia. Do you think I'll develop that next?"

"Relax, Camille. What matters is that whatever is happening is interfering with your peace of mind. You tell me what would help you the most, and I'll do whatever I can—within ethical boundaries."

"I don't know." Camille offered the open box of chocolates to Natalie.

"Choosing chocolates in the dark adds a thrill to the process." Natalie took one. "What don't you know?"

"How much is real, I guess. I swing back and forth, positive I'm getting stalked, then afraid my mind is messing with me. I'm not sure which one I want it to be."

"If you'd like to talk to someone about it, Kirk is fantastic."

"I know he is. In fact, I recommended your whole practice to someone the other day, so you're welcome. But I don't know. I hate doubting myself." Her voice firmed. "I swear someone SOS'd on my window and moved my decorations."

"I believe you. But even if—"

"I'll think about it. Maybe I need to let it stew longer. Let's switch to a frivolous topic. Mostly frivolous." She tapped her phone. "Check *this* out. I would have shown it to you weeks ago, but it's what I bought at MaryLisa's right before Wade Radcliffe died, so I ended up with all these messy feelings about it and hid it in my closet, but when I finally took it out yesterday, it dazzled me all over again. I realized I was being stupid, choosing not to enjoy it—this is my birthday present from Dante, and it's *divine*."

She held the phone out. For the first time in the conversation, Natalie accepted it eagerly. On the screen was a picture of a royal-blue silk clutch purse with silver clasps and a silver chain. The purse was decorated in miniature, glittering tiles that formed a winter scene of a frozen pond surrounded by leafless trees and evergreens with snow shimmering on blue-green branches. Tiny silver stars speckled the sky.

"That is *gorgeous*!" Natalie said.

"That's the front of the purse. Swipe to the next picture to see the back."

Natalie did so. The back of the purse was as intricate as the front, with white crystals of snow falling on a rustic cottage.

"Next week, I'm debuting it at the Chapman soiree," Camille said. "I'm sad I never went to MaryLisa's before that; they had some amazing handmade stuff. Pricey, though, so I guess it's good I stayed away."

"I have a skirt from MaryLisa's. A gift from Andrea. I never would have been able to afford it myself."

"I'm sure she made that point when she gave it to you."

"Eloquently. In fact, Felicia told me Andrea made a point of it with Wade when she bought the skirt. She rhapsodized about how thrilled I'd be with this expensive skirt, so far beyond my pitiful budget."

Camille snickered. "Flaunt that inheritance, girl." She took her phone back and looked at the picture. "A local artist made the purse. Her husband was one of Dante's insane marathon-training buddies. I'm too embarrassed to tell you how much I paid for it, even with my haggling the price down a few bucks, but it's so beautiful and so unique."

"Dante would be delighted that he showed such exquisite taste in choosing your gift."

"Right? I'm going to search for formal events to attend this winter so I'll have lots of excuses to carry it. Symphony concerts or the opera or something. Come with me sometime?"

"I'd love to."

"Speaking of the Chapman shindig, did you decide to invite Felicia to go with you?"

"Yes. I left her a message but didn't hear back. I'm assuming that means she doesn't want to come. I don't want to pester her about it."

"You tried. That's all you can do."

"I hope it wasn't tactless to invite her, but she and Wade always enjoyed it. I thought she might still be interested but wouldn't want to go alone." Natalie resumed sipping hot chocolate and scanned the sky, hunting for the Big Dipper— the only constellation she could ever find. "Did you know there's an app that identifies constellations? We should get it."

"Forget learning constellations," Camille said. "I'm going to learn Morse code. If either the stalker or my grieving imagination comes tapping at my window, I'll tap back something that will curl their hair."

CHAPTER 8

"How do you feel about Jonas being so involved in your work?" Dr. Marsh's voice was kind, encouraging, as though whatever Lacey said, she'd accept it.

"I . . . well, I'm grateful he's so supportive." Lacey settled back more comfortably in her chair. She'd come to her second therapy appointment afraid that if Dr. Marsh struck the wrong spot in her psyche, she'd shatter, but the questions weren't blows. They were soft, like a cloth cleaning spots off a window so Lacey could look through it. "But sometimes it . . . I don't like the pressure. Don't tell him that."

"I won't tell him anything we discuss. You know that."

Lacey nodded.

"In what ways does his involvement feel like pressure?"

"Um . . ." Lacey tried to figure out how to answer this question. A few days ago, she wasn't sure she could have stopped herself from exploding, spilling every horrible thought she'd had about Jonas, but today was better. This was the best she'd felt all week.

Over eight days of house arrest, she'd done everything she could to act normal, to work hard, to convince Jonas she was fine. Gradually, her strategy had succeeded—first, Jonas had left her home alone while he'd gone running; then he'd started leaving for a few hours at a time to meet with clients instead of only working from home. This morning, she'd even convinced him that Dr. Marsh had ordered her to drive herself to and from her appointment, that it was important for her mental health that she handle her sessions on her own. She'd worried Jonas might call Dr. Marsh and question this fib, but he'd accepted it and returned her car keys and wallet. Maybe he was so relieved that she was going willingly that he wasn't analyzing why Dr. Marsh would or wouldn't care how she got there.

Now Jonas was at work for the whole day. After her appointment ended, she planned to go straight to where she knew Camille would be today: eating lunch at the India Pearl buffet. Jonas and Camille had talked about how she never missed a Friday buffet. Lacey craved a dose of watching Camille.

Dr. Marsh sat in silence, still waiting for her to answer the question.

Quickly, Lacey said, "He gets concerned if he feels I'm not productive enough. He says to be successful I need to build up an inventory, so if I'm not creating enough new projects, he'll . . . well, he has a lot of good suggestions about managing time and focusing and stuff like that. It's so nice of him to be concerned about me being successful."

"Do you feel he pressures you to create your artwork at a pace that's not comfortable for you?"

"Oh, he's just trying to keep me from wasting time daydreaming." Lacey focused on Dr. Marsh's office carpet. She liked the soft gray speckled with deep blue. "I don't concentrate very well, so he's helpful about encouraging me."

"You're the artist," Dr. Marsh said. "Do you think you might enjoy your work more—and even be more productive—if you worked at your own pace, not at Jonas's?"

"I'd be too slow. I'm lucky he keeps me going." She toyed with the phone in her lap—the phone Jonas could track. She'd figured out how he'd located her last week: she'd discovered a new tracking app on her phone. She could have deleted it but didn't want him to know she'd noticed it.

"What would be the consequences of creating your artwork at a slower pace?" Dr. Marsh asked.

Hoping the gesture looked absentminded, Lacey set the phone on the strip of cushion between her thigh and the arm of the chair. She'd removed the mosaic cover she usually had on her phone so the slick metal would slide easily. "Um, I wouldn't be as successful."

"Do you feel that way, or are you repeating what he's told you?"

"Um, I can't sell as much if I don't create as much."

"Is that your goal? The maximum number of pieces sold, even if you feel the pieces could have been better with more attention and time?"

Lacey shifted in her seat, her thigh nudging the phone closer to the crack between the cushion and the chair arm. Maximum sales *wasn't* her goal, and she sensed Dr. Marsh already knew that. "I think Jonas figures the pieces are good enough now that people will buy them, and once I'm established, I can take the time to create spectacular stuff."

"That's Jonas's opinion. What do you think?"

Could she tell Dr. Marsh what she thought? Lacey felt the way she had when they'd visited that Chicago skyscraper and she'd had the chance to step into one of those tilting glass boxes to get a view of the city below. She'd been fascinated, wanting to step forward but terrified to do it.

She hadn't stepped forward.

"I, uh . . ." Lacey squirmed. "I . . . I don't know what I think. But I made this purse once . . . and that was the first time I'd tried something like that. It took ages. Just a small purse, an evening clutch, but it . . . it turned out so beautiful. It was winter scenes. Thousands of micro-tiles . . . so many hours to piece it all together. Jonas was out of town, so he didn't know I was spending so much time on one project."

"Did you enjoy being able to spend the amount of time you wanted on that project?"

"It was wonderful. I loved it."

"How did Jonas react when he returned and saw your new project?"

Lacey pushed the toe of one shoe against the carpet and drew it back, imagining transparent plexiglass beneath her feet. "He . . . thought I could have spent my time better. He didn't yell or anything. Just told me not to spend so much time on a project that would never bring in enough money to make the time worth it. He couldn't imagine anyone would spend more than fifty bucks on a purse."

Dr. Marsh smiled. "Versace would disagree."

"I told him people pay thousands of dollars for designer purses, and he said they'll only pay that if you're already famous; nobody will pay big money for an unknown artist. I know he was right. Almost right, I mean. The purse *did* sell. Not for thousands, but . . . a lot of money. To me, I mean. It was a lot to me. Nothing like how much he makes. He's a financial planner and is really good at it. He has a lot of clients." She gave her phone another subtle nudge. "I think he was surprised someone paid that much for my purse."

"How did you feel about the sale?"

"Oh, great! Except . . . " She thought of Wade Radcliffe's accident and his wife's obsession with finding out who'd bought the purse on the day he'd died. "Um, I think the store that sold it is closing, so I won't be able to sell there again. I'd like to make another purse though. I have some ideas, and if local stores don't want it, I could sell it online. But I'm supposed to be working on designs for a wall mural."

"Are you under contract for a wall mural?"

"No." She pretended to straighten her long knit skirt and bumped the phone again. One more nudge and it would be down the crack, and she could plausibly "forget" it. If Jonas checked the app, he'd think she was still at her appointment. After she watched Camille, she'd return and tell the receptionist she thought she'd left her phone in Dr. Marsh's office. "Not a contract, but . . . someone who works for Robert Chapman . . . you know who Robert Chapman is?"

"I do."

"Who in Ohneka doesn't, right? Jonas hopes he can get me a commission to do a mural for that old building Mr. Chapman's company is renovating, and he wants me working on ideas for it, just in case. It's a long shot though, and I already *have* several ideas. I just don't want to pour more time into them when it's so unlikely they'll hire me."

"Have you told Jonas you would prefer to work on a purse right now?"

"Um . . ." Lacey shifted position, bumping the phone into the crack. "He wouldn't agree with that."

"He wouldn't respect your point of view?"

"Um . . . he's a smart guy, so . . . he usually knows how best to do things."

"Do *you* respect your point of view?"

The question stuck painfully in Lacey's mind. When she tried to tug it loose, it clung with hooked thorns. "I . . . um . . . I don't know."

Dr. Marsh's hazel eyes studied Lacey. "What kind of feedback does Jonas give you when you do express your point of view?"

Lacey thought about the cinnamon apples and the raspberry sauce she wanted to make. She still hadn't told Jonas about it. "If I . . . if he thinks I'm wrong, he'll tell me, but he doesn't yell or swear or anything bad."

"If he tells you he thinks you're wrong, how do you respond?"

"Well . . . I mean . . . I don't want to argue." Lacey resisted the impulse to touch the phone one more time to make sure it was out of sight. "He always takes care of me."

Dr. Marsh had an unhurried, meditative expression on her face that made Lacey want to slow down and ponder the questions again—maybe answer them more thoroughly.

"What do you think he would do if you *did* defend your point of view instead of defaulting to his?" Dr. Marsh asked.

Lacey curved both hands around her knees, fingering her skirt. She'd wanted a different pattern of fabric, but Jonas had told her this print would look better on her. At least he'd liked the beaded scarf she'd bought. She'd been ecstatic when she'd spotted a scarf exactly like Camille's coral-and-gold one. "Oh . . . uh . . . he'd probably . . . explain again why he was right."

"What if you held to your point of view, even when he tried to persuade you he was right?"

"I don't know," Lacey said. "I've . . . never done that."

* * *

After she'd escorted Lacey to the waiting room, Natalie returned to her office. She approached the chair where Lacey had been sitting, slipped her hand into the crack between the cushion and the arm, and pulled out Lacey's phone. Lacey had been subtle when maneuvering the phone out of sight, but Natalie had noticed it; she'd been on the verge of asking Lacey if she was expecting a call when Lacey had first set it on the cushion. In Lacey's first session, she'd left the phone in her purse, and her fidgeting with it this time around had piqued Natalie's interest.

So Lacey was the local artist who had made Camille's new purse—which meant Dante's "insane marathon buddy" had been Jonas Egan. Jonas, friends with Dante? Why did that information fit so awkwardly, like shoes on the wrong feet? The fact that Jonas dominated his wife didn't mean he was an all-around jerk. Why shouldn't he have decent friends like Dante? But Camille must not have seen much of Jonas and Lacey together—the way Jonas controlled her would have driven Camille up the wall, and Camille likely would have vented about it when she'd shown Natalie pictures of the purse.

Lacey had immense talent. Natalie hoped she could guide her to the point of having confidence in her own judgment—and realizing that overbearing behavior didn't equal omniscience.

She'd debated confronting Lacey about why she'd hidden her phone but had decided to let her leave without it. If Natalie had mentioned it at the time, Lacey would have denied hiding it deliberately, and the conversation would have gone nowhere. If she let Lacey finish whatever she was planning, Natalie would have more facts to deal with and—she hoped—more luck getting Lacey to open up about why she'd felt the need to leave the phone. Natalie's guess was that she wanted a period of time when Jonas couldn't contact her or locate her. "Accidentally" leaving her phone at her therapy appointment was an excuse he might accept.

For now, Natalie would leave the phone at the reception desk. Lacey would probably come back for it later today.

Jeanne was on the phone when Natalie approached the reception area. "Could you hold for a moment?" Jeanne touched a button and lowered the phone. "Call for you. I was about to send it to your voice mail. Do you want to take it now, or are you starving?"

She was hungry but not ravenous. Lunch could wait a few minutes. "I'll take it in my office." She set Lacey's phone on Jeanne's desk. "Lacey Egan left this behind. I imagine she'll come back for it at some point."

Jeanne pulled out the pen she kept stuck through the gray-black braid wound around her head. She jotted Lacey's name on a Post-It note and pressed it to the phone. "I'll guard it for her."

"Thanks." Natalie returned to her office and picked up her office phone. She touched a button to accept the call. "Hello, this is Natalie Marsh."

A male voice spoke. "Hi, uh, this is Gideon Radcliffe. I apologize for interrupting your workday. I thought I'd be leaving a message. I wouldn't have called you at work, but I didn't have your personal number, and I didn't want to ask Felicia for it, and I hope I'm not interrupting you."

From this courteous but rambling introduction, Natalie knew he was nervous. "I'm on my lunch hour, so you have perfect timing. What can I do for you?"

"I . . . first, I want to apologize about last week. You must think I'm a kook. I would have called to apologize sooner, but I was hoping if I waited long enough, you'd forget I existed."

Natalie laughed. "I don't think you're a kook."

"Seriously, I know I must have made you uncomfortable, and I'm sorry. I honestly did want your insights on Felicia but lost my nerve. And bored you to death during dinner."

"I wasn't bored to death, but why did you lose your nerve?"

"It's an odd situation. Dicey. Ever since I drowned my dignity in a bowl of split-pea, I've been trying to reach out to Felicia, to learn more about what she's going through and how to help her. I'm not getting anywhere. She doesn't want to talk about it. Treats me like a kid, frankly, and tells me it's not my business. I'm done keeping my mouth shut. I think grief is messing with her head."

"Did she ask you to keep your mouth shut?"

"More than asked. Ordered me, and I promised I wouldn't discuss it with anyone. But for her sake, I don't think that's a promise I should keep. She's hurting, and I can't ignore that and let her struggle. Is it too late to ask to talk to you about it?"

"It's never too late. You know I'm worried about her too."

"I feel awkward about blabbing though. Is it legitimate if I discuss the situation with you and ask you not to mention it to Felicia or anyone else until we figure out which direction to go?"

"I'm the keeper of the world's secrets," Natalie said. "I'm guessing this is more of a conversation than we can have over the phone in the next few minutes?"

"I'll take whatever time you can give me. I've already made myself a pest, and I don't want to impose."

"You're not a pest. I'd appreciate more insight on how to reach out to her. Felicia was a great blessing to me as a child, and I'd like to return the favor in any way I can. Would you like to meet for dinner? That would give us some unhurried time to talk."

"Hey, yeah, that would be great!" At the surprise and relief in his voice, Natalie felt a little bad for him—he sincerely *had* been worried he'd made a fool of himself. "Are you . . . sure?"

"I'm sure," she said. "I didn't make the suggestion by accident."

He chuckled. "Unfortunately, it does need to be private, which makes me sound awkward again. 'Hi, I'm a stranger. Come meet me for another private dinner. Don't worry; my old cellmate said he'd vouch for me, and my parole officer thinks I have promise.'"

"I've had better character witnesses than your alleged cellmate. Felicia has always told me what a nice, upstanding guy you are. I didn't know your father well, but I know he was proud of you."

"Thank you for telling me that. I appreciate it."

"I understand why you're hesitant to discuss your concerns in public. Here's a compromise. Are you free on Saturday afternoon? You could come to my house. The weather's supposed to be nice, and I have a wood-fired pizza oven in the backyard. It's not worth heating it up just for me, but I'd enjoy an excuse to use it. Picnic outdoors. Out in the sunlight, where neighbors can peek through the arborvitae if they want but will be too far away to hear us."

"That's the best lunch offer I've ever had. What time Saturday?"

"Anytime."

"Anytime works for me too. You'll let me bake pizzas, right? I have some Italian blood, and I owe it to my ancestors to learn how to wield a . . . that big spatula thing."

"A peel," Natalie said. "And yes, you're welcome to. How about one o'clock?"

"Great. What can I bring? Dough? Toppings? Salad?"

"Bring whatever toppings you like. I'll provide the dough, sauce, and cheese. You bring the fun stuff."

"Sounds great."

"Give me your number," she said. "I'll text you my address, and that will give you my phone number as well."

He recited it. "Thank you, Natalie. Seriously. I still feel stupid, hounding you like this, but I'm stumped for how to help Felicia."

"I'm stumped too, so I'll be glad to get your insights. See you Saturday."

CHAPTER 9

HER TONGUE TASTING OF UNFAMILIAR spices and several pages in her notebook crammed with notes, Lacey drove back to Dr. Marsh's office. Even though there were plenty of empty parking spaces, she parked far from the entrance. She wanted to walk through the entire lot, breathe crisp air, crunch on fallen leaves, emulate Camille's stride. She wanted to get some high-heeled shoes like Camille's, but Jonas might not approve. High heels would make her taller than he was.

She entered the building, took the stairs to the second floor, and reentered the quiet reception room. The Frida Kahlo woman at the desk smiled at her and drew back the glass window. "Hello, Mrs. Egan. I'll bet you're here for your phone."

Caught off guard, Lacey still managed a Camille-smile. She hadn't expected them to find the phone until she'd prompted them to look for it. "Yes. I was hoping it was here. I couldn't think where else I would have left it."

The woman opened a drawer, took out Lacey's phone, and passed it to her. "We kept it safe for you."

"Thank you so much." Lacey headed for the exit.

Back in her car, she took her mosaic phone case out of her purse and snapped it onto her phone. As soon as she arrived home, she'd brush her teeth and swish mouthwash to clean up her breath. She didn't want Jonas smelling those spices. She hadn't thought she liked Indian food, but she'd had it only once before, and it was better than she'd remembered. She could tolerate it again. Maybe . . . next Friday, after her appointment? She couldn't leave her phone in Dr. Marsh's office again though. She'd find another hiding place. Behind a potted tree in the lobby, or someplace like that.

She pulled into the garage. As she opened her car door, Jonas's car pulled into the other bay.

Lacey's heart gave a heavy shake. He'd said he'd be at work all day. Why had he come home now? *Stay calm.* She waved at him and started for the door to the house, pawing through her purse in search of breath mints.

His car door opened. "Lacey, wait."

She turned and smiled at him, fingers closing on the container of mints. "You're home early."

Jonas approached, opened the door to the house, and held it for her.

"Thank you." Knowing she couldn't pop a mint without Jonas noticing, she let go of the tin and stepped inside. She'd better admit she'd gone to lunch. It wasn't a suspicious act—why shouldn't she grab a bite after her appointment? *Act confident. Smile like Camille did when she was chatting with her colleagues at the restaurant.*

Jonas closed the door. "Where have you been? Your appointment was at eleven."

"I went to lunch afterward. I guess I'm burned out on sandwiches. I wanted to try something different." She went to hang her purse in the closet. Jonas swiped it out of her hands, unzipped the center compartment, and pulled out her notebook.

Lacey's phony confidence splintered, slicing her heart. "That's private!"

Jonas dropped her purse on the floor and scrutinized the front and back covers of the small notebook. "What's in it?"

"It's . . . it's where I wrote my notes when I was talking with Dr. Marsh. She said not to let anyone else look at it, that it was only for me. I need it back." She tried to grab it. Jonas gripped her wrist and leaned close to her.

"What were you doing at the India Pearl? You don't even like Indian food."

"I wasn't—" Her face was chilly, his breath like hot wind against a frosted window. Had he seen . . . ?

"You were planning to meet someone there, but he didn't show up, did he? Did he chicken out?"

"I wasn't meeting anyone! I just—I decided I wanted to . . . something new . . . give the food another try. I know you like it; if I liked it, we could go together . . . " With her free hand, she tried again to snatch her notebook.

"I thought you'd never do this to me." Jonas shoved it into his back pocket and seized her other wrist. "I've taken care of you. I've protected you. I've done everything for you. This is what you give me back? Lies? Cheating?"

"I'm not cheating! Give me that notebook!"

"Tell me the truth, and I will."

"I'd never cheat on you. I just wanted to try something different."

"So you left your phone at your therapist's office so I'd think you were still there and you could sneak away?"

He'd seen her returning to Dr. Marsh's office too? And he'd realized she knew about the app. "It was an accident. I forgot my phone. I didn't notice it was missing until I was already at the restaurant."

"You're lying. You never looked for it. You didn't search your pockets or your purse or your car."

He *had* been there, watching her the whole time. Watching as she'd observed Camille and taken notes. Frantically, Lacey tried to imagine how her actions had appeared from his point of view. Did he realize she was stalking Camille? "I remembered I'd set the phone down at Dr. Marsh's and hadn't picked it up. That's why I didn't look for it. I wasn't meeting anyone."

"Trolling for a man, then? I saw you staring at a couple of guys the whole time, the men with Camille Moretti. Which one are you after?"

"I'm not after anyone," Lacey said, amazed that she could feel so relieved at getting accused of ogling other men. "I was staring into space, thinking about my discussion with Dr. Marsh. I . . . didn't even realize Camille was there. I don't know her very well."

He released her wrists and took several steps backward. "Fine," he said. "You keep your secrets. I'll read about them." He pulled the notebook out of his pocket, turned his back on her, and walked away.

"Jonas!" Lacey lurched after him. "Please don't! It's nothing about a man. I'm not cheating. It's private; it's therapy notes."

He kept walking. She grabbed the back of his jacket. "Please!"

With a wrench of his shoulders, he pulled his jacket from her grip. He jogged toward the stairs. Thoughts of what he'd see in that notebook whirled inside Lacey, a tornado inhaling everything, destroying everything.

"Jonas!" she shrieked, racing after him. Her shoes slipped on the tiled entryway, and she flapped her arms, catching her balance. "Wait!"

He raced up the stairs. Lacey tried to follow but stepped on the hem of her skirt and crashed her knee into the edge of a stair. "Jonas!" she screamed.

A door slammed. A lock popped shut.

Tears poured from her eyes and splattered the tread of the stair. He would read the notebook. He'd learn everything she'd done, how she'd followed Camille, spied on her, delighted in scaring her. Everything about Lacey's evil. Everything about her insanity.

Lacey stood and staggered toward the garage. She grabbed her purse off the floor where Jonas had dropped it, took out her phone and hurled it down the hallway as hard as she could. It smashed into something, and glass shattered; she didn't know or care what she'd broken along with the phone. She rushed to her car and drove away from the house, smearing her tears with her fingertips, driving too fast, with no idea where she was going.

CHAPTER 10

THE NIP OF THE EVENING wind reminded Natalie that it would be October soon. She pulled her silver shawl tightly around her shoulders—though the fabric was too thin to do much good—and rang Felicia's doorbell.

Yesterday's unexpected text from Felicia asking if the invitation to accompany Natalie to the Chapman soiree was still open was the most encouraging, optimistic signal Natalie had received from her since Wade's death. Felicia was reaching out—and wanted to attend a party. Natalie hoped to have an encouraging report to give Gideon at lunch tomorrow, and she could finally give Felicia the poetry book she'd bought for her.

Felicia opened the door. "Good evening. Come in."

"Thank you." Natalie stepped into the warm house. Felicia wore a long, black velvet dress decorated with rhinestones. The dress should have been stunning with her coloring, but tonight, the black magnified how pale she was—so pale that the dusting of blush on her cheeks stood out instead of blending with her skin. She must be nervous, conflicted about attending the soiree, missing Wade. Natalie revowed to make tonight enjoyable for Felicia. The party that Bob Chapman threw every autumn for his employees and for business owners who leased property from him was always entertaining. Natalie hoped Felicia wouldn't find it overwhelming.

"That's a beautiful dress." Felicia gestured at Natalie's deep-purple gown with its long sleeves, flowing fabric gathered at one hip, and a rippling ankle-length skirt. "And your shawl is stunning."

Natalie spread her arms to show off her intricate, hand-embroidered wrap. "Birthday gift," she said. She let her voice go dry and added, "From Andrea."

"Ah," Felicia said. Natalie was glad Felicia knew her family history well enough to understand how Natalie would have mixed feelings about a beautiful and expensive gift from her sister.

"Let me get my coat," Felicia said.

Natalie offered Felicia the gift bag. "This is for you. I thought you might enjoy it."

Felicia accepted the bag. "Thank you. You're so thoughtful." Her gratitude sounded weary, as though complimenting Natalie's clothes had already tapped out her energy for courtesies.

"Don't worry about opening it now," Natalie said. "Save it for when you need a pick-me-up."

"Thank you." Felicia set the bag on the couch. She stepped into black pumps and took a dress coat out of the closet. "Thank you for driving. I hope I didn't interrupt any plans you'd made."

"Not at all. I was delighted to hear from you."

They walked to Natalie's car. "I wonder what entertainment Bob has planned for this year," Natalie said as she started the engine. "I hope something quieter than the bagpipers he flew over from Scotland last year."

"It will be something unusual."

"I've heard rumors about belly dancers. And the Royal Shakespeare Company doing a 'best of.'"

"Neither would surprise me."

"Both together wouldn't surprise me," Natalie said. Tension had increased in Felicia's voice; maybe she wasn't up for chitchat yet. Natalie touched the stereo, choosing a Beethoven piano sonata. Music might be a better way to fill the silence.

She parked behind the Chapman Fine Arts Museum, and they headed toward the walkway that crossed Kahrakwa Pond to the glass-sided reception hall that blazed in the darkness, firing streaks of silver and gold light over glassy black water.

"Maison du Canard is breathtaking at night," Natalie said as their heels clicked along the walkway. "Breathtaking during the day too."

"You'd think they'd have given it a more elegant name than 'Duck House,'" Felicia said.

"I hear he named it in honor of an annoyed mallard that kept showing up to quack at the construction workers. Vintage Chapman. Give it a whimsical name but dress it up with French so people think it means something classy."

Felicia nodded.

"I went ice skating here last winter," Natalie said. "I felt like I was in a Christmas special. I wonder how the building is constructed to keep it from being damaged when the pond freezes?"

"My stepson would know," Felicia said. "He's a civil engineer."

Natalie hesitated. Should she tell Felicia she'd met Gideon last week? She wasn't sure if he wanted that encounter to be a secret, but if he *had* told Felicia, it would seem strange for Natalie not to mention it now. "Did he tell you I ran into him other night? I stopped by your house when he was raking your leaves."

"He told me."

Relieved but not daring to say anything else about her interaction with Gideon, she said, "You must enjoy having him in Ohneka."

"He's an outstanding young man. I'm glad he's rid of Tamara."

"Is that his former fiancée? You told me she . . . that they broke up."

"Yes. She was a nice girl, mostly, but I could tell there were things about Gideon she wanted to change. He's not a DIY project."

"Absolutely." Natalie felt disingenuous not mentioning that Gideon was coming over for lunch tomorrow, but since he planned to discuss things Felicia didn't want him to talk about, she didn't want to stir conflict between stepmother and stepson. *Keeper of the world's secrets.*

A man dressed in a tailcoat opened the door to Maison du Canard. "Good evening, ladies. May I see your invitation?"

Natalie took her invitation out of her silver evening clutch and handed it to the man. Felicia didn't offer hers, thought Natalie knew she'd received one. She didn't need to show it; Natalie's invitation covered herself and a guest.

The man scanned the barcode on Natalie's invitation and handed it back. "Thank you, Ms. Marsh."

Natalie and Felicia stepped through the doorway. On the dais set against one wall of the octagonal building, a jazz band was playing "Take Five." Classic jazz seemed tame for Chapman. The band must be background entertainment, not the *pièce de résistance.*

Felicia headed for the coat check. Natalie followed but kept her shawl on. It was by far the dressiest part of her outfit.

"My lady! Paragon of loveliness, sorceress of the human mind!"

Smiling, Natalie pivoted toward Bob Chapman. His white hair was so wild tonight that she wondered if he'd escaped his house before his wife had had a chance to corner him and fix it. "It's good to see you, Bob."

Chapman took her hand, bowed, and kissed it. "Ah, Dr. Natalie, it's always good to see you, especially as a glittering beauty in silver and purple. I am, alas, unchivalrous enough to mix business and pleasure, so I will take this moment to suggest a possible psychiatrist for you to court for your still-imaginary clinic. My wife recommended a doctor by the name of Marianne Avery. She knows Dr. Avery socially but has heard stellar feedback from those who know her professionally. She has a charitable heart and might be interested in donating time. Her office is in Canandaigua."

"I haven't worked with her, but I've heard her name," Natalie said. "Thank you; I'll contact her."

Felicia returned to her side. Natalie touched her arm. "Bob, this is my long-time friend—"

"Yes, indeed, I recognize her." Chapman grasped Felicia's hand. "The elegant and savvy Felicia Radcliffe, clothed in velvet and stars." He kissed her hand. "Dear lady, I was deeply sorry to hear of your husband's death. He was a treasure, and my beloved Mel will never cease to mourn the absence of his good nature, his charming inventory, and his advice."

Felicia said nothing. Natalie glanced at her. Her expression was blank and cold.

"MaryLisa's was a lovely store." Natalie jammed her own words in place of what should have been Felicia's response. "Unfortunately, just peeking in the window was enough to overdraw my bank account."

Chapman released Felicia's hand, showing no sign that he'd been offended by her silence. "Ah, *Frau Seelenklempnerin*, if you desired riches, you should have chosen a profession that paid in gold, not in the currency of satisfaction for succoring the struggling. Ladies, please enjoy the party, eat and imbibe, dance and sing, and prepare yourselves for a mind-expanding performance brought to you from the peaks of the Swiss Alps." He bowed and strolled toward the next group approaching the coat check.

"Swiss Alps." Natalie smiled at Felicia. "Do you think he's imported yodelers? Or Alpenhorns?"

Felicia didn't reply. Her gaze stayed locked on Chapman, who was greeting the arrivals with animated handshakes and graceful hand kissing.

Natalie brushed her fingers against Felicia's shoulder. "Are you all right? Parties can be overwhelming, and Bob is pretty much always overwhelming."

"I'm fine," Felicia said, her voice steady. "What did he call you?"

"What do you—oh, the German. 'Ms. Psychologist.' 'Ms. Shrink.' I made the mistake of telling him I wanted to learn German, and now he's forever throwing phrases at me. And he's right that nobody who wants to get rich goes into this profession."

"He's the expert on getting rich," Felicia said. "Excuse me, but I'd like to approach this on my own for a while. I'll wander around, see if there's anyone I feel like talking to, maybe sit in the lounge if I need a break."

"Whatever you'd like."

Felicia walked away. She stayed close to the periphery of the room, her pace slow, her gaze skimming the guests.

Hoping Felicia might find some friends—and greet them with more enthusiasm than she had Chapman—Natalie scanned the room herself. Was Camille here yet? She spotted Kirk and his wife, Deborah, talking with Skyler and Vicki and wandered toward them.

"Lookin' *amazing*, Nat!" Skyler kissed her cheek.

"Thanks. You too," Natalie said. "That must be the new tux."

"The ridiculously expensive new tux." Vicki hugged Natalie. "I'm not sure what was wrong with his old one."

"I wanted a new one. That's what was wrong with the old one." Skyler patted the satin lapels on his ash-gray jacket. "I'm a height-of-fashion man, and I'm worth every penny. Invest in making me look good and you can't lose."

"Not true," Kirk said. "I invested in Get Hudson a Decent Haircut stock and lost my shirt."

"The shirtless look got you that flabby, rotting-flesh-zombie role in the next blockbuster, so you should thank me," Skyler said.

Deborah grimaced at Natalie. "I'm so sorry for what you have to put up with at work."

"Natalie's sorry for what you have to put up with at home," Skyler said.

Vicki sighed. "Ignore him. New suits make him think he's a comedian emceeing the Oscars."

"Hey, how can I not invest in my appearance when I'm side by side with this gorgeous brunette?" He grinned at Vicki. "Just trying not to embarrass her."

"Tape your mouth shut," Kirk said. "That will prevent embarrassment a lot better than a new tux."

Natalie laughed. "Truce, guys. Vicki, that's a gorgeous necklace."

"Thank you." Vicki ran her finger along the sparkling red crystals and scallops of silver filigree.

"I have great taste, right?" Skyler said. "Got it to go with her dress."

"You gave it to her?" Natalie asked. "You do have great taste. Where did you get it?"

"Uh . . . that fancy little store downtown . . . forgot the name. You know the store, Nat; we both know . . . knew . . . the owner."

"MaryLisa's," Natalie said.

"Yep, that's it." Skyler gave Kirk's wife an impish smile. "Deb, if you want stunning jewelry for your next birthday, slip me Kirk's credit card and deputize me to do the shopping. My taste will make up for the last thirty years of irons and frying pans that Kirk's been—"

Vicki clamped her hand over Skyler's mouth. "Truce, remember? Be nice for the rest of the evening, and I'll bribe you with coconut bread. Okay?"

Eyes gleaming with greed, Skyler nodded. Vicki lowered her hand.

"Does that apply to me too?" Kirk asked. "I've heard about your legendary coconut bread."

"It applies to you too," Vicki said.

"*Wait*, Vic," Skyler said. "You're messing with me. You're climbing on an airplane at the crack of dawn tomorrow. When are you going to have time to make coconut bread? I ain't waiting a week for my bribe."

"I have several loaves in my freezer. You can have one. And take one of them to work for Kirk."

"*What?* I didn't know you had a stash!"

"Where are you traveling to?" Deborah asked.

"Boston. Marketing seminar," Vicki said.

Skyler was still goggling at her. "You're a dragon hoarding gold. I can't believe it."

"Excuse us." Vicki linked arms with Skyler. "I'll feed him. That should calm him down." She drew him toward the food tables.

Kirk gestured across the room. "Deb, there's Gwen. Better catch her before she disappears."

"Oh! Excuse us, Natalie. I've been trying to get some information about the Harvest Faire for weeks; I'd better corner Gwen now. Good to see you." Kirk and Deborah hurried away.

Natalie glanced toward the food tables. Talk of coconut bread had stirred her appetite, and the themed food at these parties was always interesting. Last year's Scottish fare had included smoked salmon, roasted partridge, butter-rich shortbread, potato scones, and haggis. Trying to think of what foods, besides chocolate, she associated with Switzerland, she walked toward the first of the food tables.

"Nat!" Camille swished up from behind her. She was wearing a royal-blue silk dress and heels decorated with blue and clear crystals. "Your *shawl.* That is divine! Where did you get it?"

"Andrea."

Camille winked. "Of course."

"Did I tell you she's trying to send me to Alaska?"

"Temporarily or permanently?"

"Temporarily. On a cruise."

"Take her up on the offer. I'll come with you." Camille held out her purse. "Here's my pride and joy."

"Oooh." Natalie tucked her own purse under her arm and took Camille's. "This is spectacular." No wonder Lacey wanted to make more of these, though she'd definitely need to find a bigger market than Ohneka.

"Isn't it breathtaking?" Camille beamed as she took the purse back. "Do you think Dante is shocked at how much he spent on my frivolous gift?"

"Dante knows that if you're serving as his gift-buying agent, you aren't going to give yourself a toaster."

"I bought the dress to match the purse." Camille held the purse against her skirt. "And I think . . . I think I might even flirt tonight, if I can find prey. I think . . . maybe I'm ready."

"Dante would approve." Natalie shifted her purse back into her hand and straightened her shawl. "Flirt away."

"I will if *you* will. If you won't, I won't."

"Oh boy." Natalie grimaced. "No pressure. If I sort of have a date tomorrow that isn't really a date but does involve a single man, does that get me out of flirting tonight?"

"Oh brother. By *that* definition, you could count the plumber coming to fix your toilet or the guy on the porch trying to sell you solar panels."

"Felicia's stepson is worried about her and wants my insights. I invited him to lunch so we can talk."

"Good job, lady! How's Felicia doing? That's wonderful that she came tonight."

"Yes, it is. She's stressed, but she's here. I'm sure Gideon will be glad to hear that she came to a party."

"His name is Gideon? I like that. It has that something-hundred-B.C.-meets-trendy flavor. Nice guy?"

"Seems like it."

"Then I can't wait for your report. Hey . . . Nat." Camille's tone went so serious that Natalie feared she'd already changed her mind about flirting and was planning to slip off to one of the lounges and scroll through pictures of Dante on her phone. "Earlier this evening, I started sorting through some of Dante's papers that I hadn't gotten to before. I thought it might be therapeutic. Filing things I wanted to keep, shredding things I didn't. Clearing out some space, I guess, physically and mentally."

"Did it help?"

"Yes . . . well, it wasn't too intense. There were things like old notes from law school and the rental agreement from his first apartment. All our current financial information is in a different cabinet, so I hadn't had a reason to look through this one. Dante was something of a pack rat. An organized pack rat, but still. I barely made a dent in his paper collection, but it *was* satisfying to get started on it. The strange thing is, I found a letter for you."

"For me?"

"It was in one of his law-firm envelopes but didn't have a full address—just your name written in his handwriting."

A sweaty, dark feeling settled over Natalie, as though she were standing in a pitch-black swamp, not a bright, climate-controlled reception hall. "Why would he write me a letter and stick it in his filing cabinet?"

Camille squeezed Natalie's arm. "I'm thinking the same thing you are. Something about your mother. I was planning to give it to you here, but . . . I'm guessing you probably don't want it at a party?"

"No." Natalie tried to fathom what Dante would have said to her in a letter he'd never delivered. She'd never dealt with him over her mother's will—why would she? She wasn't a beneficiary.

"Are you okay?" Camille asked.

"Yes. Just confused. The estate was settled before he died."

"It can't have been official law-firm business," Camille said. "He wouldn't have kept that type of correspondence in a blank folder in a filing cabinet he hardly ever used. But I do wonder . . . Dante was such a sweetheart . . . I wonder if it was a personal letter to you saying how sorry he was about your mother's behavior."

"How would he know I didn't deserve to get cut off?"

"He didn't know until he met you. He didn't know anything about you. But then he heard me singing your praises and telling him stories of what your mother was like when you were growing up. I'll bet he felt so bad for you that he wanted to express his sympathy."

"But he didn't send the letter."

"Yes . . . he would have felt terrible for you, but he was also very professional. My guess is he wrote the letter, then waffled on giving it to you, realizing he was mixing business and personal life and shouldn't go there. I'm sorry. I know this is a painful topic for you, and I know how hard you tried with your mother, and it's not something you like to dwell on. If you don't want the letter, I'll just shred it."

"If I don't read it, I'll keep wondering about it."

"Do you want me to read it first? See if it's something you'd want to see? If it's not, I can summarize it for you and destroy it and you can forget it more easily."

Natalie felt she shouldn't agree—she was a bigger chicken than Dante if she couldn't even handle opening his letter. But what benefit would she find through reading it? Even sympathetic words would embarrass her more than comfort her.

"There's not a right or a wrong answer," Camille said.

Natalie steadied herself, imagining cool wind blowing muggy misery away. "Vet it for me. Read it and call me tomorrow."

"I'll do that. Now forget about it, and let's go check out the food and talk more about who you're going to flirt with tonight."

"I thought we agreed that I—" Natalie's purse buzzed in her hand, interrupting her.

Camille poked the silver clutch. "You'll have better luck flirting if you turn off your phone entirely."

"Nice. From refusing to even consider getting interested in anyone to deciding you might want to flirt to lecturing me about flirting, all in the last fifteen seconds."

"When I decide on a goal, I go for it. And I'm teasing you about the phone. I know you get edgy if you're completely unreachable. I'm going to grab a drink while you check that." Camille sailed toward the bar.

Reluctantly, Natalie opened her purse and took out her still-vibrating phone, hoping it was a call she could ignore.

Her answering service. Not ignorable. As she lifted the phone to her ear, she hurried toward one of the glass doors that opened onto a wraparound deck. "Hello, this is Natalie Marsh."

"Hi, this is Deanna from HealthSupport. We received a call from Mr. Jonas Egan. He said his wife, Lacey, is a client of yours. Lacey has been missing since this afternoon, and he's concerned. I suggested he call the police, but he refused. He wants to talk with you. He was very agitated."

"More worried, or more angry?"

"He seemed more worried to me."

Natalie stepped closer to one of multiple patio heaters. Despite the heaters, no one else was using the deck, and she was glad she hadn't had to go far to find privacy. "Did he clarify why he's so concerned at her being gone for a few hours?"

"I asked if he thought she was in danger, either from herself or others, but I couldn't get a straight answer. He kept demanding to talk to you. I said I would pass on the message but repeated that if he feared his wife was in trouble, he should call the police."

"Okay. Thank you, Deanna." Natalie took a notebook and pen out of her purse. "Give me his number."

Deanna offered it. "Have a good evening."

"I hope so. Thanks." Natalie hung up.

Cold wind blew her hair and rippled the obsidian water. Natalie edged closer to the heater, prepped herself mentally, and called Jonas.

"Yes, hello?" His voice was curt.

"Mr. Egan, this is Natalie Marsh. I understand you're concerned about your wife. I can listen to your concerns, but please understand that I can't—"

"She's gone." Jonas's voice trampled hers. "She's been gone since this afternoon, gone for seven hours. I can't call her. She left her phone, smashed it—threw it. It broke a mirror and broke the phone. She's never done anything like that. Have you heard from her? She might call you. She said she likes you. Has she called you?"

Natalie bypassed that question; she wanted more information first. "What happened to provoke her leaving?"

"We . . . a fight. We fought. Just yelling. I didn't hit her. I'm not her psycho dad."

"She left because she was angry with you?"

"Yeah, I guess, or maybe scared . . . I don't know. She was upset, crying."

"Are any of her possessions gone? Clothes, for instance?"

"No. She took her purse though. She's . . . something's wrong with her. She's acting all strange. She needs me."

"Has anything in her behavior given you reason to think she might be in danger, either from herself or someone else?"

"I don't think she'd hurt herself. She wouldn't hurt anyone else; she's the sweetest girl on earth. Just tell me if you've heard from her."

"I haven't."

"If she calls you, let me know *immediately*."

"If I hear from her, I'll recommend that she contact you, but I won't take that decision out of her hands."

"I'm her husband!"

"She's an adult. It needs to be her choice. Let her make it."

"But she's out of her mind!"

"Wanting time alone to calm down after a fight is not a symptom of mental incapacity."

"I'm trying to *help* her."

"Then be ready to listen to her when she returns. Try to understand her point of view. Respect what she tells you."

"I checked our credit cards, and there's been no activity there and no money taken out of the bank."

His wife had stomped out after a fight, and he'd felt the need to check her credit cards to see what she was up to? Natalie pressed her lips together, sealing her mouth shut for a moment. She wanted to tell Jonas he and Lacey needed marriage counseling, but suggesting it while Jonas was this worked up wouldn't help. "So you know she hasn't hopped on a plane to Siberia. Stay calm and give her time to calm down."

"What has she said to you about me? Has she said anything about leaving home? Or about where she'd go if she . . . ran?"

"I'm not able to share any information that pertains to—"

Jonas cursed and hung up.

Natalie stowed her phone in her purse and lingered close to the heater, gazing at the dark shoreline and the glow of wrought-iron lampposts illuminating a walking trail along the perimeter of the pond. She ought to rejoin the party, but it was quiet out here, a peaceful place to think.

She actually felt better about Jonas than she had before. The marriage had huge issues, but it had potential. He seemed genuinely concerned about Lacey for Lacey's sake, not solely because he was losing control of her. He *was* afraid of losing control of her, but it wasn't his only motivation. He hadn't denigrated Lacey or insulted Natalie. Even that blast of profanity at the end had been directed at the situation, not Natalie personally.

Would he be willing to go to marriage counseling? She guessed he would, as long as Lacey was willing to push for it, which meant a lot of individual work with Lacey before she'd have the backbone to insist. Natalie didn't get the impression that Lacey wanted to leave Jonas. Then again, Lacey didn't know what she wanted; she was too convinced that her own desires and thoughts were worthless.

Natalie moved out of the circle of warmth and crossed the deck toward the reception hall. Inside, she meandered through the now-larger crowd, chatting with other occupants of her office building she didn't see often, stopping by the food tables, dipping cubes of bread into fondue, sampling a carbonated drink that tasted like passion fruit, and trying to convince herself she didn't have to try *every* type of chocolate.

A hand tapped her shoulder. "They have raclette," Camille said. "Have you tried it?"

"Is that a sport or a food?" Natalie asked.

"It's cheese. Melted, gooey cheese. And potatoes, and I don't know what else, but you need to try it."

One of the servers stopped at Natalie's side. "Excuse me. You're Ms. Marsh?"

"Yes."

"Felicia Radcliffe asked me to pass on a message to you. She wasn't feeling well and decided to go home. She called a cab, so you don't need to worry about her."

Dismayed but not surprised that Felicia had left so early, Natalie said, "She called a cab? Where is she? I can give her a ride. She doesn't need to pay for a taxi."

"I'm sorry, ma'am. She was already heading out the door when she gave me the message, and this was several minutes ago."

"All right. Thank you."

The server departed.

"Parties can be horrible," Camille said softly. "Everybody's having a good time, and you're thinking about the person not there with you."

Natalie thought of the gift she'd left at Felicia's house. Maybe it would comfort her tonight. Sitting wrapped in a blanket, quietly absorbing poetry and watercolors, and crying whenever she wanted might be a soothing follow-up to attempting a party she'd previously attended with Wade.

"Come on." Camille hooked her arm through Natalie's. "I'll direct you to the raclette."

CHAPTER II

DANDELION-YELLOW LEAVES DRIFTED FROM the birch trees in Natalie's sunny backyard, and an afternoon breeze rippled softly across her face as she opened the canister of semolina she'd set on the patio table next to the meats, vegetables, and cheeses Gideon had lined up in separate bowls.

"We're at 705," Gideon said, scrutinizing the thermometer on the dome-shaped pizza oven.

"Getting close." Natalie stuck a spoon into the coarse semolina she would use to keep the pizzas from sticking to the wooden peel.

"Gotta say, Natalie, I'm excited about this." Gideon tapped the rough mortar exterior of the oven. "After we're done with the pizzas, what are we going to bake with all that retained heat? We could roast a pig and have a luau."

"Unfortunately, you couldn't fit a pig in there."

"I'd suggest roasting a piglet, but that would sound like *Winnie the Pooh* took a dark turn."

Natalie laughed. Part of her wanted to prompt Gideon to start sharing his concerns regarding Felicia; after Felicia's abrupt departure from the party last night, Natalie was particularly worried about her. But she was reluctant to end a light conversation that included no anxiety, no loss, nothing anyone wanted her to fix. A conversation with a nice guy whose fascination with the pizza oven kept making Natalie smile. Whenever he asked a question about the oven's construction that she couldn't answer, he'd Google for information, then apologize for using his phone in her company and hastily ask a "tell me about yourself" question. They'd chat about her job or educational background or plans to learn to ski this winter until he would buckle to the compulsion to research firebricks, grab his phone again, and start talking about thermal mass.

"Have you used this oven in the winter?" he asked, checking the temperature again.

"I haven't. Can I?"

"Heck yeah. You can use it year round. Wouldn't it be great to make pizza on a snowy night?"

"*Frozen* pizza by the time I get it back inside. And frozen toes. Winter is not my favorite season."

He gave her a playful, slightly goofy grin that made Natalie want to continue procrastinating the discussion of Felicia and learn more about Gideon. The urge embarrassed her; this lunch was not about socializing, let alone flirting, plus Gideon was on the rebound.

Still, she knew she'd be calling Camille this evening to confide that she suddenly had great appreciation for her backyard pizza oven. She also wanted to hear Camille's report on last night's flirting. Camille's stamina at the party had outlasted Natalie's, so they hadn't had a chance to talk at the end. Natalie hadn't tried to call her this morning—she'd have been sleeping in.

Had Camille read the letter from Dante yet? Natalie let that thought cling to her mind for a moment, then swatted it away. Why was she so apprehensive? Whatever the letter said, it couldn't make her feel worse—or better—about her relationship with her mother. Could it?

"I thought you wanted to learn to ski," Gideon said. "That involves winter."

It took Natalie a few seconds to remember why they were talking about winter. "Maybe I should scrap that idea, and . . . volunteer as a tester for a fuzzy socks company. Or a hot-chocolate company. Unpaid, even."

"Selfless service," Gideon said. "I admire your charitable attitude."

"I'd also be willing to test space heaters, electric blankets—"

The door from the house opened. "There you are!" Andrea sauntered toward her, carrying a large white shopping bag. "Your front door was unlocked, so I hope you don't mind that I let myself in." She smiled at Gideon. "Hello. Sorry to interrupt."

"This is my sister, Andrea Collier," Natalie said. "Andrea, Gideon Radcliffe."

Gideon shook her hand. "Pleased to meet you."

"Likewise." The sunlight made Andrea's smoky-quartz eyes gleam and accented the reddish highlights in her brown hair. She was dressed for Saturday errands, which for Andrea meant designer jeans and a metallic jersey-knit shirt that was probably dry-clean-only.

"Gideon is Felicia's stepson," Natalie said, brushing flour off her apron. "Felicia, our former neighbor."

"Oh yes! We love Felicia. She made the best cookies when we were kids. I heard about your father's death. I'm sorry."

"Thank you," Gideon said.

"His store was charming," Andrea said. "I was there not long ago, buying a gift for Natalie—this layered skirt I knew she'd love but wouldn't be able to buy for herself. Natalie, did I ever tell you Mom sold Mr. Radcliffe that set of wooden bracelets, the ones with the leaves and animals that Dad brought her from Africa? Remember those?"

"I remember them. No, I didn't know she sold them to Wade."

"Right before she died. They weren't my style, but the craftsmanship was superb, and she didn't want to just give them to someone else, so she invited him over to give him a chance to buy them for his store."

Natalie maintained a cordially oblivious expression, as though she'd missed Andrea's zinger. *Someone else.* Meaning Natalie, who *had* liked the bracelets.

"Your father was lucky to get his hands on them," Andrea said to Gideon.

"They must have been exceptional," Gideon said. "He rarely sold formerly owned merchandise."

"Are you visiting Ohneka, or do you live here?" Andrea asked.

"I moved here a few weeks ago."

"That's great." Andrea set her shopping bag on a patio chair. "You guys are adorable in your matching aprons. So Felicia introduced you?"

"We ran into each other at her house," Natalie said. "I invited him to help me test this pizza oven."

Andrea winked. "That's a new pick-up line."

Blushing, Natalie glanced at Gideon and found she wasn't the only one turning red. She wanted to inform Andrea that she was misreading this but couldn't think of a way to explain the lunch date without breaking Gideon's confidence. She didn't want to talk about his concerns in front of Andrea. Despite Andrea's "we love her," she'd had no contact with Felicia in years, and her only contact with Wade had been shopping at MaryLisa's. She hadn't attended his funeral.

"How is Charlotte?" Natalie changed the subject.

"Absolutely darling. You need to come see her—she's almost crawling." Andrea opened her shopping bag. "I'll keep this quick and get out of your hair. I was sorting through my autumn clothes and culled some things I don't wear anymore. Before I donate them, I want to see if you'd like to claim anything."

"That's sweet, but I'm fine for fall clothes . . ." Natalie tried to keep the words coming, but Andrea was holding up a cranberry-red boiled-wool jacket with a chic ruffled collar.

She passed the jacket to Natalie. "This would look great on you."

"I . . . Andrea . . . I don't need—"

Andrea pulled a forest-green cashmere cardigan out of the bag. "That skirt I gave you last winter would be perfect with this."

"I don't—" Natalie ended up with the sweater in her hand.

A wide sparkling smile on her face, Andrea pulled a dress out of the bag and held it up. "Gideon, wouldn't Natalie look fantastic in this cerulean blue?"

Gideon got an uncomfortable, cornered-by-girl-talk expression on his face. "Uh, yes, she'd look great."

Natalie shot Andrea a needle-sharp glare. "I doubt Gideon—"

"The knit fabric is *so* comfortable. Perfect dress for you to wear to work, and isn't the belt darling with that gold mesh?" Andrea draped the dress over Natalie's shoulder and reached into the bag.

When the bag was finally empty, the only things Natalie had successfully refused were two pairs of jeans—she didn't like the style—boots with heels so high she'd put her life at risk if she wore them, and a maroon silk evening gown. The only time she wore a formal dress was to the Chapman soiree, which wouldn't come for another year, and she already had two hand-me-down gowns in her closet that she hadn't worn yet.

"I'll let you get back to your lunch." Andrea repacked the rejected clothes. "Great to meet you, Gideon. Say hi to Felicia for me."

"I will."

"And snap some pictures of Natalie in her cute new clothes, okay? She never wears the clothes I give her around me, so I need proof they aren't going to waste."

"Uh . . . that's . . . uh . . . up to Natalie."

"I'll walk you out, Andrea." Carrying the pile of clothes, Natalie started toward the door. To her relief, her sister followed.

Once she and Andrea were inside with the door closed, Natalie freed her irritation. "For heaven's sake, give the guy a break. We barely know each other, and you're badgering him into complimenting me and taking pictures."

"Don't be shy. It's obvious you like each other. How long have you been seeing him?"

"I'm not 'seeing' him in that way." She walked with Andrea toward the living room. "Like I said, we just met."

"He's decent looking. Polite. Might be your best option. What does he do for a living?"

"He's a civil engineer. He works for the city." Natalie laid her new clothes on the couch, ignoring the gibe about her "best option." "Thank you for the clothes."

"Keep me posted." Andrea opened the front door. "I hope you manage to hook him. You'd be so much better off with a man in your life."

"Have a good afternoon," Natalie said flatly.

"See ya." Andrea exited and shut the door.

Natalie eyed the pile of clothes on the couch, wanting to berate herself but knowing it would be healthier to shrug and laugh. Andrea offered hand-me-downs a few times a year, and Natalie always tried to refuse but ended up caving as Andrea tempted her with stylish, nearly new clothing. The plain fact was that Natalie couldn't afford anything as nice as the clothing Andrea gave her.

The plain fact was that Andrea wanted to slam that truth into Natalie's gut over and over.

In the backyard, Gideon was checking the oven temperature.

"I'm sorry," Natalie said when she reached him. "My sister is . . . herself."

"Hey, free clothes," Gideon said. "That's always a win."

"True." She knew Andrea had reveled in having Gideon as an audience for her generosity, and Natalie had no desire to explain the emotional undercurrents that tainted Andrea's giving of gifts. Then again, Gideon might already have some idea of the issues, depending on what Felicia had told him.

He stepped away from the oven. "Should we take a picture of ourselves in our adorable matching aprons? You can text it to your sister."

"I'm sorry for all that nonsense."

"I don't mind. Truth is this is the coolest apron I've ever worn." He tapped the image of a smiling human brain on the front of it. "This elegance ought to be immortalized."

"A grad-school friend made them for a fund-raiser." Natalie sat at the patio table and fiddled with the canister of semolina, frustrated that she was having difficulty climbing out of the pit of emotions a run-of-the-mill interaction with Andrea had dug. She tried to think of something light to say. What had they been talking about before Andrea had barged in?

Gideon pulled out a chair and sat next to her. "Your brain apron would look great with that cerulean dress." He held up his phone. "If you want to try it on, I'm ready to record the proof."

"Like proof of a Bigfoot sighting," Natalie said. "Proof of me wearing Andrea's clothes. I actually do wear them regularly, but if I know I'm going to see her, I choose something else. If I wear something of hers, she can't stop commenting on it, telling me where she bought it, how much she paid for it, and why the quality is superior to anything I've ever bought."

"Ah. Fun game. Let me try it." Gideon stretched his legs out. "These are Levi's. Classic 501s. I bought them on sale at JCPenney for maybe thirty-five bucks. They're made of denim, which is made of cotton, which, in my case, is superior cotton because it's been seasoned by all the salsa I've spilled in my lap."

Natalie laughed. "Well done. Text that to Andrea."

"Does she live in town?"

"She's about forty-five minutes away, in Birch Falls. Do you have brothers or sisters?"

"I don't, unfortunately. When I was a toddler, my mother had her first bout with cancer, and the treatment left her unable to have more kids."

"How old were you when she died?"

"Sixteen."

"I'm so sorry."

"She'd been sick for years. It was rough. Horrible for Dad, horrible for both of us. He met Felicia a year later. Met her here in Ohneka at some small-business-owners event."

"Where were you living at the time?"

"Rochester area. Fairport. That's where I grew up. Dad worked in merchandising for a clothing chain, but he and Mom had always wanted to start their own little store. After she died, he decided to go for it, in her honor. That's why the store is named MaryLisa's—MaryLisa is my mother."

"That's a beautiful tribute. How did he choose Ohneka as the location?"

"He'd always liked it here—his family used to vacation at the lake. And when he found that prime spot on Main Street up for rent, he jumped on it. But he didn't want to make me switch high schools, so he commuted for the first couple of years. So did Felicia, for that matter. They got married at the beginning of my senior year, and she came to live with us in Fairport." He picked a splinter of bark off the front of his apron and flicked it onto the grass. "Sorry to steal her from you."

"I was already away at college—freshman year—when they got married, so I won't hold it against your family that you filched my favorite neighbor."

"I can't believe my dad's gone now. Your parents . . . they're both gone, right?"

"Yes."

"We're a couple of orphans." Empathy filled Gideon's voice, but he broke eye contact, and Natalie suspected his discomfort wasn't due to lack of knowing what to say about their mutual bereavement.

Rather than keep wondering what he knew about her, she decided to be blunt. "What has Felicia told you about my family?"

"Not details." He lifted a slice of olive on a spoon, then let it slide back into the bowl. "I know you didn't have an easy time. That your mother was . . . difficult . . . and you were estranged when she died."

"She was mentally ill," Natalie said. "Never officially diagnosed because she'd never talk to anyone about it, but she had bipolar disorder. She was in her mid-thirties when it manifested; she was fine when I was young. After she started struggling . . . sometimes she was fine; other times she made our lives miserable. My father did his best but finally couldn't take it anymore. He left when I was a teenager and died of a brain aneurysm a few years later."

"Wow, I'm sorry," Gideon said.

"When I was in high school, I researched my mother's symptoms, talked to people, tried to persuade her to get help, but she was adamant that she wasn't 'sick' and didn't need treatment."

"Is that how you got interested in psychology? Trying to help her?"

"Yes, that's how it started. But she . . . didn't like what I was doing. When I chose to study psychology in college, our relationship got worse. She took my choice of majors personally, saying I was targeting her. And when I decided to go on for graduate work, that was the end. I was an arrogant know-it-all trying to convince her and everyone around her that she was crazy."

"Gaslighting her so you could control her?"

"Yes, that's what she thought. And at this point, I *wasn't* hounding her to get help. I just wouldn't put up with destructive behavior from her, and I'd call her on it. That was enough to get her to cut me off. For the last three years before she died, she wouldn't talk to me."

"Was she the same way with Andrea?"

"Andrea chose a different way to handle her. I tried to get her as an ally in urging Mom to get help or at least in standing up to her, but she preferred to play along. Enable her. She put up with an entire landfill's worth of garbage, but it did pay off. My mother disinherited me and left everything to Andrea."

"You're kidding. Felicia never told me that."

Natalie was grateful to learn Felicia had kept this fact confidential. "I thought she'd softened toward me near the end of her life, but . . . apparently, I'd hoped for too much."

"Did she finally talk to you?"

"No. But out of the blue, she sent me a birthday present. Soap carvings."

"Soap carvings?"

"Soap she'd carved in the shapes of flowers. It sounds like a strange gift, but it . . ." Embarrassment kindled. She was taking this too deep, offering unneeded details—painful details. More than Gideon would want to know.

"It doesn't sound strange," Gideon said. "It sounds like a meaningful gift."

The compassion and interest in his gray-blue eyes coaxed out more of the story. "Soap carving was a hobby of hers," Natalie said. "When I was a child, I was in awe of what she could create from a bar of soap—I'm still in awe. I loved watching her work."

"Definitely a meaningful gift, then. Something she knew you'd appreciate."

"Yes." A surprise gift, beautiful and personal. At the time, she'd been certain it was a sign that her mother wanted to reconcile. What else could it mean?

Natalie still didn't know.

"I have a stupid question," Gideon said. "Do you use soap carvings? Wash your hands with them or use them in the shower? Detailed carving seems like a ton of work for something that's going to dissolve."

"That's not a stupid question, and no, we didn't use the carvings. They were artwork. The ones she sent me are in a basket in my downstairs bathroom. Take a look at them when you go inside. You'll be amazed by how intricate they are."

"I'm intrigued. I've never seen a soap carving more elaborate than the fish I used to carve from Ivory Soap with a pocketknife. And I'll put my hands behind my back while I look so I don't accidentally use them."

"Don't worry. I keep them on a wall shelf away from the sink and tub so nobody gets confused."

"After she sent the gift, things still weren't better between you?"

"No. She still wouldn't answer my calls or open the door if I came to visit. And to be clear, I'm not blaming Andrea. Andrea didn't turn her against me. At most, she finessed the hostility my mother already harbored."

"Didn't want to heal the family rift, huh?"

"No. Andrea was more a fan of small lies or spin doctoring to make me look worse. She's never minded cheating in competition, and she saw our relationship as competitive. She enjoys being the winner, the favorite, beating her older sister. It wasn't just about the inheritance, though my mother had quite a bit of money."

"I don't suppose Andrea offered to split it with you after your mother died."

"Goodness, no. She's generous, but she's generous one piece at a time. Giving me expensive clothes, as you saw. Offering to send me on pricey vacations or give me a spa membership or even buy me a new car, always making it clear that she knows I could never afford these things on my own."

"Strutting the fact that she was the loved one and you were the outcast," Gideon said.

"Yes. As you saw, I'm not always good at resisting her."

"In a smackdown between pride and practicality, I root for practicality," Gideon said. "Free clothes? Bring 'em on. If she's ever wanting to ditch some expensive men's shirts, tell her to call me."

Natalie smiled. "Practicality does win sometimes." Tasteful, high-quality hand-me-downs from Andrea meant she could both dress well at work and put money she would have spent on clothing toward paying off student loans. "But I'm not letting her send me on a cruise to Alaska."

"She can send me if she's short on ways to flaunt her wealth."

"Go for it," Natalie said. "And for the next decade, you'll be hearing about how much she spent on you. I apologize for this whole tangent. I sound bitter, talking about my sister this way. It's not her fault I didn't succeed in reconciling with my mother, and this is ten times as much as you ever wanted to know about my family. You came over here to talk about Felicia. I want to do anything I can to help her."

"Yeah, me too." He drummed his fingertips on the table. "I'm sick of being useless when my family is suffering."

"Did she tell you we went to the Chapman party last night?"

Gideon gawked at her. "The Chapman party?"

Considering how stunned he looked, this must be the first social event Felicia had attended since Wade's death. "The party Robert Chapman throws every year for his local employees and for businesses that rent from him. Felicia always used to go with your father. I was glad she wanted to come, but I don't think it went well for her. She left early without—" Her phone rang. She glanced toward where she'd left it on the table.

"You should answer it." Gideon picked it up and held it out to her. "Turnabout is fair play."

"You haven't taken a call. Just conducted important research."

"Ha! 'Important.'"

Unenthusiastically, Natalie took the phone. At the sight of the number, a flick of adrenaline hit; she'd called this number last night. Jonas Egan. Had Lacey returned?

"Excuse me for a moment," she said. "I apologize for the atrocious manners, but this is work-related. I'd better answer it."

"No problem. I'll keep an eye on the oven."

Natalie answered the phone as she hurried into the house. "This is Natalie Marsh."

"It's . . . Jonas Egan. Lacey—" The turbulence in his voice shook Natalie. He didn't sound angry; he sounded terrified.

"Have you heard from her?" Natalie kept her tone calm.

"No. But she's in big trouble."

"Why is that?"

"She, uh . . . this woman Lacey knows, somebody she admires . . . When Lacey didn't come home last night, I wondered if she'd gone to see her, so today I went over there. I found a . . . There was a . . . hole cut in the glass. The glass by the door . . ." His voice creaked and stopped.

Natalie waited for him to rally.

His breathing got louder. "Like from a burglar, you know?"

"Yes."

"You have to keep secrets, right? You said it's the law. You can't blab things people tell you."

Natalie sat at her kitchen table. "In a therapist-client relationship, I'm bound to protect confidentiality, but be aware that you are not my client, so that doesn't—"

"I'm not talking about me. I'm talking about Lacey, and she is your client."

"Whether or not—"

"I thought even if she was gone, Lacey might be there. She had to stay somewhere, and she hadn't used her credit card or withdrawn any cash."

"Has she stayed there before?"

"No, but I thought she might . . . run there, feel better staying there. The door was unlocked, from whoever broke in, so I went inside."

He'd marched into an apparent crime scene? Natalie waited for him to continue, but all she heard was panting and sotto voce cursing.

"Did you find Lacey?" she asked.

"No. But the woman . . . I found her." His voice thinned. Tore. "She was dead. Murdered."

Horror seized Natalie; she struggled to shake it loose. "You called the police?"

"No, are you crazy? What if Lacey was there? What if the police think she . . . was involved?"

"Why would they think that?"

"If she was there!" Jonas snapped. "If she'd been there."

This conclusion bewildered Natalie. Lacey had never stayed with this woman before, and Jonas hadn't found her there now, but he was so worried she *had* been there that he didn't want to report a murder? "Don't jump to conclusions. You need to call the police immediately."

"She . . . Lacey . . . Something's screwed up in her brain. She grew up in hell; her dad beat her, beat her mother; her mother never protected her. She needs help. I need to find her *now*."

"I understand how worried you are for Lacey, but you can't delay reporting a murder."

"I can't talk to the cops. Let someone else find the . . . woman, the body. I'll take Lacey away somewhere and get her help."

"Be rational," Natalie said. "You don't know Lacey was involved in any way, but you know a woman is dead. You need to call the police."

Jonas cursed. "I need to find Lacey. I've got to talk to her before I talk to the cops. You're a professional. You help me find her."

"I'm a psychologist, not a detective or a private investigator. If you don't report this woman's death and the police learn you were there, how will that look?"

"You can't tell them I was there! Lacey's your client. You'll get fired!"

"*You* told me about the murder. Please stop making assumptions about Lacey's behavior and what the police will think."

"You're going to call?"

"Is that how you want to handle this?" She'd prefer to avoid the ethical minefield of reporting the murder herself while trying to protect her professional obligation to Lacey, but she didn't want Jonas to know she was anything but eager to dial 911.

Jonas said nothing. Natalie waited, pressing her thumb against one of the lumps of pizza dough shielded by a kitchen towel.

"I'll call," he said.

"Good." Natalie had guessed he'd take that option. He'd rather control the way the police heard the story than wonder what Natalie would tell them. "Do it now."

"You'd better not say anything to anyone about Lacey."

"I won't."

"If the papers publish anything about her, I'll sue them out of existence. I know they'll be grubbing for slime and gossip, wanting a big story. The woman was one of Chapman Development's rising stars."

"What's her name?"

"Camille Moretti."

The name struck Natalie like a wave of water so cold it should have hardened into ice. She grabbed the towel covering the pizza dough as though it could prevent shock from knocking her off her chair. "Camille Moretti?"

"Yeah. I'll call the cops." Jonas hung up before Natalie could push more questions past her numb lips.

CHAPTER 12

COLD. GLACIALLY COLD. DARK. INSENSIBLE. Icebound on a kitchen chair, a towel in one hand, her phone in the other.

Camille.

Camille was dead?

Murdered?

Natalie forced her fingers open and let both the phone and the towel fall to the table. After a few seconds of staring at her phone, she picked it up again. Jonas might call back.

She inhaled until she couldn't take in more air, then exhaled hard. Lacey had known Camille well enough to flee to her after a fight with Jonas? Had Camille been playing mother hen, protecting Lacey under her wing? Why hadn't Camille ever mentioned Lacey except in connection with her new purse?

Natalie dragged herself to her feet, her limbs limp and damaged, floppy stems that had frozen and thawed. She shuffled toward the french door that led from the kitchen to the patio. Through the windows, she saw Gideon peering into the oven, the ash stick in his hand.

She opened the door and stepped into the gentle sunshine. Camille would have adored today, warm, cloudless, leaves vibrant with color.

"We're ready to roll," Gideon said. "I'm pushing the embers off—" He set the tool back in the basket and hurried toward her. "What's wrong? Wait, I'm not supposed to ask that. May I ask if you're okay? You don't look okay."

She should wave off his concern and say something pragmatic about how once he'd pushed the large coals to the back of the oven, he could use the brush to clear the floor for the pizzas. She didn't want to talk about Camille. Gideon had come today because he was worried about his own family. He was grieving his father; he was anxious about his stepmother. He wanted Natalie's insight, not her pain.

Gideon started to reach toward her, then rerouted his hand toward the canister of semolina. He lifted the spoon and poked it back into the coarse flour. "Is there anything I can do for you?"

"I . . . got some . . . bad news." Her thoughts sloshed in her head. She couldn't figure out what to say, what she *could* say. "A friend. I don't know details yet. Apparently, she's dead." The words sounded strange. *Apparently* Camille was dead?

"I'm so sorry," Gideon said.

Part of Natalie appreciated the concern in his eyes while part of her obsessed about her own choice of words. *Apparently?* Did she think Jonas was lying? Or wrong?

Could he be wrong? Maybe Camille had only fainted. She'd fainted once in high school, under stage lights during a choir concert. Maybe she'd fainted today, exhausted from last night's party and upset when she'd discovered the broken window. Breathless, furious, racing around the house to see what was missing. Maybe she'd lost something important, like jewelry from Dante. Maybe Jonas had found her on the floor and assumed she was dead—even assumed murder. He was clearly prone to jumping to conclusions, and he'd been so panicked about Lacey that he wouldn't have lingered to check for a pulse or breathing.

Hope blinked in the darkness. "I need to go." Were the police at Camille's yet? They could check to see if . . . If Natalie talked to them, she could confirm—disprove . . . Jonas *could* have made a mistake . . .

"Where do you need to go?" Gideon asked.

She rubbed her floury palms against her apron. How had she gotten so much flour on her hands? She'd washed them after shaping the dough. "To her house."

"Let me drive you." He didn't ask why.

"You don't need to do that. You have enough to cope with—"

"Natalie, you just got devastating news. I'll drive you." Gideon picked up a napkin. "You have flour on your face. May I?"

Natalie stared blankly at him, not sure if she was supposed to take the napkin or if he was offering to clean her face for her.

He picked up the water pitcher she'd set out earlier, poured a splash on the napkin, and gently wiped the flour off her cheek. Natalie untied her apron and dropped it on a chair.

Gideon shed his apron and grabbed his phone and keys off the patio table. "Would you like me to lock your house or put any of the food away?"

Natalie shook her head and hurried toward the side gate that led to the front of the house. The food could rot, and thieves were welcome to whatever they could find. She had to get to Camille.

Gideon unlocked his car and opened the passenger door for her. Natalie slid inside, and Gideon rushed to climb into the driver's seat. Hurrying for her, worrying about her. She was burdening him. She should have sent him home.

"Where can I take you?" he asked.

"Haslett Street." He was new to Ohneka; he wouldn't know where it was. "It's past downtown, the . . . No, it's not past downtown, it's before—"

"I can find it." Gideon tapped the screen of his phone. "Got it." He snapped his phone into a holder on the dashboard. "We'll be there in eight minutes."

As he drove, the directions from the GPS were the only voice in the car. Grateful Gideon wasn't asking questions or trying to make conversation, Natalie watched the road with dry eyes. Hope intertwined with terror, twisting into knots so tight it was difficult to breathe or swallow.

When they reached Haslett Street, she started to tell Gideon which house but realized she didn't need to point it out. The flashing lights of two police cars and an ambulance had marked it.

Camille's radiant smile last night . . . the glee in her eyes when she'd showed Natalie the new purse . . . her jokes about flirting. Her empathy when Natalie had reacted with cowardice and avoidance to her discovery of the letter from Dante.

Please let her be alive. Let Jonas be wrong.

Gideon slowed his car and glanced at Natalie, waiting for instructions. She didn't know what instructions to give. She wanted to sprint into the house, but panic spun her thoughts into such a blur that she couldn't figure out how to explain her arrival to the police without exposing the fact that Lacey Egan was her client. She had no idea what Jonas had told them.

Whatever. She'd handle this on the fly. "Pull over," she said. "I'll go see what's happening."

Gideon parked at the curb a few houses down from Camille's. "Would you like me to come with you, or would you rather I wait here?"

"Wait here." Natalie opened her door and tried to hurry toward Camille's house. She caught the toe of her shoe on a crack in the sidewalk, skidded on an acorn, stepped out of her shoe, and had to stop to slip it back on.

Camille's front door was open, and a police officer stood on the porch. As Natalie approached him, he held up a hand. "You can't come in here, ma'am."

Natalie stopped on the sidewalk and tried to read the officer's inscrutable face. "I'm a friend of Camille Moretti's. What happened? Is she all right?"

"What is your name?" His accent made Natalie think of Europe and cold. Europe and the travel she'd wanted to do, the trips she and Camille had wanted to take someday. Scandinavia, Germany, France, Italy . . .

"Ma'am, what's your name?"

"Natalie Marsh. Camille and I grew up together. I've known her since . . ." Why was she babbling, trying to prove her friendship with Camille? "I have my ID . . . No, I don't." She had her phone, but she hadn't brought her purse. "Is Camille all right?"

The officer took a notebook and pen out of his pocket. "What's your address?"

Natalie gave it. Inside, she grew darker and darker, her mind and body a smudge of fear. If this were only a burglary, would the officer look this grim? If Camille had been unconscious but was now awake, wouldn't Natalie be able to hear her voice through the open door? She couldn't see any damage to the front door. The cut glass Jonas had described must be in back.

"What happened?" Natalie repeated, frantic for information. Or maybe she didn't want information, not unless it was good, not unless it was a miracle, not unless Jonas was delusional and the officer on the porch was imaginary and she could wake from a nightmare.

From the street behind her came the double thump of two car doors slamming. The officer gazed past Natalie, and she turned to see who had arrived. Two men strode toward the house. Their charcoal-gray suits were similar, but everything else in their appearances was opposites: one man was portly, bespectacled, black, and in his forties or early fifties. His pale, extremely tall, and much younger partner could have passed for a college basketball player.

"Scene is secure," the officer on the porch said. "EMTs are inside with Haber and Avino. Fuller's in back."

"Thanks, Rasmussen." The older man shifted his gaze to Natalie. The thumping in her heart seized control of her lungs, forcing breaths down her throat in too-quick gasps.

"This is Natalie Marsh," Officer Rasmussen said. "A friend of— A friend who arrived right before you did."

The older officer nodded and flipped open a badge to show Natalie. "Detective Jeffrey Turner."

"Is Camille all right?" Natalie asked.

"I'm sorry, ma'am. Mrs. Moretti is dead." His words swept through Natalie. "If you could wait here for a moment, Detective Bartholomew will return to take your statement." Turner walked briskly up the porch stairs.

A hand gripped her elbow. "You should sit down." This advice came in such a rich bass voice that Natalie glanced dumbly around, searching for a speaker besides the rail-thin young officer holding her elbow. There wasn't anyone else in sight except Rasmussen, the officer with the northern European accent. The deep voice was Bartholomew's.

He propelled her toward the porch. To the right of the door were Camille's pumpkins and scarecrow. Natalie had shrugged off Camille's anxious report of the repositioned decorations. She'd minimized Camille's fears that someone was watching her, following her. She'd lulled Camille into thinking she was imagining things, that there was no stalker.

Natalie pressed both hands over her mouth, smashing her lips against her teeth as though sealing her mouth shut now could undo words she'd spoken earlier.

"Right here." Bartholomew grasped her shoulders, his stringy fingers urging her toward the ground. Not the ground; the stairs. He wanted her to sit on the stairs. Natalie dropped her hands to her sides, bent her knees, and settled on the steps.

"I'll be right back." He walked past her up the steps. She watched the motion of his king-sized leather shoes, the hem of his trousers.

She closed her eyes. Inhaled. Exhaled. Inhaled. Tears would have to wait until she'd finished talking to the police. Was Jonas here? Probably not. He'd been so agitated on the phone; she couldn't imagine he'd be willing to return to the crime scene. Either the police were at his house, or he'd promised to go to the department to make a statement.

Did Camille's family know?

Behind her, Bartholomew was speaking to Rasmussen, but the conversation was too quiet for her to overhear. They must have stepped through the doorway for privacy.

A breeze stroked her hair. Dried leaves scratched whispers against the pavement.

Gideon. She had no idea how long she would be here, and she didn't want him stuck waiting for her. She pulled out her phone to text him that he should go home, that she'd call a cab when she was done, but the phone fell out of her hand, bounced off the edge of a red-brick step, and landed on the step below it.

With floppy fingers, she groped for the phone until she was able to pick it up and set it on her lap. It wasn't damaged. The case had protected it. The crimson leather phone case that Camille had given her. She thought of Camille's glittery case that she'd joked could double as a disco ball in a dance emergency.

Gideon. She was supposed to be texting Gideon. Tapping the screen in slow motion, she wrote a message: *I don't know how long I'll be. Don't wait for me. I'll take a cab home.*

Gideon answered immediately: *Don't take a taxi. When you're done, call me, and I'll come get you.*

She was about to text back to refuse the offer, but Bartholomew's rumbling voice spoke behind her. "Thank you for your patience." He sat on the step next to her, letting his long legs stretch the rest of the way down the steps and over the sidewalk. "Are you all right?"

By what standard? She didn't need the attention of the EMTs, if that was the question. "What happened to Camille?"

"I hope you don't mind if I take notes, ma'am." He opened a notebook. "I like to make sure I get everything right."

"That's fine. I'm sorry I don't have my ID. I forgot my purse."

"Not a problem, Dr. Marsh. You're a friend of Camille Moretti's?"

"Yes, I've known her since we were in elementary school. We've stayed close. Especially after her husband died . . . that was about a year and a half ago. A car accident, or rather a car-pedestrian accident . . ." She was rambling again, saying irrelevant things. She wanted to screech *What happened to her?* at a volume the whole neighborhood would hear. Why were the police so hesitant to give her information?

Think about it. You came rushing onto the scene of a homicide. Of course they're cagey with you.

"I'm very sorry for your loss," Bartholomew said. "Do you know Mrs. Moretti's next-of-kin? The person we should contact?"

"Yes. Her parents. Annette and Jacob Edison." Natalie studied a fragment of dried dough stuck to one of her cuticles, wanting to focus on anything but a mental image of Camille's parents learning their daughter had been murdered.

"Do you have their contact information?" Bartholomew asked.

"I don't think so. They moved to North Carolina several years ago, to Raleigh. I can check though . . . the information . . . Wait, I do have it. I think it was in their Christmas letter . . . I might have saved it . . ."

"Don't worry about it. We'll find it. Why did you come to Mrs. Moretti's house today?"

"I was . . . informed that she was . . . I hoped the information wasn't correct, that she was injured, not . . ." Natalie rubbed a scratch on the corner of her phone case.

"Who informed you?"

"Jonas Egan," she said. "He called me. I assume he called you."

"Why did Mr. Egan notify you?"

What could she say that wouldn't make it plain Jonas's wife was her client? Nothing. Had giving Jonas's name been too much? Should she have kept that confidential? But he wasn't her client . . . The police already knew he'd discovered Camille's body . . . This was a murder investigation . . .

Her thoughts decomposed into sludgy misery, and all Natalie could say was, "I'm sorry. I'm not free to discuss that."

"All right." Bartholomew's matter-of-fact answer caught Natalie off guard. She'd expected him to be suspicious, push her to explain—

Oh. *Dr.* Marsh. She hadn't introduced herself that way, but he'd just addressed her by her title. He knew who she was. The police had clearly done some quick research on her.

"Tell me about Mrs. Moretti," he said. "Did she have any enemies?"

CHAPTER 13

NATALIE PAID THE TAXI DRIVER AND trudged up the sidewalk toward her house. Though she'd ignored Gideon's offer of a ride, not wanting to inconvenience him, she'd have to face him anyway: his car was in her driveway. Why had he returned? Had he left something behind—a jacket or his wallet?

She opened her still-unlocked front door, feeling strange as her hand executed the simple, familiar gesture. Everything looked the same. Everything felt different.

The house was silent. "Gideon?" His name croaked out of her throat. She swallowed.

No answer. He must be in the backyard. Maybe it should bother her that he'd come to her home without her, but she didn't care. Let him wander wherever he wanted. Let him rearrange the furniture, paint the walls orange, stable a horse in the living room.

A horse. Camille had always sworn that someday she'd own a horse. A mustang, glossy black.

Natalie walked into the kitchen. The table that had been covered with flour and towel-draped balls of dough was empty and clean. No dishes waited in the sink, and the dishwasher was running. Through the window, she saw Gideon sweeping the patio. Two rows of small pizzas covered the card table Natalie had set up to hold the finished pizzas.

She opened the back door.

"Hey." Gideon leaned the broom against a patio chair and came to meet her. "Why didn't you call me?"

"I didn't want to bother you."

"It's not a bother. I like to do what I can."

With a controlled breath, Natalie inhaled the scents of woodsmoke, pizza crust, and tomato. "You didn't need to do all this."

"It's the least I could do." He waved toward the pizzas. One of them was too thick, a puff of dough. One was burnt. One was too thin, with a hole in it. The rest looked great, with perfect, light charring. "Took me a few pizzas to get the hang of it, I'm afraid. Would you like to eat? No pressure, but you must be hungry."

She felt dehydrated and headachy but didn't have an appetite. Would she feel less sick and foggy if she ate? It might help. A little.

"Here." Gideon pulled out a patio chair. "May I bring you something to drink?"

She sank into the cushioned chair. "Water. A huge glass of water."

"Got it." Gideon hastened toward the back door. In a minute, he returned with a glass filled with ice and a pitcher of water. He poured water into the glass and set the glass and pitcher in front of Natalie. "Do you want pizza?"

Natalie nodded. "I don't care what kind. Please eat, too, if you haven't already."

Gideon picked up two plates and headed toward the card table.

Her phone rang. For a surreal instant, she imagined she'd see Camille's name on the screen, as though she could think herself into the past.

She gulped water and drew the phone out of her pocket. Kirk. She took the call. "Hi."

"Natalie," Kirk said. "I heard. I'm so sorry. How are you holding up?"

"I'm holding."

Gideon, at the pizza table, caught Natalie's eye. He pointed to himself, then to the door, and mouthed, "Should I?"

Natalie shook her head and beckoned him toward the patio table. "How did you hear so quickly?" she asked Kirk. He had obviously not only heard of Camille's death but also knew Natalie knew.

"Jeanne's son," Kirk said. "He lives in the same neighborhood as Camille, and word is traveling at light speed. He called Jeanne; Jeanne called me. He heard you were the one who found her."

Apparently, the grapevine had some glitches, but that was just as well. "No. I . . . stopped by her house a couple of hours ago, and the police were already there." As she said the words, she realized Gideon would recognize that she'd cut the information about receiving word via phone. Gideon wouldn't ask about it though, and she could give Kirk a better explanation later, in private.

"Glad to hear you weren't the one who . . . Still rough for you, but at least you didn't have to see her."

Natalie wondered if she could dump the pitcher of water over her head and wake herself up to a different reality.

"I didn't know Camille well, but everything about her impressed me," Kirk said. "I know you two were best friends from childhood. I'm sorry."

Natalie licked her lips and realized how chapped they were. "Thank you."

Gideon set a plate filled with wedges of pizza in the center of the table. Natalie gestured for him to sit and mouthed, "Eat."

"Natalie, I'm in Syracuse for the day, but I called Skyler, and he's on his way to your house," Kirk said. "Don't worry if you're not home or don't want company. We just had something we wanted to drop off."

"You guys are the best," Natalie said. "I'm home."

"Do you feel up to seeing him, or do you want him to leave it on the porch?"

"I'll see him. Tell him the front door's unlocked and he can come straight through the house. I'm in the backyard."

"I'll let him know. If there's anything at all we can do for you, please let us know."

"Thank you, Kirk. I appreciate it."

"Talk to you soon." Kirk hung up.

Gideon finished his slice of pizza. He was eating eagerly enough that Natalie suspected he hadn't eaten at all while cleaning and cooking. She took a slice and put it on her plate. "A friend from work is stopping by, but please don't feel you need to leave. He's just dropping something off."

"Are you sure you don't want privacy?"

"We're not discussing anything confidential," Natalie said. "Eat, please. You've been working for hours on this food."

He took another slice.

Natalie took a few bites of pizza, and her appetite stirred. She *was* hungry. "I'm sorry about today. We were supposed to talk about Felicia, and instead you ended up as chauffeur. And cook and maid."

"I volunteered for those positions. We'll talk about Felicia later. She's struggling, but it's not urgent. Grief is a . . . long process."

She nodded. He was grieving. Felicia was grieving. Camille had been grieving for a year and a half. Natalie had been . . . was still . . . her father's aneurysm . . . her mother's cancer . . . Camille's death . . .

A bite of pizza got stuck partway to her stomach. She swallowed water, a large gulp that hurt all the way down.

They'd nearly emptied the pizza platter before the back door opened and Skyler stepped onto the patio. Natalie tried to stand but couldn't seem to remember the technique; her chair legs snagged on the stamped concrete, her knees shook, and her chair tipped.

"Don't get up." Skyler scurried toward Natalie, set a vase of cream and pale-yellow flowers on the table, and hugged her while she was still seated.

"I'm sorry, Nat." Skyler released her. "Camille was awesome." He held out a hand to Gideon. "Skyler Hudson. Sorry to come crashing in."

"I'm the trespasser." Gideon stood and shook Skyler's hand. "Gideon Radcliffe."

"Radcliffe, as in Wade Radcliffe?" Skyler asked.

"My father."

"Nice. I knew your dad. Good guy. I was sorry to hear about his passing."

"Thank you. How did you know him?"

"Worked with him in physical therapy. After he got beaned by a ball."

"Hey, right, I heard him talk about you. You did great work with him."

"Eh, I always do great work, but it's more fun with a guy like your dad. Easy patient. Worked hard at recovery. It's rotten that . . ." Skyler scowled. "Wish fate had left the guy alone."

"Me too," Gideon said.

"Skyler works part-time in our office as a biofeedback therapist, in addition to his PT work," Natalie explained.

"Good to meet you." Gideon picked up his empty plate. "I'm heading out. Natalie, please call me if you need anything."

Natalie didn't want him to feel evicted but suspected he genuinely wanted to go. He'd been through enough lately without having to witness her dumping grief on Skyler. "Thank you for everything. Take some of that pizza with you."

"I'll leave it," he said. "You can freeze it for later meals." He nodded at Skyler and headed for the gate. After it closed behind him, Skyler pulled out a chair and sat next to Natalie.

"Wade Radcliffe's son?" he whispered. "You have secrets, sister."

Natalie's laugh was abrupt and barky. She was glad Gideon wasn't there to hear it.

"Sorry." Skyler patted her shoulder. "None of my business."

"Don't apologize." Natalie tilted her head back, looking up into the blue sky. How could such a beautiful day be such a terrible day? "He moved to Ohneka after his father died to help take care of things. We're both worried about how Felicia's coping, and he wanted my input; I invited him to lunch so we'd have a private place to discuss it. That plan . . . got derailed, obviously."

"If you were having a lunch meeting with Gideon Radcliffe, how did you end up at Camille's? Kirk said you went over there and got surprised by the police."

"I didn't get surprised by them. I got a call informing me of her death; that's why I went over there. I . . . don't want to say more. I'm too muddled to decide what's ethical to say and what isn't."

Skyler winced. "You're kidding me. Professional complications on top of this? Please tell me you don't think a client—"

"I don't." Natalie touched the petals of a cream-colored snapdragon. "Thank you for the flowers. You guys broke the land-speed record for delivering a sympathy bouquet."

"We're good," Skyler said. "Jeanne organizes everything, Kirk bellows orders, and I'm the public face of the gang. We're here for you. We want you to know that."

"I failed Camille," Natalie said flatly. "She was afraid someone was following her, stalking her. I thought it was stress. Imagination."

Skyler caught her hand with both of his and squeezed it. His warm fingers made her realize how cold her hand must be. "Someone was threatening her?"

Natalie couldn't answer. A horrific yearning to go back and fix her mistake seized her—mind, soul, body—everything pushing backward, crashing against reality until hope and determination broke into rubble.

Camille was dead. She couldn't fix that.

CHAPTER 14

IRRITATED WITH HIMSELF, GIDEON EXITED the CAD program he'd been using to design his Lego model of St. Patrick's Cathedral. He couldn't concentrate well enough to design a structure that intricate. Heck, he couldn't concentrate well enough to design a simple house or a garden shed or a cardboard box. Creating a model of a thirteenth-century Irish cathedral was *way* beyond this evening's brain capacity.

He pushed back from his computer and paced around his living room/kitchen area. Finally, he settled at the table and eyeballed the beginnings of a commercially produced Lego model of the Sydney Opera House that he'd started assembling last week. He couldn't think through a design of his own at the moment, but he could follow simple instructions.

He hoped.

He flipped open the instruction booklet, found his spot, and started sorting through a heap of bricks. Lego models: the hobby Tamara had labeled "your break from adulthood." He'd laughed when she'd first said it, but the more she'd used the phrase, the more he'd suspected that beneath what appeared to be affectionate teasing was embarrassment. She thought building Lego models was childish, designing them was only marginally more impressive, and displaying them in his office was immaturity on parade.

Why did his thoughts keep reverting to Tamara's rejection? She hadn't dumped him because he found it relaxing to design models and construct them in miniature plastic bricks. She'd dumped him because a guy who had the face of Thor and the magnetic charm of a vampire had slinked into the telecommunications company where she worked and she'd decided she was more interested in flirting with a mythical creature than in remaining loyal to a nerdy civil engineer.

Good thing he'd learned that before he married her. And weird how he could feel simultaneously hurt, humiliated, *and* relieved. He'd rather make wood-fired pizza with Natalie Marsh than accompany Tamara to that gourmet cooking class where all foods on the plate had to be stacked vertically and the plate decorated with sauce hieroglyphics. What kind of hobbies did Natalie—

You self-centered oaf. Natalie's friend just got murdered, and you're thinking of her in dating terms? And why would she be interested in you?

The sight of Natalie with Skyler Hudson should have hurtled logic back into the game. Was she dating him? She hadn't tried to kick Gideon out before Skyler had arrived, but that might just mean she was too polite to evict him unfed . . .

He didn't look annoyed that you were there. He didn't kiss her. She didn't try to explain your presence.

So? Maybe she'd forewarned Skyler about her appointment with him—

You have a problem. Stop making up scenarios. Why are Natalie's relationships even your business?

Would Natalie want to date a coworker? Skyler hadn't even been the one who'd called her; she'd addressed that guy as Kirk—

You definitely have a problem.

He examined the Lego he'd been about to stick on the Opera House. Dark gray; he needed light gray. He tossed it onto the table and picked up his phone.

He'd already looked up the address where he'd taken Natalie this afternoon so he could learn the name of her friend: Camille Moretti. He hadn't sought any other information; he'd already felt guilty about searching for information Natalie hadn't shared. But the name of the murder victim would be public soon anyway—the fact that Natalie's colleagues already knew meant information was at peak flow. Camille's murder and everything about her that the media could scrape up would be big news in Ohneka. It might have hit the news already.

Murder. He still hadn't had a chance to confide in Natalie about Felicia's obsessive belief that his dad's accident was murder.

But there *had* been a murder in town now. How had Camille died?

He checked the local newspaper's website. On their Twitter feed, he found a formal statement of *Ohneka woman found dead in apparent homicide* and a few statements about a police investigation led by Detective Jeffrey Turner of the OPD. Private citizens were already gossiping and speculating. A woman in Camille's neighborhood had shared Camille's name and was posting blow-by-blow reports of what she could see of the police activity at Camille's house. Had this neighbor paused to wonder if Camille's family had been notified before she'd flung the victim's name onto the Internet? Apparently, the police hadn't released any information about how she'd died, or this neighbor would have posted it.

And here you are reading her gossip, Saint Gideon. He fought the remnant of his compunctions for a few seconds, then surrendered and Googled Camille's name. He found a picture of her: pretty face, blonde hair. He found her name in an article about lawyer Dante Moretti being killed in a car-pedestrian hit-and-run. Her husband. Poor lady, widowed as a newlywed. A couple of articles about the renovation of the Stoker Building mentioned her; she was the property manager in charge of leasing office space.

The Stoker Building. Owned by Chapman Development. Camille had worked for Robert Chapman?

Lots of people work for him. It doesn't mean anything.

Felicia's warning echoed in his head for the ten-thousandth time: "*He does things his own way, and not all those ways are harmless . . . Be careful, and don't let on that you suspect anything.*"

He set his phone down and fiddled with a pile of Legos, arranging them in a line. He had no reason to believe Camille's death had any link to Chapman. He had no reason to believe Felicia was right about his father's death.

A murder of a woman with a Chapman connection . . .

Nope. No more struggling to figure this out without facts. It was time to force a discussion with Felicia, demand specific evidence-rooted answers and not back down until he had them. No more trying to deal with Felicia's fears in a roundabout way by seeking Natalie's help. No more letting Felicia ignore his calls or make vague comments about "private matters." If she wouldn't share the rest of her information, he'd take her theories about sabotage and the nervous purse woman to the police—regardless of what excuses she gave about why she couldn't talk to them.

He called her. No answer. He texted her. No answer.

Gideon stood. He'd drive over to her house. If she was home, he'd corner her. If she wasn't home, he'd stake the place out until she arrived. Even sitting in his car waiting for her would be more productive than slouching at his kitchen table, sticking the wrong bricks on the Sydney Opera House.

Fifteen minutes later, he rang her doorbell. No answer. He stepped off the porch and went to punch in the code to raise the garage door. Two cars were parked in the garage: her Nissan and his father's Camry. She was here. She just didn't want to answer the door any more than she'd wanted to answer his calls. Tough. Feeling like his father was prodding him in the ribs to get him to hurry, Gideon trotted to the door that led from the garage to the house and opened it.

"Felicia?" he called, standing in the doorway. "It's Gideon."

Felicia's voice—strained and angry—came from the direction of the living room. "I didn't invite you in."

"I didn't ask permission."

"Go home. I'm not feeling well."

She wasn't physically ill. A cold or a headache or the stomach flu might make her irritable, but it wouldn't make her ignore his messages and snap orders to clear out. He stepped completely into the house and shut the door behind him. "I'm coming in. If you're not dressed for visitors, throw a blanket over you or wrap yourself in the curtains because it's time to talk."

No response. Gideon marched into the living room.

Felicia was sitting on the couch. She was dressed, wearing jeans and a turtleneck, but her hair was uncharacteristically messy, and she had makeup smears around her eyes. He'd never seen her so disheveled, even after his father's death.

Gideon lifted a blue gift bag from the cushion next to Felicia and set it on the floor. Was that the same bag Natalie had been holding when she'd found him raking leaves? "Sorry about storming the gates." He sat. "But we're done with secrets. I need to know what's going on."

Felicia touched her lips. They were pale and looked parched. "Nothing now," she said. "Nothing anymore."

Relieved—and feeling sheepish that he'd taken her odd warnings seriously, even momentarily—he said, "You realized you were mistaken?"

"No. I took care of it. I told you I would."

Gideon's relief backlashed. What had she done? She *did* look physically ill. Those weren't only makeup smudges around her eyes; they were shadows. From exhaustion? From sickness? "How did you take care of it?"

"Don't worry about that."

"Nice try. I'm worrying. Did you . . . uh . . . figure out who . . . killed him?"

"Yes."

This declaration startled him again. "Who?"

She shook her head.

Gideon tried another angle. "Have they been arrested?"

"It wasn't that straightforward. But what I did worked. If it hadn't worked, I'd know it by now. The rest is none of your business."

"It is my business," Gideon said. "We're talking about my father's death."

"Parents don't tell children everything."

"Methuselah might call me a child. Nobody else could."

"You'll always be my child. All you need to know is that I took care of it."

She hadn't made eye contact once. Gideon studied her haggard profile. He didn't want to threaten her with his ultimatum about calling the police until he couldn't think of any other options for persuading her to confide in him.

"Did you hear about the woman who was murdered?" he asked.

"What woman?"

"A woman who worked for Robert Chapman. You told me to be leery of anyone with ties to Chapman. Now that one of his people has been killed, are you going to explain what's going on and what Dad had to do with it?"

Finally, she faced him. Stared at him. The wrinkles in her skin were usually subtle, but today, deep creases marked the puffiness under her eyes. "Who is she?"

He didn't want to mention Camille in context with Natalie. He wasn't ready to confess he'd been talking to Natalie, intending to share Felicia's warnings. "The property manager for that Victorian office building Chapman is renovating. Her name is Camille Moretti."

Felicia's eyelids slowly dropped and slowly rose. Dropped and rose again, a sluggish, trancelike blink.

"I don't know how she died," Gideon said. "No details have been released yet, but they say it was a homicide."

"Camille Moretti is dead?"

"Yes." Given the dazed way Felicia had spoken, they weren't talking about a stranger. He made his tone kinder. "You knew her?"

"How did she die?"

He'd just told her he didn't know. If she was forgetting information within a few seconds, he'd really shocked her with this news. Even though he'd wanted to say something that affected her, he still felt guilty. "I don't know how she died," he repeated. "They haven't released that information yet."

"When did she die?"

"I don't know. Either last night or this morning, I guess."

She leaned back, a remote, unfocused expression on her face. Gideon tried to think of what to do for her. He'd wanted to shake her into speaking, but instead he'd shaken her into a stupor. He touched her shoulder. "Are you okay?"

"When did she die?" Felicia repeated her question.

Gideon scrutinized her. Did she need medical care? He'd never seen sharp Felicia go foggy like this. "Let me get you something to drink. And eat."

In her kitchen, he opened the fridge. Milk, a pitcher of filtered water, a bottle of something greenish. That was one of the reusable glass bottles she used for different fresh concoctions. He popped the lid open and sniffed. Mint? Lemon? Maybe grapefruit? He poured a glassful of the drink. The cookie jar held oatmeal-almond cookies; he took three of them and put them on a plate.

He took the snack into the living room, set the plate on the lamp table, and held the glass out to Felicia. "Here you go. You could use some energy." Second time today he'd pushed food on a grieving woman, unable to think of any other way to help.

Felicia accepted the drink and sipped. Gideon took a ceramic coaster out of the top drawer of the table and put it next to the cookie plate so Felicia would have a place to set her drink.

"I'm sorry to throw the news at you like that," he said, sitting next to her. "I take it you knew Camille."

Felicia took a bigger swallow, then set the glass aside. "A little."

"How did you know her?"

Felicia picked up the glass again and guzzled most of what remained. When she lowered the glass, she said curtly, "I knew her when she was a child. She's a friend of Natalie Marsh's. I used to see her at Natalie's house."

He hadn't realized Natalie had been friends with Camille since they were kids. No wonder Natalie was devastated. "I'm sorry." His tongue kept adhering to the roof of his mouth, and he was suddenly thirsty. He should have poured himself a glass of mint-magic-energizing-lemon-whatever-it-was. "You realize Natalie has a Chapman connection too. She's trying to talk him into funding a new mental health clinic."

Felicia nodded.

"I hear you went with her to the annual Chapman party last night. Why were you warning me to avoid anything Chapman related when you're partying with him?"

"I didn't want to go," Felicia said. "It was necessary. I *have* been cautious around Natalie."

She'd been avoiding Natalie, Gideon remembered. Why had she changed that pattern last night?

"How did you know she accompanied me to the party?" Felicia asked.

Gideon defeated an urge to lie. He couldn't fib his way into coaxing Felicia to be forthright. "She told me. She was glad you came." No lies, but he wasn't above quickly changing the subject. "I know this hurts, and I'm sorry to press you, but I need you to tell me exactly why you think Dad was murdered. I need to know what you did to 'take care of it' and if you think his death has any link to Camille's murder."

"I've told you everything you need to know."

"No, you haven't. I'm not leaving until you give me that information. I'll pitch a tent in your living room if I have to."

"Stop pushing me! I have good reasons for not sharing details. I'm not changing my mind."

His stepmother could dig her heels in so deeply that it would take a bulldozer to push her onto a different course. Time to bring on the bulldozer. "I know you think you're doing the best thing," he said. "But two people are dead. Dad's death was ruled an accident. You disagree with that. Why? Whatever you know, you can't hide it. You need to take it to the police."

"I already told you I can't do that."

"I can. I'll do it unless you give me convincing evidence why I shouldn't."

Felicia grabbed his wrist, her fingernails stabbing him. "*Don't.*"

"Tell me why I shouldn't." Gideon jiggled his wrist. "And either let go of me, or get me some Band-Aids because I'm going to be bleeding soon."

She loosened her grip enough to retract her nails from his flesh, but she didn't release him. "Promise me you won't go to the police."

"I just promised you I *would*. Unless you can convince me not to. No more secrets. Start off with why you think Dad was murdered. What happened between him and Robert Chapman?"

Felicia averted her face. Her hand was sweaty on his wrist.

The clock on the wall ticked as polished gold-and-silver gears rotated behind the glass face. Gideon watched the clock, thinking of when he'd given it to his father and Felicia a few Christmases ago. They'd loved it.

When Felicia stayed silent, Gideon said, "Do you think Chapman owns the police? Is that why you won't go to them?"

"I won't discuss this." She finally released his wrist. "I'm doing what's best."

Gideon watched the minute hand move forward. "I don't think he owns the police. Chapman may be rich, but I haven't gotten the sense that he runs the town or that people are afraid of him. I'm willing to chance going to the police."

"Don't be silly. You won't do that. You know I wouldn't warn you away from them unless there was genuine danger."

"I usually trust your word," Gideon said. "But this time, I'm worried grief is damaging your good judgment. If you have evidence, give it to me now. Otherwise, I'm calling the police."

She watched the clock as Gideon had—the mesmerizing rotation of the gears, the motion of the hands. He watched the clock with her and waited.

The second hand rotated around the clock face once. Twice.

Gideon drew his phone out of his pocket. "This isn't a bluff," he said. "Are you going to tell me what's going on?"

"Put that away," she snapped.

"Evidence, Felicia. Give me evidence."

The second hand made another rotation.

"Let me think about it," she said. "Call me tomorrow."

"You don't need to think about it. You either have evidence or you don't."

She looked at him. Her face was ghostlike. Inscrutable.

Gideon battled his instinct to ditch his demands and focus on her health. If he got diverted now, he'd have to start over. More wheel-spinning, no answers.

"Tomorrow," she said.

"Okay, the cops it is." A slack sensation in Gideon's fingers made it tricky to hold his phone steady and look up the number for the police department. He hadn't thought he'd end up doing this. Gold medal to Felicia for stubbornness.

"I'm calling the main number," he said. "I figure this isn't a 911—"

Felicia ripped the phone out of his hand.

Dumbfounded, Gideon reached to snatch it back but pulled his hand away. He'd never seen Felicia get physically aggressive, and he didn't want to flail his way into an altercation where she might get hurt.

"You foolish boy." She tossed his phone onto the lamp table. "I can't go to the police because Robert Chapman has something on *me*."

The words hit as though he'd whacked himself in the face with the hammer he'd thought he could use to nail evidence together. "Are we talking about blackmail?"

"If I turn him in, he turns me in. I've dealt with your father's murder privately because it's the only way I *can* deal with it if I don't want to go to prison. Do you understand?"

"No." He couldn't fathom Felicia doing anything anyone could blackmail her for. "He's . . . blackmailing you into keeping your mouth shut about Dad?"

"It's a standoff. We've never talked about it. But he knows what I did, and I know what he did, and I know what will happen if I go to the police."

Blackmail? This had to be grief-fired madness. "What did you do?"

Felicia's lips remained still.

"So help me, I *will* call the police." Gideon didn't want to raise his voice, but it happened anyway. "If I want that phone, I'll take it back. If you want to arm wrestle for it, fine, but you won't win."

She spoke in a whisper. "Don't do this, Gideon."

Gideon wiped the anger from his voice. "I owe it to Dad to help you. That doesn't include letting you bury yourself in secrets or fears. If there's blackmail or implied blackmail going on—let alone murder—this all needs to come out. If you're unable to give me solid information, maybe what we need is a doctor, not the police."

"I haven't lost my mind." Felicia drew a long, deep breath that deteriorated into a wheeze. "I murdered Sheryl," she said. "Robert Chapman's first wife."

CHAPTER 15

A SHOCK WAVE NEARLY DECIMATED Gideon's self-possession. "What . . . I thought his wife died in some kind of accident. What happened?"

She glared at him. "I told you enough. I told you what Chapman has against me. And his daughter, his and Sheryl's—they had a falling out after her death, and they're still estranged. He lost his wife and his daughter. Do you see why he'd take revenge by killing my husband *and* possibly by targeting you, my stepson? He'll take from me what I took from him."

Gideon struggled to stabilize his thoughts. Natalie had said it was an accident at an event Felicia was catering. "Tell me exactly how she died. We're done with secrets."

Felicia was shaking—or was it shivering? Gideon stood and grabbed the chenille throw blanket folded in a basket next to the couch. He draped it over her, covering her from her shoulders to her feet.

"Tell me what happened." He remained standing in front of her. "No point in holding out. I'll hound you until you talk, and if that doesn't happen soon, I'm taking that phone back."

She pushed the chenille blanket off her shoulders and sat folding and smoothing the edge of the blanket now crumpled on her lap.

"Felicia."

She yanked the blanket back up to her shoulders. "Swear you won't tell anyone."

"I won't promise that. I swear I'll do whatever I can to help you. I swear I'll try to do what my father would want."

"He wouldn't want everyone to know what I . . ." Her gaze returned to the clock. Gideon wanted to unhook it from the wall and stuff it behind the couch if that would help keep Felicia's attention on him.

"Okay." Gideon lifted his phone off the lamp table. "You sit there and hoard your secrets."

"Sit down," Felicia said. "Please."

He retook his seat on her left, keeping his phone in his left hand so if she wanted to steal it, she'd have to reach across him—an attempt he'd easily thwart.

"My café . . . The Chicken Noodle . . . Chapman was a fan," Felicia said haltingly. "He decided he wanted our soup and sandwiches and cookies for the opening of Maison du Canard."

"Great compliment for you."

"It was. But my food wasn't the . . . type of cuisine usually served at an event like that. Sheryl was the one organizing the program, and she . . . she was unhappy with his choice of food. Soup and sandwiches for the opening of a magical glass house on the pond."

Cautiously, Gideon set his phone on the arm of the couch opposite from where Felicia sat. "Did she try to convince him to change his mind?"

"I'm sure she tried, but he wanted what he wanted. So Sheryl was . . ." Felicia's expression transformed from haunted to ice hard. "She made it clear to me—and to everyone working on the event—that I wasn't up to her standards. I was a low-class hash-slinger and wasn't it cute how Bob got these peculiar ideas and you had to roll with them, and if he'd sink this low, next time he'd be serving people frozen fish sticks and canned spaghetti."

"Ouch."

Felicia adjusted the blanket so it reached her chin. "The day we were setting up, Sheryl mocked my food so often I worried I wouldn't get *any* positive word of mouth from the event. Nobody would want to look like a hick by praising food Mrs. Chapman despised."

Her words no longer came grudgingly. They flooded out of her, and blood began to return to her ashen cheeks. Telling this story must be a relief. Had she ever confided it in anyone—even his father?

"This wasn't the first time I'd met Sheryl," Felicia continued. "She'd come into my café with her husband and had called it an 'aspiring truck stop' in a loud voice to make sure all my customers heard her. I was fed up with her. She kept making a big deal about how elegant and tasteful the event was supposed to be and how they'd have to do their best to compensate for the 'college-student food' by making everything else extra marvelous."

Gideon was starting to wish uncharitably that this "elegant event" had involved someone splashing lobster bisque all over Sheryl's designer clothes.

"At the beginning of the celebration, she was planning to paddle across the pond in a rowboat. There was a painting she loved . . . I can't remember the artist . . . called *Lady in a Rowboat*. It was on loan to the museum at the time. Sheryl was a dead ringer for the woman in the painting—a dead ringer plus twenty-five years, mind you. She wanted to re-create the painting."

"Re-create it?"

"Yes. 'Bring it to life,' she said. She had the flowing white dress, the pink-flowered hat, the white parasol, an exact reproduction of the rowboat. She planned to paddle gracefully across the pond while all the guests watched her from the deck of Maison du Canard and a string quartet played and a narrator talked about the painting. Oh—Edward Cucuel. That was the artist's name. American Impressionist."

"Ah." Gideon tried not to look clueless. He didn't know much about art.

"Sheryl loved the spotlight," Felicia said. "Loved showing off." She went silent. Gideon waited for her to continue, but she didn't.

"What happened the day she . . . the day of the event?" he prompted.

"I was sick of her rudeness," Felicia said quietly. "So sick of it."

"I'll bet. I would have been."

Her gaze locked onto the clock again. "I knew she was scared of cats. Phobic of them."

"Of cats? Plain house cats?"

"Yes. You should have seen her when a stray wandered past when we were on the grounds talking about setup. Sheryl screamed like the cat was a rabid lion, ran inside the museum, and wouldn't come out until a security guard caught the cat and took it to the shelter."

"Huh."

"I decided to strike back—a practical joke, I suppose it was. I had a toy cat—not a toy, really. A decoration. Realistic looking. Do you remember it?"

"Yeah. You had it in a basket by the fireplace. A faux pet that wouldn't bother your allergies."

"Yes."

"So you used the cat as part of a practical joke?"

"When I arrived early on the day of the celebration, I hid it in the rowboat she was using. I figured she'd notice it when she climbed in and she'd panic and make a fool of herself in front of her audience, maybe fall in the water in her pristine, vintage dress. She would be the star at a party where everyone was privately snickering over how she'd been spooked by a fake kitty. It was childish of me, yes, but I was so tired of her, and . . . I suppose I thought immaturity was justified. I . . . didn't think she'd get hurt. I didn't want her to get hurt."

"I know that," Gideon said. "What went wrong?"

"She climbed into the rowboat with no problem. I thought someone must have noticed the cat earlier and removed it. I was disappointed but also relieved—by then, I was a little embarrassed for being so petty." She looked at Gideon. "I'm not usually that way."

"I know."

"But the cat *was* there. She was too preoccupied playing the oil-painted beauty to notice it at first. About halfway across the pond, she screamed and started whacking at the interior of the rowboat with her paddle. Then she stood up, and . . . the boat tipped over."

After another extended pause, Gideon prodded. "Did she not know how to swim?"

"Of course she did, and I hadn't been worried about that anyway because with so many people around, I knew if she did fall in, she'd get rescued immediately. But I didn't know she had a heart condition or that her panic combined with the shock of falling into cold water . . . The water wasn't *that* cold; it was early October, but apparently, you don't need freezing water to cause problems in a vulnerable person. They rushed her to the hospital, but she died before she got there. Cardiac arrest."

Gideon rested his hand on Felicia's blanket-covered shoulder. "You couldn't have known about her heart condition. You couldn't have known that would happen."

"Does that change anything? I pulled a prank that killed her."

"Robert Chapman knew you put the cat there?"

"Nobody found the cat or knew why she'd panicked. The cat must have sunk. It was fairly heavy, weighted at the bottom to sit nicely on a hearth or pillow."

"You never told anyone what happened?"

"I couldn't. I'd go to prison for murder."

"Not murder. You didn't mean to hurt her. But you said Chapman knows what you did."

"He must have figured it out eventually. Maybe he dredged the pond and found the cat and was able to link it to me. That's why he ordered Wade's death. An eye for an eye."

Gideon gave himself several ticks of the clock to evaluate what she'd told him. Up until this point, she'd been reporting what had sounded like a factual story, but now she was leaping off facts and landing in assumptions. "Felicia . . . if he knew what you did, why didn't he go to the police?"

"Because he's Robert Chapman. He does what he wants. Soup instead of caviar. Murder instead of taking his chances that the legal system would get revenge for him."

"If he did want to take revenge by killing Dad, wouldn't he have done something less chancy than tampering with a ladder? Dad might not have gotten seriously hurt, let alone died."

"He wanted to send a message but didn't want a vigorous police investigation. I imagine that was his first try, and if it hadn't worked, he would have tried again."

Imagine was the right word to use. *Imagine. Fantasize. Fabricate.* "It's way too much of a stretch to think Dad's accident—"

"I didn't realize it at first either until I found out that the day your father died was . . . would have been . . . Robert and Sheryl's thirty-fifth wedding anniversary. That's not a coincidence."

This fact unsettled Gideon, but he said, "It absolutely could be coincidence. How many years ago did Sheryl die?"

"Seven."

"If he wanted revenge, why would he wait that long? That's six anniversaries he bypassed, if he wanted to take his revenge on that date."

"I don't know why he waited. Maybe he only found the cat and figured it out recently. Maybe he wanted to wait until a significant anniversary."

"Did he contact you in any way? Send you a message to indicate that he knew?"

"Your father's death was the message."

"But you never heard from him or any of his people? Never any blackmail or threats or hints that they knew what had led to Sheryl's death?"

"Your father's death made it clear."

But where's your proof? Felicia's grieving, guilty assumptions, plus the date of death . . . none of that was solid evidence.

"When you said you 'took care' of the issue, what did that mean?" Gideon asked.

"It means I took care of it." Her voice tightened, the loose eagerness of confession gone.

"Be more specific. What did you do?"

"I got the message to Mr. Chapman that I knew what he'd done and I had proof, and if he harmed you—or me—I had prepared things so my evidence would automatically go to the police. But if he leaves us alone, I'll leave him alone. He got the only revenge he was entitled to. He can't blame me for his problems with his daughter."

Entitled to revenge? Gideon decided not to dissect that statement. "You have proof Chapman killed Dad? Courtroom-grade evidence?"

"No. I was bluffing. But I learned enough to make it appear I know more than I do. That will scare him."

"What did you—"

"I'm done talking."

"No, you're not. You need to—"

"You wanted proof of why Chapman would go after your father. I gave it to you."

"You didn't give any proof. You gave assumptions."

"They're correct. And I have . . ." Her lips closed.

"You have what?"

The color that had enlivened her face drained away again. Her pallor provoked an abrupt memory of how his mother had looked when he'd visited her in the hospital before her death.

"I have indications that Chapman got my message," she said. "You'll be safe."

"What indications? How did you send the message?"

"I'm done answering questions. If you can't stop asking them, get out."

"What about Camille Moretti? She was one of Chapman's people, and she's dead too."

"I have no idea what happened to Camille. Go home. I need to rest."

"I'm not walking out while you're still—"

The doorbell rang. Felicia jumped.

"Should we ignore that?" Gideon asked.

Felicia pulled her hand out from under the blanket and massaged her forehead. She started to stand.

"No, stay here." Gideon sprang to his feet. "I'll answer it." *And get rid of whoever it is.* He walked to the door and checked the peephole. At the sight of Natalie, fresh stress and deep relief skirmished inside him. He unlocked the door and opened it. "Hey."

"Oh, hello." Natalie's eyelids were swollen, but her eyes weren't bloodshot. "I'm sorry about the—" Apparently remembering he hadn't wanted Felicia to know they were meeting, she dropped her voice to a whisper. "How is she?"

He had no idea how Felicia was. Better? Worse? Healing? Having a breakdown?

Behind him, he heard soft footsteps. "Natalie, it's so sweet of you to stop by," Felicia said. "Come in."

Come in? She wanted Natalie's company? Yes, because she thought it would shut Gideon up. He wouldn't ask painful questions in front of Natalie.

Would he? It might be better to bring her in . . . But he still didn't know . . . Should he dig more details out of Felicia before daring to . . . What would his father . . . He flat-out didn't know *what* to do. Never in his life had he felt so far out of his depth that he couldn't find the surface no matter which direction he swam.

Natalie embraced Felicia. As Gideon watched them, he realized that in the moments it had taken him to answer the door, Felicia had cleaned the makeup from under her eyes, tucked her turtleneck smoothly into her jeans, and redone her ponytail so her hair was tidy. Her face was now slightly flushed.

He should be glad she looked better, but her healthier, composed appearance frustrated him. If she'd looked as she had when he'd entered—like she'd slept in her clothes and was recovering from food poisoning—Natalie might have asked hard questions herself, taking the pressure off Gideon.

"I'm sorry I abandoned you last night," Felicia said to Natalie. "The party ended up being more than I could handle, and I didn't want to make you drive me home and miss out."

"Don't apologize," Natalie said. "It's great that you tried it. And I didn't mean to interrupt your visit with Gideon."

"He told me about your friend. I'm so sorry."

"Thank you."

"I remember Camille. You brought her over to my house a few times. Pretty and sassy and smiley."

"Yes, that was Camille." Pain soaked Natalie's voice, but her expression remained calm.

"Come sit down," Felicia said. "Gideon was about to leave. He's helping a neighbor move tonight."

I'm doing what? Gideon kept the confusion out of his expression, debating how to react.

"That's nice of you," Natalie said to him. "I hope they don't have a grand piano or a barbell collection."

"Uh . . ." Gideon glanced at Felicia. She was attempting to use Natalie's arrival as an excuse to boot him out. So much for being "cautious" around Natalie. Should he call her on her lie? Should he sit and tell Natalie what Felicia had told him so they could both pressure her to spill the information she was still hiding?

He didn't dare. Felicia's information was too messy, too perplexing, and he wanted to clarify his thoughts and make a reasoned decision about how to proceed—not blab her story while he was still reeling.

"I'll stop by tomorrow," he said grimly, holding Felicia's gaze.

She smiled and opened the door wider. "Good evening. Thanks for stopping by."

* * *

"Would you like a cookie?" Felicia lifted a plate off the lamp table and held it out to Natalie. Natalie recognized Felicia's oatmeal-almond cookies. She loved them, but her stomach was heavy with pizza, even though it had been a few hours since she'd eaten.

"No, thank you, but maybe later." The gift bag Natalie had given Felicia last night was sitting on the carpet near the couch. The tissue paper sticking out of the top was still arranged as perfectly as it had been when the clerk at the bookstore had wrapped it, and the card resting on top was sealed. Clearly, Felicia hadn't opened the gift yet.

They sat on the couch. "How are you doing?" Felicia asked.

"I'm coping. In shock still, I think. I wanted to come see how you're doing." She couldn't do anything to help Camille, but reaching out to someone else who needed help was the best gift she could offer in Camille's memory—and she wanted to do it for Gideon too after how kind he'd been today. It was far better than sitting at home crying and compulsively checking the news to see if they'd released any information about Camille's death. Natalie would have plenty of time to cry tonight when she couldn't sleep.

"Do the police have any information about what happened to her?" Felicia asked.

"If they do, they haven't told the media." Natalie didn't want to talk about Camille's stalker fears. She'd already experienced the grueling shame of admitting both to Skyler and Detective Bartholomew that Camille had been worried and Natalie hadn't taken her seriously.

"She was an ambitious girl," Felicia said. "She leaped up the ladder in Chapman's organization."

Natalie didn't know how to respond to this strange remark. She hadn't realized Felicia knew anything about Camille's career, and what did this have to do with her death? Was she implying someone had murdered Camille out of jealousy over her promotion? Or that her death had resulted from something shady she'd done to advance her career?

"She was a smart, trustworthy, hard worker," Natalie said. "How are you, Felicia? Do you feel like talking about last night?"

"Wade should have been with me," Felicia said. "There's nothing more to discuss."

"I'm sorry."

"He was a good man. A loving man who didn't hold grudges."

"I wish I'd known him better."

"I wish you had too. You'd understand that he didn't deserve what happened to him."

Natalie stopped herself from giving Felicia an incredulous look. Felicia couldn't possibly think she *did* believe Wade had deserved to tumble from a broken ladder. "It does feel excruciatingly unfair."

"He mentioned you," Felicia said. "On the day he died."

Prickly surprise rolled across her nerves. "What did he say?"

"When he called me at the end of the day, he mentioned you. In our last conversation. He asked if I'd seen you recently. How you were doing."

Natalie wanted to squeeze Felicia's hand or touch her shoulder but didn't dare. Considering Felicia's enigmatic mood, Natalie had no idea how she'd react to physical contact. "That was thoughtful of him."

"He'd never asked me about you before. I didn't think too much about it at first . . . I tried not to think too much about it. But I have to know." Emotion— was it anger?—strained Felicia's voice. "On the day he died, why would he have asked me about you?"

Natalie held back an irritable *How would I know?* "You sound frustrated. I'm sorry; I wish I could answer your question, but I have no idea."

"I asked him," Felicia said. "He said he'd just been thinking about you, that you'd had some tough breaks in life."

"Something must have reminded him of me."

Felicia's gaze was both piercing and apprehensive, as though she was searching for something she didn't want to find. "Did you see him the day he died?"

"Felicia, you know I didn't. If I had, I would have told you at the time." Coming here hadn't been a good idea; Natalie was too overwrought herself to manage this conversation.

"Were you still close to Camille?" Felicia asked. "I know you were close as children."

"We stayed close."

"You admired her, didn't you? You followed her lead."

Was this a conversation or an interrogation? Natalie was willing to talk about Camille, but Felicia's interest didn't sound sympathetic. Was she hurting too much from Wade's death to have the ability to hurt for Natalie? "I admired her, but I don't know about following her lead. We followed our own paths."

"You followed her into Robert Chapman's orbit."

"I'm not sure what you mean. She worked for him, but I didn't. We lease our office space from his company, but I wouldn't call that being in his orbit."

"Your clinic," Felicia said. "You asked him to fund your clinic."

"Camille did suggest I contact him about the clinic, and he thought it was a good cause. I hope it all works out." Determined to change the subject to something that didn't increase Felicia's stress or increase her own desire to flee, Natalie picked up the gift bag.

"Would you like to open this now?" she asked.

Felicia peered mutely at the bag. Natalie waited for several beats, then reached to set it back on the floor.

Felicia extended her hand. "Thank you," she said quietly, taking the bag. "Thank you. I was so tired last night that I didn't get to it."

"No hurry," Natalie said, relieved at Felicia's softer tone. "I hope it's something you'll enjoy."

Felicia opened the card, read it, and gave Natalie a brief smile for the words of friendship and sympathy she'd penned. She drew the wrapped book out of the bag and unwound the tissue paper. The book came out upside down in her lap, and she flipped it over. Head bowed, gaze on the book cover, she didn't speak.

"The illustrations are by a local artist," Natalie said. "Jennifer Lacombe. You might have seen her work at the art museum."

Felicia didn't raise her head.

Natalie looked at the cover illustration, a painting of a tabby cat gazing through a window. "Each poem is illustrated," she said. "Original watercolors painted for the book."

Felicia's back was a wooden arch, hard and still as she leaned over the book.

"What's wrong?" Natalie asked gently. "If that's not a welcome gift, I'll be happy to exchange it."

Felicia didn't speak.

Natalie brushed her fingers along Felicia's knuckles, white from her grip on the book. "If you'd like to talk about anything, I'm here to listen."

"I was still trying not to believe it." Felicia's whisper was a high-pressure hiss. "Even with the evidence, I tried. Do you think this is funny?"

Natalie drew her hand back. She'd somehow taken a turn so off course that she had no idea where she was. "I'm sorry. I've upset you, but I don't know what I've done."

Felicia turned toward Natalie. "You *devil*." She raised the book and smashed it into the side of Natalie's head.

Lightning dazzled Natalie's brain, and she flopped against the arm of the couch.

Felicia jumped to her feet and moved away, her motion a smear of navy fabric and pewter-gray hair.

Stupefied, Natalie pushed away from the arm of the couch and sat up straight. "Why did you . . . Felicia . . . I don't . . ."

"How could you sell out?" Tears surged down Felicia's face. "After everything? Do you want to go back, Natalie? Do you want to do your childhood over without me?"

Natalie touched her head and found a lump swelling under her hair. No wonder Gideon had been worried about his stepmother. Holding Felicia's anguished gaze, Natalie said softly, "Tell me how I sold out."

"I loved you like a daughter." Even at Wade's funeral, Natalie hadn't seen Felicia cry, but she was almost sobbing now. "Are you getting paid for coming here tonight, or is this just professional curiosity? You're here to experiment on me? Mock me and see how I react? Chart what you can do to me before I crumble?"

The dregs of Natalie's composure trickled away. She needed to leave before she fell apart and turned Felicia's sobbing into a duet. If Felicia had deteriorated to the point of assaulting her with a poetry book, there was nothing Natalie could do for her tonight.

Bending in slow motion, she picked up the book that lay near her feet. "I love you, and I'm grateful for everything you'd done for me. I don't know why you're angry with me or what you think I did, but I'll leave you in peace now." Felicia needed professional help, but Natalie wasn't the one to suggest it, not after Felicia had accused her of running an experiment. Natalie picked up her purse and rose tentatively to her feet. Her head pounded.

Felicia took a step toward her. "You're after Gideon, aren't you? You've been playing him behind my back. I could tell you knew each other better than you should have."

"I'm not playing him." Natalie retreated toward the door. "We've talked. If you want to know what about, ask him."

Felicia advanced another step. "You can't kill him, so you'll devour him from the inside out. That's your style, isn't it? That's what your mother always said."

This endorsement of her mother's viewpoint gashed Natalie, lacerating two decades' worth of interaction with Felicia. Natalie clutched the doorknob. "I'm not after Gideon, and I would never hurt you. I hope you come to realize that." She pulled the door open, stepped onto the porch, and hastily shut the door behind her.

Legs shaking, she staggered down the stairs and headed for her car.

CHAPTER 16

GIDEON SET ASIDE THE LAPTOP displaying his search for information about Sheryl Chapman's death and grabbed his ringing phone. "Hey. How are you?"

"There's trouble." Felicia's agitated tone jostled his nerves. "Listen to me, and do what I tell you."

So much for hoping her call meant she'd become more reasonable. "I'm listening." *Not promising to obey but listening.*

"Natalie Marsh is dangerous," Felicia said. "She'll try to call you tonight, if she hasn't already."

"Uh . . . what?"

"I've been in denial about her." Felicia's voice broke. "But there's no question now."

Was she crying? Felicia hardly ever cried. "Mama Felicia. Are you okay? I'm coming over."

"No. Don't come over. I can't take more tonight; I'm going to bed." She sniffled. "Chapman bought her. They made a bargain. She helps him with his revenge, and he funds the mental health clinic she wants to open."

"She told you this?"

"Not directly, but she wanted me to know it. She came to mock me. She's been contacting you, hasn't she? She's after you."

"I contacted *her.* I was worried about you, and I wanted her input since she's known you so long."

"Gideon! What did you tell her?"

"Uh, nothing." Gideon skipped the fact that he'd intended to confide in Natalie this afternoon, but the news of Camille's death had interrupted that plan. "I didn't give her any details. Just that I was worried about you."

"I suppose it doesn't matter anyway. She already knows everything."

"What do you mean she's after me? I thought you said I wasn't in danger anymore."

"Not physically. She'll get in your head, your heart, destroy you from inside."

"But you always said good things about Natalie—"

"I thought they were true. They *were* true when she was young. She'll call you. I know she'll call you. She'll tell you I've lost my mind, that I'm insane and to ignore anything I say. It's the same story she used to give about her mother."

"Her mother . . . Natalie told me . . ."

"Roxanne disinherited her a few years ago. I'd always blamed Roxanne; I didn't think Natalie deserved it—" Felicia's voice collapsed.

Gideon vaulted to his feet and paced his apartment, giving Felicia a few seconds to calm herself. When her breathing started smoothing out, he said, "Tell me exactly what Natalie said to you. Not what you assumed."

"It was the gift—you saw the bag. She pressed me to open it while she was there. It was a cruel reminder of Sheryl's death."

"What was it?"

"A book. I don't remember the title. She took it with her. But the illustration on the cover was a cat. A brown-and-cream, green-eyed tabby. Exactly like my fake cat."

Gideon pressed his hand against a corner of the Sydney Opera House, pushing until his palm hurt and Legos broke apart and scattered over the kitchen table. "That could be coincidence—"

"Gideon, there's . . . more." Her voice trembled again, words lurching out. "The day your father . . . The day your father died, he asked me about . . . if I'd seen Natalie lately. How she was doing. Out of the blue, he brought her up . . . said he was thinking she'd had a tough time in life. Why would he suddenly be thinking about her? I don't remember him ever bringing her up before. Something must have provoked those thoughts. I could tell he was worried."

She could tell at the time, or she was conjuring that tone to his words in retrospect? "Slow down. When Natalie gave you the book, did you accuse her?"

"Yes. She took the book and walked out."

"Leaving doesn't mean she's guilty. You're assuming—"

"Hush. I know it doesn't prove anything. Didn't I tell you *I* kept fighting it myself, not wanting to believe she could . . . the sweet girl who . . ."

Felicia's weeping wakened an agonized need to call his father and ask for counsel. "Felicia—"

"The woman who died last night—Camille Moretti." Felicia interrupted him, her words now sharp and solid. "She was another Chapman stooge. She's the one who actually sabotaged the ladder."

"*What*? How do you know that?"

"The purse. The mosaic purse. I've spent weeks trying to figure out how to track the assassin down."

"And you found her?"

"At the Chapman soiree last night. I hadn't planned to go—I'd only attended in the past for your father's sake; I always hated it—but I realized the killer might be there and might bring her dressy new purse. Camille Moretti was flaunting it."

Gideon finished decimating one of the shells of the opera house. "Did you confront her?"

"Surrounded by hundreds of Chapman's people? No. I went to her house, got inside, and waited for her. When she got home, I confronted her and told her I knew what she'd done and to carry the message to Chapman to back off or I'd destroy both of them."

Pulling out a chair was too hard; Gideon thumped to the kitchen tile and sat there, eyes closed, phone flattening his ear. "You broke into Camille's house last night?"

"Yes. I had no idea she'd end up dead. She *did* send my message to Chapman. That must be . . . That has to be the reason she died. Punishment. He was angry."

At least Felicia wasn't confessing to murder. "Why would he punish her if she'd done the job he wanted?"

"The *purse*. She'd been careless and marked herself by buying that purse."

"When you confronted her, did she admit what she'd done?"

"Yes, she admitted it."

He dragged his tongue around his dry mouth. It stuck to his teeth. "You challenged a murderer on your own? That was crazy!"

"I'm not a fool. I kept her away from me until I could state my bargain and she'd agreed to it."

"How—"

"It doesn't matter."

Felicia must have had a weapon—his dad had owned an old hunting pistol. Or maybe she'd pounced on Camille and tied her up. Whatever she'd done, Camille must have felt threatened. Was her confession valid?

Had Chapman ordered a hit on Camille? Or had Felicia herself . . .

No. She wouldn't.

But she's not in her right mind.

She couldn't go that *far out of her mind.*

"Okay," Gideon said. "If you know what happened to Camille, you need to tell the police immediately. We can't let this go on any longer. I'll come pick you up."

"*No.* I told you I don't have enough evidence to convict Chapman. The only safe thing to do is keep him *thinking* I do, which means we keep this away from the police and courts. Leave it alone. I didn't want this to worry you. Keep away from Natalie; don't give her any opening to play her mind games. You'll be fine."

"Seriously? You're telling me Camille and Natalie killed my father, and I'm supposed to leave that alone?"

"Nothing will help. You know nothing will help. Wade is *dead.* You can't touch Chapman, Camille's gone, and chances are . . . chances are . . . since Natalie knew about the purse and didn't force Camille to get rid of it . . ."

"He'll murder Natalie too? I'm supposed to condone that?"

"We can't stop it. Don't you think I'd fix this if it were fixable? It's *not.* I'm leaving tomorrow morning, going to Manhattan for a few days. I need to get away from Ohneka, away from Natalie, away from . . . too many memories."

Gideon wanted to protest but didn't know what to say. He felt he was catching snowflakes out of the sky and trying to pack them into a snowball even as they melted on his palms. Maybe it would be better for Felicia to get away. Maybe it would help her think straight. Maybe it would help *him* think straight.

"Be careful," Felicia said. "Keep your mouth shut. Don't trust Natalie; don't even talk to her. You don't want to suffer through what she could do to you. Do you understand?"

"Yes."

"I'll call you when I get back. Promise you'll be smart."

"I promise," Gideon lied mechanically. Be smart? He'd never felt this stupid and useless in his life.

"Be safe, Gideon." She hung up.

Phone still in his hand, Gideon stood, shuffled into his bedroom, and collapsed on his bed. How could everything be reasonable one moment and a surreal nightmare the next?

Or *had* things been reasonable since his father died? Had they only seemed reasonable before and after?

He could sweep away everything Felicia had told him, except for one bedrock fact: Camille hadn't called the police after Felicia's visit last night. If she had called, the police would have arrested Felicia. That clearly hadn't happened.

Since she hadn't called, that meant either she hadn't wanted to call—she had reasons for avoiding the cops—or she hadn't had time. The odds that the instant Felicia had left, a random killer not connected to Chapman had barged in and slaughtered Camille before she could dial 911 . . .

There were only two logical options: Either Felicia—motherly, sensible, kind Felicia—had killed Camille herself, or—

Or Felicia's theory about his father's death was correct.

His phone rang. He checked the screen.

Natalie. As Felicia had forecast. Calling to tell him Felicia was insane.

Gideon flipped onto his back and held the phone in front of his face, staring at her name. Should he flat-out ask her if she and Camille had killed his father and see how she reacted?

Yeah, ask her. Belly flop into the water with a shark who might be getting paid to shred your heart and gnaw your sanity to mush. Confide in her. Trust her. Maybe in an act of record-breaking genius, you could completely fall for her.

At least Tamara hadn't set his mental annihilation as her goal.

Gideon dropped the phone onto his bedspread, closed his eyes, and listened to it ring.

CHAPTER 17

STOMACH GROWLING, EYES ACHING, LACEY sat in her car in the driveway, clinging to the steering wheel and staring through the open garage door at Jonas's car. She had yearned to feel safe with him, to let him handle things; she'd yearned to flee from him, speed along the freeway until her gas tank was empty, then walk along the road until *she* was empty and she could crumple into the weeds and die. She'd compromised with herself, deciding he was probably out searching for her, so she could sneak into the house, eat, wash her greasy hair, and change her wrinkled clothes. Or maybe he didn't want to find her at all; he might have moved out, wanting to escape his crazy, criminal wife. Either way, he wouldn't be home.

But he *was* home, and the thought of driving away still hungry, exhausted, and alone made her want to bawl. Twenty-four hours of blundering around Ohneka with no idea what to do was enough. She'd gotten almost no sleep last night, cold and uncomfortable in her car. This morning she'd mustered the courage to buy a heavy fleece blanket, hoping it would help her get some rest, but it hadn't worked. She'd been warm but still too keyed-up even to nap.

She'd face Jonas. She had to face him. It couldn't be worse than coming home as a teenager to face her father, and she'd dealt with that. She pulled into the garage, parked, and trudged into the house.

Why was the house so silent? Lacey stepped out of her shoes and padded along the hallway, her heartbeat an inner cascade of sounds, stones pouring into a bucket, striking the bottom, striking each other.

He wasn't in the kitchen or the living room or his office. She increased her speed and headed upstairs. In their bedroom, the bed was neatly made. She was the one who made the bed; she couldn't imagine Jonas would think of it after he'd had his life smashed by the proof that his wife was a monster. Had he not slept here last night?

What if he *had* left her? He could have taken a taxi to the airport.

She yanked his closet open. His clothes still hung on the rod, and his shoes were pigeonholed in the shoe organizer.

She could call his name, but she had a horror-movie feeling that if she made a loud noise, a killer would lunge at her. She tiptoed downstairs, along the hallway, and into the workshop he'd built for her at the back of the house.

Jonas lay on the couch in her workshop, asleep, covered with the quilt she'd sewn when she'd wanted to try creating patterns with fabric. Stubble covered his chin. His shoes—leather loafers, not the athletic shoes he usually wore on Saturdays—were next to the couch, and the part of his shoulder she could see told her he was wearing the same shirt he'd had on when he'd snatched her notebook.

He hadn't left her.

Where was the notebook? If she could reclaim it . . . Maybe he hadn't read the whole thing yet. Maybe he didn't fully know how awful she was; maybe if she could steal it back, he'd eventually forget whatever part he'd read. Where would he have put it? Maybe in the drawer of his bedside table where he kept things like his wallet and checkbook?

She pivoted and hurried toward the door. Behind her, she heard a rustle and a thump. With a yelp, she spun toward Jonas.

He was on his feet, the quilt on the floor. "Lacey."

"I'm sorry. I didn't mean to wake you up." She couldn't look him in the eyes, and she had no idea what she wanted to say. *I'm sorry I ran away and didn't come home. I'm sorry I'm crazy. I'm sorry I lied to you after the way you took care of me. I'm sorry I want to scream and punch you.*

Jonas advanced, a fast stride that made her cringe. He stretched his arms out, curled them around her, and drew her against him. She could feel the strong thumping of his heart.

He didn't speak. Lacey sagged against him.

He pulled back slightly and kissed her. Her lips were dry and her mouth sour, but from the energy in his kiss, he didn't seem to care. She clung to him, her lips clumsy against his.

"Lacey." His lips touched her forehead. "Are you all right?"

She nodded.

"Are you sure?"

"Yes." He hadn't left her. He didn't find her repulsive.

"Where have you been?"

"Can we . . . sit down? I'm so tired."

He guided her to the couch, and they sat together, his arm around her shoulders. "Where have you been?" he asked again. "Where did you spend the night?"

"In my car," she said.

"You slept in your car?"

"I . . . I didn't sleep much at all."

"What did you do? Where did you go?"

"I'm not sure. It's blurry. Drove around mostly or sat in the car."

"All night?"

"If I got too tired, I'd stop and try to doze for a while. Like in a supermarket parking lot."

"Why didn't you come home?"

"I thought you wouldn't want me after what . . . the . . . things . . . in the . . . what I was . . . doing."

"Baby, I'll always want you." Both his arms went around her in an embrace so tight her lungs felt flattened. "I'll take care of you."

Gratitude flickered and dwindled in her mind, a phantom emotion she wasn't sure she'd felt. His words, like his embrace, both comforted and constricted her, but she couldn't think how to explain that. Out of habit, she asked herself how Camille would handle the situation, but the question burned like brimstone.

"I'm hungry." She tugged against his hold.

He released her. "Yeah, you must be starving. Come into the kitchen. There's still some of that pasta you made the other night." His arm around her waist, he led her to the kitchen. Lacey sat at the table as Jonas piled pasta on a plate and stuck it in the microwave. When the scent of tomatoes and sausage reached her, her mouth watered. Coming home had been the right thing to do.

Jonas set the plate in front of her, then filled a glass with milk. He liked her to drink milk at dinner, milk for her bones. She'd never liked drinking milk with dinner, but asking for water or wine wasn't worth it right now. She wanted to eat quickly and go to bed.

The doorbell rang. Jonas seized Lacey's shoulder, a gesture that startled her into a squeaky gasp.

"Stay in here," he said. "Stay quiet. Don't come out unless I come get you."

Lacey put down her fork. "Who is—"

"Stay put." He exited the kitchen.

Confused but too weary to fret about it, Lacey continued eating. She must look so awful that Jonas didn't want a salesman to see her and ask what was wrong. Then again, Jonas looked like a wreck himself.

She heard him open the front door and male voices talking, but she didn't bother trying to eavesdrop until she heard Jonas say, "Come in." He was inviting someone inside *now*?

Footsteps. An unfamiliar voice sounded clearly from the living room. "Thank you for your time." The words were courteous but carried a vibe of authority that made Lacey think this wasn't a salesman.

"No problem." Jonas's tone was curt, and Lacey could tell he didn't want the visitor here. "Have a seat."

"Thank you." A different voice, deep and resonant. It made Lacey picture Darth Vader, only polite. Two visitors. She shouldn't be listening; Jonas hadn't wanted her to be part of this conversation.

So what? She could sit here and eavesdrop; Jonas couldn't stop her. She could even march into the living room if she wanted to.

She definitely didn't want to.

"I know you already gave some of this information to the 911 operator and to the officer who talked to you this morning," the first man said. "But if you could review the events for Detective Bartholomew and myself, that would be helpful. What led you to Mrs. Moretti's house this morning?"

Lacey's skin went scorching hot. The police. Jonas had called the police after she'd run away? And he'd been at Camille's? Had he told Camille that Lacey was—No, he wouldn't do that.

"I had an appointment with Mrs. Moretti," Jonas was telling the officers. "She was interested in buying a piece of my wife's artwork. My wife is a mosaic artist."

Lacey gaped at the kitchen doorway. Camille—or really Mr. Chapman—wanted to buy her artwork? Why hadn't Jonas told her that?

"Was your wife with you?" the first man asked.

"No, I deal with the business side of Lacey's work. She doesn't like to be involved in sales."

Lacey's wide-open eyes smarted. She blinked several times. True, Jonas liked to deal with pricing and sales and taxes and things, but if he met with customers, Lacey was always with him. She enjoyed talking to people about her work, and he wanted her there—he always said her angelic smile was an effective sales tool.

"Had you met Mrs. Moretti previously?"

"Yes," Jonas said. "I trained for a marathon with her husband a few years back. He's dead, I'm sorry to say—car accident. Camille worked for Chapman Development, and I met with her recently about the possibility of Lacey doing a mural for the Stoker Building renovation. Camille hadn't heard back from her boss on that one, but she got interested in Lacey's work for her own house. This morning, I went to show her some samples."

What? That couldn't be true. Jonas would have told her immediately if Camille was interested in her work. He for sure wouldn't have called the police on Lacey and then gone for a business meeting with the woman she was stalking—without even shaving or changing his clothes.

"When I got there, Camille didn't answer the doorbell or her phone. I went to the backyard to see if she was there since it was a nice day. The glass on the back door had been cut—I figured she'd been robbed. I went inside to see if she was there, to make sure she was all right. I found her body and called 911."

Lacey gasped and gasped again, but no air seemed to reach her lungs. Camille's body . . . she was *dead?*

"The operator asked you to wait in your car until the police arrived," the man said. "Why did you leave?"

"Sorry. I wasn't thinking straight. I'd never seen anything like that before, and I wanted to get out of there."

Lacey's elbow hurt. She massaged it. Had she whacked it against the table?

"I don't know anything that could help anyway," Jonas said. "I didn't see anyone or anything suspicious except for that hole in the glass. Was it a burglary that went south?"

"We're still determining what happened. Do you have any idea who might have wanted to hurt Mrs. Moretti?"

"No idea at all. I didn't know her that well."

Lacey laid her fork on the table so carefully that metal against wood made no sound. Jonas must have gone to Camille's to search for Lacey, thinking he'd find her hunkered down in the bushes or crouching behind storage bins in the garage.

Did he think Lacey had . . . ?

She would never . . . But she had enjoyed scaring . . . She'd *never* . . . *Had* she . . . ? She remembered driving past Camille's house, but she hadn't stopped there. Driving past a few times. Maybe twice? Was it more than that? She did remember thinking how much better she'd feel if she could scare Camille, make her shriek, prove that Camille had weaknesses too, that Lacey wasn't the only one who was afraid.

Voices still spoke from the other room, but words disintegrated into senseless noise. Camille, Camille's house, the way glass would fragment as it hit brick steps. Camille's strong voice, her laugh, Lacey's pen flitting across notebook pages. Jonas snatching the notebook from her purse. The rawness in her throat.

"Lacey." Jonas jiggled her shoulder. She focused on his face, bewildered. How had she not noticed him approaching her? Was he truly that pale, or did her eyes now see everything as bloodless and dead?

"Do they want to talk to me?" Lacey whispered.

"They're gone." Jonas took both her hands. "You'll never have to talk to them. I've taken care of things." His gaze was as strong as his fingers, immobilizing her. "It's not your fault."

"I didn't . . . Jonas, I didn't . . ."

"You'll be all right. No one will ever find out."

"I don't think . . . I never wanted—"

"I'm sorry, baby. This isn't your fault. It's my fault for not taking better care of you."

Lacey's thoughts kept splintering and mixing together. How had Camille died? Did Lacey already know that? Was there a picture of Camille stored in her head, strong Camille bloodied and limp?

No. She couldn't have hurt her. "Dr. Marsh . . . I need to . . ."

"You can't talk to her now, not while the police are investigating." Jonas pulled her chair out from the table and lifted her to her feet. "I'll call her office and cancel your appointment for next week. Let's get you to bed. You need to rest."

CHAPTER 18

As NATALIE PASSED THE RECEPTION desk, Jeanne rose to hug her. "I'm so sorry, sweetie. How are you holding up?"

"I'm okay." Over Jeanne's shoulder, Natalie saw Kirk and Skyler speeding out of their offices. They stopped near the reception desk. When Jeanne released her, Kirk stepped forward and embraced her.

"I'm sorry," Kirk said. "Anything we can do?" He stepped back so Skyler could approach.

"No, but thank you." Natalie hugged Skyler. "And thank you all for the flowers."

"What are you doing at work?" Skyler asked. "I told you you should take time off."

"To do nothing? I'd rather be here. Clients are counting on me."

The phone rang. Jeanne lifted the receiver, and Natalie, Kirk, and Skyler moved down the hallway for privacy.

"Do the police know what happened yet?" Kirk asked quietly. "Was it a robbery?"

"They've issued a couple of statements," Natalie said. "How much do you know?"

Kirk glanced at Skyler as though seeking another male opinion on whether or not to bluntly state what he'd learned.

"We read that she died of strangulation." Skyler took the initiative. "It's being treated as a homicide, and time of death was between 1:00 and 3:00 a.m. Saturday. The news reports didn't say anything about . . . reasons."

"That's all I know too. They haven't said anything about suspects or motives." Natalie realized she was rubbing her throat. She dropped her hand, wishing she could shake the recurring, miserable question of how much Camille had suffered. "Skyler, did you . . . tell Kirk?"

"About her stalker worries?" Skyler asked. "Yep. Hope you aren't mad at me."

"Listen hard, lady," Kirk said sternly. "You have good judgment. If you didn't take her seriously, it's because her concerns didn't warrant it."

"She's dead," Natalie said shortly. "Her concerns were serious."

Kirk shook his head. "Her death might have had nothing to do with a so-called stalker."

"That makes for a big coincidence," Natalie said. "She was scared, and now she's dead, but those facts aren't related?"

"Maybe not," Kirk said. "Coincidence is more credible than the theory that over a few days, somebody escalated from rearranging pumpkins to strangling her."

"I tried to tell Natalie that," Skyler said. "This could be a random crime or connected to some issue that had nothing to do with Camille's notion that Jack the Ripper was peeping at her in the deli department. Rotten stuff happens. You can't blame yourself."

Natalie wanted to absorb their words and feel better, but she couldn't yet.

"If she'd told me the things she told you, I would have thought it was melodrama and nonsense," Kirk said. "Maybe there was a stalker, but given the evidence, I would have recommended therapy, not police involvement." He scratched his jaw through his trim beard. "Poor Camille. Deborah and I took the kids for a walk at Lake Ohneka yesterday, and I kept thinking of you talking about how you and Camille liked to go stargazing there. At Beau Lac pier, right?"

Natalie nodded.

"That's where we were. Nice area. I'm sorry."

"Thank you. I need to get ready for my client." Blinking, Natalie hurried toward her office. Just thinking about stargazing with Camille made her eyes fill up. If she tried to tell Kirk she and Camille had been at Beau Lac a few days ago, she'd crumble.

"Any time you want to talk, I'm ready to listen," Kirk called after her.

"For his usual rate of a hundred fifty bucks an hour," Skyler added, and Natalie smiled over her shoulder at her colleagues, glad for a glimmer of humor.

She entered her office, closed the door, and settled into her favorite chair. Instead of reviewing her client notes, she lifted her hand to her head and gingerly traced the bruise hidden by her hair. The swelling had started to recede, but a significant bump remained where Felicia had struck her.

She'd tried to contact Gideon about the incident, but he hadn't answered his phone or returned her voice mail or texts. If he was ignoring "Please call me as soon as possible" and "Felicia's behavior was frightening and erratic" and "Your stepmother needs help," he too must have decided Natalie was some type of traitorous conspirator. She could call Felicia and ask for an explanation, but if Felicia were rational enough to explain, she would have already called Natalie to apologize.

Natalie hadn't done enough to help Camille, and Camille was dead. She'd tried to help Felicia, and Felicia was falling apart. Here she sat in her office with her comfortable furniture and serene landscapes and soothing gray-blue paint, waiting for people to write her checks in exchange for her guidance.

She pressed a fingertip harder against the bruise. Pain twined around her scalp and neck.

". . . right now! This can't wait!"

"Please calm down. You need to—"

"I need to talk to her. Now!"

Natalie opened her eyes and tuned in to the muted sounds of an argument.

". . . can't wait for my appointment, and I think my husband canceled it anyway. She's here, isn't she? This is important!"

Lacey Egan. Natalie opened her office door so she could hear more clearly.

"Why don't you have a seat?" Jeanne suggested. "I'll bring you a cup of tea. You can relax a moment while I check Dr. Marsh's schedule and we figure out a good time for you to see her."

"I can't wait! What if he checks on me? He told me not to leave the house. I need to—"

"Can I help?" Skyler's voice.

"Thank you," Jeanne said. "Could you escort Mrs. Egan to a seat while I—"

"This can't wait!" Lacey shrieked.

"Ma'am, we can't have this disruption," Jeanne said. "Other clients will be arriving soon. If you can't calm down, I'll need to call the police."

"*No.* Please—"

"No worries; we don't want the cops," Skyler said. "They'll eat the best donuts. Come sit down."

Natalie hurried toward the door that led to the waiting room. Standing behind the reception desk, Jeanne spotted her approaching and whispered, "Do you want me to call for backup?"

"No. I'll talk to her and see if I can settle her down."

"Do you want me to contact your first appointment to see if we can reschedule? You have an opening this afternoon with that cancellation."

Natalie zipped through an instantaneous mental evaluation. The first client on her schedule could roll with a delay; it wouldn't be a problem. "Yes, do that."

She opened the door to the waiting room. Skyler was artfully backing Lacey away from the reception window. "Let me get you something to drink. Coffee? Tea? Water? Mountain Dew from my secret cache?"

Lacey and Skyler both saw Natalie. Skyler stepped between them, ready to intercept Lacey if she lunged.

"Hello, Lacey," Natalie said. "What's going on?"

"I'm sorry." Lacey tried to step around Skyler. He moved sideways with her. "I'm sorry, I know this isn't the right way to do things; I'm not supposed to come in like this, but I don't know who else . . . No one else can help me." She wiped her face with the sleeve of her blouse. Though it was a cool, rainy morning, she wasn't wearing a jacket. "Please don't call the police."

"I won't," Natalie said, "if you demonstrate that you can control yourself. Lacey, this is Skyler Hudson, our biofeedback therapist. I don't think you've met him."

"Nice to meet you." Skyler held out his hand. Fingers quivering, Lacey shook it. "Would you like coffee?" Skyler asked. "And we really do have donuts. I brought some this morning. May I get you one? We have Boston creams."

"Oh . . . um, that's nice of you, but no, thank you." Lacey's cornered-animal mien was softening. "I don't want anything."

"Come in." Natalie gestured Skyler and Lacey through the doorway. When they stopped at Natalie's office, Skyler grinned at Lacey. "Holler if you change your mind about the donuts."

"Okay."

Skyler strolled away. Lacey entered the office, and Natalie closed the door. "Have a seat."

Lacey collapsed into a chair. "I'm sorry. I'm really sorry I yelled at your receptionist. I know I'm acting horrible. I can't stop thinking about this, and you were the only one . . . There's nobody else I can tell."

Natalie felt weary and sluggish as she sat down, her professional instincts distorted by pain. Was Camille's death part of the reason Lacey was so agitated today? It still surprised Natalie that Lacey had been close enough to Camille that Jonas had searched for her at Camille's house.

Could she continue as Lacey's therapist while both of them mourned the same friend? That didn't seem like a good idea, but on the other hand, could she, right now, inform Lacey that she had a conflict of interest and Lacey needed to see a different therapist? Natalie imagined herself handing Lacey a referral and telling her to pack up her tumult of emotions and haul them to a stranger. She'd been terrified to begin therapy in the first place.

The best course was to find out what was going on with Lacey this morning so Natalie could make a decision that was wise, ethical, and compassionate. "Tell me why you're here. What upset you?"

Lacey wiped her eyes. Her hair was clean and brushed, and she wore nice jeans, a ruffled pink blouse, and a gold heart locket. In contrast to her neat clothes, her face was a mess of makeup and tear blotches.

"Um . . ." Lacey poked at the sleeve of her blouse where she'd smeared mascara on the fabric. "I'm afraid I'm . . . I'm . . . crazy for real."

"Why do you think you're crazy?"

"Is it possible to . . . to . . . do something horrible and not remember it?"

"Do you think you did something horrible?"

"I don't know. I didn't think I . . . but . . . I know I did *some* bad stuff, so maybe . . ." Her lips pinched closed, popped open, pinched closed as though she couldn't decide whether or not to let the rest of the words emerge.

"Would you like to tell me what 'bad stuff' you did?" Natalie asked.

"It's . . . weird," Lacey mumbled.

"I'm here to listen to you, not judge you."

"I guess I don't know how to say it." She picked at a ruffle on her blouse.

"Say it in any way you'd like. You're sharing something in a safe setting. You don't have to give a speech."

"True . . . well, there was this person I met a few years ago. I'd pretty much forgotten about them, but then I met them again recently and was . . . really impressed with them. Fascinated by them, I guess."

An affair. Jonas must have suspected it; that was why he'd wigged out when Lacey had disappeared. If he'd found proof and confronted Lacey this morning, no wonder she was hysterical.

"Did you act on those feelings?" Natalie asked.

"Well . . . yes. I thought it was harmless, that it would help me, but . . ." She trailed off again. This time, Natalie didn't nudge her. After a few seconds of silence, Lacey said, "I think it *did* help me in some ways, but I had trouble keeping it under control, I guess. I got . . . I got obsessed."

"How did this person respond to your interest?"

"Oh, they didn't know."

"You never shared your feelings with them?"

"I couldn't. They'd think I was crazy. I didn't want them to find out. I don't think they ever did find out. I thought I could . . . you know . . . keep my distance but watch. Learn."

This wasn't going the direction Natalie had expected. "What did you want to learn from them?"

"Everything. I . . . well, like I said, I admired this person—this woman—too much. Not romantic-like. Like an idol, I guess. I'd watch her for anything that might help me."

"Help you in what way?"

"To . . . be stronger. Things she did or said or expressions on her face or what she was wearing or how she walked. Then I . . . I . . . well, I'd practice. When Jonas was gone, I'd see if I could do the things I'd watched her doing, like if I could sound like her, not like me."

"How did you feel when you imitated her?"

"Oh, that depends on how good of a job I did. If it was pathetic, I felt silly. But if I nailed something, I felt strong like her."

"You said this was something bad. Why do you feel it's bad to admire someone and privately imitate her?"

"I guess I . . . pushed it too far." Lacey squirmed in her seat, facing one way, facing the other.

"How did you push it too far?"

Lacey froze, gaze anchored on Natalie, then started fidgeting again, looking around the office. Fear had engulfed the determination she'd shown in the waiting room.

Natalie spoke gently. "Are you afraid of what I'll think of you if you tell me?"

"This was dumb," Lacey whispered. "Jonas told me not to talk to you."

"That's not his decision to make. You wanted to talk to me. You demanded to talk to me so insistently that you alarmed Jeanne and Skyler."

"I'm really sorry. I'm sorry about that."

"Have you changed your mind? Do you want to keep silent and take all your fears home with you?"

Lacey moaned. "I'm crazy for real. I'll get locked up."

"You're not crazy. Let yourself say what you came to say. How do you feel you pushed things too far with this woman?"

Lacey strained forward and leaned back as though she wanted to stand but was bound to the chair. "Like . . . I followed her. Spied on her."

"All right. What else?"

"I even . . . well, a few times . . . went to her house. Outside it, I mean, like hiding behind the bushes. That's horrible, isn't it?"

"I'm not judging you. What else?"

Lacey stopped shifting position and sat with hunched shoulders. "I started . . . I know this wasn't nice, but I started scaring her."

Natalie's thoughts jounced and high-centered on an obstacle she should have seen long before she hit it. "Scaring her?" she asked, tone matter-of-fact and mind frantic to find out her assumption was wrong. "In what way?"

"Little things, like tapping on her window and running away. Silly stuff. I admired her *so* much—I shouldn't have liked spooking her, but . . . I mean, here was this amazing woman who didn't let anyone push her around, but I could shake her up by tapping on her window!"

Lacey hadn't been Camille's friend. Lacey had been Camille's stalker. That was why Camille had never mentioned Lacey except in the context of the purse—she hadn't known Lacey that well. Natalie had dismissed Camille as overimaginative and overstressed even as her own client had been rapping an SOS on Camille's window.

Natalie used every speck of her training to keep her panicky, guilt-wracked thoughts veiled. Lacey had opened herself in a way that left her excruciatingly vulnerable. If Natalie handled this poorly, the damage to Lacey would be brutal.

Lacey's panic and desperation when she'd stormed the reception desk. Her question to Natalie: *"Is it possible to do something horrible and not remember it?"*

Like commit murder?

You need to end this session now. Tell her you can't continue as her therapist. This is an ethical nightmare. Don't ask more questions. End it.

Lacey shriveled in Natalie's silence. "It's awful, isn't it?"

Don't ask her. Don't ask her. The words boomed in Natalie's head, but her mouth opened anyway: "Lacey . . . you . . . asked if you could do something horrible and not remember it. What horrible thing do you think you did?"

"I don't remember doing anything. But the woman who I was following, she . . . she's dead. Jonas thinks I . . . killed her."

Stop. Don't go on with this. End the session. "Why does he think that?"

"He found my notebook where I wrote about this woman, about all the times I'd stalked her or whatever, all the things I admired about her, the times when I'd scared her. Then he learned that she . . . she'd been murdered. Killed on the night I ran away from him, when I freaked out because he took my notebook. I remember driving past her house that night, but I never stopped or went inside. I don't *think* I stopped. But what if I . . . Could I do something like that and forget it? I know my . . . my mind is a mess."

Natalie felt stuck, kicking in midair, scraping her toes along the impossible rock she'd attempted to scale. *You know what you need to do. Do it. Let go. Get your feet back on the ground.*

"Lacey," she said quietly. "I asked you this question at our first session, but I'm going to repeat it now. Are you worried you might hurt yourself?"

Annoyance overshadowed the anxiety in Lacey's face. "No, I still don't want to do that. I got hurt enough from my family; I'm not doing their work for them."

"I apologize for the repetition. My primary concern is your safety, so I have to ask. Are you worried you might hurt someone else? I'm not asking if Jonas thinks you might have harmed someone. Are *you* worried that when you walk out of here, you might be a danger to anyone?"

"No, I've never worried about that. I don't want to hurt anyone. I guess . . . well, sometimes I imagine hitting someone, or something like that, but I know I'll never do it. That's why it's so weird, but I *was* stalking her, so maybe something happened inside me that I don't know about? But I hate . . . I really hate violence."

"All right. Thank you for your patience and your honesty. I'm so sorry about this, but I can't continue as your therapist. I have a conflict of interest."

Lacey gasped, air screeching down her throat. Her reaction exposed her terrified conclusion: Natalie believed she was a murderer and didn't want a murderer for a client.

Natalie spoke rapidly. "Please listen to me. I'm not assuming anything about your guilt or innocence. Did Jonas tell you he called me when you were gone, after you argued?"

Lacey shook her head.

"He told me he went looking for you at Camille Moretti's," Natalie said. "That's who you're talking about, isn't it? The person you were obsessed with?"

"He *told* you what I wrote in my notebook?"

"No. He didn't say anything about your notebook. He told me you were friends with Camille and that's why he thought you'd gone there."

"He found her body," Lacey whispered.

"He told me." Natalie hesitated, wondering how much detail to give but knowing if she didn't explain, Lacey would keep thinking she'd scared Natalie away.

"I knew Camille." Grief knifed Natalie, as it did every time she referred to Camille in the past tense. "We were close friends, lifelong friends. My connection with her could affect my ability to provide you with the best possible therapy, and I won't take that risk. I want you to get the most effective care."

"You were friends with Camille?"

"Yes. That's not a healthy situation for a therapeutic relationship. I'm so sorry."

"Jonas is protecting me," Lacey said. "I heard him lying to the police for me. He thinks I killed Camille when I was . . . I don't know, in a trance, I guess, or that I blocked it out afterward. Can that happen?"

"What I hear you saying is that it was Jonas's assumption that made you doubt your memory, not your own experience or perceptions. Is that correct?" *Stop. Why are you asking her questions? You just told her you couldn't continue therapy with her.*

"Yes, I guess. I didn't *think* I'd hurt Camille. I never *wanted* to hurt her, and I don't remember hurting her, but . . . Jonas is smart, and I *am* messed up inside. And I did like scaring her."

"That doesn't mean you hurt her." Natalie rose, walked to her desk, and took a business card out of her center drawer. "Tori Hendershot is a fantastic therapist, and I know she'd welcome you as a client." She handed Lacey the card and sat in the chair next to her. "With your permission, I'll call her and arrange for you to transfer to her. In fact, I can call her right now and leave her a message. She'll get back to you today. I recommend that you see her as soon as possible."

Lacey fiddled with the card. "Jonas . . . he didn't want me talking about this to anyone."

"This is about you, not Jonas. What do you want?"

"Are you going to tell the police I was stalking Camille and that Jonas thinks I . . . that it's possible . . . ?"

"No. The only reason I could break confidentiality would be if I thought you or someone else was in danger. Do you think you're in danger?"

"No."

"Do you think anyone else is in danger?"

"I . . . don't think so. I don't know of anyone in danger."

"I know you won't like this suggestion, but I strongly recommend that you contact the police immediately. They're conducting a murder investigation, and you know Jonas is not being honest with them."

Lacey's eyes were frozen blue patches of horror in her frozen white face.

"Will you think about it?" Natalie asked.

"Um . . . yes, I'll think about it." Lacey scanned the bent card in her hand. "Could you . . . wait a little while before you call Tori? I'm not sure I'm ready to start with a stranger. Could I maybe call you in a day or two and tell you my decision?"

"You were very agitated when you came in here this morning," Natalie said. "Do you feel able to make a decision that will be best for you, especially if Jonas objects?"

"I feel a lot calmer now." Lacey gripped the arms of the chair and hoisted herself to her feet. "I'm thinking . . . with all the stuff I wrote in my notebook, I never wrote anything about wanting to commit murder or wanting to hurt Camille. I don't *think* I wrote anything like that. If it were in my subconscious, wouldn't it have shown up in my notebook?"

"That's something Tori will do an excellent job of exploring with you." Natalie kept her tone kind, mentally grappling with the compulsion to sit Lacey down and wring out every trace of information she had about Camille's death. Information Natalie wouldn't be able to pass on to the police anyway.

Lacey took a tentative step toward the door. Natalie rose to follow her.

"I don't think I wrote anything about hurting her," Lacey repeated. "I wish I could read my notes again to be sure I'm not remembering wrong."

"What happened to your notebook?" Natalie asked.

"I don't know," Lacey said. "Jonas won't tell me what he did with it, and he won't give it back."

CHAPTER 19

NATALIE STEPPED OUT OF HER shoes, dropped her purse and jacket on the table in the entryway, and slumped on the living room couch. She needed ibuprofen for her headache, she needed dinner, she needed something hot to drink, she needed a blanket. She needed Camille's voice: *"Gee, Nat, holding court in your Freud chair all day sure takes it out of you. Good thing you don't have a job where you use actual muscles."*

Her own client—now former client—was Camille's stalker, the stalker Natalie had assumed didn't exist. What a train wreck, personally *and* professionally. She shouldn't have talked with Lacey at all today except to tell her she needed to transfer to a different therapist. Jonas's fear that the police would view Lacey as a suspect should have forewarned her that the connection between Lacey and Camille wasn't a simple friendship. But when terrified Lacey had crashed into the office, could Natalie honestly have stuffed Tori's business card in her hand and booted her out the door without even letting her speak? Or worse yet, told Jeanne to call the police on her? She'd consulted with Kirk after Lacey's departure, and he'd agreed that she'd behaved appropriately, so that was some comfort. She'd also spent an extensive amount of time documenting every detail of her interaction with Lacey, knowing a judge's subpoena might land those notes in court and Natalie's interaction with Lacey would be legally dissected.

She closed her eyes and pressed her fingers against her eyelids, trekking through a futile attempt to process what had happened without getting mauled by guilt. *Was* Lacey Camille's killer as well as her stalker? Lacey strangling Camille? Lacey was a tall woman but wispy; in a struggle, Camille could have flung her halfway to Long Island. And Natalie was dubious about the dissociative-amnesia label Jonas had apparently pinned on Lacey's lack of murderous memories. Jonas might be panicking or even gaslighting her, using her alleged guilt to control her.

Whether or not she'd killed Camille, there was nothing Natalie could do about it but try to persuade her to talk to the police and meet with Tori. No matter what she'd done, she needed help. If she'd had the guts to see Natalie against Jonas's wishes, maybe she'd have the guts to see Tori even if Jonas didn't want—

Jonas didn't want her to talk to a therapist? He'd been the one to haul her to Natalie's office in the first place, but now he wanted to keep Lacey away from her. Did he think he was protecting Lacey, that Natalie would betray her to the police? Or was he afraid a professional would prod Lacey to question his accusations—or even question his innocence? Had he "found" Camille's body because he'd killed her? How seriously were the police investigating him?

She stood, shuffled into the kitchen, and opened the fridge. A Ziploc bag filled with leftover pizza awakened thoughts of learning mid-pizza-prep that Camille was dead. She reached for the bag anyway. Shoving it to the back of the fridge wouldn't reduce her grief. She was hungry and tired, and pizza was quick.

Her phone rang. She returned to where she'd left her purse in the entryway and retrieved her phone.

Andrea. Just what she needed. "Hello?"

"Why on earth didn't you tell me about Camille?" Her sister's voice sprayed over her like lukewarm water, sympathetic but not quite warm enough to be comfortable. "I found out from my cleaning lady, for crying out loud!"

"I didn't feel up to talking about it," Natalie said. "I was going to call you later."

"That's such a horrible thing to happen to her," Andrea said. "Do the police know who did it?"

"I don't think so. The news reports haven't said much."

"You must have theories about what happened. Did she have a jealous boyfriend?"

"No. She wasn't dating anyone."

"Why not? She's always had guys chasing her."

"It hadn't even been two years since Dante died. She didn't feel ready."

"That's a long time to wait."

"People mourn in their own ways and at their own pace."

"True. And I can see why she was heartbroken over Dante. He was a prize. Mom always told him if she were thirty years younger and not dying, she'd sweep him away to the Bahamas."

Natalie made a small effort to think of something about that statement that wasn't either creepy or morbid. "He was a charming man."

"And gorgeous!"

"Yes." Natalie chose three small slices of pizza and put them on a plate.

"I can't believe Camille got *murdered*. I know there are scary people everywhere, but you only expect strangers to be victims."

"It's surreal." Natalie set her plate in the microwave.

"Are you okay? You must be freaked out."

"I'm sad, not scared."

"Do you think it was a robbery? Camille had expensive tastes. Did she own a lot of valuable stuff?"

"Some. She only bought what she could afford."

Andrea laughed. "I don't think Dante held back. I saw that pile of diamonds on her hand!"

"I don't know if robbery was involved," Natalie said brusquely.

"I'm sorry," Andrea said. "You must be heartbroken. You two were besties since you were kids. Can I do anything for you?"

"You're sweet to ask, but I don't need anything right now."

"You must be lonely. Do you want to come stay with us for a week or two? Being with family might help you feel better."

"Thank you, but I'm okay." Natalie hoped her voice didn't reveal too much of what she was thinking: *Two weeks of you sounds anything but comforting. I'd rather sleep in the graveyard.*

"Are you sure? Charlotte misses her Aunt Natty."

"I'd love to see her. I'll come by sometime soon."

"Did you see that picture I posted of her? Can you believe that expression on her face?"

"It was darling." Given that Andrea posted multiple pictures of her baby every day, Natalie didn't know which picture she was talking about, but it was safe to assume it was darling.

"Call me if you need anything," Andrea said. "Even if you need money to hire help for a few weeks so you don't have to worry about laundry and stuff."

"Thank you. I appreciate the offer. Thank you for checking on me, but I need to hang up now. I'm exhausted."

"I understand. You poor thing. I hope the police figure out who killed Camille before the murderer goes after someone else—like you. I could hire you a bodyguard."

"Please don't. I doubt we have a serial killer in town."

"But you were her best friend, so the murderer might be worried you know something."

Natalie tapped the microwave controls. "I don't know anything."

"Have the police questioned you? Are you a suspect? I know you'd never hurt her, but family members are always prime suspects, and she was like your sister. Do you need a lawyer? I'll hire one for you."

Could Andrea make it any plainer that she was ravenous for drama—and Natalie's getting arrested would be the most thrilling drama of all? "Thank you, but I'm not a suspect. I'm going to eat dinner now. Say hi to Austin and Charlotte."

"Natalie, you need to let me do something for you. You're going to be adrift without Camille. You and Camille used to talk about taking a European tour. I could send you—"

"Thank you, but I'm too busy to leave anytime soon. I'll keep it in mind though. Talk to you later." Natalie hung up and took her reheated pizza to the table.

Are you a suspect? Andrea's question reminded her of Felicia's accusations. *Selling out*, whatever that meant. *Devouring Gideon from the inside out*—an accusation Gideon apparently believed, or he would have called her back.

She couldn't help Felicia, but Gideon could, and he needed Natalie's side of the story, whether or not he wanted to hear it. She'd ram it into his brain, walk away, and pray that he'd guide his stepmother to the help she needed.

She reached for her phone but changed her mind and kept eating her limp pizza. She wasn't calling or texting him this time, another contact he could ignore. She'd talk to him face-to-face.

The doorbell rang. Natalie wiped her fingers on her napkin and went to answer it.

On the doorstep stood rangy, pale Detective Bartholomew and his older, heavier black companion, Detective Turner.

"Good evening, Dr. Marsh." Turner showed her his badge. "We met at Mrs. Moretti's."

Natalie nodded. "Has there been progress?"

"We're doing our best," Turner said. "If you have a few minutes, we'd like to talk to you."

"Come in." Natalie tried not to let thoughts of Lacey's stalking and Jonas's suspicions escalate her stress. Even though she couldn't say everything she'd like to say, she still wanted to talk to the police to learn everything they knew—or at least everything they were willing to tell her.

The detectives sat on the couch; Natalie sat in her easy chair. Detective Bartholomew opened his briefcase, took out a file folder, and brought it to Natalie.

"We'd like you to look at this," he said in his remarkable bass voice. Fleetingly, Natalie pictured him on stage performing in *The Marriage of Figaro*. "It contains photographs of an envelope we found in Mrs. Moretti's home."

The letter from Dante. Apprehension and eagerness tussled inside Natalie; apprehension prevailed. She wanted to see the letter, but she didn't want to discuss it with the police. *Yes, Dante was my mother's attorney. Yes, my mother despised me.*

Bracing herself, Natalie opened the folder.

The first photograph was of a manila envelope, bulky with what was obviously not merely a sheet or two of paper. Her name was handwritten on the front.

The second picture was of the back of the envelope with the flap opened. Next to it were stacks of cash. Natalie squinted at the image. The top bills on each stack were twenties or fifties. How much money was this? Thousands of dollars?

"This money was in the envelope?" she asked.

"Yes," Turner said.

Natalie scrutinized her name on the envelope. That wasn't Camille's handwriting. "Where in the house did you find this?"

"In a filing cabinet in the office formerly used by Mr. Moretti," Turner said. "At the back of the bottom drawer."

The filing cabinet Camille had finally started searching. She definitely hadn't found *this* envelope.

"Why was there an envelope with your name on it containing $16,040 in cash in the Morettis' filing cabinet?" Turner's firm tone wasn't accusatory, but it sent the message that anything but a full, honest answer would bring consequences Natalie wouldn't enjoy.

"I have absolutely no idea. Camille . . . She told me . . ." Natalie exhaled hard, trying to vent emotion before it shook her voice. "The night she died, as I told Detective Bartholomew, we'd been at a party together. At the party, she told me she'd finally started searching through Dante's old filing cabinet, and she'd found a letter to me. She *wasn't* talking about this envelope. A plain letter, in an envelope from his office stationery. Did you find that in her house?"

"A letter to you from Mr. Moretti?" Turner raised his eyebrows. "We didn't find anything like that. Did she mention where she put it?"

"No."

"Why didn't she bring it to you that night if she knew she'd be seeing you?"

"She thought about it, but she knew I might not be excited to see it. She offered to read it first so she could prepare me for it." Wishing she didn't have to explain this but aware the situation would be incomprehensible if she didn't, she added, "Dante was my mother's lawyer. My mother and I had a falling out, and she wrote me out of her will. I assumed if Dante had written me a letter, it had something to do with that."

"I'm sorry," Turner said. "When did your mother pass away?"

"Two years ago."

"I'm sorry for your loss," Turner said kindly.

"Thank you."

"What was the cause of the estrangement?" Turner's attitude, unyielding but infused with caring, reminded Natalie of her neuropsych professor—a man who'd do everything he could to help you pass but wouldn't hesitate to flunk you if you were lacking.

"My mother was mentally ill," Natalie said. "I urged her to get treatment, which she resented."

"A difficult situation," Turner said. "Regarding this letter from Mr. Moretti, if it was professional correspondence, what was it doing in his home filing cabinet two years after his client's death?"

"I don't know if it was professional correspondence, strictly speaking. I didn't know Dante well—only through Camille—but he was a nice guy. I imagine he felt bad about my mother's decision. Maybe he wrote me a note to say so but didn't deliver it."

"We didn't find it in Mrs. Moretti's house or car," Turner said.

"I suppose she could have shredded it. If she read it and knew it wasn't something I'd want to see, she might have destroyed it."

"Without your permission?"

"She knew me well. She'd be confident in deciding if it was something I'd want to read."

"Mrs. Moretti's wallet was missing from her house, along with her evening bag. I believe she was carrying a fancy evening purse at the Chapman party?"

"Yes, a beautiful, handmade purse." Guilt slapped her at the thought of Lacey. "It's missing?"

"Yes."

"So it was a robbery," Natalie said, feeling marginally less culpable. "A random crime."

"We don't know," Turner said. "According to her sister-in-law, the purse is the only significant thing missing. Her jewelry was still there, cash, small electronics. You say she spoke of the letter while at the party. Could she have had it with her, in that purse?"

"I don't know. It's a small clutch purse; she would have had to fold the envelope to tuck it in there."

Turner pointed to the pictures in Natalie's hands. "Do you recognize the handwriting on that envelope?"

"I know it's not Camille's."

"Our graphologist identified it as Dante Moretti's. Do you have any idea why Mr. Moretti kept an envelope filled with cash and labeled with your name?"

"As I said, I have no idea. I don't even have a ridiculous guess. But I'm sure Camille didn't know about the cash, or she would have told me."

"Did you ever have any business transactions with Mr. Moretti?" Turner asked.

"None. He was my mother's lawyer, not mine."

"He didn't owe you any money?"

"No. I never loaned him money or sold him anything."

"Thank you," Turner said. "If you think of anything that would help us understand this, will you let us know immediately?"

"Of course," Natalie said. "Could you do the same for me? I'd like to understand what's going on."

"We'll let you know what we find out." Turner glanced at Bartholomew, and both men stood. Natalie escorted them to the door and returned to her cold pizza.

She picked an artichoke heart off one slice, not sure she felt like eating anymore. Sixteen thousand dollars stashed away, somehow connected to her? That made no sense. Could Dante have been involved in something illegal? Could his activities be linked to Camille's death?

What about illegal acts linked to Dante's own death? A car-pedestrian accident—what if someone had deliberately run him down?

What if you're cartwheeling into distorted thinking, labeling everything as sinister? Besides, no explanation about smuggling drugs or mob bonuses or bribing judges could explain why Dante had written Natalie's name on the envelope.

Why didn't anything make sense? She poked a curled-up slice of pepperoni and contemplated Jonas and his assumptions, Lacey's stalking behavior, Felicia's loss of control and her wild accusations, Gideon's stonewalling.

Gideon. She'd wanted to talk to him. If she confronted him, maybe she could get a couple of pieces of this jumbled puzzle to fit together.

Natalie lifted her phone and looked up his address.

CHAPTER 20

HE'D CALL THE POLICE. HE'D do it. He'd do it immediately. Tonight. Now. Gideon paced his living room, snapping Legos off the section of the Sydney Opera House he'd repaired until it again looked as though a Lego tornado had demolished the building.

It was Monday evening, and Felicia was still in Manhattan. He'd called her several times. She wouldn't answer her phone, but she'd text back with brief comments like *Stay calm. Everything will be all right. Keep quiet. I'm fine. I'm safe here.*

How in blazes could Felicia expect him to take everything she'd told him, lock it into a virtual safe deposit box, and act like nothing had happened? Ignore his father's murder—if it was murder? Stay silent because an eccentric multimillionaire allegedly had so much control over Ohneka that if Gideon made waves, he'd get murdered? Chapman . . . Camille Moretti . . . Natalie Marsh . . .

Was Natalie that devious, that ruthless? Lying to make Felicia—and her own mother—appear insane? Selling out to Chapman and helping her friend commit murder so Chapman would fund her clinic? Did that even make sense—simultaneously wanting to help people and destroy them? Maybe she'd rationalized that his father deserved to die and the benefits were worth more than his life. Maybe she was power hungry, wanting to rule her mental health kingdom. Maybe she'd despised Gideon and relished Chapman's order that she target him. Felicia had probably told her about Tamara, so she'd know that his track record with women showed him to be a gullible, witless sap.

Or maybe Felicia had conjured all this in a mind misshapen by grief and scarred by secrets.

But Camille hadn't called the police. That was the redwood that had fallen across the road, and he couldn't drive past it. Either she'd called Chapman and he'd sent an assassin, or Felicia was lying about leaving her alive.

Felicia, a murderer? No.

No? Was he certain?

"Call the cops, idiot," he said aloud. "Call the cops. The cops who live in Robert Chapman's pocket."

There goes my last marble. All marbles lost. Dad, time to do the Hamlet thing and appear to tell me what happened.

The doorbell rang, startling Gideon. He hoped the visitor hadn't heard him talking to himself—unless the visitor was the ghost of his father. He put his eye to the peephole. Natalie.

Oh boy. Pretend you're not home. Go back to pacing and muttering to yourself.

Confusion and frustration stealing control of his muscles, Gideon twisted the dead bolt and yanked the door open.

"Hi," he said. "If you're here to destroy my mind and soul, bring it on. At least that will settle things."

Outwardly unfazed, Natalie glanced at his hands, probably checking for weapons, and scanned his face, probably checking for sanity. "I'm not here to destroy anything."

Did she react with such composure because she was already desensitized to her guilt? Or because she was trained to deal with people whose brains had jumped the rails, which Gideon's had?

"Felicia warned me about you," he said recklessly.

"I figured she had. I have no idea why she thinks I'm out to 'devour you,' as she put it. If you have any insights on my scheme, I'd appreciate your sharing them."

Gideon started laughing. It was a nitwit response, but no worse than trying to respond rationally when his brain was completely drained of rationality. And logic. And certainty.

He stepped backward.

Natalie accepted that movement as an invitation; she stepped inside and closed the door. "Do you want to search my purse for weapons?" she asked.

"Not really. But I'm planning to call the police. Tonight."

"You're telling me that now? Rookie mistake. You're supposed to tell me you've already called them. If the villain knows you have secrets you haven't revealed yet, you'll be dead before the end of the chapter."

"Good point."

They surveyed each other in a silence that twisted in two directions inside Gideon: tension and amusement. He cursed himself for how much he wanted to trust her. Or maybe he should trust her. Maybe it was Felicia he shouldn't trust. Maybe he should get the word *maybe* printed on his forehead; it summed him up.

"What are you planning to tell the police?" she asked. "What have I supposedly done, and why is it the business of law enforcement?"

Blunt question time. "Did you help Camille Moretti murder my father?"

"Murder your father!" Natalie finally sounded baffled. "I thought he died in an accident."

"Felicia says Camille sabotaged the ladder. Camille was at MaryLisa's right before he fell."

"Why in the world would Camille want to hurt your father?"

"Because Robert Chapman paid her to do it?"

She teetered slightly as though his words had bumped her. "Why would he want your father dead?"

"Long story."

"You think Camille killed your father? Camille and I?"

His thoughts rotated again, her question applying so much torque that some part of him was going to crack. "I don't know what I think. I'm losing my mind."

"I'll second that."

"Will you sit down?" He pointed toward the couch. "Let's talk."

"Should I keep my hands in sight at all times? No sudden moves?"

Gideon wanted to laugh again but held it back. "Yeah, that works."

Natalie walked toward the couch. She was wearing a long coat with a big drapey collar. He ought to offer to hang it up for her—or check to see if she was hiding a shotgun inside it—but he said nothing as they chose seats on opposite ends of the couch.

Gideon floundered to think of a way to explain. Would he be making a fool of himself, telling her secrets she already knew? *More of a fool of yourself than you already have? Not possible.*

At his hesitation, she spoke first. "I don't know what Felicia told you, but I'll share what I came to say. Saturday evening when I was at her house, after you left, she was behaving strangely. She asked me odd, almost belligerent questions about Camille's ambition and Camille's influence on me. I wanted to get the conversation on a better track, so I urged her to open my gift—the one I tried to bring by the first time we talked."

He nodded.

"It was a poetry book, poetry about animals, illustrated with watercolors. I thought it was perfect for her. It wasn't. She smashed it into the side of my head."

"She *struck* you?"

"Yes. Hard enough to set off brain fireworks." Natalie touched her hair. "You can still feel the lump, if you want evidence, though I can't prove I didn't walk into a lamppost. Then she started making incoherent accusations about how I had sold out and I was playing you, trying to hurt you. I couldn't get her to explain or calm down and didn't have the emotional stamina to handle her, so I took the book and left. And tried contacting you. Several times."

Gideon debated whether or not to feel guilty over not responding. Was Natalie telling the truth about Felicia's attack? He thought of her uncharacteristic aggression in snatching his phone away.

"Your stepmother is in serious need of professional help," Natalie said. "I recommend both a physical and a psychological evaluation. I know some excellent people, if you want suggestions. People who don't sabotage ladders."

"Good to know," Gideon said blankly.

"Could you please explain why Felicia thinks Camille and I killed your father—and why you obviously think she might be right?"

"It's . . . a long story."

"You said that."

"Yeah." Gazing across the room at the wreck of the Sydney Opera House—easier than looking into Natalie's eyes when he couldn't decide whether to feel stupid or wary—he related the things Felicia had told him about Sheryl's death and Chapman's revenge.

"Oh my goodness," Natalie said hoarsely. "Oh, Felicia. This secret has been chewing her up for seven years?"

Gideon evaluated Natalie's anguished expression. "She was afraid to tell anyone. She was sure she'd go to prison."

"Instead, she let it eat her alive." Natalie didn't seem disconcerted by Gideon's stare. He wanted to look away but wouldn't let himself do it; he wanted to see if her compassionate demeanor failed.

"There's nothing suspicious in the fact that Camille paid cash for that purse," Natalie said. "She wasn't covering her footsteps. She'd been setting aside cash, a little at a time, planning to use it to buy herself an indulgent birthday present from her late husband. That gift was the purse. And there's nothing suspicious about the fact that she seemed edgy that day and that she holed up in the restroom. She was having trouble keeping her composure. She hates crying in front of people, and shopping as proxy for Dante—her husband—stirred a lot of grief."

Gideon didn't comment. He didn't know what to say.

"Felicia's entire theory of Bob Chapman's revenge is absurd," Natalie said. "She'd know that if she hadn't let guilt make a wreck of her thinking."

"I don't know the guy, but I hear he's a nut."

"He's brilliant and quirky and stubborn, and if you disappoint him, he won't do business with you again, but he's a good man overall, not a mob boss ordering hits. And he holds people accountable for their *own* mistakes. He doesn't go after their associates. Or family members."

"Felicia thinks differently."

"I've known Felicia for twenty years—longer than you have—and this doesn't sound like her at all. She's ill."

Gideon focused on a few Legos that had fallen to the carpet and thought of clicking them into place, logically assembling pieces until he had a complete, recognizable structure.

"You know there's no hard evidence for anything she told you," Natalie said.

"I noticed. But she was my father's wife. She's a wonderful woman, and I've always respected her. Trusted her."

"So have I. Until two days ago when she hit me and accused me of being the manipulative devil my mother always said I was."

"She's always had common sense." Gideon blistered inside at how insulting to Natalie that sounded but finished making his point anyway. "She's never been a drama queen or a conspiracy theorist. It's hard to dismiss what she's told me when I don't have proof it isn't true."

"I agree that she's always had common sense. I'm also suggesting it's possible for guilt and grief to cause a glitch in normal behavior. You know her behavior isn't rational."

Gideon didn't respond.

"A few days ago, you trusted me enough to want my help with her. Now— with no hard evidence—you're willing to believe I'm so toxic you can't even risk answering my messages. All this because I gave her a poetry book with a cat on the cover?"

The heat of confusion and humiliation inside him could have melted tungsten. What was he supposed to say? *I can't risk trusting you because I was starting to like you. I can't be that degree of idiot again.* "You're Camille's friend," he muttered. "You're linked to Chapman."

"I had absolutely nothing to do with your father's death, and I'm certain Camille didn't either."

"She didn't call the police after Felicia's visit," Gideon said. "That's key. She didn't call."

"If she didn't, it's because she didn't have a chance."

"Or because she called Chapman instead, and he ordered her death."

"Is that what you think happened?"

Silence. The most asphyxiating silence Gideon had ever experienced, permeated with fear that seared his lungs.

"Felicia would never deliberately hurt someone," he said doggedly. "She was already in agony over Sheryl's death. Camille must have called Chapman."

Natalie's keen, grieving gaze made him feel she was discerning his pain and echoing it. "So I'm a conspirator in your father's death."

"Not necessarily. Maybe Camille acted alone and you weren't involved. The cat poetry book was coincidental bad luck."

"So I'm not playing spiteful games with you, trying to mangle your soul."

"Uh . . ." His desire to trust Natalie flipped over, and Tamara's betrayal faced upward, a betrayal he'd been too dense to see coming. He shoved the heels of his hands against his eyes, pushing against the pain that spiked through his skull. "I have no idea. I don't know."

Natalie said nothing, but Gideon's mind filled in what she must be thinking:

"You don't know? You let me into your apartment and didn't check to see if I was armed. You told me everything Felicia told you and all your suspicions. You admitted you haven't given any of this information to the police. Now you're sitting here with your hands over your eyes, all defense systems offline. I think you do know."

That thought hit like he'd dropped something into a cup of superheated water. He sprang to his feet, wanting to yell a protest, but the scalding steam in his brain didn't form words. He stalked away from the couch, into the kitchen, to the front door, past his decimated Lego project, back into the kitchen. With no idea where he wanted to go or what he wanted to do, he looked back at Natalie.

She wasn't watching him. She sat with her eyes closed, head slightly bowed, her face a color that made Gideon unwillingly imagine a cadaver.

Guilt? Or was she grappling with the suspicion—the likelihood—that a woman she'd trusted as a surrogate mother had murdered her best friend?

No. He struck at the conclusion, but it was as useless as trying to punch a hurricane. Felicia's behavior had been uncharacteristic from the moment she'd brought up her theory that his father had been murdered. A healthy Felicia wouldn't have been secretive, obstructive, vague. Not about something critically important. Given the facts, he couldn't take the responsibility of determining what had happened to Camille. That was for the police, maybe for a jury.

Drenched in new grief, he slogged back to his end of the couch and slumped onto the cushions. "I can't call the police without talking to Felicia first. Out of respect for her and for my father."

Natalie looked at him. From the distress in her eyes, he guessed she was deciding whether she wanted to burn in the agony of turning Felicia in or the agony of protecting Camille's murderer. "Do you know if she's home?"

"She's not. She's in Manhattan."

"Why?"

"To get a break. Get away from you and Chapman-ville."

Natalie's eyes closed again. She pulled the shawl-like collar of her coat closed as though the room was chillier than the wool could handle. Gideon wondered how she could be cold; he was sweating.

"I don't think calling her is a good idea," Natalie murmured, sounding exhausted. He ought to recommend that she go home to bed, but part of him didn't dare let her out of his sight until he was certain she wasn't guilty of—

He stared at her coat. An object was slipping out of the pocket, bright and metallic, catching the light. Adrenaline fired, but within a nanosecond, alarm became irritation. *That isn't a gun, you imbecile. It's some glittery, girlish—*

Glittery. Felicia's description. A royal-blue silk mosaic purse, the purse his father's assassin had purchased.

He reached toward Natalie's pocket. Her eyes remained closed, her arms folded.

Carefully, he closed his fingertips on the corner of the item and gave it a discreet tug. More of it slid out of the pocket, enough for him to see miniature mosaic tiles forming a pine tree layered in snow.

Natalie opened her eyes. Gideon yanked the purse all the way out of her pocket and glanced at the winter scenes on either side of it.

"Camille's purse," he said, this curveball discovery slamming even anger out of his head. With composure that felt inhuman—robotic—he rose to his feet and stood in front of Natalie. "I hope you have a fantastic explanation for why your murdered friend's purse is in your coat pocket."

CHAPTER 21

NATALIE COULD HEAR HER OWN breathing and feel air moving into her lungs, but she was still suffocating. Fuzziness spread, dulling her brain, tingling along the sides of her face, prickling her neck and shoulders.

She clawed at the silk lining of her coat pockets. In the right pocket, she found her brown leather gloves; the left was empty. Empty now. She remembered noticing bulk in the pocket when she'd put on the coat and thinking vaguely that there was a hat or rolled scarf in there. She hadn't cared enough to check.

Gideon loomed in front of her, gripping Camille's evening bag. She pressed her hand against the outside of her left pocket, flattening the wool. She wanted to accuse him of pretending to find it on her, but she knew he hadn't. Something *had* been in her pocket earlier, it was gone now, and she'd felt the friction of him grabbing it away.

"I didn't kill Camille or your father." Could Gideon even hear her, or had her voice disappeared into the chasm of suspicion between them? "I have no idea how her purse got in my pocket. The police . . . Detective Turner . . . he said Camille's evening bag was missing from her house." Useless words. Of course the purse would be missing if Natalie had stolen it when she'd murdered Camille.

Felicia had admitted to being at Camille's the night she'd died. Had Felicia killed Camille, taken the purse . . . But when could she have put it in Natalie's pocket? And why would she do that?

"This is the first time I've worn this coat since Camille died," Natalie said, wishing Gideon would speak instead of wordlessly observing her, hoping she'd fumble her way into a confession. She focused on the sparkling purse in his hand, Camille's purse, the purse she'd bragged about while they'd sat on the pier at Beau Lac, the purse she'd been excited to show off to Natalie at Maison du Canard, the purse Lacey Egan had made.

The purse Felicia thought identified the assassin. Camille as an assassin and Natalie as her sidekick; Natalie then killing Camille on Chapman's orders . . .

killing Camille, murdering her closest friend . . . Did Gideon believe that? If she had murdered Camille, why would she carry her purse around? Was it a trophy? Penance? A subconscious desire to get caught?

Hysteria built inside Natalie. She wanted to grab the purse and clutch it to her chest as though Camille's soul were inside and she could summon her like a genie, babbling questions and wishes for the gift of time travel so she could prevent Camille's murder. Gideon could stand and watch her disintegrate, then call the police to haul her to the hospital. Turner and Bartholomew would visit her in the psych unit and ask questions about the purse, about Felicia's accusations, about wads of cash in Dante's filing cabinet, labeled for Natalie—

The cash. The letter. Turner had asked if Camille might have had the letter with her, if it might be in the missing purse.

Natalie managed a coherent sentence. "Open the purse."

"Why?"

"There might be a letter in there to me. Camille said she had one, and the police didn't find it when they searched her house."

"Why would Camille have a letter to you in her purse?"

Explaining would take more patience than she had; she wanted to screech at him to just open it. But she shouldn't ask him to handle the purse more than he already had. If there were fingerprints on it, he'd already smeared some of them.

"Never mind," she said. "I'll call the police." She reached for her own purse where she'd set it on the carpet.

Gideon sprang toward her, sending another slug of adrenaline into Natalie's already-overloaded system. He snatched her purse and jumped back.

Natalie raised her hands and tried to breathe deeply and steadily. "I was reaching for my phone, not a gun. You call the police, then. I don't care who does it. And you're welcome to search my purse."

Gideon set both Natalie's and Camille's purses on the coffee table, opening neither of them.

Natalie lowered her hands to her lap and interlocked her fingers, keeping her hands in plain view. "I have a business card from Detective Turner, the lead detective on the case. But it's in the pocket of my slacks, and I assume you don't want me to reach for it."

"Do you usually carry his card around?" Gideon's voice was low, falsely neutral. Whatever emotions he was feeling, he didn't want to show them.

"He and his partner visited me this evening," Natalie said.

"Why?"

At this point, she didn't care what he knew. At worst, new information could make her sound incrementally guiltier than she already appeared, and what did that matter? "When they were searching Camille's house, they found a manila envelope in her husband's filing cabinet, a cabinet Camille hadn't gone through since his death. The envelope was filled with thousands of dollars in cash and had my name written on it. I have no idea where the money came from or why the envelope had my name on it. It was written in Camille's husband's handwriting. Dante Moretti died about eighteen months ago."

"An envelope of cash."

"Yes."

"This isn't the letter you were asking about."

"No. Please call the police."

Gideon took his phone out of his pocket. "I'm calling Felicia."

Natalie wanted to lie on the couch. Or rest her head on her knees. Or start crying, or throw up on Gideon's carpet. "Even if you think I'm the killer, you know she's not stable right now. She's alone in a hotel five hours away, and you're going to call and warn her that all her secrets are going to the police?"

"She won't do anything rash . . ." Scowling, Gideon lowered his phone. "This is ridiculous. I can't just throw her to the wolves. I owe it to my dad . . . He adored her . . . After Mom died, he was devastated, and Felicia . . . " His expression turned decisive. "I'll go get her, talk to her face-to-face. I'll let her know it's time to report everything."

Natalie felt preternaturally cold, her face chilling the air around her, her linked hands freezing together. "Am I coming with you? And if so, am I riding in the passenger seat or tied up in the trunk so I can't make a break for it?"

Gideon grimaced but didn't answer. She doubted he'd come up with any plan for what to do with suspected-murderer Natalie if he wanted to delay calling the police until he could meet with Felicia.

"One more thing to consider," Natalie said. "You should . . ." She paused, trying to remember what she'd wanted to say. It was difficult to connect and verbalize her thoughts. Something about bribery. Chapman. Controlling the police. "If Felicia's theories are correct, Chapman owns the police or has at least part of the force on his payroll. I doubt there's anything you can say that will persuade her it's a good idea to go to them."

"Yeah, I know."

"Even if she weren't afraid that Chapman is bribing them, she's admitted to breaking and entering and threatening Camille the night she died. When you tell her you're reporting this, she's not going to handle it well. She'll get angry. She may panic. Be careful and be prepared to stay with her until the police arrive."

"I'm not planning to summon the NYPD to her hotel. I'll bring her back—" He stopped.

Natalie didn't urge him to state what she could see in his face: if Felicia didn't cooperate, he had no idea what he'd do.

Gideon sat in the middle of the couch, closer than before. She doubted it was a sign of trust; he wanted to be close enough to tackle her if she pulled a knife.

"Are you okay?" he asked.

The compassion in his voice crashed against her self-control, cracking it. "No," she said, sinking her fingernails into the backs of her hands. Shedding tears in front of Gideon was *not* going to happen. "But neither are you."

"You look bad. Seriously, do I need to call the paramedics?"

"No. I'm calling the police. Now. There's nothing you can do to make this easier for Felicia. If you don't want me touching my purse, bring me my phone."

"Wait." The word was anguished but absent; he was doing last-ditch analysis, not fully listening to her.

She shifted forward on the couch. "Bring me my phone, or I'll get it myself."

He held up a hand. "Take it easy. I'll call." He took his phone out of his pocket. His face was cement-gray; if she appeared as sickly as he did, no wonder he was talking about paramedics.

"You know you might get arrested," he said.

She nodded but didn't let his words sink in. She couldn't think about that or about anything else. One step at a time.

He looked up the number, tapped it into his phone, and switched the setting to speakerphone so Natalie could listen.

A friendly female voice answered the call. "Ohneka Police Department, this is Tasha; how may I help you?"

"This is—" Gideon shifted and held his phone in both hands. "My name is Gideon Radcliffe. I have information about the murder of Camille Moretti."

* * *

"I didn't kill Camille." Lacey punched the air with this statement, no warning, no warm-up. Jonas's full spoon tipped. Butternut squash soup splashed the table.

Lacey couldn't restrain a grin, even though smiling seemed insensitive to Camille. She'd done it. Said plain, stark words that stated plain, stark truth.

"I didn't kill Camille," she repeated. "You think because I was stalking her, I killed her. I heard you lying to the police for me. You don't need to lie. I didn't kill her."

Jonas set his spoon in his bowl and reached across the table to take her hand. "Baby, stay calm."

"I *am* calm. I did drive past her house the night she died, but I didn't stop there. I didn't go inside. I never went inside Camille's house at all, ever. Just her garage." How strange that she could talk about her stalking like it was a normal topic instead of horrible and humiliating. She knew she was blushing, but she didn't feel a frantic compulsion to run away or change the subject.

"I went to see Dr. Marsh today," Lacey added.

"Lacey!" His hand clamped around her wrist. "I told you not to talk to her. I told you not to leave the house."

"I did anyway." Lacey wanted to look him in the eyes but ended up focusing on his jaw instead. *Close enough.*

"What did you tell her?" Jonas asked.

"Everything. That you thought I'd killed a woman and I didn't think I had, but I wasn't sure."

Jonas swore under his breath. "What did she say?"

"She pointed out that it was your suspicion that got me questioning myself. *I* didn't think I killed Camille until I realized you thought so. That's where I got confused."

"You can't be sure what you did. You're messed up."

"I know I am. But I didn't kill her. There's no evidence that I killed her."

"Baby." He released her wrist and intertwined his fingers with hers. "There *is* evidence."

"My notebook? I didn't say anything in there about wanting to hurt Camille." She bit her lip, hoping he'd confirm that.

He didn't. "You were out of your mind the night she died," he said. "You're not responsible for anything you did."

"I wasn't *that* out of it. What evidence is there that I killed her?"

"Honey, we don't want to talk about that. If you've forgotten, I don't want to remind you. It's better if you don't have those pictures in your head."

Uncertainty chiseled at her flimsy self-confidence. "What's the evidence? What if the police—"

"They won't find it. It's safe. You've got to listen to me, let me help you. I know you like Dr. Marsh, and that's great, but now's not the time to see her. You need to cancel any future appointments."

"I don't have any future appointments," Lacey said. "There was a problem today."

Urgency spiked in Jonas's voice. "What problem?"

"I didn't tell her Camille's name, but when I told her about . . . about the stalking, she figured out who I was talking about. She knew Camille. They were friends, so she had to stop the session."

Jonas gripped her hand with both of his, all but crushing it between his palms. "What do you mean stop the session?"

"She said it was a conflict of interest, her knowing Camille. That it wouldn't be right for her to continue as my therapist. But she recommended another therapist, one she said is really good, and she'll contact her for me." Lacey didn't add that she hadn't yet given Dr. Marsh the go-ahead to make the call. It had taken her all afternoon to decide she *did* want to meet with this new psychologist.

"A conflict of interest?" Jonas rubbed her fingers. "You don't realize what she was saying. She was saying that counseling a murder suspect is beyond her scope."

"She didn't say I was a murder suspect."

"Did she say you were innocent?"

"She . . . well . . . we didn't have much time because she had to stop the session early—"

"Because she was scared. That therapist she's referring you to will be a police psychologist. Baby, she's trying to get you to turn yourself in."

A fissure split the decision she thought she'd made. Dr. Marsh *hadn't* said she thought Lacey was innocent. No matter what, she knew Lacey was guilty of stalking and scaring her friend. She wouldn't want Lacey to get away with that. *Was* she trying to trick her into giving herself away? She *had* told Lacey to go to the police.

"I asked you to stay home because I want you to be safe," Jonas said. "See why I was worried?"

"You're the one who made me go see Dr. Marsh in the first place."

"I thought you were stressed out and needed someone to tell you how to feel better. I didn't know you were doing dangerous stuff that could get you locked up."

"I didn't kill Camille!"

"It's okay, baby. I'll take care of you. You'll listen to me now, right? You'll stay away from shrinks and cops, and you'll keep out of sight?"

Lacey wriggled her hand, trying to pull it free. She didn't want to be taken care of for something she hadn't done.

It's my fault. She'd done so many awful things to Camille that no wonder Jonas thought . . .

What evidence did he have? Was it more than the notebook? Should she demand that he tell her? Did she want to know?

It's better that you don't have those pictures in your head. What kind of pictures? Sickening, nightmare pictures.

"Just do what I ask, and you'll be fine." Jonas released her hand and started eating his soup.

Lacey hid her hands under the table so he couldn't grab them again. The evidence must be in her notebook—at least Jonas *thought* it was evidence, but maybe he was reading dangerous things into it out of worry for her. She needed to read it again herself to see if she'd written any violent threats toward Camille. If she'd written awful things she didn't remember—if she'd done awful things she didn't remember—she needed to pay for that. She couldn't murder a woman and hide unpunished.

"Eat your soup," Jonas said. "You need nourishment."

She fumbled to lift her spoon. "I want my notebook back. I told you that before."

"Don't worry about the notebook. The police won't get their hands on it."

"It's mine. I want it back. You don't have the right to keep it from me."

"Baby, you don't need it. Reading all those things about Camille would upset you." He gave her a soothing smile that made her want to claw him. "I'll keep it safe."

CHAPTER 22

NATALIE SHUT HER CAR DOOR and watched Gideon step out of his car, parked a few slots away from hers in the lot at Chapman Development. She hadn't had a chance to talk to him after their visit to the police department last night. When Detective Bartholomew had finished interviewing her and she'd left, she'd seen Gideon's car still in the lot. She hadn't dared call him later to find out how things had gone. She'd known he'd be raw from betraying Felicia's secrets to Detective Turner, she'd had no idea what his current opinion was on her own guilt, and she'd been so drained she hadn't had the energy to do anything except fall asleep.

"Hey." Gideon approached her, a leery, questioning expression on his face. "How did it go last night?"

"I'm not out on bail, in case you're wondering," she said. "They didn't arrest me."

"I didn't think they did."

"Do you think they should have?"

"No."

His decisive response brought a reprise of the relief she'd felt last night when Bartholomew had told her she was free to leave. "Thank you."

"You decided to do lunch here too, huh?" he said.

"Yes. Bob told me he'd invited you. I wondered if you'd come."

"Summoned me is what he did. Through his secretary. Didn't tell me why though."

"I assume you don't think he called you here to shoot you."

"I figured he'd be sneakier about it if murder were his goal. But I wore my Kevlar plaid shirt and tactical Dockers just in case."

They stood facing each other. Gideon had gray circles under his eyes, and Natalie doubted he'd gotten more than an hour or two of sleep last night.

"Have you talked to Felicia?" she asked.

"No, but Detective Turner called me late last night. Felicia's on a psychiatric hold. Apparently, when the police confronted her in her hotel room, she . . . fell apart."

"I'm sorry." Natalie didn't admit she was grateful to hear that Felicia had hit the point where she couldn't conceal her torment and would—Natalie hoped— have to face the reality that she needed help. "I hope this leads to healing for her."

Gideon ground a twig under his heel, spreading bits of bark across the asphalt. "I've never seen Felicia lose it. She's always levelheaded. But Turner said she was screaming about how Chapman controls the town and has a squad of assassins and you're one of them and you killed my father and you killed Camille and you're controlling me, turning me into your zombie serf."

"Zombie serf?"

"Okay, those aren't her words, but that was the idea. Brainwashing me, getting me to do your bidding, including betraying her. It was complete breakdown."

"I'm so sorry."

"I feel like a fool for muddling around instead of getting help for her the instant she started talking about a mysterious woman tampering with Dad's ladder."

"You're not a fool—and you're new in town. The idea of Bob Chapman as a vengeful, evil man wouldn't sound as strange to you as it would to people who know him. And how could you know whether or not Camille and I had dirty secrets? You'd never met her, and you'd barely met me."

"I still should have known better."

"At least you were able to connect with Felicia, and you did your best. I didn't know how to get through to her at all."

"I'm sorry for the way I've treated you. Crazy suspicions. Accusations."

"You have nothing to apologize for. Even when damning evidence was falling out of my pocket, you were never unkind." Natalie had fought all morning against the compulsion to keep checking her pockets and purse to make sure no other evidence had appeared. "Did Felicia say anything about Camille's purse?"

"About if she planted it on you? I don't know. Turner didn't give me that much detail. I don't even know if they're charging her with Camille's murder. It's going to take time to get a rational statement from her. What did Bartholomew say to you about the purse?"

"He asked where the coat had been, who had had access to it, had I noticed any hints of a break-in at my home—which I haven't. I must be high on their list of suspects, but when we're face-to-face, they're always polite . . . and hard to read."

"Yeah, I know what you mean." Gideon trapped a dried leaf under the toe of his shoe and pulverized it. "I need to let my family know about Felicia. My dad's brother and his wife, especially."

"Do they live locally?"

"No. Dallas. It'll have to be a phone call, and I'd better make it today. If they find out through other channels, Dad will return from the dead and murder me. Dad and Uncle Ron were close; they talked often."

"I'm sorry. It's difficult to share bad news."

"Yeah, not my favorite thing to do. Have you talked to Camille's family?"

"Yes, to her mother." The call had been heart-wrenching enough, even without having to break the news. "I'll go see them as soon as they're up for visitors." Natalie beckoned to Gideon and started walking toward the five-story granite and glass office building. "Bob is big on punctuality. We'd better not be late."

"Or he'll send his goons after us?" Gideon joked bleakly. "One broken bone for every etiquette violation?"

"Exactly."

"Why *do* you think he called us here?"

"To ask us about Felicia," Natalie said. "While we talk about her, he'll assess both of us. You don't have anything to worry about."

"Do you?"

"Maybe." She didn't want to mention her concerns about what effect this fiasco would have on her hopes of a Chapman-funded mental health clinic. Gideon was dealing with the personal pain of his father's death and his stepmother's suffering; he didn't need to hear Natalie fretting about the clinic.

When Chapman's invitation had come early this morning, she'd dreaded facing him, but a prework chat with Kirk and Skyler had eased some of her apprehension. She hadn't planned to confide in her colleagues this time, but she hadn't been able to hold an *I'm fine* demeanor with them either, and when Kirk had badgered her, an overflow of tension had gushed through the spillways. She'd told them about Felicia, Gideon, Chapman, and the incriminating purse. To her relief, their response had been incredulity, sympathy, and, on Skyler's part, stupid jokes. They obviously thought she was innocent and assured her Chapman would agree.

Would they have still believed she was innocent if she'd told them about the money from Dante's filing cabinet?

The main doors to the building slid open, and Chapman loped toward them. His white hair flapped in the wind, and he was wearing a flannel shirt, cargo pants, and boots. He looked like a mini lumberjack.

"Ah, *meine schoene Sinn Zauberin.*" He took Natalie's hand and kissed it. Natalie had no idea what he'd called her; this was a new one.

He extended his hand to Gideon. "Mr. Radcliffe, noble designer of roads and bridges. Thank you for bestowing your presence on me."

"No problem." His expression befuddled, Gideon shook Chapman's hand. Natalie had to stop herself from smiling. Even in stressful circumstances, it was entertaining watching someone meet Chapman for the first time.

"Come inside." Chapman led the way into the building, through the reception area, and down a hallway. He stopped in front of a door and pressed his thumb to a control panel. The lock clicked open. He waved Natalie and Gideon inside and closed the door.

The room was so far from what Natalie had expected that she goggled at it. Instead of the modern elegance she'd seen in public areas of the building or in areas she'd visited with Camille, this room resembled a queen's drawing room. Intricate gold-leafed plasterwork decorated the ceiling and walls; swags of lustrous brocade fabric framed the windows. Thousands of diamond-bright prisms dangled from chandeliers. Chapman tromped across the ornate floral rug toward a round table set for three, his outdoorsy clothes even more of a clash with the room than Natalie's sweater, slacks, and fringed linen scarf.

Chapman pulled out a chair for Natalie and waved Gideon to a seat. Given the atmosphere, Natalie would have expected cucumber sandwiches, crumpets, and scones, but instead, the platters in the middle of the table carried the fixings for hamburgers.

"A classic American repast," Chapman said as he sat. "Chosen in honor of my dear late wife, Sheryl, who would have publicly despised it, then crept into the kitchen at the full moon and feasted on the leftovers when no high-income friends were watching. Eat up, children; serve yourselves."

They followed Chapman's example in filling their plates. "I'm sorry about your wife, Mr. Chapman," Gideon said.

"Ah, lad, I appreciate the sympathy, but let's slice to the heart of the matter. I don't hold you responsible for your dear stepmother's prank gone wrong." Chapman scooped baked beans onto his plate. "Detective Turner met with me last night and informed me of the unfortunate event behind Sheryl's fate and your stepmother's certainty that I'd executed a sadistic revenge. I presume that, like Detective Turner, you'd like to know if I ordered a hit on your father?"

Gideon squirted mustard on his burger. "As long as telling me the truth doesn't include killing me because now I'm a threat."

Chapman chuckled. "Mr. Radcliffe, I'm not a mob boss or a drug lord or a supervillain, though if I had to choose one of those careers, I'd take the third option in hopes of wearing outrageous costumes. I'm simply a businessman who's made a lot of money, not a farthing of which have I ever spent on paying someone to harm someone else. Murder jibes with neither my style nor my conscience, and frankly, I haven't an inkling how to hire a hit man. Do I post a job listing describing the qualities desired in an assassin? Is the position generally temporary or is a man in my position expected to have assassins on staff?"

"Uhhh . . . I'd guess on staff," Gideon said. "Unless you don't want to pay benefits, so you use only part-timers."

"Camille Moretti was my full-time employee, but I adamantly did not order her to kill your father. I'm told he died from a fall. I'm sorry for your loss. Deeply sorry. My wife—my current wife, Mel—was a great fan of MaryLisa's and spent so much money there that I felt your father should have placed a brick in his sidewalk with her name engraved on it. Onion rings?" He held out a basket to Gideon.

"Thanks." Gideon took it.

"And I'm deeply sorry that instead of owning up to her ill-fated practical joke, your stepmother let guilt erode her mind until good judgment and even sanity teetered. Random misfortune is now viewed as punishment for her crime, and I am the fist of justice. Is that an accurate analysis, Dr. Marsh?"

"I'm sorry that I never realized what she was hiding," Natalie said instead of answering his question.

"Ah, please, yes, join the game and claim a share of guilt before it's gone. You bear no fault either. *Sind Sie ein Gedankenleserin?*"

"I did finally sign up for an online German course," Natalie said. "But I'm afraid I haven't progressed past *Hallo, meine name ist Natalie.*"

"I asked if you were a mind reader. Are you? You're not. You couldn't have known; your friend was determined to hide her guilt. Let me answer your questions before you ask them: I had no idea Felicia had played a joke on Sheryl that led to her death. I never knew why Sheryl panicked while daintily paddling across the pond, but I didn't meditate over it much because she was prone to overreaction. Perhaps a large insect had buzzed past her face; perhaps she felt a tickle and thought a wasp was crawling down her neck. I tip my hat to Felicia; the stuffed cat was cruel but clever. I love cats myself, but Sheryl had what Dr. Marsh would call a phobia. I have two cats now: Artaxerxes and Beebee the Claw."

"She had no idea the prank would harm Sheryl," Gideon said. "She wanted to embarrass her, not hurt her."

"I'm aware of that, and had she taken up a collection to fund her prank, she would have found a significant number of people slipping cash into her pocket. I'll be candid: dear Sheryl had become a self-centered woman who reveled in making demands, spending money, and flaunting her elegance. More lemonade, Dr. Marsh?"

"Thank you."

Chapman refilled Natalie's glass. "I had become atrociously embarrassing to Sheryl, despite the fact that I had earned the gold that swept her to association with the rich and famous. But I wasn't inclined to divorce her. I've always condemned the trading of older wives for younger women who lack wrinkles and integrity. She was my wife, she was faithful to me, and I prayed she would once again . . . someday . . . appreciate me as she had when we were living on student loans and canned soup. Mr. Radcliffe, lemonade?"

"Please."

"Money is a powerful thing," Chapman said, pouring the lemonade. "I enjoy it, but it didn't bring out Sheryl's better qualities, though she did have many talents and virtues. I don't condone your stepmother's prank, but it doesn't surprise me that Sheryl grated on her nerves. Since secrets are erupting in abundance, I'll continue the theme of confession. There were two reasons I insisted The Chicken Noodle cater the opening of Maison du Canard. First, the food was delightful, and second, I wanted to tweak Sheryl's increasingly high-brow sensibilities. Sadly, I did a poor job of anticipating the reaction of a humiliated caterer."

"Felicia was terrified of what would happen if she confessed," Gideon said.

"Sheryl's death was accidental, and though the legal system would doubtless have held Felicia accountable in some measure, I can't imagine that any legal consequences would have equaled even a millionth part of the guilt she's endured while keeping her secret."

"True," Gideon said.

"I'm a happy man." Chapman added more pickle slices to his burger. "I did love Sheryl, may she rest in peace, but Mel is a delight who indulges me in my eccentricities and couldn't care less if the gossips know I eat Cheetos."

"Felicia also worried you'd blame her for your estrangement from your daughter," Gideon said.

"Ah, yes. I do regret the course of my relationship with Tessa. But we didn't get along well before Sheryl's death. Tessa was perpetually furious that I wouldn't fund all her desires. Without Sheryl to run interference, our relationship went up in flames, as they say, and we went for a time without speaking. But she's maturing, and Mel has been an angel at reaching out to her. I don't blame Felicia for that estrangement. It was a long time coming and had many roots. It was not the result of a stuffed cat in a rowboat and an unfortunate heart condition."

"Thank you for your candor," Gideon said.

"It's your turn to return the candor, son. Do you think your stepmother killed Camille Moretti?"

Gideon took a bite of hamburger and chewed slowly—stalling for time, Natalie figured. She was curious what he would say and hoped it wouldn't be *"Actually, I think Natalie did."*

"I don't know," Gideon said finally. "I'd like to say no, absolutely not, and I would have said that up until two days ago. But she admitted to being there the night Camille died. She thought Camille had murdered my father and was an ongoing danger to me. She's clearly suffering a mental breakdown. I don't know."

"Frau Seelenklempnerin? Your expert opinion?"

"I don't have an expert opinion," Natalie said. "Gideon knows much more about Felicia's state of mind than I do."

"The police asked about you as well." Chapman tipped back in his sculpted mahogany chair. "They were interested in how well I knew you and what I knew about your friendship with Camille. Confess, my dear. Why are the knights of the realm investigating you?"

Natalie tried to answer this painful question matter-of-factly. "Last night, I found Camille's purse in my coat pocket, her evening bag that she carried at your party the night she died. I definitely didn't bring it home from the party with me—I wasn't even wearing that coat. I have no idea how it ended up in my possession."

"Intriguing," Chapman said. "*Eine Dame der Geheimnisse.* A lady of secrets."

"Me or Camille?"

"You tell me." Chapman cut one of the remaining hamburger patties in quarters and stabbed a quarter with his fork so he could eat it plain.

"I didn't kill Camille." She loathed those words. Why did she have to keep saying them?

"Do they have other reasons to suspect you?" Chapman asked.

Natalie hesitated. She'd been hoping he wouldn't ask that question. She was embarrassed enough at her confession about Camille's purse; she didn't want to talk about the envelope of money too. "I don't know what the police would want me to discuss."

"If they didn't forbid you from discussing it, assume you're free to share it—which the expression on your face makes it plain you don't want to do. If it would comfort you, I can summon the captain of the guard to haul Mr. Radcliffe out and chain him in the dungeon where he can't overhear your confession."

"As long as I can take my onion rings with me," Gideon said dryly.

"He doesn't need to step out," Natalie said. "He's aware of the situation."

"Ah. Then this is something less than a secret. If you're concerned about discretion, rest assured that I have the wisdom not to spread your scandals. If you fear damaging my thus-far promising opinion of you, know that you're guaranteed to inflict severe damage by withholding the truth. With full confession, a happy ending is still a possibility."

"I'd feel better if I understood the evidence myself," Natalie said.

"Then allow me to help you interpret it. I assume it has something to do with your finances, since Detective Turner grilled me about your proposed clinic, the monetary backing you seek from me, and if I have ever bestowed any bags of gold upon you."

"The police found an envelope of money with my name on it." Resigned, Natalie told him about the cash Dante had marked for her, the letter Camille had found, and the reasons Natalie had been reluctant to open it. Chapman listened, shrewd concentration in his eyes.

When she finished, he studied Gideon for a moment. Was he checking for any giveaway discomfort in Gideon's face indicating Natalie had lied about something? Gideon didn't speak. Natalie kept her eyes on Chapman.

Chapman redirected his gaze to Natalie. "Ah, *mein Schatz*. My dear. Was your mother your only connection with Dante Moretti? Previous to his marriage to our beloved Camille?"

"Yes, but it wasn't a direct connection. I'd heard my sister mention him, but I didn't meet him until he and Camille were engaged."

"I met him not long before that." Chapman wiped his hands on a cloth napkin and focused on the gold-leafed ceiling. "That was a difficult year for Mr. Moretti."

"A difficult year?" Natalie asked.

"A failed real-estate venture. He had invested a significant amount of money in building some sort of nonsensical cross between a state-of-the-art health club and an amusement park. A key investor withdrew, and there was dishonesty and ugly dealings. Not from Moretti; he was more of a victim. His money disappeared, and the project collapsed."

"I didn't know that," Natalie said. "Though I vaguely remember my sister telling me about the health club."

"I doubt the financial mayhem got much publicity. I know of it because Mr. Moretti came to my company to try to persuade us to take over the project. We declined; we didn't think it feasible, and though I don't like to see a man reduced to bankruptcy, I keep my business and my charitable donations separate."

"This must have been before he married Camille," Natalie said. "I didn't realize he'd had such a rough patch."

"Not long before he married her. He met her in my office when he came to beg for capital. He lost his shirt but gained lovely Camille, which was a superb bargain. Camille was a gem."

"That makes this money with Natalie's name on it even stranger," Gideon said. "If Moretti was in financial straits, why would he hoard a pile of cash at all, let alone mark it for his wife's friend?"

"A weighty question." Chapman's gaze locked onto Natalie. "To which there are nearly zero answers that don't involve unsavory activity. That's not an accusation. It's an evaluation of current evidence."

"I understand. I know it looks suspicious. I have no idea what's going on."

"Let's hope the police are able to solve the puzzle," Chapman said. "I strongly recommend that you do everything possible to aid them, including offering any and all puzzle pieces from your own life."

Reddening at the certainty that both Chapman and Gideon were speculating about what sordid pieces she was hiding, she said, "I have, and I'll continue to offer anything new that I can think of."

Chapman rose to his feet, walked to a smaller side table, and picked up a bakery box. "I like and respect what I know of you, but unfortunately, I haven't known you long enough to invest full trust in you. Again, this is not an accusation. But there are countless good causes, and even I can't fund all of them. I work with people I trust. Prove to me that you're in that category, and we'll do business. Otherwise, my attention will go elsewhere."

"I understand." Natalie's nearly realized dream of the mental health clinic swayed above her, ready to topple and bury her. She had nothing else to say: Chapman didn't want to hear a whiny refrain of "*I don't know what's going on.*" He wanted evidence.

"Mr. Moretti had a reason for sticking sixteen thousand dollars in an envelope and writing your name on it." Chapman set the bakery box on the table and opened it. "If you know the reason, consider the cost you might pay for keeping that secret. Secrets did not go well for Felicia Radcliffe."

"I'm not keeping secrets."

Chapman took a thick chocolate-chip cookie out of the box, placed it on a napkin, and handed it to her. "If you aren't keeping secrets, there's someone in your life who is. It's time to excavate those secrets, *mein Schatz,* before that person destroys you."

CHAPTER 23

As soon as Lacey heard the garage door close behind Jonas's car, she slithered out of bed, crawled to the window, and peeked to make sure he was driving away. She didn't know how long he'd be gone, so she needed to hurry.

After a sleepless night, Lacey had had difficulty focusing on her work, but she'd forced herself to stay with it, diligently placing tiles on a simple undersea design she was making for a friend who wanted an ocean theme in her nursery. Lacey had spoken to Jonas as little as possible, though he'd stayed with her the whole day, sitting on the couch in her workshop, usually working on his computer—he hadn't dared go to his office and leave her alone.

At dinner, she'd felt a swish of relief when he'd told her he needed to go meet with someone and he wanted her to stay home. She'd sworn she wouldn't leave the house and had even urged him to take her car keys. He'd nodded, and she'd thought that was enough until, as they'd been eating mint-chocolate-chip ice cream—another food she was sick of—he'd set a brownish-pink pill on the table next to her glass of milk and told her to swallow it. A sleeping pill, to give her a good night's rest.

Never mind that it was hours until bedtime—it was even early for dinnertime. She knew what he was thinking: he didn't want to leave unless she was too doped up for any mischief.

She'd played along, giving a fake yawn and claiming she did want to go to bed early. She'd put the pill in her mouth and gulped milk. He'd smiled. She'd said she wanted more chocolate syrup and had gone to get it from the fridge so she could turn her back on him and dig out the bitter, gooey pill disintegrating between her cheek and gum. She'd left the slobbery tablet in the fridge, hidden under the pickle jar. She'd clean it up later.

Sweaty under her nightgown, she hurried out of the bedroom and down the stairs. All day, she'd been thinking about her notebook and what Jonas would have done with it. If he'd burned it or shredded it or tossed it into a random

Dumpster like people did on police dramas, he would have said so. He hadn't destroyed it. He wanted to keep it, but he wanted to keep it *from* her.

Why? In case he needed to use it to control her? If she balked at what he ordered her to do, would he threaten to show it to the police? How incriminating *was* her writing? If she had to spend any more time wondering if she'd subconsciously recorded violent thoughts about Camille, she'd end up even nuttier than she was right now. She had to find out exactly what she'd written.

What if she had murdered Camille? Could she ever have peace knowing what she'd done and not owning up to it?

No. If she found proof against herself, she'd call the police. She'd rather get locked up than go the rest of her life carrying a secret so heavy it pressed on her back like a bag filled with scrap glass. Twenty pounds, fifty pounds, a hundred, a thousand. Enough to crush her.

If Jonas wanted to squirrel the notebook away in a spot she'd never search, where would he put it? His safe was an obvious spot, but it would be obvious to the police too. If they ever got a warrant to search the house, they'd force him to open the safe, and they'd be curious about why he'd locked up a flowery notebook like it was diamonds.

If Jonas wanted to keep the notebook from Lacey but also didn't want the police to think it was anything interesting, where would he put it?

The basement. Where Lacey never went. The one time he'd taken her down there to show her it wasn't dangerous, she'd cried and clung to him like a toddler, arms and legs both wrapped around him lest the soles of her shoes touch the floor. He'd never tried again, and Lacey had never even opened the door to the basement. Jonas would be confident he could leave her notebook there and she'd never find it. He could even leave it in plain sight on that cold concrete floor with the drain in the middle or leaning against a wooden wall stud strung with spider webs or in a dark corner with roaches and mouse droppings. He'd know Lacey wouldn't go near it—not if it meant flashing back to the basement where she'd hunkered down as a child, listening to her mother's screams from upstairs; not if it meant remembering the grimy water in the bottom of that open sump pump and her nose nearly touching it as her father had forced her head into the basin, yelling that he'd drown her.

If she wanted the notebook back, she had to go down there, and she had to do it immediately. If she stalled, she'd lose her chance.

Following the plan she'd worked out in her mind, she scuttled to the coat closet. Ignoring the tears already running down her face, she yanked on her snow pants, shoving and bunching her nightgown inside them, then stepped into her boots. She pulled on a knit cap that covered her hair, wrapped a scarf around her mouth and nose, and put on her heavy coat. As the last piece of her armor, she put on her gloves. The winter clothing would shield her, protect her from any dust or spiders or rodents. If she didn't have to touch anything with her skin, maybe it wouldn't even feel like she was in a basement.

She clomped into the kitchen, grabbed her hand lotion off the windowsill and unscrewed the top so she could breathe in the scent of fresh apples. She'd thought the scent was too strong when Jonas had bought it for her, but now she was glad it was powerful, almost headachy powerful. She held it in front of her scarf-covered nose. If she smelled anything through the scarf, it would be apples, not dank basement.

I can't. She stood in the kitchen, pressing the open lotion bottle against the scarf already damp with her tears. She couldn't do this. She'd go climb back in bed, safe.

Safe? Safe without knowing if she was a murderer? Safe with Jonas controlling everything about her, including her memory?

She inhaled a deep breath of apples and took fast, shaking steps toward the basement door. She grabbed the doorknob, twisted it, and wrenched the door open so savagely that the doorknob slammed into the wall. She didn't check to see if the collision had left a dent; if she paused, she'd lose the one shredded scrap of nerve she had. She pawed the wall on either side of the basement stairs, not sure where the light switch was. Her gloved hand touched it; she flicked it on.

Go. Lacey pressed the lotion bottle against her scarf-covered nose and took one heavy, wavering step downward. Another step. Another step. The wooden tread squeaked, and Lacey yelped. She should grab the stair railing to keep herself from falling, but even with thick gloves on, she didn't want to touch anything she didn't have to.

Another step. Sweat rolled down her back. Her nightgown would be soaked before she was done. She'd have to change into a different one. Would Jonas notice? She'd tell him she'd spilled her bedside water glass down her front, and she'd wad this nightgown in the bottom of the hamper in case any basement smell had penetrated her winter clothing and contaminated it.

She stopped on the bottom step and stared at the concrete floor. There was a crack in it, a small crack. Filled with spiders or roaches or maybe blood. Someone might have died down here.

Go. She jumped to the ground, both boots striking at once.

She should have brought a flashlight; the light in here was weak. But a flashlight would let her see *more* details, and she didn't want more details. She wanted only the notebook.

Cardboard boxes labeled in black marker were stacked against one wall. She squinted but couldn't read the labels from here. One step closer to the boxes. Two.

Her legs jiggled, and her heartbeat boomed. What if she stumbled, or fainted? What if her face touched the floor? What if she lay here while cockroaches and spiders—

One more step. Did the floor feel gritty under her boots? Gritty with what?

One more step. She squinted at the boxes. She could almost read the labels. Jonas had square, neat handwriting.

One more step. Something tickled her cheek. Lacey screamed, flailing her arms, but couldn't see anything. It must have been a spider web. Was there a spider on her? She swatted her head, face, and shoulders, trying to knock any creatures away.

A glob of lotion from the open bottle had streaked across the back of her glove and arced across the floor. She needed to clean that up, but the thought of touching the floor made her feel panicky-sick. With the toe of her boot, she smeared the lotion around, hoping the scent would fade before Jonas came down here again.

Three boxes were stacked on top of each other, each labeled "Books." If Jonas didn't want the notebook to look suspicious, a box full of books was a perfect place to hide it.

Lacey's upper body arched backward as she pushed her legs forward. The thought of opening a box in here made her afraid she'd vomit, but she wasn't quitting after getting all the way down here.

So sweaty and hot she felt her clothes were filled with steam, Lacey picked at the edge of the packing tape Jonas had used to seal the top box. Her gloves were too thick to let her grip the edge of the tape.

It's new tape. You can see it's new tape. It's not even dusty. You can touch it. Hurry.

Letting herself whimper, Lacey stowed the lotion bottle in one large coat pocket, hoping it wouldn't spill, and yanked off her right glove. The basement air was clammy against her wet skin, clammy and dirty.

With slippery fingers, she clawed at the tape until she finally caught the edge and ripped the tape off. After putting her glove back on, she opened the flaps of the box.

Her notebook was there, right on top. Lacey grinned behind her soaked scarf. That was easy. Or not easy. Horrible, but she'd done it. She snatched the notebook, pressed the flaps of the box together, and did what she could to stick the now-crumpled tape to the cardboard. If Jonas got close, he'd know she'd been in the box, but at least it wouldn't be flapping open, drawing his attention.

She tucked the notebook in one pocket and reached into the other pocket for her lotion bottle. Inhaling the fake apple scent, she turned away from the book boxes. She wanted to run for the stairs, but her legs were too wobbly. She took a careful step toward the stairs but stopped and wheeled toward the box she'd spotted in her peripheral vision. It was a tall wardrobe box labeled "Lacey." This must be where Jonas put the clothes he confiscated from her closet, telling her they didn't look good on her or they made her look too old or too young or whatever. When she would object, he'd assure her he wasn't getting rid of them; he was putting them in storage in case she wanted them later, which always bugged her because she'd tried to tell him she wanted them *now*.

Was her blue skirt in here? She'd loved that full skirt that swirled and rippled with layers of tulle and silky lining, but Jonas had declared it too childish, too much like a costume.

Forcing her legs to plant her boots firmly against the concrete, she walked toward the box. She didn't dare bring the skirt up to her closet yet, but she wanted to see if it was here. If she'd mustered the guts to come down here once, she could muster the guts to come down here again. Someday—soon—she'd reclaim the skirt, even if Jonas thought it made her look like a fairy godmother.

She opened the flaps of the box and fingered through the hanging clothes. The blue skirt was there, fabric shiny and whimsical even in this dingy basement. Maybe she *should* take it upstairs now. If she stuck it in the back of her closet, Jonas wouldn't notice it for a while.

She started to unhook the hanger from the rod. A scarf folded over the hanger next to it drew her attention. Her new coral scarf with the gold beads! The scarf like Camille's. She hadn't noticed it missing from her closet. Why had Jonas confiscated it? He'd liked this scarf; he'd said it was classy.

Annoyed, Lacey snatched the scarf off the hanger. The silk was wrinkled, with bulges where the fibers had stretched. How had *that* happened? She'd been meticulous with this scarf, handling it tenderly and smoothing it out before hanging it up. Even if Jonas hadn't been that careful in culling it from Lacey's closet, he wouldn't have been so rough that . . . He couldn't have damaged it this severely . . .

Damaged. Stretched, yanked, twisted.

Twisted around Camille's neck? Camille had been strangled.

Twinkles of dizziness filled her head. Had Jonas seen the scarf on Camille's lifeless body and stolen it because he'd thought it was Lacey's—the proof of her crime? Was the scarf, not the notebook, the reason he was so sure she'd killed Camille?

But Camille had a scarf identical to this. The scarf could be hers, not Lacey's. Jonas had made a mistake.

Clutching the scarf, Lacey galloped across the basement, up the stairs, and up the second flight into their bedroom. Sweat trickling into her eyes, she wrenched her closet open and pushed clothes apart until she found the hanger that held her dressy scarves.

The gold-beaded scarf was gone.

Lacey dropped the scarf she'd found in the basement, ripped off her sweaty gloves, hat, and coat, and searched between every item of clothing on the rack, on the floor, behind the shoe rack, on the shelf. In all her drawers. Under the bed.

No second scarf. The only beaded coral scarf here was the scarf that must have strangled Camille.

Lacey's scarf.

* * *

After the door to the waiting room had closed behind her last client of the day, Natalie offered Jeanne a smile that felt more weary than genuine and bent her body forward, trying to stretch stress-tightened back muscles.

"Post-work yoga?" Jeanne asked as Natalie rested her palms on the carpet.

"Sore back," Natalie said, standing straight.

Jeanne rose from her desk. "You look wiped out, hon. You okay?"

"More or less," Natalie said.

"I hope you're taking it easy tonight."

"I'm heading home as soon as I finish a few notes." Natalie didn't add that she wasn't planning to stay home, and even if she did stay home, taking it easy—at least mentally—wasn't a possibility.

Skyler strolled toward the counter. "Me—I'm hoping that when I get home, I'll find a roast beef dinner a generous stranger left on my doorstep. Steaming-hot mashed potatoes. Homemade gravy. Apple pie. With Vicki out of town, my standard of living is not up to par."

Jeanne picked up her purse. "I read in the paper how someone has been sneaking around delivering home-cooked meals to random strangers."

Skyler's eyes bulged. "They have?"

Jeanne snorted. "Stop and grab yourself a burger if you want hot food, sonny. Or cook it yourself." She waved and headed toward the exit. "Have a good night."

"Was that a nice thing to do to me?" Skyler asked. "Get my hopes up?"

Kirk stopped at Jeanne's desk and grabbed a pen to write something on a business card in his hand. "How did it go with Chapman today?" he asked Natalie.

"He was kind," Natalie said. "And blunt."

"The clinic?" Kirk asked.

"Nothing definitive, but if the police don't get some breaks soon . . . Let's just say there's a lot of competition for his financial support."

Kirk gave her an encouraging smile. "The cops will sort it out."

"Did Sir Gideon Radcliffe show up for lunch?" Skyler asked.

"*Sir* Gideon?" Kirk asked.

"Yeah, don't you think his name sounds like it belongs to a British aristocrat?"

"I think it sounds like the Bible guy who blasted down the walls of Jericho with a trombone, or whatever he did."

"You're thinking of Joshua," Natalie said.

"Oh." Kirk removed his glasses and tucked them into his shirt pocket. "Which one is Gideon?"

"Gideon's the one with trumpets and lanterns, whose men spooked an army into panicking and self-destructing," Natalie said.

"I feel for them," Skyler said. "I panicked once when I saw Kirk pick up an accordion."

"Yes, Gideon Radcliffe was there." Natalie pulled the conversation back on course. "Bob made it clear he has only sympathy for Felicia, and he certainly didn't murder Gideon's father."

"I hate to say it, but that's a let-down of an ending," Skyler said. "I was on board for the mob-boss scenario."

"Shut your mouth," Kirk said. "This isn't a joking matter to Natalie."

"It's fine," Natalie said. "I'd rather use humor to deal with it than . . ." She blanked on any other coping mechanisms. "I need to finish up. See you guys tomorrow."

"Take it easy, Nat," Skyler said.

In her office, Natalie finished her client notes. Work done, she straightened her spine, braced her feet flat on the floor, and opened her desk drawer to retrieve her phone.

Andrea had answered the text she'd sent in the few minutes she'd had free before her final client had arrived. *Of course! Come by around eight.*

Natalie set the phone down and evaluated her own emotions. Relief? No, the feeling seared more than soothed. Satisfaction that she was moving forward? Satisfaction plus dread. All afternoon, whenever she'd had a moment, she'd thought about Chapman's words, about who in her circle might know something that could guide her.

Andrea.

She wanted to learn everything Andrea could tell her about Dante and the Marsh family's interaction with him. It would take a while to chisel away Andrea's drama and passive-aggressive gibes to excavate anything helpful—if Andrea knew anything helpful. But even if the content of the conversation was useless, Natalie could check one archeological dig off her list.

She knew Andrea had the wrong idea about why she wanted to visit. Natalie's text had been artfully vague: *Could I stop by tonight? I need your help.* Andrea would automatically think the help she sought was financial. She'd be eager for Natalie's visit, thrilled that Natalie had finally humbled herself and was coming to petition her for a speck of her wealth. Andrea off her guard would be easier to handle than Andrea armed and ready—though this might end up being a conversation Andrea enjoyed, if it included discussing how their mother had lambasted Natalie in Dante's presence.

Natalie picked up her phone. Did she want to update Gideon? When they'd parted after Chapman's lunch, he'd told her he'd keep her updated on Felicia and had urged Natalie to let him know if he could do anything to help her. Did he want to help her—or did he want to keep her under observation, waiting for her to give herself away? Even though he knew Felicia's accusations weren't rational, that didn't mean Natalie was trustworthy; she might be guilty of shady dealings with Dante.

He'd be more likely to trust her if she showed she trusted him. Natalie texted him: *I'm visiting my sister this evening to ask what she knows about Dante.*

Natalie slid her phone into her purse, packed up her things, and walked into the cool evening air. The sky was clear, and the night sky would be cloudless and star-filled. Less than a week ago, she'd sat on the pier with Camille, stargazing and listening to Camille's worries about a stalker.

Don't. Natalie walked faster and climbed into her car. She couldn't bring Camille back to life. The only thing she could do was seek justice for her—and freedom from suspicion for herself.

Natalie's house appeared grim and deserted in the twilight as she steered into her driveway. The days were getting shorter. She should put the lights on timers so both the interior and exterior of the house were illuminated when she got home.

She'd never worried about that before.

She pulled into the garage and hurried toward the door that led to the house. She tapped the button on the wall to close the garage door, but the door lowered only partway before the motor stopped and reversed.

She pivoted to see what had shifted into the path of the door. A man in a blue jacket was standing at the threshold, one leg planted forward far enough to trigger the electric eye.

Jonas Egan.

She grabbed the doorknob that led to the house, but it didn't turn; she'd forgotten she'd started locking this door after Camille's death. She shoved her hand into her purse, reaching for the keys she'd already stashed there.

"Wait," Jonas said. He hadn't moved farther into the garage.

Keys now in hand, Natalie eyed him, her apprehension dropping a little. "What are you doing here?"

"I want to talk to you."

"This isn't the place or the way." She didn't ask how he'd learned her address. It was unlisted, but she doubted a savvy snoop would have trouble locating it. He might even have followed her from work.

"It's the only place I can talk to you, since you kicked my wife out of your office," he said.

Since Jonas was keeping his distance, Natalie held off on rushing into the house. "I'm not free to discuss anything related to my interaction with clients, but please know I would never terminate therapy without ensuring that a client has access to the help he or she needs."

"You ditched her because you're scared of her."

"That's not true. You need to leave now. Tracking me to my home is inappropriate."

"I'm not your client. You have no authority to tell me what's inappropriate."

"You're trespassing. I'll have the police tell you what's inappropriate if you don't get out of my garage."

"You'd better not be playing games with Lacey. Did you ditch her so she's not your client and you're free to blab everything about her to the cops?"

"Any professional interaction I've had with clients, whether current or former, remains confidential."

"You'd better not betray her." Jonas still hadn't moved toward her, and his voice wasn't louder, but it was harsher. "If you say one word to the cops, I'll sue you for so much money you'll be broke for the rest of your life."

"Mr. Egan, let me tell you what's *not* confidential: you tracking me here and confronting me in a way meant to intimidate me. I understand you're worried about your wife, but aggression and hostility won't help her."

Jonas lifted a foot and brought it forward, then drew it backward as though deciding whether or not to advance. "What did she say to you about the woman who died?"

"I can't confirm I've even spoken with your wife. If I have, anything we discussed is confidential. Think about what you're asking. You threatened to sue me if I violate confidentiality, and now you're asking me to violate confidentiality."

"I'm her husband!" He took the step forward. "I'm trying to take care of her. That's different."

Natalie shoved her key into the lock. "It's not different."

"If you messed with her mind, you won't get away with it. She said you claimed Camille Moretti was a friend of yours. Is that true?"

"You need to leave." Natalie twisted the key. "Now."

"If you think you can play—"

Footsteps thumped on the driveway. Jonas spun around.

"Hey." Gideon strode toward the garage, a grocery bag in his hand. "Sorry, didn't mean to interrupt. I have something to drop off for Natalie." He stopped next to Jonas and held out his hand.

"Gideon Radcliffe." Even from several yards away, Natalie could see his smile was as soft as a steel beam bent into a curve. "Who are you?"

Jonas ignored him. "If you hurt her in any way, you'll answer to me," he said to Natalie. He stalked toward the street. Gideon stayed at the front of the garage, watching him retreat. Not until Jonas had driven away did Gideon face Natalie.

"Thank you," she said. "Good timing."

Gideon walked into the garage. He was wearing running shorts, a sweaty T-shirt, and Nikes. "I was out for a run when I got your text. I decided to stop by to bring you this." He opened the grocery sack and removed a bag of chocolate-covered blueberries. "For the drive to your sister's house."

"That's very thoughtful." She took the candy. "Thank you."

"Full disclosure," he said. "I was on the other side of the street when you got home, and I saw that guy pull over and head toward you. He didn't look friendly, so I went ninja and approached from the side so he wouldn't see me. I overheard a chunk of your conversation, overheard it on purpose, I mean. Eavesdropped. I hope that doesn't offend you. If it does, I apologize."

"It doesn't offend me. I'm glad you showed up, because I was ready to bolt into the house and call 911."

"Is that Jonas Egan? The guy who found Camille's body?"

"Yes." For an instant, Natalie was bewildered that he could identify Jonas, then realized he'd been named in the news reports—and Natalie had addressed him by name during their conversation.

"I'm not going to ask you what his deal is," Gideon said. "I picked up enough to understand that it's a complicated situation for you. But there are no complications for me, so heads up: I'm calling our cop friends and telling them I saw Jonas Egan show up at your house and he was angry and aggressive. So, yeah, I'm confessing to snooping, *and* I'm confessing in advance for interfering, but your friend is dead, and my stepmother has a possible murder charge hanging over her, and I just witnessed a guy with connections to the case getting hostile with you. I'm not keeping my mouth shut."

"I understand." Natalie restrained the impulse to add a heartfelt *thank you*. She'd known she needed to report Jonas's behavior but was glad to have Gideon start the process without her having to pick through an ethical snarl. "Would you like to come in?"

Gideon grinned and tugged the hem of his damp shirt. "You don't want me inside your house right now. They almost evacuated the grocery store when I showed up. But if you're worried that guy might come back, I'll lurk in your garage."

"Thank you," she said. "No, he won't come back tonight. He said what he had to say."

"What time do you leave for your sister's place?"

"In about an hour."

"Good luck," Gideon said. "I hope it's helpful."

"It'll be excruciating," Natalie said. "But as long as it's helpful, too, I can cope with it. I'll call you tomorrow and report."

"Sounds good. Talk to you then."

Natalie watched him jog away, belatedly pondering the words she'd spoken. Why had she promised to report on the meeting?

Because Gideon was an ally. Because she trusted him.

Because she ached to have him trust her.

CHAPTER 24

"How are you doing?" Andrea swooped through her doorway and embraced Natalie on the front porch as though unable to wait until Natalie had entered the house. Natalie hugged her back, debating if she wanted to hope that Andrea's fervor indicated sincere sympathy. No. Natalie had nailed together too many rickety hopes already; she wasn't in the mood to fantasize about an improved relationship with her sister.

Andrea released her. "Come in. Austin is putting Charlotte to bed, so we have privacy." She escorted Natalie to the living room and offered her a platter holding miniature lemon tarts. "These are delicious. Try one."

"Thank you." Natalie took a tart.

Andrea didn't take one. She sat on the couch next to Natalie. "New bakery in town. Outrageous prices but worth it. Have the police learned anything about Camille's death?"

"Not that I know of."

"You must be so lonely in Ohneka now. Come to Birch Falls. We'll help you find an affordable place. I'm sure there are nutcases here who could use your services." She smoothed her highlighted hair behind both ears, a gesture meant to show off new earrings—gold hoops paved with rubies.

Natalie neither complimented the earrings nor took the bait of Andrea's crass remark about "nutcases." "I have no plans to move at this time. How are Austin and Charlotte?"

"Very well, thank you! Motherhood gets so crazy sometimes, and my house ends up a wreck—it took the cleaning service four hours yesterday, and there were three of them! But I love being home with Charlotte, and with Lindy coming in to nanny a few hours each day, that gives me a breather. Austin is jealous, stuck at his office."

"I'm glad you're enjoying it. Charlotte is a sweetheart. I'm sorry I missed seeing her."

"You'll have to come before her bedtime next time. I thought about keeping her up late for you, but I didn't know how stressed you'd be and didn't want her picking up on your stress and being cranky." Andrea rested her hand on Natalie's arm. "What can I do for you? Is it student loans? I know you're buried in them."

"I'm not buried."

"I'm happy to help. I can send you home with a check tonight. Not for all of it, of course, but we can get started."

"I didn't come to ask you for money. I came to ask you about Dante Moretti."

Andrea frowned and drew her hand away. "Why do you think I'd know anything about him?"

"You were living with Mom at the time he was working with her on her will. You accompanied her to her meetings with him. You gave me extensive descriptions of how handsome and witty he was."

"You're single! I would have introduced you, but Mom didn't want you around. If I hadn't been engaged to Austin, I would have been interested myself. I had no idea he was dating Camille. Why would you ask me about him? You knew him yourself after he married her."

"I didn't know him very well even then. I'm interested in your impressions of him at the time he was serving as Mom's lawyer."

"Oh, Natalie." Andrea patted Natalie's shoulder, then reached to take a lemon tart. "He didn't persuade her to cut you out of the will. You know that. It was all her."

"Let me explain why I'm asking. The night she died, Camille told me she'd started to clean out Dante's old filing cabinet. She found a letter addressed to me. She was going to give it to me but died before she could."

A chunk of crust and lemon curd broke off the tart in Andrea's hand and landed on her blouse. She set the broken tart on the coffee table and grabbed a napkin. "A letter addressed to you?"

"Yes. The envelope was work stationery."

Andrea scrubbed at the stain on her shirt, though clearly a napkin wasn't going to expunge the stickiness. "Did you hire him as your lawyer for something? I didn't think you could afford him."

"I never had a business connection with him."

Andrea took another napkin and wiped each manicured nail. "Isn't the letter still in Camille's house?"

"No. The police couldn't find it."

Andrea plucked a crumb off the couch. "It must have been trash, then. Camille realized what it was and threw it away."

"Trash?"

"Junk mail. Like a fund-raising request for whatever charity he supported."

"Why would Dante have kept a fund-raising letter for me in his filing cabinet instead of delivering it? Why would he approach me for fund-raising at all?"

"Because you're Camille's friend. He probably sent letters to all their associates but stashed yours there and forgot to give it to you, or realized you didn't have money to donate. Why are you obsessing about a letter? What does it matter what it said? He's dead."

"Among the contents of his filing cabinet, in a drawer Camille hadn't sorted, the police found something else with my name written on it in Dante's handwriting. A manila envelope containing over sixteen thousand dollars in cash."

"Sixteen thousand dollars!"

Natalie had expected this news to shock Andrea but not to the point that she looked like she'd stepped on a downed power line. "Yes."

"You're making this up."

She hadn't expected to be called a liar either. "Why would I make it up?"

"To make yourself feel special? To feed some guilty fantasy about your friend's husband?" Andrea's tone was so caustic that it sounded to Natalie like lousy acting more than genuine derision.

"I'm telling you what the police told me," Natalie said. "I can give you the detective's number if you'd like to speak with him. Do you have any idea why Mom's lawyer would have a stack of cash labeled for me?"

"How would I know? Maybe he was crazy. You're the shrink; you tell me. Some kind of money psychosis."

"Money psychosis? I don't think so." Natalie scrutinized Andrea. Her cheeks had turned blood-crimson. "Why does this upset you so much?"

"I'm not upset. I'm irritated that you're asking ridiculous questions. The money must have been from Camille. She felt bad that you were hurting for cash and Mom cut you out, so she was saving it for you. A surprise."

"It wasn't from Camille. It was Dante's handwriting, and Camille wouldn't plan some over-the-top pity donation when she knew I was fine financially."

"Maybe Dante would though." Andrea took another lemon tart but didn't eat it. "You said you didn't know him very well."

"And he didn't know me very well. I'm asking you to brainstorm with me. Let's go back to your interaction with him. You were there when Mom discussed her will."

"What does that have to do with it? I thought you wanted my help, not to waste my evening."

"I do want your help. Think about those discussions. My name must have come up. What was Dante's reaction when it did? Did he ever say anything about me?"

"I don't remember any reaction at all. Do you hope he had a crush on you? Now that Camille's dead, do you want to dream Dante loved you, not her?"

"If you're concerned about wasting time, stop making accusations you know aren't true," Natalie said.

"I don't know what you want." Andrea slapped the now-cracked tart onto a napkin and wiped her palm. "How would I know anything about secret money?"

"Did you know Dante was having financial struggles at the time Mom was writing her will?"

"No. How would I know his business?"

"I thought you might have heard rumors."

"I didn't. Why would I care?"

Why was Andrea so defensive? So much for thinking she might relish talking about Dante and the will. "I'm sorry this topic is bothering you, but it's important. Can you please think back and try to remember if Dante ever said or did anything that might hint at why—"

"He *didn't*. Why would he? Why would we have discussed you? Mom had already made up her mind, and it took her three seconds to say 'My other daughter isn't an heir.' Can't you deal with that yet?"

The more insulting Andrea got, the more interested Natalie got. Andrea was being deliberately vicious, working to make the subject so hurtful that Natalie would drop it.

"Do you know if there were other lawyers in the firm who were close to Dante—colleagues he might have confided in?" Natalie asked.

"How would I know?"

"Are you afraid the sixteen thousand dollars was from Mom? That she entrusted it to Dante to give to me later?"

Andrea leaped to her feet, dropping the marred tart on her immaculate carpet. "Why would I care? That's a few pennies compared to what she gave me."

"If you didn't care, you'd rationally explore this with me, not get angry and rude. Is being 99.999 percent the winner not enough for you?"

"Don't you *dare* analyze me."

"I'm not—"

"She didn't leave you *anything*. She despised you. She would have burned every dollar she owned before she'd have given it to you. I'm done with this visit. I didn't invite you here so you could make up fairy-tales about money stashes."

Natalie didn't react. Andrea bent and clawed crushed pastry bits into a napkin. Sweat circles were forming under the arms of her silk blouse.

"What's wrong, Andrea?" Natalie asked softly. "*Did* Mom say something about a gift for me? Did you talk her out of it—or think you had?"

"I said I'm *done*!" Andrea shrieked. "Get out before I scream for Austin."

"Fine." Natalie stood. "I'll find other ways to pursue this. Call me if you decide to explain why it upsets you so much. Or if you don't want to share it with me, share it with the police. They're curious about the money. I'll suggest they contact you." She picked up her purse and strode out of Andrea's elegant house.

CHAPTER 25

NATALIE FELT TOO EMOTIONALLY RUMPLED for smooth hair, a tweed pencil skirt, and a sleek red sweater, but showing up to work in a hoodie and pajama pants with her hair in a sloppy ponytail wouldn't elicit much confidence from her clients. She had a responsibility to look competent and professional, and she *would* achieve that no matter what emotions stormed inside her.

She'd deliberately arrived early so she could hide in her office before any of her colleagues arrived, and now, instead of being productive, she sat slumped in her chair, reviewing things she wished she'd never had to think about in the first place.

Had the police talked to Jonas yet in response to Gideon's report? If Jonas—or Lacey—was clearly guilty and the money in Dante's filing cabinet had nothing to do with Camille's murder, would the police continue to investigate the money and Natalie's connection to it? She had no idea. A hoard of cash was odd, but if they couldn't link it to a crime, they'd probably turn to more important cases.

Whether or not they wanted answers, Natalie did, no matter how much Andrea didn't want her to find them. She had no idea if Andrea's over-the-top reaction indicated anything besides her desperate need to make sure everyone—especially Natalie—knew she'd been so favored that every cent of the family wealth had gone to her. Regardless, today Natalie would mention her conversation with Andrea to the police. It wouldn't be wise to abandon the possibility that Andrea knew something until Turner and Bartholomew had investigated her.

Granted, the cost of notifying the police would be Andrea haranguing her for the next decade for being so spiteful and jealous that she'd called the police on her own sister. *Fine. Send me that bill.*

Natalie had never told Andrea about the birthday gift their mother had sent a few months before her death. She assumed Andrea didn't know—if she'd known, she would have done her best to taint the gift, maybe by claiming Mom had been doped up on painkillers when she'd sent it and didn't know what she was doing or that she'd gloated about unloading old soap flowers on Natalie because Natalie didn't deserve anything of value.

But their mother had known Natalie loved the intricate soaps she'd carved. There must have been *some* affection when she'd decided to send them, some desire for connection.

Could that money in Dante's filing cabinet have been from her mother? A trace of acknowledgment, a farewell wisp of affection for Natalie, something her mother had arranged with Dante independent of her official will? Could it be money she had wanted presented to Natalie several years down the road, maybe on a significant birthday or as a wedding gift?

If so, why an unconventional, secret approach with no backup plan—resulting in the money remaining undelivered in Dante's filing cabinet? Had their mother been attempting to avoid conflict with Andrea?

How domineering had Andrea been in those last months of their mother's life? Roxanne had always been able to stand up for herself, but how much had cancer weakened her willpower? Had Andrea achieved such control over her at the end that Roxanne had taken a roundabout path to leaving a gift for Natalie, skirting Andrea's pressure and manipulation?

If she wanted to talk to someone who'd witnessed the dynamics between Andrea and their mother near the end of her life, she should talk to Skyler.

The only time they'd talked about Roxanne was the first time they'd met, when he'd come to the office to discuss the possibility of joining the practice. Since Andrea had told him about the opening and recommended him, he'd known Natalie and Andrea were sisters. Natalie had told him her mother had appreciated his skill and had praised him abundantly—not mentioning that she knew her mother's opinion only through Andrea since Roxanne wouldn't speak to her. Skyler had smiled and commented on Roxanne's strength and grit without revealing if he knew anything of their estrangement. They'd never brought up the topic again. Natalie hadn't wanted to discuss it; she'd figured anything Skyler could tell her would involve bitter humiliation.

She was willing to risk humiliation now if there was a chance of getting information that could help her figure out Andrea's attitude. Was Skyler at the office this morning, or was he at the physical therapy center? If he wasn't here yet, she'd check with Jeanne to find out today's schedule.

She located him in the break room, toasting a bagel.

"'Morning, Nat," he said. "You doing okay?"

"Yes." Natalie came to stand next to him so she wouldn't broadcast her question to the entire office. "Do you remember my sister, Andrea? She always brought my mother to her PT appointments."

"Sure do."

"I had a . . . somewhat incomprehensible argument with her last night, and it relates to my mother. I understand you can't give me any medical information, but that's not what I want. I want to know what you thought of Andrea and my mother, the interaction between them. Anything you can tell me."

Skyler peeled open a packet of cream cheese. "What was your argument about?"

"Good morning, folks." Kirk strolled through the doorway. "Where's the coconut bread, Hudson? Vicki's famous coconut bread. You swore you'd bring it today."

"Yeah, oops. I was going to pick some up from her apartment last night, but I forgot again. I'll bring it tomorrow, all right?"

"Great. I'll starve to death." Kirk set his oversized coffee mug on the table. "That bread was my breakfast. Are you going to share that bagel?"

"Not a chance." Skyler plucked it out of the toaster.

Jeanne wandered into the room. "What smells so good?"

"A bagel he won't share." Kirk settled into a chair and started scrolling down his phone.

"Top-of-the-line blueberry." Skyler smeared cream cheese on the bagel. "Get your lazy carcasses to the bakery and buy your own."

Natalie took an apple from the basket on the counter to make it appear she'd had a reason for standing shoulder-to-shoulder with Skyler. She'd have to corner him later. This wasn't a conversation she wanted to have in front of anyone else, even Kirk and Jeanne.

Skyler sandwiched the bagel halves together, caught Natalie's eye, and started toward the door, holding his breakfast in a napkin. She followed.

In the hallway, he said quietly, "I'm thinking this isn't a workplace conversation. I can call you later, or you know what? Face-to-face would be better. What's your schedule tonight?"

"I'm flexible."

"Would it work if I drop by your house? I'm not sure if I know anything that would help you understand whatever Andrea's up to, but I'll tell you whatever I can."

"I'd appreciate that. What time?"

"Eight?"

"Fine."

"Text me your address." He took a bite of his bagel and headed back into the break room. Hoping he wouldn't mention her question to Kirk and Jeanne, Natalie headed back to her office.

Her cell phone was buzzing on her desk. She picked it up. "Hello, this is Natalie."

"Dr. Marsh, this is Abe Bartholomew from the Ohneka Police. We have a few questions for you. Would you be able to stop by the police department some-time today?"

Partly desperate for an update and partly afraid this meant they were closer to arresting her, she said, "I could come either on my lunch hour or after work." At least this would be a good opportunity to discuss Andrea.

"Let's go for the lunch hour. What time?"

"I could be there at a quarter past one."

"See you then. Thanks for your help."

"You're welcome." Natalie hung up and stashed her phone in her desk. She hoped Jeanne wouldn't have to notify her afternoon clients that their appointments were canceled because their therapist was in jail. *That* wouldn't help anybody's progress. *You can trust me. Yes, I'm a felon in my spare time, but let's talk about you.*

At lunchtime, Natalie pulled out the sandwich she'd planned to eat quickly before leaving for her interview, then stowed it back in the fridge, not wanting to combine a ham sandwich with a nervous stomach. She'd eat after the interview. If she was feeling better then. If she wasn't behind bars.

Bartholomew met her in the lobby of the police department. "Good after-noon," he said. "How are you doing?"

"I haven't figured that out," she said.

"Understandable." He led her to the same comfortable room where he'd talked to her the other night when she'd come with Gideon. Pale green walls, padded chairs, an oak table, the smell of new carpet.

"Have a seat," he said. "To get the formalities out of the way, you're not being detained. You're free to leave at any time."

"Thank you." How had her life become so screwy that the message that evoked the most positive emotions was "We're not arresting you yet"?

"Dr. Marsh. May I call you Natalie?"

"Of course. We've been friends long enough to use first names."

He grinned and passed Natalie a chilled water bottle. He opened two plastic containers and set them in the middle of the table: one contained grape clusters, strawberries, and pineapple chunks; the other contained cubes of cheese and different types of crackers.

"I haven't eaten lunch, and I'm guessing you haven't either." He sat on the opposite side of the table. "Feel free to help yourself while we talk."

"Are you sure you're doing this right?" Natalie asked. "I thought the bad-cop part was supposed to come first."

"Yeah, usually, but Turner's busy right now."

Natalie laughed. Turner had never been remotely bad-cop either.

"Gideon Radcliffe called us," Bartholomew said. "He reported witnessing Jonas Egan coming to your house and speaking to you in a threatening way."

"His manner was aggressive, but he neither touched me nor verbally threatened my safety."

"Mr. Radcliffe said he warned you not to betray his wife's confidence or play games with her. He said there seemed to be a professional relationship between you and Mrs. Egan."

"I can't confirm that."

"Understood. Mr. Radcliffe also said Egan asked if it was true that you were friends with Camille Moretti."

"Yes, he asked me that, but I didn't give him any information about our friendship."

"We spoke to Mr. Egan this morning," Bartholomew said. "He told us Lacey was a client of yours and you'd been treating her for anxiety."

"I can't confirm that."

"Understood. We didn't speak to Mrs. Egan directly; Mr. Egan said she was ill."

Natalie wasn't surprised Jonas had prevented Lacey from speaking with the police. He would want to filter Lacey's information to keep her from incriminating herself . . . or incriminating him. That strategy wouldn't last. Eventually, the police would demand to speak directly with Lacey.

"Mr. Egan insisted he wasn't threatening you," Bartholomew said. "He simply wanted to ensure that you behaved in a professional manner regarding your interaction with his wife."

"His demeanor was intimidating, as was the fact that he showed up at my unlisted address, but he kept his distance. His only direct threat was to sue me."

Bartholomew slid the food closer to Natalie. She took a cube of cheddar and a sesame cracker.

"Are you free to give me an update on the investigation?" she asked.

"Neither of the Egans is under arrest. The investigation into Mrs. Moretti's death is ongoing. That's all I've got for you right now."

"Thank you." She didn't ask how serious of a suspect either of the Egans was; Bartholomew wouldn't hand her that information. She swallowed a final bite of sesame cracker and picked up another one, mulling over how best to bring up Andrea. She didn't want Bartholomew to think she was being vindictive or ridiculous, urging the police to get involved in a spat between sisters.

Bartholomew waited until she'd finished the second cracker before he spoke again. "Natalie, as you know, we found an envelope in Dante Moretti's filing cabinet that contained a large amount of cash and was labeled with your name. In trying to discover the significance of the money, we got a warrant to examine Mr. Moretti's bank records."

Perspiration dripped down Natalie's spine. How did people ever pass polygraph tests? She hadn't committed any crimes, but she still had wet hands and a racing heartbeat. "Did you learn anything?"

"Starting a little less than two years ago, over the course of several months, there were eight deposits made into Mr. Moretti's account, each for twenty-five thousand dollars. We traced the deposits. The checks came from a bank account belonging to Andrea Marsh, now Andrea Collier."

"From Andrea!" Natalie gripped her water bottle, cooling her sweaty palm. Never mind figuring out how to start a discussion of Andrea—Bartholomew had that covered.

"Do you have any idea why your sister would have paid Mr. Moretti two hundred thousand dollars?" he asked.

"As I told you before, Dante was my mother's lawyer. Andrea was taking care of Mom at the end of her life but would have paid bills from a separate account. And I can't imagine Dante did two hundred thousand dollars' worth of legal work for my mother."

"This money was deposited into Mr. Moretti's personal account, not his business account."

Mystified, Natalie tried to think why Andrea would have paid Dante for something non-work-related. Had she bought a luxury car from him? Or a boat? If she had, why hadn't she bragged about it to Natalie?

"I have no idea why she paid him so much money," Natalie said. "But last night, I visited her to see if she knew anything about the cash you found in Dante's filing cabinet. She claimed she didn't but had a disproportionately angry—almost hysterical—reaction to my questions. When I tried to find out why the topic upset her so much, she threw me out."

"That's interesting." Bartholomew popped a grape off the stem. "We talked to her this morning and asked her about the deposits to Mr. Moretti's account. She told us she'd paid the money to protect you."

"Me! Protect me from *what*?"

"Your mother had told you she was excluding you from her will, which was going to cost you a couple million dollars."

"That's old news. What does it have to do with protecting me?"

"Naturally you were upset about getting disinherited. You started coping by using prescription drugs. Using, then abusing."

"She told you *what*? I have no idea what she's talking about. I've never had a drug problem."

"Right before your mother died, you tracked Dante Moretti to his home," Bartholomew said. "You were high, out of your mind. You barged into his house, yelled at him, struck him, and said he'd better say your mother wasn't legally competent to write a will and get the will invalidated. If he didn't, you had friends who'd break his legs and arms and throw him in the lake."

Natalie rested her elbows on the table and braced her forehead on the heels of her hands. "And?"

"Andrea found you there and hauled you away. Mr. Moretti was furious and ready to call the police and have you arrested on a list of charges. Andrea was desperate to protect you, so she offered a bribe: if Moretti would forget what had happened, she'd pay him a large sum of money once she received her inheritance. Moretti was in financial trouble due to a real-estate deal going belly-up and was frantic for money. They bargained. Andrea swore to keep you under control and to pay the bribe."

Natalie didn't lift her head. Her sister had lied about her to the police. Not little fibs, not exaggerations or distorted facts, but enormous, malicious lies aimed to get Natalie in severe legal trouble.

"Natalie?" Bartholomew said.

She met his gaze. To her relief, he didn't look ready to pull out the handcuffs. The expression on his bony face was cordial and businesslike.

"After this hair-raising story, are you sure I'm not being detained?" she asked.

"Yes, ma'am. I'll let you know if and when that changes."

"Did Andrea have an explanation for why Dante would leave me sixteen thousand dollars in an envelope after I attacked him and threatened to have him murdered?"

"She said she didn't know but had a theory. Moretti was a competitive athlete, a runner willing to do anything to win races. Since you had underground drug connections, once the whole inheritance issue was water under the bridge, she suspects he offered you a pile of cash in exchange for performance-enhancing drugs, but the transaction didn't go through before he died."

Oh, Andrea. Really? Now Dante's a drug user too? "What about the letter?" Natalie asked. "The missing letter Camille told me about. Did Andrea have an explanation for that?"

"She didn't know but guessed it must have been something incriminating," Bartholomew said. "Because the night Camille told you about it was the night she died."

Bartholomew's words beaded on the surface of her thoughts. Natalie tried to hold them there, seal her mind against them, but they sank, heavy and poisonous. "She's saying I killed Camille. To hide the information in that letter."

Bartholomew plucked another grape and ate it, not confirming her words.

It would have been strenuous enough facing a police detective and struggling to keep her head above a flash flood of lies, but knowing the lies came from her sister, that Andrea had painted her as a conscienceless drug addict who'd murdered her best friend while Andrea had portrayed herself as the heroine who'd surrendered a chunk of her inheritance to protect her troubled sister . . . that she was lying in hopes that Natalie would be charged with murder . . .

That was what Andrea was willing to do to her. What Andrea was *trying* to do to her.

"None of her story is true." Natalie forced herself to speak evenly, forced herself not to scream and pick up a chair and slam it into the wall again and again, breaking the chair, breaking the wall, breaking reality.

Bartholomew ate another grape.

"No, there's one part that's true, or I assume it's true," she amended. "I can't verify personally that Dante was in financial trouble, but yesterday, Robert Chapman told me Dante had lost a lot of money in a real-estate debacle around that time. But I have never abused prescription drugs or used illegal drugs. I never even talked to Dante about the will, let alone threatened him. He never contracted with me to buy performance-enhancing drugs. And I did not murder Camille." Natalie wanted to add more meat to these statements but wasn't sure what else to say. She didn't have an alibi for the time Camille had died, but Bartholomew already knew that.

"Thank you," Bartholomew said. "Tell me about your relationship with your mother. You had been estranged for several years. She'd made it clear you wouldn't be a beneficiary in her will."

"Yes. Many times. It was a favorite weapon." A weapon Natalie had always pushed away with words her mother had never seemed to hear: *"I don't care about your money, Mom. I care about you."*

"Toward the end of her life, did she ever say anything about changing her will to include you?"

"Not that I heard. Not according to Andrea."

"Did she show any desire to reconcile? Did she contact you?"

The direction Bartholomew was leading this conversation surprised her. She'd expected questions asking her to prove her innocence. "She didn't contact me or return my calls, but she did send me a birthday present."

"A birthday present?"

"Yes. One of her hobbies was soap carving. She made lovely, detailed carvings, mainly of flowers. She sent me a basket of them."

Bartholomew's long fingers fiddled with an empty grape stem. "Was this gift unexpected?"

"Yes. She hadn't acknowledged my birthday for several years, and out of the blue, she sent the soap carvings. No card or note, but it was her handwriting on the envelope and on the wrapping paper."

"How long was this before she died?"

"About three months. I hoped this was a sign that she wanted to reconcile. She was proud; I thought she couldn't humble herself enough to reach out with words. But when I tried to visit her after that, she still wouldn't see me. Or answer my calls."

"Her will showed no sign of any desire for posthumous reconciliation?"

"No, and from what Andrea said . . . not that Andrea's word holds any credibility anymore . . . Mom hated me until the end."

"Thank you." He rose to his feet. "I appreciate your cooperation. I know this is a difficult topic for you."

Was she being excused, or had Bartholomew hit a button to summon backup officers? "Would you like me to take a drug test? I'm willing to do that."

"I appreciate that," Bartholomew said. "We'll let you know if that would be helpful."

Meaning that a drug test now wasn't going to prove she'd been sober two years ago. "Is that all the questions you have for me?"

"For now. Thank you for coming in."

Grateful, Natalie stood. Andrea must have expected her to get arrested today on the basis of her lies, but apparently, a war between sisters with no proof on either side didn't qualify as probable cause. Had Andrea considered that once the police started investigating her accusations, they'd find no proof? And once they found no proof, they'd explore—were probably already exploring—what she was trying to conceal by telling such whoppers?

What *was* she hiding? Two hundred thousand dollars paid to Dante. Bartholomew's questions about Natalie's relationship with her mother. Andrea's wild accusations.

The pieces popped into place. The police were wondering if Andrea had bribed Dante, not over Natalie's alleged crimes but over the will. Had she bribed him to keep Natalie out of it—even if that wasn't Roxanne's desire any longer?

"Food for the road?" Bartholomew gestured at the boxes on the table.

"Thank you." Natalie took a strawberry and a cube of Swiss cheese, then Bartholomew escorted her to the lobby. She controlled her pace all the way to her car, feigning calm.

Once the door was shut and the engine running, she set her strawberry and cheese on the center console and texted Andrea, fury making her fingers so ungainly that only the phone's autocorrect function made the message readable. *Thanks for all the lies. You'll be sorry to know they didn't arrest me.*

Knowing Andrea wouldn't respond, she threw her phone on the passenger seat and started to back out of her parking place.

Changing her mind, she pulled back in, picked up her phone, and called Gideon. She didn't know if sharing what had happened was wise; she didn't know how he'd react; she didn't know if she wanted him to see the dirt Andrea had dumped all over her.

She *did* know that if she tried to deal with this alone, clear-headedness would darken to stifling misery, and she wouldn't be able to help herself or anyone else.

CHAPTER 26

"NICE TRY, ANDREA." THE DISGUST in Gideon's voice heartened Natalie. "Doesn't she realize the police will need concrete evidence—not just her word?"

"I don't think she does yet." Natalie took a final bite of the salad Gideon had created with whatever vegetables he could find in Felicia's fridge. "I think she's panicking and struggling to take control. Lies are the only strategy she could come up with."

"Panicking because she's hiding something." Gideon picked up the rest of the grilled sandwich on his plate but scraped at a bit of crisped cheese stuck to the bread instead of taking a bite. "I'm sorry, Natalie. That's a brutal blow—your own sister lying to the police about you."

"It hurts," Natalie said. "Andrea's not an amateur at spinning the truth, but this is outrageous."

"Have you talked to her about it?"

"I tried. I called her before I came over here. She didn't answer . . . not that I thought she would." She smiled at him, a meager smile but genuine, unlike the smiles she'd faked all afternoon. "Thanks for listening to me vent."

"Anytime. Thanks for meeting me here this evening. I . . . was actually planning to call you." Gideon rose to his feet and took his plate to the sink. Instead of returning to his chair, he stayed facing the kitchen window. From her seat, Natalie could see a few bright slashes of coral-pink sunset, but she doubted the beauties of nature had entranced Gideon.

"You probably didn't expect to get roped into straightening up Felicia's house after a police search," he said, still facing the window.

"I'm happy to help, and it doesn't look like it will be much work. The police were careful about it. Thank you for dinner."

He returned to the table and took the empty salad bowl and sandwich platter. "Felicia would appreciate your eating her food," he said. "She'd hate it if the stuff in her fridge went to waste."

"True," Natalie said. Gideon's tone was casual but distant—he was thinking about something other than what he was saying. "If you were planning to call me, I doubt it was because you wanted help straightening drawers and finishing off Felicia's radishes and arugula. Did the police find anything in the search?"

His mien troubled, Gideon sat. "They asked about my father's gun. He had a hunting pistol, an old Colt Woodsman, that they found in a drawer in Felicia's desk. They asked me if that was where the gun was usually stored. I told them no. My father kept it locked in a box in the basement, and I've never known Felicia to so much as touch it."

Natalie swallowed. Imagining Felicia holding a gun on Camille made her feel as though the barrel of the gun were pressed against her own windpipe.

"It's not good news that she'd moved it," Gideon said. "It wasn't a self-defense thing because it wasn't loaded. The ammunition was still locked in the basement."

"So if she used it to threaten Camille, she used it unloaded." Natalie wished this were definitive evidence that Felicia hadn't wanted to hurt Camille, but it was only definitive evidence that she hadn't wanted to shoot her.

"It doesn't make things worse, I guess," Gideon said. "We already knew she must have had some means of keeping Camille under control; an unloaded gun is a good prop. But it feels worse."

"It does."

"That's not what I wanted to tell you though," he said. "I spoke to my aunt and uncle this morning, to tell them what was happening with Felicia, including the part about you. I hope that doesn't bother you."

"I'm part of the facts of the situation," Natalie said. "Of course it doesn't bother me." That was almost true—his sharing straight facts didn't bother her, but she couldn't stop herself from wondering what commentary he'd added.

"I mentioned how Felicia had come to suspect you, both because of your friendship with Camille and because Dad had mentioned you—out of nowhere, Felicia said—on the day he died. Uncle Ron recognized your name. He—"

Abruptly, Gideon stood. "Come into the living room."

A new surge of dread flooded Natalie as she rose to her feet. If this was momentous enough of a discussion that Gideon didn't want to have it while staring at dirty dishes, that was a bad sign.

They sat on the couch. Perched stiffly on the edge of a cushion, Gideon said, "You know how my dad and your mom had the same physical therapist? The guy I met at your house?"

"Yes, Skyler Hudson. My mom recommended him after your Dad's concussion."

"My dad told Ron that . . . uh, once near the end of your mother's life, in the waiting room, your Mom started talking to him. About you."

"Lovely," Natalie said. "Your uncle must think I'm a demon."

"Not at all. But your mother told Dad—they were alone in the waiting room—that she had a secret, but he had to swear not to tell anyone, even Felicia. He gave his word."

"Because he was too polite to tell her he had no interest in her dramatic secrets," Natalie added.

"Yeah, that's probably true. She told him . . ." He flashed a rueful smile. "It feels weird telling you this, but I'm sick of secrets, and considering what Andrea's up to, you need to know this. She told Dad she was changing her will, that she'd decided to split things fifty-fifty between you and Andrea."

This knockout blow left Natalie flattened. She couldn't even focus on Gideon's face, let alone speak.

"She said you didn't know. She didn't plan to tell you; she wanted to surprise you after her death," Gideon said. "So Dad kept his mouth shut, like he'd promised. After the estate was settled and everything went to Andrea, he figured your mother had been toying with him, just enjoying the attention—maybe hoping Dad *would* tell Felicia and then Felicia would end up disappointed for you."

Natalie groped to locate sensible words to speak. "That might be the case. She and Felicia were cordial, but they didn't like each other."

"He confided in Ron but never did tell Felicia," Gideon said. "He figured it would just hurt both of you if he shared your mother's malicious joke."

"I can understand that." At least Roxanne hadn't been malicious enough to give this false news directly to Natalie.

"Dad also said some things to Ron about your sister. One of the things your mother mentioned to him was how livid Andrea was about her plans to change the will, and when Andrea arrived to pick her up, Dad could see there was tension between them."

"That . . . wasn't abnormal." Natalie wished her heartbeat would slow.

Gideon hunched forward, elbows digging into his thighs, hands locked together so tightly that his fingertips dug into his skin. "Ron said the whole deal bothered Dad. He didn't like drama, was annoyed at everything about the situation, and felt sorry for you. Your mother and Andrea both rubbed him the wrong way. Ron remembered Dad joking—Ron *thought* he was joking—about how Andrea was so proud of showing off her wealth that maybe Roxanne *had* meant to change her will but Andrea had killed her before she could."

Natalie winced. "I can't imagine her committing murder. Unless she rationalized that Mom was dying anyway and it was a mercy killing. Which . . . isn't as impossible to believe as I wish it were."

"I told Ron it was something he should pass along to the police. Maybe they could find out if there was any evidence that your mother's death could have been hurried along. But after what you told me, it looks like there's an additional angle. The money Andrea paid Dante Moretti."

A bribe? Or blackmail? Had their mother told Dante of her plans, but when she died before she could change the will, Dante got suspicious?

"I feel guilty even wondering if Dante could have been involved," Natalie said.

"Because of Camille, yeah. How well did you know Dante?"

"Not well." And Dante had been in financial straits at the time of her mother's death. Two hundred thousand dollars might have sounded tempting. "I have a hard time believing Camille would be naïve enough to marry someone that cold-bloodedly unethical."

"Maybe he regretted it," Gideon said. "The sixteen thousand dollars marked for you? Was that the start of an effort to pay you back? The letter you never got to read? Could that have been a confession he was trying to get up the guts to deliver?"

New ideas, connections, fears, questions all whirled through Natalie's mind in dark, cold patterns. "Your father," she said. "If he asked Felicia about me on the day he died, he was probably thinking about the will. Do you think he was considering telling me everything? Or even telling the police?"

"Like he truly had started to suspect foul play?" Gideon frowned. "And died in an accident before he could share that suspicion?"

"Or not an accident?" Natalie felt paranoid suggesting this. How had she ended up echoing Felicia?

Gideon stared at Natalie. "You mean he told someone his intention, and they didn't want him to go through with it."

"You don't need to say 'someone,'" Natalie said. "We both know we're talking about Andrea. She did shop at MaryLisa's occasionally. She could have been there that day."

"If Dad did suspect Andrea murdered your mother, he wouldn't have been dumb enough to say so to her face and then let her go fool around in the back of his store."

"If he truly did suspect murder, he would have called the police long ago," Natalie said. "He couldn't have had solid suspicions about anything. You said Andrea rubbed him the wrong way. Maybe she got on his nerves, insulting his inventory or what have you, and he said something irritable about how Mom had mentioned changing the will and he wished she had? I don't know."

Gideon shook his head. "It still doesn't sound like Dad. He was always courteous to customers, even difficult ones."

"My imagination is getting carried away." Bizarrely carried away—yes, Andrea was a liar, but that was worlds away from being guilty of double murder.

"I'm meeting with Skyler Hudson tonight—that's why I told you I needed to be home at eight. I have some questions for him about the dynamic between Mom and Andrea. His fiancée is out of town, so he has some free time." Needles of embarrassment poked Natalie. Vicki's business trip was irrelevant; she'd mentioned a fiancée to make it clear that Skyler and Natalie had no romantic connection. Even worrying about that seemed ridiculous at the moment, and she hoped the tangential comment hadn't registered with Gideon. "Mom adored him," Natalie continued. "She might have confided in him."

"Good thinking. Maybe he can help sort this out." Gideon sagged back against the couch. "This whole thing is punching the life out of my brain."

"Mine too," Natalie said, knowing Gideon wished as desperately as she did that their intellects were the only part of their minds and spirits getting pummeled. No matter what these fragments of evidence meant, when they melded together, the full truth would be heart-shattering.

* * *

Natalie set a glass of chilled water and her phone on the lamp table and settled into her recliner. Before she could even start to relax her muscles or process what she'd discussed with Gideon, her phone rang. She picked it up and saw Jonas Egan's number on the screen. A conversation with Jonas might escalate her emotional status from overheated to core melt, but the chance to assess his reaction to the police visit drove her to answer the call. "This is Dr. Marsh."

A female voice quivered through the phone. "It's . . . it's Lacey Egan. I'm sorry to call you when it's not business hours."

"It's fine." A rivulet of hope cooled a part of her anxiety. "I'm glad you called."

"I thought about seeing the therapist you talked about. I'd like to see someone, and I'm sure the person you're suggesting is great, but . . . I don't think I'll be able to go."

Natalie's hope evaporated. She wished she'd given Jonas an unprofessional piece of her mind when she'd had the chance. "Why do you think you couldn't go?"

"Um . . . well . . . I . . . don't think I'll be free that long. I . . . called to tell you something."

"I'm happy to listen, but as I told you, it's not possible for me to continue as your therapist. Is this something that would be better shared in therapy?"

"I don't care about that, if you're talking about the confidentiality thing. Tell the whole world; you have my permission. It'll be headlines soon anyway." Lacey inhaled a noisy, hoarse breath. "I killed Camille Moretti. I'm so sorry."

This confession was a too-bright light flashing in her eyes, leaving spots in her vision. "Do *you* think this, or did Jonas convince you that you did it?"

"It wasn't him. I found . . . the . . . the murder weapon. It was . . . my scarf."

Tongue dry, Natalie picked up her glass of water. It slipped out of her hand, struck the edge of the table, and splashed water all over the carpet and side of the recliner. She slouched back in her chair, not bothering to retrieve the glass.

"How do you know your scarf was used to strangle Camille?" As she asked the question, Natalie tried to sweep all images out of her head. No imagining allowed, no pictures. Only objective words.

"Jonas told me he had evidence that I'd killed her but that he'd keep it safely hidden and I shouldn't worry about it. I thought he was talking about my notebook. When he was gone last night, I searched for it—I went down to the basement. I can't believe I went down there—basements scare me to death—but I knew that's where he'd hide something from me. I found the notebook, but I also found my scarf. It was . . . damaged."

"Damaged?"

"It had been twisted. Stretched. Jonas must have . . . when he went to Camille's searching for me, he must have seen my . . . He recognized . . . He must have taken it so the police wouldn't find it."

The thought of Jonas unwinding Lacey's scarf from Camille's cold, bruised throat made Natalie feel she was drowning in a maelstrom of regret. Lacey *had* killed Camille. Her own client.

"I still don't remember doing it," Lacey said. "I guess I blocked it out. I don't even . . . Well, I have no idea how I had the scarf with me."

"What do you mean?"

"I know I wasn't wearing it when I ran out of the house after Jonas took my notebook. I'm sure I wasn't because that was the day I spied on Camille at that Indian restaurant, and no way would I have worn that scarf when I knew she might see me. It was exactly like her scarf—that's why I bought it. I didn't want her to notice me copying her."

Natalie picked up the water glass from the soaked carpet, wanting to refill it but sure she'd walk into walls or trip if she tried to listen to Lacey while carrying the glass to the kitchen. She set it on the table. "Your scarf was exactly like one Camille owned?"

"Yes, a coral one with gold beads."

The coral scarf. Natalie remembered it. "If the scarves were identical, how do you know it was *your* scarf at Camille's? It could have been hers."

"That was the first thing I thought," Lacey said. "When I found it in the basement, I thought it must have been her scarf and Jonas had freaked out thinking it was mine. But . . . it's mine. If it weren't, mine would still be hanging in my closet, and it's not there."

"If you weren't wearing the scarf when you left home, how do you think you came to use it on Camille?"

"I have no idea. I couldn't have grabbed it before I left because Jonas had locked himself in our bedroom. I guess I must have come back for it later? I don't remember."

Natalie assimilated the details of Lacey's story. She'd run without the scarf but had decided to return home—while terrified of facing her husband—to take the copycat scarf and use it to strangle Camille. She'd been meticulous enough about the murder that she'd sought a specific weapon, yet she remembered none of what she'd done.

Had Lacey thought about the fact that she wasn't the only one who could have used that scarf to murder Camille?

Natalie spoke quietly. "Is Jonas listening to this conversation?"

"No. I'm hiding in my workshop so he won't hear me talking to you. He's in the shower. He doesn't know I have his phone. He doesn't want me to talk to you at all, but I can't . . . I can't live like this. The police came again this morning, and Jonas made me stay in the bedroom while he talked to them, and I thought I was going to die, I felt so horrible. I knew I had to tell you the truth. It's okay for you to call the police."

If Lacey truly wanted to turn herself in, why hadn't she called the police instead of Natalie? Because she wanted someone else to take control? She usually passed that responsibility to Jonas; now she was pushing it on Natalie. Or was she hesitating because she knew in her heart she *wasn't* the killer—and she knew who was, but facing that possibility scared her more than accepting blame?

"I'll do everything I can to help you," Natalie said. "But you need to be honest about what's scaring you. You know you weren't the only one with access to your scarf. The way you described that day, Jonas could have taken it more easily than you did."

Lacey's tremulous voice went shrill. "He wouldn't."

"Do you feel responsible for Camille's death because you think Jonas killed her to keep her from finding out you were stalking her?"

"No!"

"Lacey, stay calm. I'll call the police. Don't tell Jonas you called me. Lock yourself in the bathroom, or—" A shriek from the phone made Natalie jump. "What happened? Can you answer me?"

"Jonas—*no*—give that back—"

The call disconnected.

CHAPTER 27

JONAS CHECKED THE SCREEN AND stowed his phone in his hip pocket. "That was Natalie Marsh, wasn't it? Don't you understand how dangerous it is for you to talk to her? Why can't you listen to me?"

Lacey backed away, her gaze skimming her workshop. A room she loved now seemed like an arsenal. Metal tools, sharp glass, stone. Countless weapons that could hurt or kill her. Jonas's face was inert—white tile surrounding cold brown eyes.

"She's calling the police," Lacey said. "There's no way for you to stop her. I'm . . . I'm turning myself in. I'll tell the police I killed Camille."

His face contorted, dislodging fragments of his stony expression. "Baby, no!"

"I . . . found the scarf. My beaded scarf. In the basement."

"You went in the basement?"

"Last night, while you were gone. I didn't swallow that sleeping pill. I wanted to search for my notebook."

"You never go down there!"

"I had to find out why you thought I killed . . . I had to find the evidence."

The evidence. A scarf Jonas had had better access to than she'd had. And a notebook she'd reread in the bathroom this morning while she'd run the water so Jonas would think she was indulging in a long shower. She'd confirmed the notebook included no references to violence, no words about harming Camille. Only words Lacey remembered writing.

She still didn't remember murdering Camille. Because she hadn't done it.

"You've always taken care of me," Lacey said. "I shouldn't have stalked Camille. I caused this trouble. You thought you didn't have a choice, that you couldn't let Camille find out what I'd done. I swear I won't tell the police the truth."

His mouth gaped, a hole in the white-tile mosaic of his face. "You're saying I killed her? Why the devil would I kill her?"

Lacey edged farther away from him. "I'll tell them I did it."

Jonas wasn't moving to seize her or grab something sharp. "I took the scarf from around her neck, but I took it to protect *you*. It's a distinctive scarf—I couldn't let the police trace it to you. And you might have gotten your fingerprints on those beads."

"Well, they're there *now*, anyway."

Jonas ran his fingers through his wet hair, disheveling it into messy spikes. "You'd been stalking her. You wrote about how you followed her and spied on her and broke into her garage and liked to scare her. When I took your notebook, you ran off, and . . . she died."

"When I ran off, *you* were locked in our bedroom where my scarf was. How could I have come back to get it when I was too scared to face you?"

"You're saying I took it and strangled her with it? Lacey! If you didn't kill her, why did you buy a replacement scarf before you came home?"

"What do you mean?"

"The new scarf, the one you put in your closet. So I wouldn't notice the other one was gone."

"What?" This conversation was random colors and shapes tossed together, no design. "There's no scarf in my closet. I checked."

"I *know*. I got rid of it. Those beads might have made distinctive marks on Camille's throat; you wearing that scarf around town would have been dangerous. I would have thrown away the damaged one, but I was afraid I'd need it."

"Need it! Why?"

"You couldn't remember what you'd done. I kept it to show to you in case you were too messed up to listen to me and I needed proof to convince you."

Lacey tried to pick up each phrase in her mind and set it into a spot where it made sense with the other phrases. "You found a scarf in my closet *after* she died?"

"You don't remember buying it? Baby, I was keeping an eye on the credit cards. You spent money at Townsend's Saturday morning before you came home. You told me that's where you originally bought that beaded scarf."

"I *did*, but I didn't buy another one on Saturday. I bought a blanket. I was freezing in the car and thought a blanket might help me sleep."

"Then where did the replacement scarf come from?"

Lacey lifted a drawing that lay on her worktable, one of the possible Stoker Building mural designs. It was hideous. She crumpled it and tossed it on the floor. "I bought the scarf—the first scarf—because it was exactly like Camille's. I was copying her. If you found a scarf in my closet after she died, *that* was my scarf. The one around her neck was hers."

"Camille had a scarf like yours?"

"I had one like *hers*. She had hers first. I guess you never saw her wear it." Lacey stuck her hand into a bowl of iridescent purple tiles and stirred them.

If Camille had been strangled with her own scarf, maybe Jonas hadn't had anything to do with her death. "How can you think I'd kill her?" Lacey threw a handful of tiles on the floor. They hit with painful cracking noises. "I wanted to *be* Camille, not kill her."

"Why would you want to be someone else? You're prettier than she was, prettier than anyone."

"Who cares about *that*?" Lacey dumped the whole bowl. The clatter was earsplitting. "I'm not talking about her face; I'm talking about her *self*. She was strong. She knew how to stand up for herself, to be herself, to deal with people. She wasn't weak and stupid." Lacey kicked at the pile of tiles; they skittered across the floor.

"You don't need to be strong," Jonas said. "I'm here to take care of you."

"That's what I'm *sick of*." Lacey screamed the words. "I can't *stand* it anymore."

Jonas's face should have been deeply familiar, but Lacey had the dreamlike impression that she didn't recognize him. From the befuddled way he was staring at her, he didn't recognize her either.

"You're sick of me?" he said.

"Not of *you*. I'm sick of you telling me what to do, running every part of my life, telling me what to cook and which shirt to wear and which project I should be working on and whether or not I should call Dr. Marsh. I'm sick of you telling me when to stay home and when to go out. I'm sick of you thinking it's okay to read my private notes and take my keys and treat me like I'm a child or a prisoner."

Jonas looked so punch drunk that Lacey wasn't sure he understood what she was saying. "I'm sick of you *meaning* it when you call me 'baby,'" she said. "I'm an adult."

He spoke unevenly, as though straining to heave each word from his mouth. "I . . . thought you . . . liked it when I took care of you. That's what you wanted. I rescued you. I kept you safe. I've given you everything you need."

"I was eighteen when you rescued me from my nightmare family. I'm twenty-six now."

"You . . . want to leave me?"

"No. I just want you to . . . to . . ." How could she explain this? She'd imagined herself talking to Jonas about this hundreds of times, but she could remember hardly any of the confident, intelligent phrases she'd wanted to say. The ones she remembered were in Camille's voice, not her own.

"I want to be myself," Lacey said. "If I want to wear that sparkly blue skirt, I don't want you hanging it in a box in the basement because you think it looks like a Cinderella prop." Silly Lacey words gushed out. "I want to make raspberry sauce for breakfast. I want to make more mosaic purses, and I don't want you to tell me I'm wasting my time. I want to help decide where we go on vacation. I want you to listen to me instead of acting like I'm a dummy because I never went to college. I want you to respect me. I want to take a kickboxing class. I'm sick of making waffles. I—" At the wail of sirens, Lacey's rant collapsed. "The police," she said. How could she have forgotten the police were on their way? She kicked more tiles across the floor. "Um . . . did we decide which one of us is the killer?"

"You're not going to prison," he said.

"Neither are you!" she yelled.

With weighty, cautious steps, Jonas moved toward her. He stopped about a foot away, agony and confusion in his face, as though he didn't know how he'd been injured. "I love you," he said. "I'll always love you. I didn't know you wanted those things from me."

"Neither did I," Lacey said. "Not for a long time. I'm still figuring it out. I want us to get help. Both of us."

"I'll do anything you want," he said. "Except let you take the blame for Camille's death."

"We'd better just tell the police the truth," Lacey said. "The total truth. And . . . I guess we hope they believe us."

Jonas nodded. As the sirens grew louder, Lacey stepped into his embrace and curled her arms around him, pressing her cheek against his.

* * *

Not until a brief, kindly text from Detective Bartholomew assured her that Lacey was safe could Natalie finally set her phone aside instead of frantically staring at the screen, desperate for news. What was happening with the Egans now? Unless Jonas had flat-out confessed to Camille's murder, Natalie was still a suspect herself. Then again, with the Egans' fraught marital dynamics, even a confession might not be enough. Turner and Bartholomew might think Jonas was trying to protect Lacey, even as Natalie had thought Lacey was trying to protect Jonas.

Let the police do the investigating; neither of the Egans was her responsibility at this point.

Stretched out in her recliner, Natalie scanned the comfortable clothes she'd absentmindedly changed into after arriving home from Gideon's: a faded sweat-shirt, ragged-but-not-on-purpose jeans, rubber-soled felt slippers. Classy. Skyler would be here soon—maybe she should have stayed in her nicer clothes? No. Who cared? Skyler wouldn't.

She closed her eyes, tightened the muscles in her scalp for several seconds, then relaxed them. Facial muscles. Jaw muscles. Neck. Shoulders. Working out tension through progressive muscle relaxation was a better use of her time than spiffing herself up.

Arms: tighten, release. Hands. She was tightening the muscles in her toes when the doorbell rang. She slid out of her chair and padded to the door.

"Hey, Nat." Skyler held out a loaf of bread. "Coconut bread, fresh from the freezer. Don't tell Kirk."

"Thank you." Natalie claimed the ice-cold loaf. "Come in and explain how I'm supposed to defend the castle when Kirk storms the walls to steal this."

"Eh, don't worry. I have another loaf I'm defrosting for work tomorrow, and this time, I'll remember to bring it. That'll hold him off." Skyler stepped inside. "When I told Vicki we were meeting tonight, she told me to bring you a loaf, even though it's frozen. She figured you'd want it for breakfast, so that's time to thaw."

"Perfect," Natalie said, not even curious what Skyler had told Vicki about why she'd wanted to talk with him. Vicki probably already knew about her dysfunctional family. "Thank you, and please tell Vicki thank you."

"You doing okay? You seem okay at work, but I'll bet you're faking it."

"I'm sort of okay and mostly faking it. Have a seat."

Skyler sat on the couch. Natalie returned to her recliner.

"What can I do for you?" he asked. "Teach you to control your sister with your mind powers?"

"Could you? Biofeedback therapy is a more powerful tool than I thought."

"I'm kidding. Remote-controlling minds is outside my area of expertise. Talk to the CIA."

"Thanks for the tip. And I have no idea how much you already know about my relationship with my sister . . . which, to be honest, makes this uncomfortable for me."

"I get it."

"I realize you have to respect patient confidentiality—"

He held up a hand. "Here, I'll give you what I've got. I worked with your mom for . . . can't remember how long, but it was over a year. From after her cancer surgery until it was plain nothing was going to fix her and the best we could do was manage pain and keep her functional as long as possible. We got along great. She enjoyed the appointments. The physical therapy helped with her pain and mobility, and my handsome face, ripped abs, and charisma were a bonus." He flexed one arm. "Check out these biceps. Wouldn't they cheer any woman up?"

"How did she feel about your super-sized ego?"

He grinned. "In all seriousness, she *did* like me. She talked to me. She didn't seem fazed by the fact that she was dying—seemed to like talking about it, actually. Shocking people with it because she didn't look that sick. She'd throw it at other clients or receptionists. I got the sense she liked watching them try to respond to lines like"—he switched to falsetto—"'Well, dear, I'll try to have a nice evening, but I have so few days left that every sunset is depressing. I have terminal cancer.'"

Natalie sighed. Yes, her mother would have enjoyed the power of leaving strangers feeling flustered and guilty. "What did she talk about with you besides her death?"

"Money was a favorite topic," Skyler said. "Your family was well-to-do, huh?"

"Not by Forbes standards. But yes, we had some money. She did well in the divorce settlement, then when my father died, she was the sole beneficiary of both his estate and his life insurance."

"Even though they were divorced?"

"Yes. He had a lot of guilt about divorcing her, and one way he assuaged that was to assure her that even though he couldn't live with her anymore, he'd still take full financial responsibility for her, including updating his post-divorce will to ensure she remained his beneficiary. I suspect he planned to change the will eventually, if he married again or when we were older. Andrea and I were only teenagers when they divorced, and he thought he'd be around for decades. He ended up dying when he was fifty."

"Brain aneurysm, right? Roxanne told me about it. Said it was caused by all his air travel for work. Pressure changes weakened his arterial walls."

"Oh, for heaven's sake. She invented that story because it made it sound like his abandoning her for work travel had led to karma smiting him down. Did you tell her to drop the nonsense and that air travel doesn't cause aneurysms?"

"Are you kidding? I made a sad face and said 'Wow,' or something like that. No point in getting her mad at me. She described your father as a heartless, workaholic monster, which I'm guessing isn't true."

"It's not. He was a good man, and he loved us."

"She did give him credit for making a lot of money. Money, money, money."

"Did she talk about her will?"

"You bet. Favorite topic. Told me all about her heartthrob young lawyer."

"And about Andrea and me, I assume."

"Yeah . . ." He paused. "Okay, I'm kinda losing my nerve here. Maybe—"

"Say it. I won't be shocked."

"Bombs away, then. She said her older daughter was a conniving devil who tried to make her believe she was crazy. She said you wanted a doctor to lock her up and dope her into a trance so you could take all her money."

None of this was new to Natalie, but hearing it from Skyler scraped old wounds raw. What had he thought of her at the time—and what had he thought when he'd met her?

"Don't worry," Skyler said. "I figured it was fairy tales. But I'd act horrified or say 'Wow, aren't you being too hard on her?' and she'd say 'Nope, she's bad news.'

She thought you became a psychologist so doctors would believe your lies about her and do what you wanted. Gotta say, Nat, an evil scheme that requires a PhD sounds like a lot of unnecessary work. You could have done something easier, like poison her. No dissertation required."

Natalie gave a tired smile. "Too late now."

"She criticized Andrea too but mainly about the guy she was engaged to . . . Forgot his name . . ."

"Austin Collier."

"Oh yeah. Andrea was spending too much time with him, or she was secretly making wedding plans when she'd promised to wait until after Roxanne was gone to get married, or whatever."

This was new to Natalie. "My mother didn't want Andrea to get married before she died?"

"My sense of it was that she didn't want more of Andrea's time and attention going to Austin. She wanted her as full-time nurse until the last moment."

"I didn't realize that." If their mother had been interfering with Andrea's relationship with Austin, that was another possible reason for Andrea to want to hurry her death.

"She liked using her money as a chain around your sister's neck," Skyler said. "Andrea would come to pick her up, and she'd say things like 'You're late—every minute you make me wait is another hundred thousand dollars I'll leave to charity instead of you.'"

"Oh, please. She didn't want to donate any of her money. She always talked about how she would only pass money along her bloodline."

"Yeah, she told me that too, but she liked yanking Andrea around. I could tell Andrea was trying hard not to upset her."

"Did she tell you she was writing me out of her will?"

"Yup. I'm sorry, Nat."

"She never said anything about softening toward me? About changing her will?"

"I'm sorry. She didn't."

Natalie's heartbeats felt draggy and echoing, a bleak thumping in her chest. So much for hoping Skyler could be a second witness to what Wade Radcliffe had told his brother. "Did you ever see any signs that Andrea was manipulating her? Controlling her?"

"Seemed the other way around, actually."

"She never said anything about setting aside some money for me? Not money in the will but a separate, small gift administered through her lawyer?"

Skyler raised one eyebrow—or both; she couldn't see the other behind his angled bangs. "No. Why?"

It seemed futile to withhold information about the sixteen thousand dollars. She'd already told Gideon and Chapman, and if she did end up getting arrested, the whole city would know. Besides, details might jog Skyler's memory. "The police found sixteen thousand dollars in cash, in an envelope in Dante Moretti's filing cabinet," Natalie said. "My name was written on the envelope."

"Are you kidding?"

"They want to know what it means. So do I."

"Wow. I wish I could help, but your mom never said anything about setting money aside for you. Any money at all. Sorry." Skyler brushed his hair back. "You told me you and Andrea argued last night. What was that about?"

"I asked her about Dante and the money, hoping she knew something that would explain it. She got upset—furious—and threw me out."

"That's bizarre." Skyler picked a lint ball off his sweater. "Sounds like she felt under attack from you, but I don't have a clue why."

Natalie debated if she should tell him the aftermath of that confrontation. No. She wouldn't gain anything by sharing Andrea's vicious accusations. If Skyler had no idea why Natalie's questions had upset Andrea, he wouldn't know anything useful about her lies or about the money that had passed from her to Dante.

"Why do *you* think she flipped out?" Skyler asked.

"I don't know. There's a lot I'm trying to figure out." Natalie told him the information Gideon's uncle had shared. "Whether or not Mom was sincere in planning—at least at that moment—to change her will, I have no idea."

"All righty, my mind is blown," Skyler said. "That's not even close to what she told me. Could she have been fooling around? Thinking it was fun to whisper a big, fake secret?"

"Possibly."

"Harsh. I wish I knew more. But my candid two cents is that she was full of it. Never planned to change the will. If she'd had some juicy new information about her will, she'd have hissed it in my ear, and she never said anything about splitting the inheritance. Sorry. I don't want to hurt your feelings, but that's my take on it."

"Thank you for being honest with me."

"Not a problem, and no worries—I'll keep all this confidential. Any other questions for me?"

"No. Thank you for your help. I appreciate it."

"Sorry it was a pitiful amount of help. Here's one job I can do for you—I have a friend whose wife works at the same law firm as Moretti did. I'll talk to her and see if she has any clue about that 16K. Maybe your mother did decide to leave you a little surprise off the record? Not sure how that works legally, but it's got to be possible. I'll see what I can dig up."

"Thank you. That's very kind."

"No problem." Skyler stood. "You look hammered. I'll clear out so you can rest."

She walked him to the front door. Skyler hugged her. "Hang in there. I'll let you know what I find out."

"Thanks." She stood, too drained to even close the door, and watched as he walked away. She stayed there, breathing the brisk autumn air as his headlights lit the dark street, then swooped around the corner. The neighborhood went dim.

CHAPTER 28

GIDEON SHOVED THE VACUUM INTO the closet and scanned his apartment for something else he could clean. He'd tried to contact Felicia, but they weren't yet allowing calls or visits. He'd tried to answer work e-mails and had typed nonsense; he'd tried to work on the plans for the ribbed vaulting of his Lego St. Patrick's cathedral and had designed a jumble; he'd tried to read a biography of James Madison and had gotten distracted by random imaginings about live-tweeting the Constitutional Convention. Cleaning was the only activity he seemed able to accomplish.

He headed into the kitchen and started scrubbing under the stove burners, his brain an electrical storm of worries for Felicia's sanity and Natalie's safety. What was Andrea frantically trying to hide with her lies about Natalie? If her lies didn't work, what would she do next? And what if that Jonas Egan character came after Natalie again?

He couldn't help Felicia right now, but what could he do that would help Natalie? Stand guard over her house? Follow Andrea or Jonas Egan around?

The murderer might be neither of them. The murderer might be in a psych hospital in Manhattan.

The doorbell rang, opening the gates on enough adrenaline to fill the Grand Canyon. Gideon threw his dishcloth into the sink and sprinted to open the door.

For an eye-blink, his addled mind identified the visitor as Natalie, but recognition immediately escalated to fear. Andrea. She'd come to bring bad news about Natalie; why else would she visit Gideon? "What's happened to Natalie? Is she all right?"

"Yes, but I need to talk to you. Let me in."

Fear lifted partway; he could still feel it, but it wasn't crushing his rib cage. "Uh . . . sure, come in." Had she decided to repeat her lies about Natalie to Gideon? Why?

She stepped hurriedly over the threshold and clapped the door shut.

"May I take your coat—your cape?" he asked. She was wearing a black hooded cape that covered her to the ankles. Either it was cutting-edge fashionable, or she was auditioning for *A Christmas Carol.*

She ignored the question and sat on his couch. Warily, he joined her. "What's going on?"

"You care about Natalie, right? I know she cares about you. That's obvious."

Gideon was tempted to ask how Natalie had made it obvious, but he kicked the question to the back of his thoughts. "Have you changed your mind about the lies you told the police about her?"

"Natalie's in danger. Do you want to help her?"

"Yes. What can you tell me? Truth only, please. I'm out of patience for nonsense."

Andrea's gloved hands repeatedly tweaked the clasps on her cape. "She needs to get out of Ohneka for a while."

"Who is she in danger from?" Gideon asked. "What do you know?"

"I know she needs to leave. You need to get her out of here. Take her to Hawaii or something."

"Take her to Hawaii! You're kidding. I've never even taken her to a movie, and I'm supposed to sweep her away on a tropical vacation?"

"You want her," Andrea said coldly. "And you're a reasonably handsome guy who isn't a creep and who has a good job. She's a lonely old maid. It'll be the most thrilling thing that's ever happened to her."

"Seriously? Not only do you insult her, but you borrow insults from 1932?"

Andrea shrugged. "She's not that old, I guess, but lonely. Desperate for a man."

"I don't think you know your sister very well. She's—"

"I'm trying to help her." In Andrea's throat, a vessel throbbed so perceptibly that a nurse could have taken her pulse by looking at her. "I'm here risking myself to help her. Take her away for a few weeks until I can settle things down."

"Until you can settle what down? Do you know who killed Camille Moretti?"

She turned her face toward the wall shelf. Gideon doubted his Lego models interested her. She didn't want to meet his eyes. "No," she said.

"So you're changing your story about Natalie being the murderer?"

"I never said she killed anyone. Shut up and listen. Natalie has done some stupid things. I don't blame her. It was hard for her, getting rejected by our mother. But she's in debt to dangerous people, and they're fed up with her stalling. I would have paid what she owed long ago, but she wouldn't admit to me that she was in trouble—she *still* won't admit it; she claims she's clean, hasn't abused drugs in years, which is ludicrous. You need to get her out of here. With a little time, I can pay off her debts plus some extra to calm things down."

"If you know she's in danger, why aren't you talking to her directly?"

"She won't listen to me."

"She won't listen to you? Or you don't want to talk to her because that would include admitting to her face that you lied to the police about her?"

"You hardly know her! How could *you* know what she's done?"

"I haven't known either of you very long, but she seems a lot more credible."

Andrea gave him a derisive glance. "Because you're infatuated with her."

"No. Because you strike me as manipulative and hungry for drama, and she doesn't."

Andrea flushed. "I don't care what you think of me." She unfastened her cape, reached underneath it, and brought out a thick envelope. "I know she can't afford Hawaii, and you probably can't either, so here." She slapped the envelope onto the couch cushion between them. "That will more than pay for the best Hawaiian vacation you've ever dreamed of, including airfare. And separate hotel rooms if you want to be prudish."

"You are out of your mind. Natalie would never go for this, and even if she did, neither of us can fly to Maui on a whim. We have jobs, and there's an ongoing police investigation. They might not want—"

"Who cares what they say? She's not under arrest. They can't stop you. Don't ask permission. Just go. If you think she'll refuse, don't ask her. Just take her, surprise her, don't let her know what's happening until you're at the airport."

"There is no way we can leave without—"

"Don't worry about your stupid jobs! I'll get you new jobs. I'll pay for whatever you need."

I'll get you new jobs? Did Andrea think her bank account could erase the consequences of their flaking out on professional responsibilities?

"Don't you care about her?" Andrea asked.

"Yes," Gideon said flatly. "Do you?"

"Why else would I be here? I could mind my own business and let her die."

"You could tell the police what you know. If you know the guys to pay off, you know who's after her. What are their names?"

"I can't tell you that. It's too dangerous."

"You'll shield drug dealers, knowing they'll kill your sister if they can?"

"This isn't my fault!" Her agitation was mounting; Gideon sensed she was struggling not to shout. "I didn't start it. It's none of your business anyway. Do what I told you. You know you want to do it. Get her out of here!"

Déjà vu regarding his enigmatic conversations with Felicia tripled Gideon's frustration. "If you care about Natalie, *tell me what's going on.* Do you know who killed Camille?"

Andrea jumped to her feet, grabbed the envelope, ripped it open, and dumped the contents on Gideon's lap. Hundred dollar bills, fifties, twenties. Stray bills floated to the carpet around his feet.

"See *that*? See how rich I am?" Her voice squeezed tight, then split. He looked up to see tears cascading down her face. "I can give you this and not miss it. I can give you more than this. Do you want a Ferrari? I could buy you a Ferrari!"

"I don't want a Ferrari."

"Whatever." She cleared tears off her cheeks with hard swipes of her gloved hands. More tears flowed. She retreated a few steps and turned her back on him.

Gideon wasn't a tear expert, but her crying seemed genuine, not theatrics meant to soften him. She *was* scared for Natalie, but she was lying about why. "Andrea," he said. "Whatever secrets you're keeping can't be worth more than your sister's life. Tell me the truth. Let's fix this the right way, not try to dodge it with some hare-brained scheme to whisk Natalie to Hawaii."

Her shoulders jiggled; she was trembling. "I'm doing everything I can."

"No, you're not."

She spun to face him, her cape whirling around her legs. "If you're too selfish to help her, say so. Don't waste my time."

"Who's after Natalie?"

She moved toward him. Anger writhed in her dripping eyes, so much anger that Gideon prepared himself to ward off a slap. "You're useless." She snatched her money off his lap. "I'm leaving."

"Wait," Gideon said as she bent to gather bills off the floor. If she walked out of here with her secrets, what proof would he have for the police that they'd had this conversation? He couldn't even prove she'd been here. She'd kept her tight leather gloves on the whole time, so no fingerprints. This late at night, he doubted any neighbors had seen her.

He needed to stall.

He started helping Andrea gather scattered twenties and fifties. "Listen, I want to help Natalie. I'm not completely opposed to Hawaii." He picked up a hundred-dollar bill and stacked the money he'd collected on the couch cushion next to him. "Sheesh, this is a lot of cash."

Andrea slapped the money she'd collected on top of his stack. "Do what I ask and it's yours."

He started removing bills from the pile one by one and setting them in a new stack, pretending to count them but focusing none of his attention on keeping track of the numbers. "I could buy us matching hula skirts to go with our matching aprons."

"So it's a deal?" The relief in her voice was the most appealing tone Gideon had heard her use. "You'll get her out of here for a couple of weeks?"

"I don't know," Gideon said. "Does that Ferrari offer go along with it?"

"I didn't say I *would* buy you one. I said I could. Keep Natalie safe, and I'll be grateful. When I'm grateful, I'm generous. You'll be happy."

"Huh. I've never been to Hawaii. Always wanted to go."

"So it's a deal." She stepped backward, shrinking toward the door. Gideon could read her: she wanted to get out of here and tell herself she'd done everything she could. Gideon would take it from here, and if Natalie got killed, it wasn't her fault.

"Hang on. This is good for the trip." He tapped the money. "But I want more specifics about afterward. What if it takes you a while to use your connections to find me a new job after I get fired for going AWOL?"

"I can handle it."

"I want some guarantees. Sit down for a minute. Do you want something to drink?"

She wiped her face. "I need to go."

"Go then. I'll get you a police escort for the ride home. I'll tell them you're planning to pay off drug dealers but won't share their names."

She lurched toward him and grabbed the stack of cash. "If you do that, you won't get a cent."

"Hey, hey, don't panic." He eyed the money in her hand. "Let's nail down the details. We can be quick."

She sat on the couch, still clutching the money. "Get me a drink then. Just water. Sparkling water if you have it, which you probably don't."

"I have it." He rose to his feet. "Hungry? I have some fudge-brownie ice cream—"

"No."

He headed into the kitchen area. He opened the fridge, squatted so the breakfast bar hid him from Andrea, and pulled out his phone. With his knee, he bumped jars and bottles so it sounded like he was searching for the water. With his fingers, he texted as fast as he could.

Message sent, he reached for a bottle of salsa on the top shelf and knocked it to the floor. It struck the tile. Glass smashed, and salsa spattered Gideon's shoes.

"What is your problem in there?" Andrea asked.

"Sorry. Broke a jar. Hang on." Gideon headed to the pantry to get the broom and to the counter to fetch paper towels. He wiped up a clump of salsa with a paper towel, carried it to the trash, and returned to wipe up the next clump. When only salsa-stained glass was left, he swept the floor, scrupulously shoving the bristles in every corner and resweeping the area nearest the fridge three times.

"Forget the mess," Andrea snapped. "Get back in here and finish our discussion."

"Almost done." He put the broom away, wet a paper towel, and went to wipe the remaining smears of salsa off the tile.

When the floor was clean, he washed his hands, filled two glasses with sparkling water, and brought one of the glasses to Andrea. "Sorry about that."

"Good thing Natalie will put up with a klutz," she said irritably, taking the glass.

"Sorry. I'm, uh, a little distracted." He raised an eyebrow at the envelope Andrea had refilled with the money and placed on the coffee table.

"Let's get this over with and you can have it," she said.

Gideon sat and gulped from his glass, frizzling his tonsils with carbonation. "First thing I want to know is—is this going to be dangerous for me? If a killer is after Natalie and I'm her escort . . ."

Andrea snorted. "Don't be a coward. He won't bother you. *You* didn't cheat him. You have ten minutes to settle this, and then I'm leaving."

Gideon set his glass down on the coffee table. He picked up the envelope of money, peered inside it, and rubbed his thumb along the stack of bills. "Still sounds like a dicey job."

"I thought you cared about Natalie."

"I do, but I care about staying alive too. No wad of cash could bounce me out of the grave."

"I should have known Natalie would go for a wimp. Do you sit here every night alone playing with Legos?"

"Pretty much. It's safe. They aren't dangerous unless you step on them with bare feet."

"Listen, clown. You're not in danger." Andrea lifted her glass and drank. Gideon wished she'd drink it all; otherwise, she'd probably throw the rest of the water in his face if he pushed her too far. She set her glass on the table. "This is a . . . private thing, a personal vendetta. You're not involved, you won't get hurt, and if you get Natalie out of here, she'll be fine."

"Okay, good enough. But how soon do we need to go? It'd be nice to have a little time to pack and plan and research which island would be the most fun—"

"You *idiot*." Andrea made a convulsive up-and-down motion as though wanting to spring from her seat but fighting to stay still until she'd locked down his cooperation. "You're running away, not planning a honeymoon. The sooner you can get her out of here, the better. Forget packing; buy new stuff when you get there. Go get her *tonight*, bring her here, leave as soon as you can get a flight out."

Gideon held his palm flat, set the envelope in it, and hefted it as though weighing it. "She's going to wonder what the rush is. I won't be able to get her to cooperate without telling her you hired me to keep her safe."

Andrea's tone changed from impatient to venomous. "How can you be this stupid? If you do that, she'll never leave with you. She'll stomp over to my house and yell at me. She's in denial. If you want her out of danger, *lie* to her. Make it all impetuous and romantic—if you have any idea how to do that."

"Fine, I get it. Calm down."

"Are we done?"

"Getting there." He sniffed the money in the envelope.

"Hurry!" Andrea ripped the envelope out of his hands. "What other questions do you have?"

Good thing she was too worked up to critique his acting, which had to be atrocious. "This is cash to cover the vacation, right? What about . . . let's call it a salary. I'm doing you a favor, doing your family a favor. That doesn't seem like it should be a freebie. It'll be a real pain for me to leave—"

A knock came at the front door. Gideon jumped; Andrea gasped. She moved to hide the money under her cape, but Gideon snatched it away from her. The last thing they needed was a "get a warrant" argument as to whether the money existed.

"I'll hang on to this," he said.

"Don't open the door," she whispered. "Are you insane?"

"It might be important."

"At least get that out of sight." She gestured urgently at the cash. "Do you want to get robbed?"

Gideon shoved the envelope in the back waistband of his pants. Andrea darted to the far side of the living room, out of sight of anyone on the doorstep.

Gideon opened the door. "Come in," he said. "You guys are fast."

Detective Turner stepped into the room, followed by Bartholomew.

Turner nodded at Andrea. "Good evening, Mrs. Collier."

Andrea stood with her mouth pinched shut, her eyes murdering Gideon.

Gideon took the envelope, removed the money, and set the envelope and stack of cash on the coffee table. "I texted Detective Turner and told him you had information about Camille's murder, that you know Natalie's in danger, and you're trying to pay me to whisk her out of here. Now, how about you share the details?"

CHAPTER 29

NATALIE WANTED TO SLEEP, BUT she didn't want to go to bed and end up tossing and turning, wide awake, her stress burgeoning as sleepless hours passed. Instead, she wandered between the living room and kitchen, made herself hot chocolate, sat in her recliner and tried to read, wandered back into the kitchen for a fresh glass of water, tried to watch TV, walked back to the kitchen for a piece of toast, then went back to her recliner to stare at a cobweb she needed to sweep down from the light fixture.

She closed her eyes and pictured grief and anger as the tiny white petals blown from blossoming trees. Twirling on the breeze, scattering, sifting down between blades of grass still brown from winter. Floating along a stream, sweeping over rocks, slipping down waterfalls, lingering momentarily in pools, but drifting, finally, to where crystalline water flowed over—

She twitched in her chair, knocking her book to the floor. She rubbed dry eyes, not sure if she'd heard a thumping noise or had dreamed it.

The thump came again: a knock. On the back door. At . . . what time was it? Too late for visitors. She grabbed her phone and crept toward the doorway to the kitchen.

Outside, leaning close to the glass with a wry grin on his face stood Skyler. She stalked over, unlocked the door, and yanked it open. "You'd better have another loaf of coconut bread for me. Or a year's supply of filet mignon."

"I don't, but I'll herd a whole cow to work tomorrow if you'll give me my wallet."

"Your wallet?"

He entered the kitchen and closed the door behind him. "Yeah. It must have fallen out of my pocket on your couch. Sorry about that."

She massaged her forehead. "Why didn't you text or call me instead of giving me a heart attack?"

"I did call, twice. It went to voice mail. Is your phone off?"

She squinted at her phone screen. It didn't show any missed calls, and the ringer was on. "It didn't go through."

"Stupid carriers. Anyway, I decided to drive by to see if your lights were on. I saw the kitchen light was on and thought you might be having a midnight snack—that's why I came to the back door."

"I'd like to feed you to a bear for a midnight snack. How could you tell from the road that the kitchen light was on?"

"Side window." He pointed at it. "Could see it when I was driving up."

"You realize there's a murderer in town, and you think it's good manners to creep around like the bogeyman?"

"Sorry. Didn't want to scare you. But I already searched my house and my car, so if the wallet isn't here, I must have lost it when I was out to dinner. I need to know whether or not to cancel all my cards, which would be a giant pain in the neck."

"I understand," Natalie said grudgingly. "And I was still awake. Sort of." She walked toward the living room with Skyler trailing her. "That better be a good cow you bring me tomorrow."

"USDA Prime from head to tail."

"Search." She waved at the couch. "If you find any loose change, you can keep it for your donut fund."

"Nice," Skyler said, but he stayed behind her. Natalie glanced over her shoulder. All her nerves sparked with sharp, bright pain, and she whirled to fully face him.

"Sorry." He swished the gun he was holding, tracing an apologetic downward curve with the barrel. "I'm sorry, Nat." He extended his other hand. He was wearing gloves—sleek, close-fitting black gloves. "Give me your phone."

She *was* asleep. She drew a deep breath, wiggled her arms and legs, blinked. Nothing changed. "Skyler—"

"Phone."

She held it out. He took it, flicked the switch on the side to silence it, and stuck it in his hip pocket.

Natalie stared at his index finger resting on the trigger of the gun. "What's going on?"

"You know how things can start small and end up huge and ugly and you have to do whatever you can to control them? That's where I'm at. I don't have anything against you. I like you."

Natalie gathered every scrap of composure and met his gaze. "You don't want to do this. Put the gun down."

He grinned. "Shall we explore my feelings about you? Or about firearms? Or about my daddy or my self-esteem?"

"We're friends. I care about you. You know that."

"I killed Camille Moretti," he said. "Do you still care about me?"

The words slashed through her calm façade, tearing into her soul. "Why would . . . I don't understand why—"

"I didn't have anything against Camille either. She was great. Here's the thing: I'm a guy who likes taking risks. Life's a bore without them, right? But sometimes they pay off; sometimes they don't. Sometimes you need plan B, and plan B usually isn't the greatest."

This had to be a nightmare. "What was plan A? What 'small thing' started this?"

"Money. Money was the glorious plan A. Nobody getting hurt. Where's your laptop?"

"It's . . . still in my bag from work. In the entryway."

"Get it. And your purse too."

"Why?"

"Because if you don't, I'll shoot you. That's what the gun means."

With slow steps and her ears attuned to Skyler's footsteps behind her, Natalie fetched her computer and purse.

Skyler directed her to the couch and sat next to her. He braced the gun on his thigh, tipped so the barrel pointed at her chest. "Open the computer and angle the screen so I can see it too," he said. "You're going to buy an airline ticket."

"To where?"

"You have a current passport, right?"

"Yes." A passport she'd planned to use on international adventures with Camille.

"France," Skyler said. "You're going to France. Find yourself a flight that leaves early tomorrow morning. Doesn't matter which airline."

"Why am I going to France?"

"Because you don't need a visa, and it's a good place for American fugitives to hide. Did you know that?"

"I'm not a fugitive."

"You will be." He touched the muzzle of the gun to her temple. "Find a flight. Now."

The chill of the gun seemed to draw all warmth from her body. She'd never imagined what it would feel like to be one tiny muscle contraction away from death. "A flight for both of us?"

"Just for you."

Natalie started typing. "What went wrong with the money-only plan A?"

"I tried to blackmail the wrong guy. Awkward, right?"

"Who?"

Skyler withdrew the gun and rested it on his thigh again, now aimed so a bullet would hit her in the side. "See, I lied tonight when I told you your mom never said anything nice about you. She did. Toward the end, she started saying things like maybe you meant well and you were actually a nice girl in some ways and really smart. She told Wade Radcliffe the truth; she *did* change the will."

Natalie gawked at him, forgetting about the search for flights, almost oblivious to the gun. "She told you she was changing her will?"

"Fifty-fifty between you and Andrea. It would be her posthumous big reveal. She hadn't told anyone, she said, except her lawyer, Andrea, and me—didn't mention Wade; he must have been a later impulse blab. She thought it was hilarious how angry Andrea was, how hard she tried to convince your mom that only *she* cared about her, but she had to be so polite because she was scared your mom would boot *her* out of the will. Poor Andrea."

Poor Andrea, who had insisted their mother had wholeheartedly despised Natalie up through her final heartbeat.

"Her fantasies were great theater," Skyler said. "She pictured you collapsing in Moretti's office and sobbing out thank-yous. You ought to be flattered—at the end of her life, the thing that thrilled her most was imagining your reaction when you found out she'd bestowed a pile of money on you." He tipped his head toward the computer screen. "That first flight on the list is fine. Book it."

She clicked on it. Her fingers were fragile sticks, buckling, nearly snapping as she tried to type her information into the boxes and kept misspelling her name. "She died before she could change the will?"

"No, she did change it, and that's where plan A started. See, I *knew* she'd changed it."

"Why did she tell you all this?" Natalie glanced at him and answered her own question. "Because she needed an audience to gloat to."

"Yeah, that's what I figured. I was her hunky, charming, listening ear; I was a neutral party, and I was paid to be polite. After she met with her lawyer, she gave me a full report of the meeting and how Andrea had looked so grim, but it didn't matter. Roxanne had made up her mind; too bad for Andrea. Chattered my ear off the whole time I was working with her."

"But weren't there witnesses? Don't witnesses have to sign a will?"

"Sign it, yeah, but they don't have to know the content. The witnesses were employees at Moretti's firm, and Roxanne didn't tell them a thing." Skyler took Natalie's purse with his left hand and clamped it between his knees so he could unzip it and root through it with one hand. He brought out her wallet and handed it to her. "Buy the ticket."

She opened it and removed a credit card, wishing futilely she had a canister of pepper spray hidden in her wallet. "Did Andrea pressure her until she changed the will back?"

"Nope. I didn't even realize anything was wrong until after Roxanne died and all the legal nonsense was finished and I heard through the grapevine that every penny had gone to Andrea. Which shorted out my brain because that *wasn't* what Roxanne had told me, and I was working with her right up until she was so weak she couldn't speak a full sentence, so it was hard to believe she'd changed her will at the last instant. Nat, that's the third time you've erased your card number and started over. Quit stalling and finish the transaction."

"Put the gun down, and maybe I won't have so much trouble typing accurately." She started again on the card number.

"I didn't like Andrea," Skyler said. "Truth is I didn't like your mother either. For all her rambling about her wealth, she never gave me so much as a gift certificate for a burger. Tacky, right? The cheapskate. I'd hoped if I charmed her, it would pay off, but nope. So I was mad anyway, and then after I heard Andrea got it all, I got suspicious, wondering if she'd pulled a fast one. I decided to gamble, and I confronted her. I told her I knew Roxanne had changed the will to include you. I asked her how much she'd paid the lawyer to get him to destroy the altered will."

Natalie sat paralyzed.

"Yeah, I was fishing," Skyler said. "But it made sense, and her reaction was a giant squid on the hook." He wriggled his fingers like tentacles. "I told her that for a fee, I'd keep my mouth shut. That seemed fair."

Natalie tried to stuff her credit card back in her wallet but couldn't fit it in the slot. "You blackmailed Andrea?"

"Eh, it wasn't that sordid. I asked for a well-earned bonus. Come on, half that inheritance didn't belong to her. She stole it through bribery and fraud. Nothing wrong with taking it away from her, right? I deserved a cut after everything I did for your mom. I figured Andrea was a total amateur and had paid Moretti off in a way the cops could trace, so she'd be desperate to keep me happy. Yep, she was. We made our bargain, she paid, and I got what I'd earned. No harm done, right?" He held out his hand. "Give me that."

Natalie passed him the wallet and credit card. Andrea *had* bribed Dante to cut Natalie out.

Skyler tucked the card into the slot and returned her wallet to her purse. "I gotta fess up. Getting money from Andrea was such a breeze that I couldn't resist trying it again. Seemed like a small risk for a big payoff."

"You blackmailed Dante Moretti."

"Tried to. You know how sometimes a great idea bombs? Since Andrea had already admitted to their dirty dealing, I thought he'd give me a quick payoff to keep himself from getting disbarred and worse. Turned out the guy had too much of a conscience. He'd already spent most of Andrea's money to pay off debts, but guilt was tearing chunks out of him—especially since he'd married Camille and had actually met you, his wife's friend, so now it was personal, not some stranger he'd cheated out of her inheritance. When I told him to pay up or I'd tip off the cops, he lost it—said go ahead, tell them, he was done with this. Do you have wireless printing?"

"Yes."

"Print out your flight information."

Natalie obeyed and heard the printer in her office respond. "When he refused to pay, what did you do?"

"I made the case that I could ruin his life, but for the bargain price of fifty grand, he could live happily ever after. He said I could kiss the seat of his Armani pants. I said the first person I'd tell would be his wife. He said he'd tell her himself; he was sick of hiding it. He threw me out of his office."

"He didn't tell Camille," Natalie said.

"Nope. Because when he was walking home that night, I ran him down."

Black horror filled her throat, filled her eyes, choking and blinding her. Camille *and* Dante? She was supposed to be trained in understanding and reading people, and she'd seen Skyler multiple times a week for the past year—and had always thought he was harmless. Vain, a little self-centered, a little materialistic, but a nice guy.

"I swear I didn't want to hurt the guy," Skyler said. "I honestly didn't. But the way he'd acted, I didn't think he was bluffing. I was driving around, trying to figure out how to save my neck and thought, 'Hey, he took a bribe once before; maybe if I offer to bribe *him*, he'll cool down and remember he doesn't want to go to prison.' I started toward his neighborhood, and there the guy was, walking home, walking fast—angry body language, right? No way was he going to take my measly bribe. Nobody around—just trees. I hit the gas. It was a panic move, right? I didn't plan it, and, wow, I did feel like garbage afterward. But come on, the guy was corrupt. Kinda deserved it."

He murdered Dante. He murdered Camille. Natalie felt Skyler lift her computer off her lap. He snapped it shut. "Time to pack for your European get-away."

"Wade Radcliffe." Natalie looked at Skyler. "Did you have something to do with *his* accident?"

"Yeah, unfortunately. See, I'd gone to MaryLisa's to get that necklace for Vicki, the one she wore at the Chapman bash. Nice necklace, right? Wade was talking to me—Andrea had been in there a few days earlier and had been a real diva, and I said, 'Wow, money's not good for her, huh?' He said seeing me again got him thinking about what Roxanne had told him when they ran into each other in my waiting room. He told me about Roxanne's 'secret' and asked if she'd ever said anything to me about including you in the will. Caught me off guard. He said he didn't trust Andrea, and maybe he'd blown it by never telling you or his wife what Roxanne had said and he was going to talk to Felicia and ask her opinion. It was another panic moment, right?"

"You didn't want him setting an investigation in motion. What did you tell him?"

"That informing you of your mom's shenanigans wouldn't do any good and would hurt you. But he was going all crabby grandpa, saying he never should have played along with Roxanne and he should have told you two years ago. I didn't plan to kill him—I was just stalling, wanting time to think of how to persuade him to drop it, so I asked if I could use his restroom. While I was in the back, I spotted his ladder. I knew he'd be on the ladder later that day; when I'd arrived at the store, he'd been talking to another customer about the new inventory he'd be unpacking after business hours. He'd joked about how dumb he'd been to store a heavy box of pottery on the top shelf. Lightbulb moment, right? It was an old ladder. I tinkered with some of the bolts. I didn't think a fall would kill him—just thought it would hurt him enough to distract him so he'd temporarily drop the idea of spilling Roxanne's secrets and I could figure out what to do. Oops. Guess he fell the wrong way. Rotten luck." Skyler poked her in the shoulder with the gun. "Where are the suitcases?"

She focused on the gun. Skyler's aim was steady. "Why did you think I was a danger to you?"

"Wow, Nat. You're on the hunt for information, you're learning critical stuff, and you don't know why I think you're dangerous? Best case, you'll keep searching for why that money was in Moretti's filing cabinet, and that's bad news for me."

"What *was* the money doing there?"

"I couldn't swear to this in court—not that I'll have to—but my guess is that it was what remained of Andrea's bribe, that he set it aside for you and planned to add to it. In that letter you never read, he confessed to taking Andrea's bribe and said how sorry he was and how he needed time to make it up to you. That was back when he was trying to fix things without wrecking his life. Probably hoping you wouldn't want to send your friend's husband to prison."

"You read the letter?"

"Catch up. Why do you think I had to kill Camille? I heard you guys talking at the Chapman party. I didn't know what was in the letter, but the fact that he'd written anything to you sounded like a problem. I bailed on the party—told Vicki I was feeling sick to my stomach. I dropped her off at her apartment and broke into Camille's house. Did the cliché cut-the-glass burglar thing. I searched but couldn't find the letter. Then whack-a-doo Felicia Radcliffe walked in the front door, and I had to hide behind the couch—thought I was going to be stuck there all night; I had no idea why she was lurking there. *Then* Camille came home, and the loony bird accused her of tampering with the ladder—good guess, wrong villain—and Camille tried to talk her down, but it sounded like Felicia had a gun, and Camille finally ended up playing along. At least that part was fun to listen to. Then Felicia left."

"Why did you kill Camille? She didn't know anything dangerous."

He sighed. "I was out of options. When the loony bird left, I knew the first thing Camille would do was call the police. If she did, I was going to be stuck behind her couch until they left—maybe get busted if they searched the place. Even if I could sneak away, I wouldn't have another chance to find that letter before Camille read it and told you what it said. No choice, Nat. I had to do it. I jumped her, knocked her phone away, and demanded the letter. She gave it to me—it was sitting on the kitchen counter, which it hadn't been when I'd searched, so she'd brought it in with her. She must have had it in her purse or left it in her car at the party. I took the letter, grabbed a scarf that was hanging over the back of a chair, and . . . it wasn't fun. I really didn't want to do it. I'm still having nightmares. Maybe I should see a therapist."

Natalie interlaced her fingers and squeezed hard to keep herself from punching him. He'd get a bloody nose, and she'd get a bullet in the chest. "But she wasn't a danger to you until you confronted her. Dante never made it home after you tried to blackmail him, so he must have written the letter earlier. It couldn't have mentioned you."

"But it mentioned Andrea. Think about it. If Andrea's bribery came to light, do you think she'd have kept her mouth shut about me?"

No, she wouldn't, Natalie thought. She'd have tried to strike a bargain by offering the police information on Skyler's blackmail, or if that didn't work, she would have spilled the information anyway, venting her delayed fury at him.

"The main problem now is we need a fall guy," Skyler said. "Your sister is panicking since the cops know she paid big bucks to Moretti. *I'm* panicking because if she goes down, she'll make sure I get it worse than she does. She told me about her idea of convincing the cops you were a drug addict and how she'd bribed Moretti to keep that secret. It's not the greatest yarn, but she already gave it to the cops, so I told her I'd run with it and build some evidence against you."

Realization made Natalie too numb to move, too numb to blink. "Andrea sent you to kill me."

"No, actually, she made me swear I wouldn't hurt you, and I swore I wouldn't. See? You're safe."

"You're lying."

"Not about what Andrea said."

At least Andrea hadn't intended to send a hit man. But Natalie doubted she'd object to Natalie's death if the other option was getting herself arrested. "Why the charade of buying a plane ticket? You're planning to kill me, not put me on an airplane."

He gripped her arm and stood, hauling her to her feet. "Suitcases?"

"Basement," she said. Skyler knew she wasn't naïve enough to think he'd let her live. He was counting on her cooperating in an effort to buy time. For now, she'd keep cooperating; she didn't want to challenge him until she had a wisp of a chance at escape.

"Lead the way," he said, releasing her arm.

She plodded toward the basement stairs. "You're making it look like I planned to leave the country. Why am I running away?"

"Because you know the cops are sniffing you out. They know about that suspicious money in Dante's filing cabinet and that Camille died right after she told you about Dante's letter. Andrea told them about your addiction and your under-the-table dealings with Dante. We'll give them a little more evidence, and you'll look like a top-of-the-line killer."

"If I didn't want the police to know I was dealing drugs to Dante, why would I have told them about the letter Camille found?"

"Because you didn't know who else Camille had told about it, and you didn't want the police thinking you were hiding things."

"Did I kill Dante too?"

"Nah, that was still an accident, an unsolved hit-and-run. Why would you kill him when he owed you money and you wanted the dough?"

The unfinished basement was cold concrete and gloomy lighting. The suitcases sat on a shelf at the far end of the room, and she hoped Skyler wouldn't see them right away. She wanted a moment to scan the basement for anything she could use as a weapon. Skis and ski poles leaned against the wall to her right, a gift from Andrea she'd never used. She drifted in that direction. If she grabbed a pole—

The gun touched between her shoulder blades, and she halted. "If you try anything, I'll shoot you. I don't want to shoot you, and it will be more complicated for me, but if you want plan C—or are we up to plan D?—we can do plan D right now. What's your vote?"

She didn't answer.

"Get a suitcase, the biggest one you have. Don't touch anything else."

She headed for the suitcases, grabbed an empty one, and trekked back up the stairs, the gun periodically tapping her on the back. Skyler varied where the muzzle made contact as though sending the message that there were a multitude of sites into which he could blast a bullet: between her shoulder blades, at the base of her neck, low on her spine, in the middle of her back.

"We'll go to your bedroom now," he said. "Fit everything you can in that suitcase, but don't make it too organized. Make it looked hurried, like you stuffed everything in there in a panic."

At least making it appear that she'd packed in a panic would come naturally. Was there anything in her room she could use for self-defense? No baseball bats or concealed handguns or even a sharp umbrella. *Be creative. Think. There has to be something.*

Good luck. It doesn't matter what you find; nothing will help you while he's holding a gun against your spine. She needed to put distance between them. Every yard would make it harder for him to hit her with a lethal shot, especially if she could distract him with some chaos, screaming, throwing clothes and shoes, whatever would unnerve him. She doubted Skyler was an expert marksman.

"Unzip the suitcase, and put it on your bed," Skyler said.

She did so. "Sit down and relax," she said acidly, waving toward the padded bench at the foot of her bed. "It's going to take me a few minutes to decide how many pairs of heels I'll need for my life as a fugitive."

"Nice try." Skyler pointed at the closet. He stayed directly behind her as she walked to the closet and slid the door open. "Make any sudden or suspicious moves and I'll shoot. Startle me and I might pull the trigger even if I don't mean to. Grab some clothes; don't be picky about it."

Natalie yanked shirts, slacks, and skirts off hangers. Skyler herded her to the suitcase. She heaped the clothes inside. He marched her to the closet for shoes.

"You haven't thought this through." She unloaded an armful of shoes into the suitcase. "Even with me gone, that won't be enough to keep the police away from Andrea. Like you said, if Andrea goes down, so do you."

"Eh, I think it'll work. Haven't you wondered why I stopped by earlier tonight, then left and came back?"

She'd forgotten to wonder about that. She'd been distracted by a gun in her ribs and a double-murder confession. "Why did you?"

"First time I came, I parked in your driveway, brought you bread, didn't try to hide that I was here. Second time, trust me, nobody saw me approach. This means later I can tell the cops that I saw you this evening and you were agitated and irrational and babbling about Camille. I'll testify you were wigging out, Andrea will testify you were wigging out, and the cops will inhale our stories because they'll be able to stamp *Case Closed* on Camille's murder." He pointed at her dresser. "Pack some socks and underwear, whatever you women need."

She walked to the dresser; he followed her. As she gathered underclothes from her drawer, terror darkened the last of her hopes. Soon, she'd finish with his instructions and he'd kill her. She had to do something to disrupt his plans and give herself a chance.

She shoved underclothes into the suitcase, her gaze flicking around the room in search of ideas. Maybe the suitcase itself was her best weapon. He'd make her carry it—he wouldn't want to drag its weight while trying to keep the gun trained on her. When she pulled it off the bed, she could swing it to the side, bashing him in the legs—

No, that wouldn't work. She'd packed so much into the suitcase that she was going to struggle to lift it, let alone wield it as a quick weapon.

"Toothbrush and makeup and whatever all you travel with." He used the gun to nudge her toward the vanity area opposite her closet. She opened the medicine cabinet and began to sort through her makeup.

"Take it all," he said. "Hurry."

She shoved items into a makeup bag. In the mirror, she could see his face—still placid but colder than before.

Back at the suitcase, she added her overfull bag of toiletries.

"Put this in your suitcase too," he said, reaching around her. In his gloved hand was a prescription-style pill bottle, unlabeled but full. "For your drug addiction."

Natalie didn't bother to investigate what type of pills it contained. She probably wouldn't recognize them anyway. She threw the bottle into the suitcase.

He passed her another prescription bottle. "Open this one."

"Why?"

"Cravings," he said. "Open it."

She popped the lid off and peered at dozens of blue pills. "What is it?"

"Swallow two of them. You're feeling anxious, right? This will help. I don't want you all stressed and miserable."

"No, thanks." She moved to snap the lid back on the bottle. He dug the muzzle of the gun into her ribs. Bottle in one hand, lid in the other, she stood rigid.

"Look at it logically," he said. "Do you want to die peacefully? Or do you want agony and terror and blood and drama?"

"Do I want to make it simple for you, you mean?"

"This won't knock you out. It'll only relax you."

"It'll fill my bloodstream with drugs for them to find when they do the autopsy. It'll shore up your lies."

"It beats getting ripped apart by bullets, right? C'mon, Nat. Don't make this nasty."

"You strangled Camille. That was nasty."

"Yeah, I'm sorry she went through that. If you cooperate, I promise not to let you suffer."

She rattled the pill bottle and tipped it from one side to the other, pretending to evaluate her options. She didn't care what threats he made. She wasn't swallowing something that would make her less able to fight him. "I can't take pills without water."

"Sure you can. Put them at the back of your tongue and gulp."

"I'll gag on them. My mouth is dry. They'll get stuck. If you want me taking these, get me some water."

"Get it from the sink. I saw you have a glass there."

Natalie headed toward the vanity area. Skyler shadowed her. Her legs felt weak enough on their own, but she exaggerated their fragility, letting them wobble, making herself stumble. The gun was no longer touching her, but he was still directly behind her.

Internally, she steeled herself. If he shot her, he shot her. If he was at the point of forcing her to drug herself, she was finished playing along. She took another shaky step and let herself sway as though losing her balance. The medication bottle spilled, scattering pills across the carpet.

Her knees buckled. He seized her arm. "Stand *up*—"

"Dizzy . . ." she gasped. He couldn't hold her upright with one hand while her body was jelly; he released her. She landed on her knees. Hunched low, she instantly spun toward him, fists interlocked, arms swinging to strike him in the knees, knock him over—

Her arms struck nothing. Her momentum threw her to the carpet; she landed hard on her back, legs flailing, spine twisting, hands still gripping each other. Before she could unsnarl herself, Skyler landed crosswise on her, crushing her stomach and ribs, knocking her remaining breath away.

Writhing, she tried to inhale. Skyler dug one elbow into her ribs, his face toward her feet. She grabbed his arm, fighting to pull that skewering elbow away. Pain poked the front of her thigh, followed by a stinging sensation.

An injection.

"Yup." He leaped to his feet. "I figured that was where you'd balk. I should have been a psychologist, right?"

Gasping for air, she blinked at Skyler, who was standing far enough away that she couldn't hit or kick him. He stuck the cap back on the syringe in his hand and slid it into an inside jacket pocket. He no longer held the gun.

"Want some help putting your luggage in your car?" he asked. "Maybe France is out, but we'll go stargazing at the lake. I hear you and Camille had a favorite spot there. Good place for you to go while you're crazy with guilt over killing her."

CHAPTER 29

"WHAT'S YOUR PROBLEM?" ANDREA GLARED at Gideon with bloodshot eyes. "I come here seeking help for Natalie and you turn on me and start lying to the police. What did Natalie tell you to make you believe I'm the bad guy?"

"What kind of help were you looking for, Mrs. Collier?" Turner asked.

"Treatment," Andrea said. "I want to get Natalie into an in-patient program. That's the only thing that will help her. But she won't agree, and I know she's friends with Gideon, so I came to ask him to help me persuade her. Apparently, he'd rather help her destroy herself."

Gideon battled a turbulent surge of anger. If he started yelling at Andrea, she'd stand there sorrowful and innocent, drawing sympathy from Turner and Bartholomew. "You'd rather let your sister die than tell the truth?"

"I'm trying to *save* her life. You're the one enabling her." She gestured at the cash on the coffee table. "I'm always offering to help Natalie financially, but she'll never accept money from me. I thought if I gave this to Gideon, he could use it to wine and dine her, get her to trust him so he could coax her into treatment. The money would also pay for the initial costs of treatment."

"If that were true, why would you bring cash?" Gideon asked. "If you had legitimate motives, you would have written me a check."

"*What?*" Andrea was so obviously offended that Gideon couldn't help feeling he'd genuinely insulted her. "You're the one who told me to bring cash. I offered to write you a check, and you said *cash.*"

Gideon glanced at Turner and Bartholomew. Both men were observing the argument with unreadable expressions on their faces. Adults watching two children bickering, waiting to see if they could work it out on their own.

"I didn't tell her to bring cash," Gideon said. "I didn't tell her to bring anything. I didn't know she was coming tonight."

"Oh, really," Andrea said. "Just because that park was busy doesn't mean no one noticed us. There must be witnesses."

"What park?" Gideon knew he was an idiot to get sucked into an argument with a liar, but he was so worried for Natalie that he was having trouble handling this logically.

"We ran into each other at Kemper Park a few weeks ago," Andrea said to the detectives. "I'd come to town to see Natalie, but she wouldn't talk to me. I was walking in the park, trying to figure out what to do, and Gideon saw me and approached because of my resemblance to Natalie. We started chatting. That's how this all started."

"Not true," Gideon said. "I met Andrea for the first time last week. At Natalie's."

"Natalie can't hear you, Gideon. You might as well tell the truth. When we talked at the park, you agreed she needed help but said you didn't have the money to do anything for her."

Gideon wanted to protest, but this back-and-forth was useless. He bolted his mouth shut and waited for one of the detectives to speak.

Tense silence compressed the room—or at least it was tense for Gideon, and from the anxiety in Andrea's face, it was tense for her.

"This is a waste of my time," Andrea said. "I should have known you're the type of worthless friend Natalie would dredge up." She grabbed the envelope and pile of cash from the coffee table. "Since obviously the deal is off, I'll take my money back."

"Mrs. Collier," Turner said. "I'd like to speak with you." He glanced at Gideon. "In another location, of course."

They don't believe her, Gideon thought, relieved.

"No, thank you," Andrea said. "I'm done talking with the police. If you have more ridiculous questions, send them through my attorney."

She walked past Turner and Bartholomew, heading for the door. Gideon expected one of them to stop her, but neither moved as she exited.

"Hey!" Gideon started after her.

Bartholomew snagged his arm as he passed. "I don't recommend pursuit. I doubt there's anything legal you can do that would persuade her to talk to us."

Gideon wanted to shout that at this point, he was willing to do something illegal, but that was an idiotic thing to say in front of police officers. "Fine." He shook his arm free. "You believe her nonsense?"

Turner closed the door. "The investigation is ongoing."

"Listen. This is exactly what happened tonight, straight truth." As quickly as he could, Gideon described Andrea's warnings, her agitation, and her demand that Gideon take Natalie out of town. "Even if you're still sorting everything out, how can you let her walk away? She knows things—maybe who murdered Camille."

"Unless she's under arrest, we can't detain her," Bartholomew said.

"You detained me."

"Would you rather be dealing with an assault charge?" Bartholomew asked. "That's what would happen if you so much as touched her."

"I wasn't going to tackle her."

"What were your plans for confronting her?"

Gideon stood brainless and wordless. His plans. What plans?

"Yeah, you're welcome," Bartholomew said. "We have enough paperwork without arresting you. Stay away from her."

He wanted to ask if they believed his word over Andrea's but knew he'd get another "*The investigation is ongoing.*"

"I'm calling Natalie," he said. "She needs to know about Andrea's visit."

"We'll be speaking to Dr. Marsh as well and keeping an eye on her," Turner said. "Please don't assume that because arrests haven't been made, we're spinning our wheels."

Gideon nodded, still infuriated that Andrea had marched away with critical information inside her and there was nothing the police could do to force her to surrender it.

"We'll be in touch," Turner said. "If anything else happens, call, no matter the time."

"We don't believe in sleep," Bartholomew added.

"Thanks," Gideon said grimly. As soon as he closed the door behind the detectives, he grabbed his phone and called Natalie, not caring that it was nearly midnight. He couldn't spirit her away to Hawaii, but maybe he could convince her to stay with friends or in a hotel. She couldn't stay alone in her house any longer.

The call went to voice mail. He tried twice more. No response. He wrestled against panic, reminding himself that Andrea had thought there was time to get her out of town so the threat wasn't immediate. Her phone was probably off. She was asleep.

He called again.

* * *

Still short of breath, Natalie staggered to her feet. She was hyperconscious of the burning in her thigh but was no longer afraid of the gun. He wasn't going to shoot her. He'd set the stage; he wouldn't wipe out his work with a noisy, messy bullet.

"They'll see the needle mark," she said. "They'll know I didn't drug myself."

"Yeah, they'll see it," he said. "But once you're a little calmer, we'll get your fingerprints where they belong on the syringe. And we'll try a few unsuccessful stabs at a vein." He tapped the crook of his elbow. "It'll look like you were going for the turbo IV effect, weren't experienced enough with a needle, and got impatient and jabbed yourself in the thigh. We'll leave a few of the spilled pills on the floor." He picked up the drinking glass from the vanity, held it high, and dropped it into the sink. It shattered, shards scattering across the vanity and bouncing to the floor. "You were freaking out, doing anything you could to numb your guilt."

She backed away from him. How long before the drug's effects hit her? "This isn't going to work."

He shrugged. "If it doesn't, that's not your problem."

He was several feet away, not standing between her and the door. She lunged out the door and flew down the stairs, hearing his tread behind her, wanting to scream but lacking air. He caught up fast. His fingers brushed her upper arm, but when he tried to seize her, he missed. She wasn't going to make it outside or to the kitchen for a knife or even another ten feet before he could grab her. She plunged through the nearest doorway—the downstairs bathroom—slammed the door and jabbed the lock button.

He grabbed the handle and tried to turn it. She pressed her body against the door, expecting the wood to rattle as he pounded it, but the only noise was her own panting for air.

"Nat." He spoke from the hallway. "You realize this is a lock a five-year-old could spring. And you have no outside window."

She didn't answer. Yes, she'd cornered herself, but it was that or get tackled in the hallway. At least this gave her a few seconds to figure out a way to . . .

A way to extract the drug her hammering heart was spreading through her body at top speed? A way to defend herself with a hand towel, toilet paper, and a soap pump? Maybe she could fling the basket of her mother's carved-soap flowers in his face and hope a carnation knocked him cold? There were no weapons in here, no way to shout loud enough for neighbors to hear her, no way to stop him from . . .

Stargazing. Stargazing with Camille. He was taking her to the pier at Lake Ohneka, to Beau Lac. Pitch-dark, deserted at this time of night, isolated by trees. He'd kill her there and toss her body into the lake. Unless Andrea spoke up, the police would never suspect him. Why would they think he'd had anything to do with her death or Camille's? Whatever way Andrea had paid Skyler's blackmail, Natalie was certain it wasn't easily traceable like her bribe to Dante. Skyler wouldn't have let her create flagrant evidence.

Trying to camouflage any noise she was making, she turned the sink faucet on high. She removed one of her silver stud earrings and snatched a carved-soap lily out of the basket. With the post of the earring, she scratched words into the soap petals. *Skyler Hudson killed Camille and Dante.* She grabbed a rose and scratched more words. *He blackmailed Andrea over the will. He killed me at Beau Lac Pier.* She set the rose and lily in the bathtub and grabbed another rose.

The door handle jiggled and metal scraped metal. Skyler had found something to use to spring the lock.

"This is trickier than I thought," he said through the door. "Be patient. I'll rescue you soon."

She didn't have time to write more information. She threw her earring in the trash and grabbed the basket holding the rest of the soaps. When the lock clicked again, she screamed as though the noise had startled her and dumped the basket into the tub with the message flowers a little separate from the rest. She hoped he'd think she'd panicked and knocked the basket over. He wouldn't know it usually sat on the wall shelf across the room, not on the side of the tub.

She unscrewed the top of the soap pump, held it under the stream of water, shook it, and dumped soapy water on the floor. As the door opened, she jumped behind it.

"Ohhhkay," Skyler said. "So I'm supposed to slip during our bathroom chase scene?" He turned off the tap. "If you're waiting behind the door to club me with a toilet plunger, I can always stand in the hall for a few minutes until you're too woozy to aim straight. You'll be feeling it soon, if you aren't already."

With the hand not holding the soap pump, Natalie gripped her thigh as though she could seal the veins, trapping a drug that had already spread. The towel ring jiggled—was he taking the towel to mop the floor? She couldn't give him too much time to straighten up, to wonder if she'd deliberately dumped the basket into the tub, to notice the messages.

"Can we make a deal?" she asked. "There must be a plan E that can work for both of us."

"Could be," he said. "Come out from behind the door, keep your hands up, and we can talk. If you have something of value to offer, maybe we can negotiate."

She was starting to feel heavy. Tired. Still scared but not as keenly frightened, as though the danger had lessened. *Stay focused. Stay focused.*

"I'm going to pull the door away from you," he said. "If you want to attack, you have one last chance. Go for it."

He yanked the door back. Natalie dropped the useless plastic soap pump and lunged at him. The motion turned her brain to swirling stars and her limbs to noodles. She skidded on the soap puddle and flailed, colliding with Skyler more than hitting him. He caught her, keeping her from crumpling.

"Okay, not bad; good try." He dragged her into the hallway and laid her on her back.

She pressed her palms against the carpet, pushing herself to a sitting position.

"Hey, no, the fight's over." He caught her wrists and pulled her bracing hands away from the floor. She flopped backward.

He pushed the sleeves of her sweatshirt up, crossed her wrists, and wound something soft around them, multiple layers of white. A gauze bandage. "Nice and cushioned," he said. "Don't want to leave marks, right?"

She tried to tug her hands out of his grasp.

"Relax. This won't hurt." He wrapped something else around her wrists and pulled it snug. A zip tie. "Now's the easy part, where you get to rest."

"I . . . won't . . . rest . . ."

"I guess I can't stop you from haunting me." He bound her ankles together. "But you'll be a friendly ghost, right? You're a nice person. Gotta admit, I'm a little scared of Camille."

"You . . . monster . . ."

"Since you made a wreck of the bathroom, let's use that as your drug den." He entered the bathroom and returned carrying a towel.

"You're right-handed, correct?" He sat next to her on the hallway floor. "Yep, right-handed. I'm thinking of you making notes in meetings." He pushed the left sleeve of her sweatshirt up past her elbow and removed the empty syringe from his pocket.

With his gloved fingers, he pressed the fingers of her right hand around the barrel and her thumb on the plunger. Shouldn't she be thrashing around, making this difficult for him? Yes . . . but Skyler wasn't scary. He was a friend, and it was a relief lying down, resting. The carpet was thick. She liked the plushy carpet in this house. *Stay focused. Fight him. He's going to kill you.*

She moaned and strained to roll away, awkwardly kicking her legs. They didn't move correctly; what should have been self-defense ended up a feeble fish-flop.

"Easy does it." He repositioned her so she again lay on her back. "Almost done here. Why don't you sleep? Close your eyes; take a nap."

"Don't . . . Skyler . . . don't kill me . . ."

"Don't worry about that. Just rest." He gripped her bare arm, twisting it against the zip tie so the inner surface was accessible. A sting. A second sting. A third sting, more painful. She winced. Warm liquid tickled her skin. Blood.

"Done." He wiped her arm with the towel, then wrapped the towel around her elbow and left it there. He tossed the syringe through the bathroom door. "You take it easy while I get your stuff in the car."

He walked away. She was alone. She could escape. Could escape . . . How? . . . Roll over . . . hands and knees . . . Crawl . . . No . . . that wasn't working; her legs wouldn't move. Army crawl. She dropped her body to the ground and inched forward on her elbows. Where was she going? The door. The front door. She could open it . . . scream . . .

Jeans and athletic shoes and her suitcase moved past her eyes. Dimly, she heard a door open. The door to the garage. He was putting her suitcase in her car.

The keys. She had to get her cars keys, hide them. They were in the entryway, on the table. She scooted forward another inch. If she hid the keys, she'd slow him down, disrupt his scheme. Skyler's scheme. He was a nice guy. She pillowed her cheek on the carpet, wondering why she'd never napped in the hall when it was softer than her mattress.

Move! Get the keys.

"All right, let's see how you're doing." Skyler was kneeling next to her, unwinding the towel from her arm. She was lying on her back again. When had that happened? "Yikes, sorry about that. That's a prize-winning bruise and more blood than I wanted, but we were aiming for amateur attempt, right?" He pulled her sleeve down. Blood trickled beneath the fabric.

He dropped the bloodied towel so it lay across the threshold from the hallway to the bathroom. "Time to go." He worked his arms beneath her and picked her up. "We'll leave the lights on. Adds to the effect." He carried her toward the garage. "You doing okay?"

"Yes," she murmured.

"Hope that needle didn't hurt too much."

"It's fine." Blearily, she tried to remember why she was scared of Skyler.

He set her in the passenger seat of her car. "I'll drive, okay?" he said. "You rest." He pulled her seat belt across her body and clicked it into place. From the backseat, he picked up her long winter coat and draped it over her like a blanket. Why was her winter coat in the car?

"I don't want you to get cold," he said.

"Thank you."

He climbed into the driver's seat and stuck her keys in the ignition. Keys. Her keys. She'd wanted to hide her keys.

"To Beau Lac," he said, reversing out of the garage. "Your favorite spot for tranquility and communion with nature."

"That's a nice place," she said. "Camille and I like it."

"I know."

"You shouldn't have killed Camille. Or Dante. In the accident. You killed Dante. And Wade."

"I didn't want to kill any of them. But you get stuck on some roads, and there's no exit for miles, right? So you keep driving. No choice."

"You're going to kill me," she murmured.

"Yes," he said. "I'm sorry, Nat."

CHAPTER 30

STILL NO ANSWER FROM NATALIE. Gideon shoved his phone in his pocket. Time to go ring her doorbell and pound on her door. If she called the police on him, fine. He could treat Turner and Bartholomew to a late-night slice of pie before they arrested him for disturbing the peace.

He grabbed his keys and jacket and sprinted to his car.

At Natalie's house, the porch light was off, but interior lights were on. He rang the bell. Nothing. Pounded. Nothing. If Natalie had gone to bed, would she have left lights on?

Knowing he was long-jumping past civilized behavior, he tried the door-knob. Locked. He rang again.

No answer.

He headed for the side gate and rushed to the back door. The kitchen lights glowed. Through the glass panes on the door, he could see the kitchen was empty. He knocked loudly on the glass.

Nothing happened. He tried the handle. Unlocked.

Lights on, back door unlocked, no response from Natalie? She was in trouble.

Gideon opened the door and stormed into the kitchen. "Natalie?" he yelled.

Silence. He hurried through the house, alert for any hint of her presence—or hint of an intruder. Nothing in the living room. Downstairs hallway—nothing. As he passed the bathroom, a white towel lying halfway out the door snared his notice.

White streaked with red.

He yanked his phone out and called Turner. As the phone rang, he stepped carefully past the towel into the bathroom. The floor was wet, and an empty hypo-dermic syringe lay in the puddle. An empty soap pump was on the floor, and the basket of carved soap flowers had spilled into the tub. Her mother's soap flowers, her last gift.

"Turner." The detective answered the phone. "What's up, Radcliffe?"

* * *

A few old lampposts made weak gray patches of light on the asphalt, but the rest of the parking area at Beau Lac was dark. Natalie sleepily scanned the black trees surrounding them. The city should install better lighting. No, too much light would interfere with stargazing.

"Camille and I liked to stargaze here," she said. "Not in the parking lot though. By the lake, off the old pier."

"Yep, the stars are great." Skyler pulled the keys out of the ignition, reached over, and stuffed them into the pocket of the coat draped over Natalie. "You're going to need these."

The keys. Yes. She would need the keys to drive. She tried to look at her wrists, but her coat was in the way. How could she drive with her hands tied? Maybe she should ask him to free her.

He won't. Focus. He's going to kill you.

Skyler exited the car and closed his door. Natalie fumbled to reach the keys. Keys could be a weapon. They were metal and pointy.

Skyler opened her door. "You doing okay?"

"You can use keys as a weapon," she said.

"I've heard." He had an open pocketknife in his hand. She studied it in the illumination from the car's dome light. A short blade, shiny and sharp. It would be a better weapon than her keys.

He sawed through the zip tie around her ankles, then removed the winter coat spread over her, and freed her wrists. Good. It would be easier to drive now. No, she shouldn't drive. She was too woozy. Why was she woozy?

"Let's walk to the lake." He released her seat belt. "You can show me where you and Camille liked to stargaze."

Camille. He'd killed Camille. Fear swelled, pushing awareness into her brain. She didn't want to go with Skyler. She couldn't go with Skyler.

He took her arm to help her out of the car. She pulled out of his grasp, flopped across the center console, and clutched the steering wheel.

"Let go," Skyler said. "We need to get to the lake."

Get to the lake. Why? It was night.

Stargazing. But Camille was dead.

Skyler leaned through the door, gripped her arm, and tugged with more force.

Scream. You need to scream. Natalie inhaled.

Skyler released her arm. Had she screamed? She couldn't remember. She should scream again. She'd love to sleep right now, though the edge of the center console pressed into her side. She could tip the seat back. That would be more comfortable . . .

"All right, relax your hands." Skyler stood on the other side of the car, leaning through the driver's door. His gloved hands massaged her fingers, peeling them off the steering wheel. She wanted to hold on, but her muscles were cramping, and she was tired. Why was he wearing gloves? It wasn't that cold tonight.

Skyler dragged her past the steering wheel and out of the car. Her feet touched the ground, and she tried to stand, but her shoes wobbled. High heels. She shouldn't have worn heels, no matter what Camille had said about the way they flattered her legs. No, she wasn't wearing heels. Felt slippers. They had rubber soles that were good for traction, but the felt would get dirty.

"I need to change my shoes," she said.

"Your shoes are great. Let's put your coat on." He helped her into her coat and buttoned it for her. Her thicker winter coat, not her new coat with the shawl collar. The police had that coat. Camille's purse had been in the pocket.

She leaned against her car and gazed upward. The sky was black with tiny star-sparkles. "*Beau Lac* means 'beautiful lake,'" she said. "In French."

"I know." Skyler drew her arm across his shoulders and clamped his other arm around her waist.

"I don't speak German," she said.

"Me neither." Skyler prodded her forward. She took a few steps, but the asphalt squished and jiggled under her feet.

"I need to sit down," she said.

"You can sit down at the lake. You can lie down if you want. Lie on the pier and find constellations."

A cool wind smelled like dried leaves and pine needles. She was too hot in her coat. Why was she wearing her heaviest coat tonight?

Skyler steered her toward the paved trail that led down a slight hill to the water.

"Stop dragging your feet," he said. "You can walk."

"Once I saw a fish jump all the way out of the lake," she said. "Like on a *National Geographic* special. It wasn't a dolphin though."

"Girl, you are completely loopy. Walk. Pick up your feet."

"That was nice of you to bring me coconut bread."

"No problem."

"Kirk wants to try it."

"I know."

She stopped. "Why are we going to the lake?"

"To stargaze." He tried to nudge her into motion.

She pressed the treads of her shoes harder against the ground. *Stay focused.* Focused on what?

Don't go with him. She tried to twist away from his arm, to head back toward her car.

"Wrong way. Hey, no, we're going to the pier."

"I don't want to."

Skyler pushed her forward. She pushed backward. "I want to sit down."

Skyler bent and lifted her off her feet. She didn't want him to carry her, but it was easier than walking. She closed her eyes, enjoying the night breeze against her face. Her head drooped back.

"Put your arms around my neck and hold on," he said, panting. "Come on, you're dead weight."

She steadied her lolling head and wrapped her arms around his neck. "This isn't appropriate," she said. "You're engaged to Vicki. Thank you for the coconut bread."

"Vicki won't mind. She'd want me to carry you if you got tired. I'll put you down when we get to the dock."

"I like Gideon."

"Good choice. Seems like a decent guy."

"I need to change my shoes."

Skyler grunted and kept lumbering along the trail. Natalie realized her head was on his shoulder. She didn't want it there but didn't know where else to put it. Her neck couldn't support it.

Rocks gritted and clicked beneath them, and Skyler staggered, jarring Natalie, almost dropping her. She clung to his neck; he cursed, regaining his footing on the rocky beach.

Boards creaked as he stepped onto the pier. Moonlight glimmered in a silver stripe across the lake. Skyler carried her to the end of the pier and set her on her feet.

With her arms still around his neck, she tried to steady her legs. The wooden planks beneath her gave familiar squeaks.

"Pretty . . . moon . . . right?" Skyler was out of breath.

"Yes." Sitting here with Camille, looking up at the stars. Meandering along the shore, dipping their toes in the cool water. It wasn't summer though, and the water would be cold. Deep and cold. Felicia and Sheryl Chapman and an overturned rowboat. An impressionist rowboat.

"Felicia didn't mean to kill Sheryl," she said.

"Uh, right." His hands closed around her forearms. "Let go of me."

"The rowboat was an accident. I mean the cat. The cat on the book with the poems."

"Natalie." He tugged at her arms. "Let go."

"I thought Felicia killed Camille. She didn't."

"Uh-huh." He kept tugging.

"I don't want to fall in the lake. Felicia thought I'd killed Camille. I didn't kill her either."

"Let *go*." Skyler's voice stayed quiet, but it roughened. "I don't want to hurt you."

Hurt you. Hurt Camille. Skyler had murdered Camille.

Skyler released her forearms and locked his gloved fingers around her wrists. Gloves. He wore gloves because he didn't want to leave fingerprints.

"Did you wear gloves when you killed Camille?" she asked.

His hands were vise-tight around her wrists, pulling hard. She interlocked her fingers. The lake. He'd brought her to the lake. If she fell in the water, she'd die. Like Sheryl Chapman.

That had been an accident. Dante had died in an accident. No, that hadn't been an accident. Skyler had wanted to kill him. Wade's fall hadn't been an accident either.

Skyler ducked, trying to escape the loop of her arms. She clung tighter, lowering her body with his. If she let go, she'd lose her balance and fall into the water, cold water; she'd sink, her heart would stop, she'd drown, Skyler killed Camille, killed Dante, killed Wade, killed Natalie wearing gloves, silver moonlight, the needle in Skyler's hand drugging her . . .

Bright, fizzing lights filled her head. Pain smashed into her stomach, and she was airborne, flying, zero gravity.

Double gravity, falling.

Ice engulfing her, her clothes anchor-heavy, her thoughts twilight darkness.

* * *

Gideon's tires screeched as he sped into the parking area at Beau Lac. Natalie's car was the only one in the lot. He swerved close to it, stomped the brake pedal, and jammed the gearshift into park. He ripped his keys from the ignition and raced toward the trailhead, straining his muscles, pouring every trace of strength into galloping toward a nightmare. He was too late . . . he'd waited too long to check on her . . . she was dead . . .

He sprinted along the trail, a sloped path illuminated by the light on his phone and an occasional security light so useless that if there was anything in his way, Gideon would trip over it.

At the end of the trail, he shot off the pavement onto the lakeshore. Pebbles and larger stones rolled under his shoes; he flapped his arms, stumbling as he tried to keep up his pace on unstable ground. The pier wasn't lit at all, but the moonlight exposed it as empty. He halted and shone the light from his phone around the beach.

"Natalie!" he yelled.

Through his panting for air, he heard a softer version of the same noise he'd made: a fast gait disturbing rocks and pebbles, momentary silence when feet hit sand, more thudding and scraping of rock against rock. Following the sounds, he swung his light to the left, but the beam didn't hit anyone. Beyond the light, he glimpsed a black silhouette running along the edge of the water. One shape, not two, and too big to be Natalie. Skyler Hudson. Instinctively, Gideon leaped to pursue him but stopped; Hudson didn't have Natalie, and if there was any chance she was alive—

Gideon rushed onto the pier, lungs and legs scorched from overexertion. He swept the beam of light over the water. Not far from the end of the dock, just beneath the surface, he saw dark fabric, dark hair, a white face tilted upward, arms spread wide.

He dropped his phone, tore his jacket off, and plunged into the water. With a few frantic strokes, he reached her. He seized her from behind and hoisted her head and shoulders above the surface of the water. Kicking hard, he paddled toward the pier, Natalie limp against him. He wanted to scream her name but didn't want to waste effort on noise. Was she alive? He thought he'd seen her arms moving, but that might have been the motion of the water or his own wishful thinking.

The star-speckled sky overhead went black, and the splashing of water echoed. What was—*you idiot.* Swimming backward in the darkness, he'd swum right under the pier. Cursing himself, he swam to the side until he cleared the pier and could see stars again. Natalie's long coat kept twining around his legs as he kicked, but it would be impossible to simultaneously get the coat off her and keep them both afloat.

He didn't know if there was a ladder from the pier to the water; he'd be better off heading straight for shore. He glanced around to orient himself to the dim trail lighting and saw instead blazing lights. Footsteps thumped on the pier, and light flashed across the water.

"Radcliffe!" Bartholomew bellowed his name. "Catch!"

Gideon turned his head toward the detective's voice. A pale shape flew through the air and smacked him in the shoulder. A life preserver. Gideon looped one arm through it, shifting his grasp on Natalie to keep her head above the water.

"Got it!" he yelled. Natalie's head lolled from side to side, then fell onto his shoulder. In the strong beam of Bartholomew's flashlight, Gideon saw her eyes were open but unfocused. "Natalie," he said. "Can you hear me?" As the police towed them to the pier, Gideon bent his head, trying to get his ear near enough to her mouth to hear if she was breathing; he held his own breath so he wouldn't hear himself inhaling and exhaling.

Her streaming hair stuck to his cheek, and her head tipped forward. Frenziedly, Gideon jolted her, tipping her head back, adjusting his one-armed hold on her, and locking his arm more securely around the life preserver. Her face turned toward his neck, and against his icy skin, he felt the lightest brush of air. Warmer air. Was that—

A rasp, nearly obscured by the splash of the water. Another rasp.

"She's alive!" he called, the words more of a wheezy squawk than a yell. "She's breathing."

A flashlight shone in his face; he averted his eyes. The light shifted to the side, and he squinted at Bartholomew, suit coat off, lying on his belly with half his torso over the edge of the pier. Behind him and next to him were the shadows of other officers.

"There's no ladder," Bartholomew said. "Hang on to that life ring, and we'll pull you up."

Gideon doubted the physics of this plan were going to work. Without the buoyancy granted by the water, he wouldn't be able to cling one-armed to the life ring and support the weight of two waterlogged people. "You'd better drag us to—"

The ring moved upward, hauling Natalie and him out of the water. Before either of Gideon's arms could fail, Bartholomew reached downward, grabbed the ring, then grabbed Gideon's arm. Another cop grabbed the front of Natalie's coat, and multiple hands hoisted them onto the pier.

Two of the officers lifted Natalie out of Gideon's grasp. He sat dripping, winded, trying to see what was happening. Bartholomew stepped into his line of sight.

"I saw—" Gideon swung his left arm toward the shore. "Someone running away, that direction."

"Turner radioed," Bartholomew said. "Skyler Hudson. They got him. He slipped in the dark, hurt his ankle. Nice job on noticing those notes Dr. Marsh left. Does Turner need to get his ears checked, or did you really say they were carved on soap?"

"Soap, yeah." Gideon's teeth chattered. He couldn't decide if he'd be warmer in or out of his soaked sweatshirt, but his aching arms were heavy. Peeling off a wet sweatshirt would be too much work.

More flashlights flickered on the path to the lake, and a flashing display of red and blue lights illuminated the sky above the parking lot. Footsteps jarred the pier: two paramedics were racing toward Natalie.

"How'd you even notice soap?" Bartholomew asked.

"Long story," Gideon said. "They were . . . carved soap, a gift, important to her. When I saw that towel in the bathroom doorway, blood on it . . . I checked the bathroom . . . needle on the floor . . . the soaps weren't where they were supposed to be . . ."

"Good eye. You okay?"

"Yeah," Gideon said. "As long as Natalie's okay, I'm great."

CHAPTER 31

"I SHOULD HAVE BROUGHT FLOWERS." A flush polka-dotted Gideon's neck as he stood on Natalie's porch. Behind him, a quiet afternoon rain drizzled on her leaf-strewn lawn. "Or chicken soup or something. I flunked out of class school. Uh, the school of class. Classiness training."

Natalie's gratitude, joy, and straightforward delight at seeing Gideon instantly tangled with sorrow and pain. Her tongue knotted into silence, and her thoughts knotted into nonsense. The best she could do was gesture him into the house.

Brow wrinkling, he scrutinized her as he stepped over the threshold. With shaky hands, she closed the door behind him.

"Are you all right?" he asked.

She nodded. She ought to welcome him. Shake his hand. Thank him for saving her life. Invite him to dinner. Start a scholarship fund in his name.

She grabbed him. No warning, both her arms locking around his body in an embrace so fast and tight he had no chance to react. Vaguely, she knew she should release him, step back, apologize, but she was too consumed in damming a threatening flood of tears.

"I wish I could have seen you sooner," he said, his arms closing around her. "I tried, but first your doctor wasn't allowing visitors, then the police were running interference, then Deborah Valdez was guarding you."

Natalie could imagine Deborah shooing all visitors away. She and Kirk had picked Natalie up from the hospital, transported her to the guest room in their home, and offered deep compassion, gentle care, and enforced rest.

"How are you doing?" Gideon asked softly.

Her defenses broke; sobs seized her in the same sudden, crushing grip she was using on Gideon. His arms steadied her as her body shook and tears splattered his jacket. "I'm sorry," she whispered. "You don't want to deal with this."

"Of course I want to deal with it," he said. "That's why I wore a waterproof jacket."

She laugh-sobbed. "I'm sorry. I've been . . . trying to . . . trying to . . . avoid this."

"Bad strategy," Gideon said. "Stockpiling everything instead of dealing with it. Boom, it all blows at once."

"I know . . . I know. I'm . . . I'm excellent at handling other people's tears. I'm a wreck at handling my own."

"Don't worry. I've got this one." Gideon guided her toward the couch, sat next to her, and held her while tears streamed from her eyes.

"Did the police tell you . . . what Andrea was up to?" she asked.

"Yes. The will, the bribery, Hudson's blackmail. Did they tell you she came to me, wanting me to spirit you away to Hawaii because you were in danger?"

"Yes."

"She did care about you," Gideon said. "She was upset. Honestly afraid for you."

At least Andrea hadn't hated her, and Natalie was glad Gideon didn't add the observation that, ultimately, Andrea had chosen her own freedom over Natalie's life. But her clumsy warning and impractical plan to protect Natalie *had* lit the fuse of Gideon's actions. Natalie tried to dwell on that.

"There are tissues in the drawer of that table to your right; will you grab them?" she asked.

Gideon tipped toward the lamp table and found the Kleenex. He handed the box to her. She wiped her face while he took off his jacket.

"I'm sorry," she said. "I ambushed you—" Another surge of tears poured from her eyes, emotions hurrying to escape before she wrenched the valves closed.

"You don't need to apologize." He eased her back into his arms. "Let yourself cry."

"How are . . . how are *you* doing? Your father's death . . . Skyler . . ."

"I'm angry, but let a judge and jury deal with him. I'll focus on helping Felicia cope."

Natalie laid her head on his shoulder, letting tears drip across her face and rain on his shirt. "Good thing he admitted what he'd done before he doped me. My memories of the part after I started getting woozy are a jumble, and I'm not much of a witness."

"Do you remember the lake?" Gideon asked.

"A little of it. Mainly I remember this compulsion to hang on to Skyler. I have this memory of my face pressed against his jacket—I even remember smelling his aftershave, the way he always smelled at work, and him pulling at my arms and saying 'Let go,' but it's murky. Then I remember being cold. From what Detective Bartholomew said, they think he was attempting to throw me into the water without visibly injuring me. He needed the drowning to look accidental or like suicide, and if I'd plainly been attacked beforehand, that would be a problem for the scenario he'd built. But when he saw your headlights at the top of the hill or heard you on the trail, he must have panicked and started punching."

She lifted her head and pulled back so she could look him in the eyes. "You saved my life, and you think you lack class because you didn't bring flowers?"

"Uh, well, it wasn't just me who saved you. The police . . ."

Tears kept welling, but her loss of composure no longer bothered her. "I'm grateful for their help as well, but they told me what went down. You tried to contact me and got worried when I didn't respond. You drove over to my house to investigate. You went inside to search for me, and you called the police. You noticed my mother's soap carvings in the tub and found my incoherent scratchings."

"Yeah, I . . . You'd told me about the soap, how you never kept it near water, so it caught my attention. But your delaying Hudson, hanging on to him at the dock, everything you did—it saved your life. Gave me time to get there." Gideon tried to smile, but his face had gone bloodless; he must be reliving his arrival at the lake. "How are you doing physically?"

"I'm doing well. The concussion was minor. My stomach is still sore where he punched me, but it's much better than it was. Plus, after two days of Deborah not allowing me to do anything, I've had a lot of rest." Natalie had *thought* she was rested, but now she felt depleted—depleted but light, as though she could truly rest, not sleep to hide from memories.

She sat up straighter and wiped her face. Gideon lifted his arm from around her shoulders and straightened his posture as well.

A gap of a couple of inches now separated them. Natalie wanted to scoot so their shoulders were touching or ask him to put his arm back around her, but she didn't want him vaulting out the window in terror. "How is Felicia doing?"

"I talked to her on the phone," Gideon said. "She's improving. She's still in the hospital but not on a hold. She wanted to stay. She admitted herself voluntarily, and the police are fine with it. They've got enough to sort out, and they're happy to let her work on getting stabilized before they nail down charges and so on. Robert Chapman sent her flowers, by the way."

"He did?"

"Yeah, Felicia said it was like three dozen roses in about a dozen different colors, with a card saying he bore no grudges and she should put the past behind her. They won't let her keep them in her room, but the nurses station has never looked so elegant. Did the police tell you she admitted to planting Camille's purse in your coat?"

"No, I didn't know that."

"She found it in her house but insists she didn't steal it from Camille. She thought *you* had put it in her house to mock her. That's why she thought turnabout was fair play and sneaked into your house to stick it in your coat. Did you know she taught herself to jimmy locks? The Internet for the win, I guess."

"Skyler must have put the purse in her house," Natalie said. "I know he overheard her conversation with Camille. At that point, he must have figured framing her was a good idea, or at least a back-up plan."

"She handled it pretty calmly when we talked about how Dad actually died. The idea that he was murdered was . . . anything but new to her, as you know."

"I'm sorry she has to deal with this. Is she starting to realize I'm not out to destroy you?"

"She's getting there. We didn't have much time to talk, and I figured telling her about Skyler Hudson was stress enough, so I didn't ask directly. But it's starting to dawn on her how screwed up her thinking had become. She knows she needs help. She'll get it."

"Thank you," Natalie whispered. "Thank you."

Gideon rested his hand on hers in a comforting touch; he must know she was thinking about her own mother. For a few seconds, he was silent, probably waiting to hear if she wanted to pursue the topic. She didn't. At the moment, she was simply grateful to know Felicia was dealing with her challenges.

Gideon released her hand. "Is Skyler talking?"

"I don't know. I doubt it. But Bartholomew did tell me Andrea has admitted to bribing Dante over the will and paying blackmail to Skyler. She's adamant she had no idea he'd murdered Dante and Camille. Apparently, that's why she got so upset when I went to talk to her—she was starting to wonder if Skyler might be guilty of worse than blackmail, and she panicked."

"So she's admitted she knew Skyler was going to kill you."

"I don't know. I'd guess the most she's admitted is that she was worried—she can't completely deny that after the way she came to you. She'll probably be out on bail soon. Long-term, I don't know what the consequences will be, but she'll do prison time, no matter how brilliant her lawyer is. I feel sorry for her husband and daughter."

"Yeah, me too."

"And I'm frustrated that I never caught on to what kind of guy Skyler was. I feel terrible for his fiancée."

"It's gotta rip you up, finding out the guy you planned to marry is a blackmailer and a murderer." Gideon offered a resigned, uneven smile. "Makes me feel like I got off easy with, uh, my experience. Are you . . . feeling better, knowing your mother didn't cut you out of her will after all?"

"I am, but it doesn't feel as good as I thought it would. How much of it was love for me, and how much of it was a new game? Then again, maybe it was the only way she could bring herself to reach out to me . . . too stubborn to do it directly, too proud, maybe too embarrassed. I don't know. I guess I won't ever know her motives, and I'll have to live with that."

"That's tough."

"Honestly, loving, face-to-face conversations would have meant more to me than whatever ends up in my bank account once the courts get the will sorted out. But if her will was the only way she could reach out to me, I'm grateful she did. To be practical about it, money is useful."

"Sing it," Gideon said.

Natalie smiled but didn't speak, wanting a chance to let roiling emotions settle. Gideon didn't speak either, and for a lengthy moment, they sat in silence. The quiet soothed her, and she felt she could sit with him for hours, comfortable and wordless.

"That's new." He pointed to a small, square mosaic on an easel that Natalie had set on the lamp table.

"Yes." Natalie looked at the blue, white, and gold image of a starry sky. "A get-well gift."

"From Lacey Egan? The one who made the purse? I read about her in the paper."

"Yes." In the drawer of the lamp table, Natalie had placed Lacey's note, a greater treasure than the lovely mosaic. *Thank you, Dr. Marsh. I'm doing okay. We're working with the police, and Jonas got us a good lawyer. I called Tori. I'm going to see her on my own, and Jonas said he'll come with me for couples counseling. We're trying to work things out. Neither of us really knows how to be different with each other, but I know he's really trying, and I am too. I think we'll make it.*

"Hey . . . uh . . . listen," Gideon said. "This is horrific timing, but . . . sometime this week . . . or the next couple of weeks . . . okay, you probably aren't interested in . . . I mean, would you like to do dinner? Here, or at my place, if you don't want to go out?" His neck flushed crimson. "Heck, this sounds tackier than tacky. You need to rest—"

"Can we go to your place?" she asked. "Tonight? I'd love to spend a quiet evening eating takeout."

"Are you sure?"

"Definitely. I saw you have a bunch of Lego models. Got anything I could help with? That would be *sehr entspannend*, as Bob Chapman would say."

"*Sehr* what?"

"Very relaxing."

His lips curved, then straightened as though he wanted to conceal his enthusiasm. "Are you sure you want to? No pressure."

Natalie laughed. "I flattened you with a hug, cried all over your shirt, and have been glued to your side ever since you made the mistake of ringing my doorbell. Does none of that give you a hint of how I feel about your company?"

"I . . . know you're grateful for . . . I didn't want to assume anything."

"You can assume I like you. I felt that way before you scooped me out of Lake Ohneka. I want to get to know you better. I just want to make sure *you* don't feel obligated because you're worried about me. Or because you're afraid I won't let go of you long enough for you to escape."

He grinned and shifted closer to her, settling his arm around her shoulders. "You can assume I like you too," he said.

ABOUT THE AUTHOR

STEPHANIE BLACK HAS LOVED BOOKS since she was old enough to grab the pages and has enjoyed creating make-believe adventures since she and her sisters were inventing long Barbie games filled with intrigue and danger or running around pretending to be detectives. She is a four-time Whitney Award winner for Best Mystery/Suspense Novel.

Stephanie was born in Utah and has lived in various places, including Arkansas, Arizona, Massachusetts, and Limerick, Ireland. She currently lives in northern California, plays the violin in a community symphony but never practices enough, and enjoys spending time with her husband, Brian, and their family. She is a fan of dark chocolate, milk chocolate, homemade chocolate chip cookies, thick chocolate brownies, and of putting chocolate chips in pancakes.

Stephanie enjoys hearing from her readers. You can contact her via e-mail at info@covenant-lds.com or by mail care of Covenant Communications, P.O. Box 416, American Fork, UT 84003-0416. Visit her website at www.stephanieblack. net and her author Facebook page at www.facebook.com/stephanieblackauthor.